A Riddl

CW00818728

Book one in the Mysteries in Metal series

Copyright © Simon Haynes 2019

www.spacejock.com.au

Stay in touch!

Author's newsletter:
spacejock.com.au/ML.html

facebook.com/halspacejock
twitter.com/spacejock

Works by Simon Haynes

All of Simon's novels* are self-contained, with a beginning, a middle and a proper ending. They're not sequels, they don't end on a cliffhanger, and you can start or end your journey with any book in the series.
Robot vs Dragons series excepted!

The Hal Spacejock series for teens/adults
Set in the distant future, where humanity spans the galaxy and robots are second-class citizens. Includes a large dose of humour!

Hal Zero (a prequel)
Hal Spacejock 1: A Robot named Clunk*
Hal Spacejock 2: Second Course*
Hal Spacejock 3: Just Desserts*
Hal Spacejock 4: No Free Lunch
Hal Spacejock 5: Baker's Dough
Hal Spacejock 6: Safe Art
Hal Spacejock 7: Big Bang
Hal Spacejock 8: Double Trouble
Hal Spacejock 9: Max Damage
Hal Spacejock 10: Cold Boots
Hal Spacejock 11: Atmosteal (TBA)
Also available:
Omnibus One, containing Hal books 1-3*
Omnibus Two, containing Hal books 4-6
Omnibus Three, containing Hal books 7-9
Megabus One, containing Hal books 1-5
Megabus Two, containing Hal books 6-10
Hal Spacejock: Visit, a short story
Hal Spacejock: Framed, a short story
Hal Spacejock: Albion, a novella
*Audiobook editions available

The Dragon and Chips Trilogy.
High fantasy meets low humour!
Each set of three books should be read in order.

1. A Portion of Dragon and Chips*
2. A Butt of Heads*
3. A Pair of Nuts on the Throne*
Also Available:
Omnibus One, containing the first trilogy*
*Audiobook editions available

The Harriet Walsh series.
Set in the same universe as Hal Spacejock. Good clean fun, written with wry humour. No cliffhangers between novels!

Harriet Walsh 1: Peace Force
Harriet Walsh 2: Alpha Minor
Harriet Walsh 3: Sierra Bravo
Harriet Walsh 4: Foxtrot Hotel (TBA)
Also Available:
Omnibus One, containing books 1-3

The Hal Junior series
Written for all ages, these books are set aboard a space station in the Hal Spacejock universe, only ten years later.

1. Hal Junior: The Secret Signal*
2. Hal Junior: The Missing Case
3. Hal Junior: The Gyris Mission
4. Hal Junior: The Comet Caper
Also Available:
Omnibus One, containing books 1-3
*Audiobook edition

The Secret War series.
Gritty space opera for adult readers.

1. Raiders
2. Frontier
3. Deadlock (TBA)

Mysteries in Metal series.
Ghostly goings-on in Victorian London!
1. A Riddle in Bronze
2. An Enigma in Silver (2020)
3. A Conundrum in Gold (TBA)

Collect One-Two - a dozen short stories by Simon Haynes

All titles available in ebook and paperback. Visit spacejock.com.au for details.

Bowman Press

V 1.03

This edition published 2019 by Bowman Press
ISBN 978-1-877034-49-7

Text © Simon Haynes 2019
Cover art © Bowman Press 2019
Stock cover images copyright depositphotos.com

Dedicated to my two closest and dearest friends, a father and daughter who... well, let's just call them Roberta and The Professor, shall we?

— I —

A dozen people were crowded into the gloomy sitting room, some reclining in armchairs while others were perched elbow-to-elbow on a pair of upholstered rosewood couches. As my gaze flitted across their faces, careful not to settle on any one of them for an unseemly length of time, I wondered whether my rivals were as desperate for this job as I was. Some returned my gaze in a rather belligerent fashion, and I imagined the chaotic scenes should the applicants decide to forgo the wait and instead engage in a scuffle amongst the over-stuffed armchairs and the side tables crammed with knick-knacks.

But no. We were all bookish types, not given to bare-knuckle fisticuffs. Sarcastic rejoinders were our weapon of choice, and we would no more call each other out than order red wine with fish.

'Mr Arthur Staines.'

We all turned to look at the speaker, a severe-looking woman of advancing years who had appeared in the doorway with no sound nor warning of her impending arrival. Mrs Fairacre was her name, and she was housekeeper to Professor Twickham, the man we were all waiting to see. Dressed in black from head to toe, with iron-grey hair and an expression that brooked no nonsense, she was a formidable presence.

A young man stood, his face reddening as all now turned their attention to him. He was clutching a leather document case under one arm, and with his polished round eyeglasses and the intelligent cast to his features, he looked the ideal candidate...damn him.

The applicant strode to the door, and was promptly whisked away to the unseen interior of the house.

'Curse that rotter,' I heard someone growl. 'He'll take the job before we're even seen.'

'Agreed,' said another. 'So why don't you leave now and save yourself a wait?'

I heard a laugh, quickly stifled, and we resumed our patient vigil.

To be fair to the others, I had no business being there. The advertisement in that morning's newspaper had sought an experienced bookkeeper, with membership of a professional accounting body and a minimum of three years experience at a respectable firm. I matched none of these qualifications, not one, and it had taken a certain amount of barefaced cheek for me to present for an interview in the first place.

Cheek, or rather desperation.

I'd arrived in the city two months earlier, twenty-four years old and eager to make a name for myself. Unfortunately, there were a thousand more of my age just as eager, if not more so, and *they* had qualifications to match their ambition.

My parents, bless them, had warned me of the dangers. 'You might have a head for numbers, son, but these big city companies want proof. Without qualifications to your name, I fear you will be spurned.' My father had gone on to dispense vague advice about the dangers of the flesh, a subject we both found equally embarrassing.

My mother, far more practical, gave me a pork pie for the journey, wrapped in a fresh square of muslin. I'd always been a gangly youth, tall and somewhat ungainly, and my mother tended to fuss over my nourishment. Once I was alone in the big city, she no doubt expected me to starve within the first week, and so I reassured her, convincing her I would eat like three horses. After bidding my family farewell, I'd taken my place in the pony trap for the long ride to the station.

Eight weeks later, I had barely a farthing to my name. I was living out of a doss-house, sleeping in a grimy attic which hadn't seen a cleaning brush since the Emperor Napoleon himself threatened these shores, and this job interview was my last chance of remaining in the city. Fail today, and I would be begging my parents for the train fare home, my dreams and hopes dashed.

Idly, my gaze turned to a side-table, just out of reach. A ray of sunshine pierced the tangled rosebushes just outside the narrow bay windows, shining upon the table's polished surface. There, I could see an eclectic assortment of items, including a pair of miniature picture frames, stylised wood carvings of unfamiliar animals, and a plain candlestick holder fashioned from brass. But the item that caught my eye was a metal cube, four inches to a side, its polished surface gleaming in the sunshine as though the box were illuminated from within. The surface was not uniform, covered as it was with fine traces and indents, and as I moved my head these patterns caused a hypnotic effect.

Near-blinded, I turned away, and as my eyes adjusted I saw other similar cubes everywhere I looked. At first I thought they were after-images, burned into my vision by the glare, but these cubes were different sizes, and were embossed with different patterns. There were cubes on every side table, these sited beside the chairs and sofas the applicants were sitting in. There were three on a nearby bookcase, and two more above the fireplace, sitting on the mantelpiece as though they'd sprung from nowhere. When I looked towards the bay windows, which afforded a view of the front gardens between the matted, thorny stems, I saw another three cubes stacked in a pyramid arrangement.

Had they been there before, or had I been so concerned at the course of my interview that my gaze had passed over them, unseeing?

My eyes turned to the first cube, the one nearest me. I wanted to hold it, to examine it, but to do so I'd have to stand up, walk to the table and pick the thing up. This was someone else's house, my prospective employer's no less, and such a liberty was unthinkable. I could no more touch another's belongings without permission than pick the housekeeper's pocket.

Even so, I felt an overwhelming compunction, and before I knew what was happening I was on my feet, reaching for the gleaming object. I heard a murmur behind me, either disapproval or condemnation, but I ignored it.

The shiny metal cube was warm to the touch, and it filled my hand as I took my seat once more. Turning it over, I noticed the pattern was different on every side. There was an obvious sequence to the spacing of the lines and indents, one which I instinctively recognised, but which stubbornly refused to reveal itself. Figures floated across my mind, accompanied by diagrams from books, and snatches of voices from my years of schooling.

'Mr Jules Hartlow,' said the housekeeper, who'd appeared as before without warning.

Quickly, I hid the cube behind my back, and I stared out of the bay windows with a look of intense concentration which couldn't have been any more pronounced had the tangled, matted rose bushes started speaking to me in tongues.

I heard the next applicant crossing to the doorway, and when I judged it was safe I risked a glance, to see whether the housekeeper had noticed the cube. She was just turning away, albeit looking directly at me, and I saw a flicker of ...*something* ...in her gaze. Was it disapproval? Was it suspicion? Or was it...relief?

'Oh, this could take *hours*.' I heard the creak of a chair, and looked round to see another applicant picking up the cube nearest to herself. She studied it casually, dismissively, then put it back again. 'I've a mind to find myself some lunch before I wilt.'

'Please do,' said another. 'We'll be sure to fetch you if your name is called.'

I ignored the banter. The housekeeper having departed, I was examining the cube once more. The small indentations I dismissed, since they formed no discernible pattern, but the lines were intriguing. There was a set of three, then a gap, then one more, and then – here I paused to count – another four, so tightly packed it was hard to distinguish one from another. 'Pi!' I exclaimed.

'Pie or sandwiches, I would gladly take either,' said the woman seated nearby. 'And with any luck, a pot of tea to accompany them.'

I paid her no mind, because I'd found an indentation in the surface of the cube which had a certain amount of give, as though it were a button or a catch. With a nervous, shaking finger, I pressed it in until it stopped, at which point there was a faint *click* from within. The button was still recessed within the device, leaving a hole in the surface, and with a feeling of alarm I realised it was going to stay there.

I stared at the cube in horror, fearing I'd broken the device. Then I glanced at the nearby table, wondering whether I ought to replace the cube quickly, with the newly-created hole face down against the wooden surface. Unfortunately, such an action would be observed by the other applicants, and if questions arose as to the vandal responsible for the mishandling of the artifact, I had no doubt they would point their accusing fingers at me.

Quickly, I turned the cube in my hands, and that's when I noticed a slight protrusion on the opposite face to the button. It was standing proud by an eighth of an inch, no more, and I had missed it in my state of alarm. I pressed it gently, fearing I might damage this side of the cube also, making my crime all but impossible to conceal, but to my relief the surface smoothed with a *clack*, and when I turned the cube over I saw the button had emerged from its hole once more.

The cube now in its original configuration, with neither holes nor protrusions, a wise soul would have replaced it on the table and sat back to await the housekeeper's calling of their name.

Well, I may be proficient with numbers, but nobody ever accused me of being wise.

Click, clack! Click, clack!

'Oh, *do* stop playing with that thing,' called one of the other applicants. 'If the housekeeper spies you toying with the professor's belongings, we'll *all* be out on our ears.'

I was engrossed in the cube, and his words were as rain to the ocean. For, after three cycles with the button and the protrusion, I'd found a corner which differed from the rest. With the deep engraved line traced across three faces, the corner resembled a pyramid, and I discovered it could be rotated upon its axis. One face of the pyramid had a tiny round marker, and I saw engravings on the larger faces of the cube to match, in a sequence of I, II and III. The marker was currently pointing to III, and so I turned it until it matched the I.

Ting!

I almost dropped the cube as the clear note rang out, and, looking around the sitting room, I saw the others eyeing me with a mix of exasperation and annoyance.

'To take such liberties,' muttered the young woman who'd yearned for lunch. 'Can you credit such behaviour?'

'Leave him be,' said another. 'He's only fashioning a noose for his own neck.'

The others brightened at that, and I turned away to resume my inspection of the clever little device. After my most recent action, I'd found a newly-loose cover on a fresh side of the cube. The little plate slid open on well-oiled tracks, and underneath there was a toggle switch, much like a Morse key in miniature. Holding my breath, I placed my finger on the raised end and pressed it four times.

I wasn't sure what I was expecting, but what I got was...nothing.

I turned the cube, inspecting it once more, but there were no fresh changes. I was certain the cube was a puzzle, and the answer was Pi. So far I'd conveyed the numbers three, one and four using the cube's intricate mechanisms, but there were more to Pi than three digits. Far, far more.

Then, struck by a sudden thought, I turned the pyramid all the way round, past II and III and back to I again. The cube *tinged* twice in rapid succession, and, confident now, I enacted another five presses on the tiny lever.

Two things happened in quick succession. First, the cube squirmed in my hands, as though suddenly alive. Shocked, this time I really *did* drop the thing, and as it landed on the thick carpet I saw the buttons, panels and protrusions all return to their original positions.

The second occurrence was less troubling, for there was a protracted ringing noise in the distance, coming from somewhere deep inside the house. At first I thought the two events were connected, impossible though that was, but then I heard one of the applicants nearby complaining.

'It seems we must wait even longer,' he said, settling back on the sofa with an air of resignation. 'I believe that was the Professor ringing for his lunch,'

'Some have all the luck,' muttered the young woman.

'Mr Septimus Jones. Would you come with me please?'

We all started, shocked by the housekeeper's sudden presence. Once again she'd appeared without warning, catching us unawares. I started more than most, since it was *my* name she'd called. Quickly, I pushed the cube under the side table with the side of my shoe, trying to make the gesture look like I was stretching my long legs. Then I got up and hastened across the room.

The housekeeper waited for me, her face emotionless, but before leading me away she turned to the rest of those waiting. 'Thank

you for your time, but you can all leave now. The position has been
filled.'

'I d–don't understand,' I stammered, as I followed Mrs Fairacre down a corridor lined with solemn-looking portraits. 'If the position is filled, where are you taking me?'

'The professor wishes to speak with you.'

I remembered the metal cube, and the way Mrs Fairacre had caught me tinkering with the device, and my heart sank. Jules Hartlow, the most recent applicant to be interviewed, must have been such a favourable candidate that he'd secured the job on the spot. And, having found the employee he was looking for, it seemed Professor Twickham now wanted a little word with me about the cube I'd mishandled.

I'd yet to meet the professor, but as we trod the creaking wooden boards in the long hallway I formed a detailed mental image. He'd be well over six foot tall, slightly stooped, with a bald head and a fringe of white hair. Spectacles, naturally, and a great beak of a nose. His eyes would be piercing and intelligent, for this would not be the absent-minded buffoon of popular fiction, and his sweeping gaze would miss nothing. I imagined him being softly spoken, for large men rarely needed to raise their voices, and his imposing figure would command the respect of all around him. He would also be a stickler for accuracy, a trait of his profession, and he would not suffer fools. I also imagined him using an ivory-handled cane for support, thanks to an old injury, and that cane would conceal a gleaming rapier with which to stick footpads and villains and job applicants who fiddled with his belongings.

My wild imaginings having completely run away with themselves, I almost walked into Mrs Fairacre, for that good lady had come to a halt directly ahead of me. We'd stopped at a solid oak door, the timber dark with age, and the housekeeper raised her hand and knocked twice.

There was no reply.

The housekeeper knocked again, harder this time. 'Professor?'

'Yes? What is it?' demanded a reedy voice, barely audible thanks to the wooden door.

'I bring the applicant. The one who toyed with your puzzle cube.'

I swallowed, for there was no longer any doubt. My hopes of employment were dashed, and I was to be roundly admonished by this professor before the housekeeper ejected me into the street.

'Send them away, Mrs Fairacre,' came the muffled reply. 'I cannot deal with them now. There is much to do!'

Relieved, I turned away from the door. Punishment was postponed, and as I never intended to set foot in that house again, it could remain so indefinitely.

But the housekeeper had other ideas. She took my elbow with a grip that would have put a dent in a cast iron lamppost, ignored the professor's protestations and opened the door wide. 'Professor, this is Septimus Jones.'

Standing directly behind her, my first impression was that she was addressing an empty room. Under the light of a wall-mounted gaslight I spied a large desk, bookcases stuffed with all manner of tomes and documents, and, to one side, a bench covered with intricate equipment. There was, however, no sign of any professor.

'I said I do not wish to be disturbed!'

The voice was high-pitched, as already noted, and it appeared to come from thin air.

Then Mrs Fairacre stood aside, all but dragging me into the room, and I realised the professor had been there all along. My mental image of an imposing giant with a deep voice was swept away like a candle flame in a gale, for the man who stood before me barely topped five feet. His grey hair was cropped short, and as he turned to glare at us I saw his piercing blue eyes were red-rimmed with fatigue. 'Why does nobody pay me attention these days?' he demanded, in a petulant, reedy voice.

There was a crackling sound to my right, and I turned to see a bolt of lightning passing between two slender metal rods. I was all too familiar with lightning, having been raised in a part of the country where storms were commonplace, but I have to confess that indoor lightning was a new experience for me. The crackling blue strand was sustained for several seconds, so bright it illuminated the entire room, and then there was a bang and a puff of smoke. The metal rods vanished, vaporised instantly, and the rest of the delicate equipment slowly toppled over with much creaking and groaning and shattering of glass tubes.

'Heavens, my experiment!' shouted the professor. 'You've *ruined* it!' He ran to the bench, where he plucked pieces of equipment from the wreckage, flapping at the smoke as he carefully inspected each piece before setting them aside. All the while he kept up a stream of complaints, directed either at myself or the unfortunate Mrs Fairacre. 'Never should have hired you in the first place...interfering busybody...no peace...stale bread in my sandwiches...toying with my belongings...'

'I shall leave Mr Jones here for when you're ready,' said the housekeeper, completely unruffled by the professor's outburst. And then she was gone, firmly closing the door behind herself.

The professor was still rescuing bits and pieces of charred equipment from the ruins on top of his workbench, and to him I no longer existed. For my part, I had absolutely no intention of revealing my presence. I did wonder how long I might have to stand there before I could safely inch the door open and depart, and as the seconds began to drag I glanced around the room. The professor was busy at his workbench, to my right, and a gaslight hissed on the wall above. The large desk was about ten feet away, ahead of me, and behind it stood an enormous bookcase which covered the entire wall. To my left was a wardrobe, and beside it a glass-fronted cabinet, with another of the patterned cubes on the top shelf. The other shelves in this cabinet were filled with rows of tiny metal cylinders, none bigger than my thumb, each with a handwritten label, the details of which I could not discern. These cylinders were an impressive feat of engineering, with smooth sides and perfectly rounded ends, and they were arranged in varnished wooden racks. The cylinders gleamed with reflected light, and I was still wondering at their purpose when the professor's reedy voice broke my reverie.

'So, you activated one of my cubes, did you?'

The professor spoke without turning round, his voice calm, and for a moment I thought he was addressing the failed experiment. Then I realised the question could only have been directed at me. 'Yes, sir. I apologise for my actions, and I promise to make good any damage I might have caused.'

'You are well spoken,' he said, and I detected a hint of approval. 'But tell me, what made you pick up the cube in the first place?'

I thought back to the instant before I'd stood to retrieve the device. 'The side table was illuminated by a beam of sunlight.'

'The entire surface?'

'Yes sir.'

'There were two picture frames, a candle holder, and several wooden carvings of exotic animals. Why the cube, and not one of those?'

I was surprised at his recollection of the precise contents of the table, given the variety of such items in the sitting room, and I found myself revising my opinion of the professor. At first he'd appeared impatient and more than a little scatterbrained, not to mention acerbic and ill-tempered, but now I realised his wits were sharper than I'd thought. 'Sir, my eyes were drawn to the cube. It was as though it spoke to me, strange as that sounds.'

The professor still had his back to me, and was yet sorting through components on the workbench. The smoke had mostly cleared now, but there was still an acrid, metallic smell to the air...not unpleasant, but somehow out of place. 'And so you stood, crossed to the table and picked it up.'

'I'm sorry, sir.'

'Why do you keep apologising?'

'I had no right to touch your belongings.'

'Had you not, Mrs Fairacre would have dismissed you with the others.'

Exactly, I thought.

Now, finally, the professor turned to face me. His appearance was startling, for he'd donned a pair of glasses with heavy lenses, each of a different hue. One was as red as the finest ruby, and it glinted in the light from the nearby lamp. The other was as dark as the night sky, and unlike its twin it reflected not the slightest hint of light. Instead, it seemed to grow darker the more I looked at it, as though it were draining my vision. 'What do you make of this?' asked the professor, and he threw a small object at me, underhand.

I tore my gaze from those unusual spectacles and caught the item in mid-air. It was heavier than I expected, and as it lay revealed on my palm, a frown creased my brow. It looked like a playing piece from a draughts board, a disc perhaps a quarter-inch thick, with smoothed edges. However, rather than ivory or teak, this item was fashioned from metal, and to my eye it appeared to be solid bronze. Then, even as I was studying the piece, I felt it...*move.* The strange twisting sensation was like that of the cube in the sitting room, as though the inert, warm metal contained a living, breathing organism.

Hastily, I tipped it from my hand, and the metal disc fell to the floor, where it landed on the rug with a solid thud. There was no bounce, and the disc merely lay there, inert. 'Wh-what trickery was that?'

The professor chuckled. 'You call it trickery, but I prefer to call it a mystery. One which I am working to solve!'

'But...metal does not move of its own accord!'

'A mystery indeed. Now, will you take a seat?'

I swallowed, because my hour of reckoning had arrived. The strange properties of the metal disc had taken my mind off more important matters, however briefly, but now there was no avoiding them. Slowly, unwillingly, I took the nearest chair, perching on the very edge as though I might flee at any second.

Meanwhile, the professor removed his spectacles and sat behind the desk, facing me across the broad surface. 'I will pay two hundred a year, less ten shillings a week board and rent. Of course, you may wish to live elsewhere, in which case the board and rent will not apply.'

Caught off-guard as I was, my mouth opened and closed in the manner of a fish.

'Surely you did not expect more?' the professor asked me gently. 'Why, a lowly recruit in the armed forces earns only–'

'Sir, I accept the position,' I said quickly. My wits had been scrambled by the unexpected turn of events, but they were not *that* scrambled. *Two hundred per year!* With that amount, my troubles were over, and I'd have enough to send a monthly stipend to my parents, easing their own situation. I felt a surge of relief so strong, so powerful, that I was completely unable to speak. Here I'd sat, thinking the professor was to chastise me, when instead I'd landed the position. Frankly, I couldn't believe it, and I wanted to leap around the study, shaking the very rafters with my joy. Then the reality of my situation hit me, staining my joy like a bucket of slops across a line of clean washing.

I had applied for the position under false pretences. I was not the man the professor thought me to be. I was a fraud.

The two hundred a year vanished with a pop. The money I'd send to my parents...gone. My new lodgings and those three square meals a day were cruelly snatched from my grasp. I had to own up, whatever the cost. 'There is one small detail I should mention, professor,' I said, all the while thinking of three very large details.

'Oh?'

'I don't match the requirements in your advertisement. Not entirely, that is.' I was still dancing around the matter, for I hoped to introduce each of my failings one after the other, in an attempt to soften each blow.

The professor gestured impatiently. 'Those requirements were of little consequence.'

'They were?'

'Of course. You're the man for this job, Jones. I knew it the moment I saw you.'

I thought back to the clouds of smoke and the professor's cries of anger as the housekeeper interrupted his work. The professor hadn't even looked upon me until he'd turned to face me with those peculiar spectacles. Either he was revising the facts to suit the outcome, which made him a very poor scientific man indeed, or he genuinely believed in the memories he'd just fabricated, in which case he was deluded. Neither spoke well of my new employer, but then I thought of the two hundred a year, and I decided I could live with his little foibles.

In any case, with no other prospects I had no choice in the matter. One way or another, my future was bound up with this eccentric little man.

— 3 —

I was about to ask what my duties might be, and whether the professor wanted me to get started immediately, when there was a sound of approaching footsteps from the hall outside. It was a heavy tread, which discounted Mrs Fairacre, and I wondered whether one of the other applicants had come to plead their case.

Instead, the door opened and a young woman strode in without having paused to knock. 'Father, have you...oh!'

The newcomer was around my age, with long dark hair tied up in a rough bun, in the way of a washerwoman or a market stall-holder, and she was wearing a set of bib overalls covered in soot or a similar fine black powder. Heavy work boots completed her outfit, and I would have taken her for a chimney sweep had it not been for the way she addressed the professor. Then I studied her face, and in that instant it was as though the mirror atop the great lighthouse of Alexandria was reflecting sunlight directly into my unshielded eyes.

I do not speak of radiant beauty or other such romantic frippery, but rather the sheer life force and strength of character apparent within the person standing before me. This was a woman who stood for no nonsense, and her clear, intelligent eyes would miss no detail, however small.

Then she gave me a warm smile and held out a slender hand. 'A pleasure to make your acquaintance, Mr Hartlow. I'm Roberta Twickham.'

So taken was I by the radiant smile that I had already extended my own hand before I became aware of her error. 'Ah, er, it's Mr Jones, actually. Mr Septimus Jones, at your service.'

Roberta withdrew her hand. 'Father,' she said, with an edge to her voice. 'Tell me you did not hire the wrong bookkeeper.'

There was no reply, and I turned to see an extraordinary sight. The professor had risen from his desk and was rubbing his hands together nervously, all the while exhibiting a ghastly smile. 'Well, ahem, you see–' he began.

'Father!'

'Yes dear?'

'I told you which applicant was the most suitable. I wrote his name down for you, lest you forgot. Master Jules Hartlow of the Stuanton Hartlows.'

'I interviewed that young man, Roberta. He was most unsuitable.'

'Who cares a fig for suitability?' snapped Roberta. 'His family is worth five thousand a year, and their introductions alone would have paid his wages of one hundred a year twice over. Do you not recall our conversation?'

'I do seem to recall the figure of one hundred a year twice over,' said the professor, and he gave me a warning glance.

I understood his meaning perfectly. Not only was I the wrong applicant, he'd offered to pay me double the amount he was supposed to. Still, even if he was forced to revise my wages, I had to admit that one hundred a year was better than nothing.

Roberta turned to me. 'I'm sorry, Mr Jones. Father gets a little mixed up sometimes, and I'm afraid we've wasted your time. I'll have Mrs Fairacre show you out.'

I stared at her in shock. 'But...the professor already offered me the position. I accepted!'

'He believed you to be someone else.'

'No I didn't,' called the professor.

'Father, please leave this to me.'

'Roberta, I refuse to be pushed around like a creaky old handcart,' said the professor. He spoke sharply, and I could tell his own temper was now beginning to fray. 'The applicant you suggested was a pompous, stuck-up fool.'

'He exceeded all of our requirements, and when you add his family connections–'

'I wouldn't have employed that buffoon if he offered to work for free!'

'So instead you seized on this poor fellow.' Roberta whirled around to face me, and I understood how the Spanish had felt at Trafalgar when confronted by the formidable guns of the *Victory*. 'Where were you employed previously?' she demanded.

'I–I managed the books for several businesses in West Wickham.'

She didn't look surprised. 'You were not with a company in the city then?'

I remembered the advertisement and the requirements therein. 'Alas no.'

'I see.' Her silence was as eloquent as any comment she might have made, and the withering look she gave her father would have felled a weaker man. 'Tell me, of which professional accounting body are you a member?'

'I am not fortunate enough to belong to such, my lady.'

'No membership and no experience.' Roberta turned to her father in triumph. 'Bad enough to hire the wrong candidate, but the man you selected is not even qualified. It seems Mr Jones applied for this position under false pretences, and that makes showing him the door all the easier.'

'Now wait just a moment,' said the professor, with a frown. 'I believe this young man is ideal for the job. Why, he solved the riddle of the cube!'

Roberta gestured dismissively. 'I did likewise as a child of seven. Would you hire a street urchin for this position?'

'If that was my choice, then yes indeed.' The professor's voice rose. 'And furthermore, you would live with it!'

'I would, would I?' demanded Roberta, advancing on him. 'How is it you lived this long without me ending your miserable existence?'

'I rue the day you were born!' cried the professor. 'You are nothing but a vicious harpy plaguing my household and sucking the very life from my bones!'

'You don't have any life, you withered old goat!' shouted Roberta, bunching her fists.

The professor didn't back down, and with a feeling of horror I realised they might actually come to blows. 'I'll do the job for fifty a year,' I cried.

Mid-argument, they ceased shouting at each other and turned to look at me.

'I mean it,' I said. 'I know I lack the desired qualifications, but–'

'When can you start?' asked the professor.

'Immediately, sir. This very minute!'

'Excellent. Sign here please.' The Professor slid a sheet of manuscript across the desk and plucked a quill from the stand, passing it carefully so as not to mar the document with spilled ink.

I glanced down at the page and saw numerous paragraphs in legal boilerplate. I signed at the foot of the document, and the professor blotted the page and folded it in two, tucking it away in a desk drawer.

'There now. That's all done,' said Roberta calmly.

Neither of them showed any signs of the rage which they'd exhibited just seconds earlier, and I looked from one to the other in total confusion. Then, having recalled that my name, the date, and wages of precisely fifty pounds a year had already been filled out on the contract, I realised that I had, indeed, been done.

I was still musing over the savage cut to my wages when Roberta took my elbow. 'Come, Mr Jones. I'll show you to your room.'

It seemed to me that Mrs Fairacre, the housekeeper, would be more suited to that task, but I wasn't going to argue. I had just been outmanoeuvred by a master tactician, and I wanted to know more of Roberta Twickham.

I followed her further down the hallway until we reached a narrow wooden staircase rising from the left, where Roberta bid me lead the way. We climbed flight after flight, turning at regular intervals, until we emerged on the top floor. Here there were two doors, side by side.

I was flushed and a little out of breath after the climb, but I noticed Roberta had not been affected in the slightest.

'One is a store room of sorts, while the other is yours,' said Roberta, and she pushed open the left-hand door.

The ceiling had a sharp incline, nestled as it was just beneath the sloping roof of the house, but the room itself was generous. There was a desk, a bookcase with numerous well-used volumes, and a trim-looking bed in the centre. And there, sitting in the middle of the bed, was my own suitcase, battered and much-used.

'I had your things brought over,' said Roberta. 'I hope you don't mind.'

I shook my head, for I'd been dreading a return to my previous lodgings. 'That was good of you.' At the time I didn't question how she knew where I'd been staying, and exactly how much she and the professor had learned of my past before they hired me. No, I was merely grateful.

Roberta crossed to the sloping window, and as she stood there, illuminated by the afternoon sunshine, I took the opportunity to study her at length. She was a sturdy, well-built sort and her face was more rounded than classic oval, but pretty all the same. And, as mentioned, she possessed a lively intelligence which promised long, stimulating conversations on just about any topic.

'Do you like what you see?' she asked, without looking round.

'Very nice,' I said.

She smiled at me, radiating warmth, and much later I came to see this as the moment I lost my heart. At the time, though, I only recognised my feelings as those of one intrigued by another person.

Roberta and her father had tricked me into accepting fifty a year instead of the promised two hundred, and right then I would gladly have torn up the contract and worked for free as long as I could remain under the same roof.

Then I realised she'd closed the door upon entering my room. Even with the purest of intentions, such behaviour was frowned upon, and I felt a growing alarm as she showed no signs of leaving. If the housekeeper found us enclosed together, I'd be cast out as a rake of the worst sort. Casually, I moved to the door and eased it open, such that my behaviour could not be questioned. Then, as I returned to my former position near the bed, I heard it swing to and close firmly behind me.

'Mr Jones, do you fear I will corrupt you?' called Roberta, from the far end of the room.

'Indeed not, but–'

'Would you behave inappropriately towards me?'

'Never!' I remembered the way she'd advanced on her father, fists clenched. 'And, should I be foolish enough to try, I believe you might pitch me through that window.'

She laughed. 'Then why do you care if the door stands open or not?'

'Society expects–'

'Oh, society can go hang.' Roberta left the window, the floorboards creaking gently as she strode towards me. 'You and

I will be working together, Mr Jones. We shall be facing perils, and dangers, and creatures more foul than those from your darkest nightmares. I cannot have you worrying about the niceties of polite society.'

Foul creatures? Dangers and perils? 'B–but I thought I was employed to keep your books? The advertisement–'

'You are not the only one who lied about the circumstances.' Roberta folded her arms. 'We need someone who can work with numbers, yes. But also someone intelligent and loyal. Someone able to keep certain...facts about our business to themselves. I believe you to be that person, and I hope you won't disappoint me.'

I looked into her eyes and was surprised to see a raw vulnerability behind the tough exterior. Had someone treated this woman cruelly, or let her down when they were most needed? 'I won't,' I said gently. 'You have my word on it.'

'Excellent. Then perhaps you'd care to unpack your things, and I'll inform Mrs Fairacre that we shall have one more for dinner from this day forward.'

She left, the door closing automatically behind her, and I was deep in thought as I crossed to the window. This talk of perils and monsters had to be a fancy of some kind, or perhaps a tease. I wanted to dismiss her warnings, but I could still remember the movement of both the cube and the metal disk in my hand, as if the very metal were coming to life.

I looked down and saw a dense, tangled jungle of a back garden, stretching thirty or forty yards in every direction. Opposite was the rear of another house, smaller than the professor's, and a row of similar dwellings stretched away in both directions. These had no gardens, just tiny yards enclosed with brick walls, with a narrow alleyway running the length of the row.

Many of the windows had curtains, but one or two gaped at me, empty and black.

As I gazed upon these lifeless windows, I remembered the curious spectacles the professor had been wearing when I first met him. The ruby lens had been unusual, nothing more, but when I envisioned its sinister, jet-black twin I felt a shiver up my spine.

Suddenly, Roberta's talk of peril and danger didn't seem so fanciful after all, and I wondered exactly what I'd signed up for.

— 4 —

When I awoke the next morning, sunlight was just starting to peep through the curtains, creating long, intricate patterns on the sloped ceiling above me. I could hear bird calls, and the distant cries of barrow boys, and the clop of horses hauling carts for early-morning deliveries, the iron-shod wheels giving that distinctive rumble. There was also a faint clanking sound I couldn't place, which I put down to a device at the City docks – a winch, most likely.

I'd slept well, although the memories of a curious dream were only just slipping from my mind. The unsuccessful applicants of the day before had been pointing and laughing as I struggled to open a simple pocket watch. The chain had somehow wrapped itself around my neck, and the more I struggled with the watch, the larger, and heavier, and tighter that chain had become. It threatened to choke me, until the professor appeared in the guise of a music-hall magician and tapped his wand on the side of my head. At that point, everything had been sucked into a dark, bottomless hole, leaving me alone and helpless.

I shook myself, dispelling the morbid thoughts, and got up from my bed. There was a nightstand against the wall, and I shaved in a basin of cold water before inspecting my appearance in a small mirror. The mirror was set low, and as I reached out to change the angle I felt a warmth radiating from the wall. Curious, I laid the flat of my hand on the plaster, and was forced to withdraw it quickly as I felt the heat. This was no product of the early morning sun, which was gleaming through the window to my right. In any case, the house was in a terraced row, and this was an interior wall. No, there had to be a chimney behind this wall, and a goodly fire below to stoke such warmth.

I was pleased at this, because my room had no fireplace and I'd feared it would be unpleasantly damp and cold in the depths of winter. Now, it seemed, I would have no cause for complaint.

Dressing quickly, I left the room and made my way downstairs. Passing the sitting room, which I recognised from the day before, I followed my nose beyond, to the dining room. A small fire crackled in the grate, but it was the smell of food which had tempted me.

The professor was seated at the head of the table, almost hidden behind the pages of an enormous newspaper.

'Good morning sir,' I called.

'Hrmph.'

I guessed this was either the professor's usual greeting, or a comment on the state of the nation. When the pages rustled and another snort met my ears, I decided it was the latter.

The professor had a plate before him, containing a single slice of toast. He hadn't touched it, nor the gently steaming teacup sitting on the saucer nearby. I looked around for a breakfast of my own, and my spirits rose as I saw the feast laid out on the sideboard, with slices of fried potato, kidneys, a tureen of poached eggs, an entire platter of glistening sausages and a rack full of toast. I was already pleased with my pleasant room at the top of the stairs, and my dinner the night before had been excellent. Now, it seemed, breakfast was also a meal to be reckoned with.

Filling my plate, I returned to the table and sat down.

'Tea, sir?' said a low voice, barely more than a whisper.

I looked round and saw the Twickhams' maid at my elbow, holding a tray. Elsie was a thin, nervous-looking girl of fourteen or fifteen, and I tried to set her at ease by affecting a bonhomie which was alien to me. 'Why yes, thank you. And just a dash of milk, if you please.'

'Hrmph,' muttered the professor, and he shook his paper again.

Having poured my tea, Elsie left with her tray, and I set about the food on my plate, enjoying the excellent cooking. I glanced around the room as I ate, eyeing the rather severe portrait above the fireplace, and the heavy drapes drawn back on either side of the bay windows. As with the sitting room, there was a tangle of rose bushes just outside, these lending a greenish cast to the room as they filtered the light.

After twenty minutes I had no further room for eggs, nor toast, nor the tiniest sip of tea, and I sat back in my chair, replete. By my estimate it had just gone nine in the morning, and I was a little surprised there'd been no sign of Roberta at the breakfast table. I wondered whether she was a late riser, but she didn't seem the sort to waste the best part of the day in bed. I glanced at the professor, but decided not to trouble him. He was holding the newspaper like a defence against stubborn invaders, and I suspected this to be part of his morning ritual.

Then Elsie returned with her tray, only this time it bore a slim envelope. She didn't speak to the professor, just took the missive and laid it on the table next to the untouched breakfast things, before retreating once more.

Eventually, the professor lowered his paper and opened the letter, scanning the contents quickly. Then he took out a pocket watch, much like the one in my dreams, and there was a distant ringing noise as he touched something inside the lid.

I recalled something similar happening when I'd activated the metal cube the day before. I was not versed in physics, nor chemistry, nor any of the branches of science connected with the natural world, but even I knew that such a thing was unheard of, and yesterday I'd put the simultaneous ringing of a distant bell down to pure coincidence.

Now, though, I was forced to accept the truth, for impossible though it seemed, the professor's watch was somehow linked to a bell in another part of the house. I'd seen him press a contact, and I'd heard the bell at the same instant. There could be no coincidence, only a mystery yet to be explained.

I wanted to quiz the professor about his watch and its curious power, but at that moment I heard footsteps approaching. Not the light tread of Mrs Fairacre, nor the near-inaudible footfalls of the maid, but the thump of solid work boots. My spirits rose, for this could only be Roberta putting in an appearance at last.

She came in wearing the same outfit as the day before, possibly with even more of the sooty dust around her person. There was a streak of the stuff down one side of her face, and her ruddy cheeks looked like they'd been exposed to a substantial heat source. Meanwhile, the professor had returned to his newspaper, and he said nothing as his daughter entered the dining room.

'Good morning,' I said, getting up.

'Are you leaving already?'

I'd always been taught to stand for a lady, but as I'd discovered the day before, Roberta didn't set much store by the customs of polite society. 'I, er–'

She smiled. 'Relax, Mr Jones. I'm teasing you.'

'Ha-rumph,' muttered the professor from behind his paper.

'And a good morning to you too, father,' called Roberta. 'Are you not rising to greet me too?'

The paper rustled, but from the professor there was no reply but a stony silence.

'He's such a grump in the mornings,' said Roberta conversationally, and having fired this broadside at her father she strode to the sideboard to assemble her breakfast.

When she returned she sat alongside me, and then she tackled the food as though she hadn't had a solid meal for the past three days. As for myself, I wanted to ask her something, but I didn't want to interrupt her breakfast. I was also conscious of the raised newspaper at the head of the table, which looked like the prow of a ship aiming to run me down.

'Speak, Mr Jones,' said Roberta, as she chased a piece of egg around her plate with a fork. 'You have a question, I'm sure.'

'It's about your father's watch,' I said, in a low voice. 'Can it really cause a bell to ring at a distance?'

She smiled. 'You heard him summon me, then?'

'Yes, just after he received the letter.'

Roberta paused, the fork halfway to her mouth. Then she turned to the head of the table. 'There was a letter, father?'

The professor lowered his paper. 'A missive from Lady Eames. I will deal with her case this afternoon.'

'I think not.'

'I am perfectly capable of–'

'Father, do you recall the last time you visited a client on your own?'

There was a strained silence, during which they attempted to stare each other down, and then the professor's will broke. Without uttering a word, he busied himself with the newspaper once more.

The battle resolved, I raised the subject of the watch once more.

'What do you know about the properties of metal?' Roberta asked me, in a low voice.

'Precious little, if I'm honest.'

She launched into a brief explanation of melting, pouring and casting, and as she spoke I wondered whether this was the reason for her worker's garb, and the soot, and her flushed appearance. However, she was speaking in an animated fashion and I didn't care to interrupt.

Eventually, however, she reached the end of her brief explanation. I guessed she had omitted much of the detail, for her purpose was not to educate me, but to give me a grounding so that she could move on to the next part: how a common pocket watch could make a distant bell ring on command.

'It's my father's greatest discovery. Castings from the same pouring are connected, you see, and this connection can be fortified by the addition of certain elements and other...ingredients.'

'Such as?'

'Oh no, Mr Jones,' she said, with a laugh. 'We do not give our secrets away so lightly.'

Professor Twickham grunted from behind his newspaper, this time in agreement.

'Suffice to say,' continued Roberta, 'we have not yet perfected the process, nor have we discovered all the many combinations of metals and additives that might react in new and interesting ways. So far, we have but a handful of discoveries to our name, but in time they will grow, you can be sure of that.'

'But this is immense,' I said, as I realised the implications. 'Why, the military uses alone...'

The professor came alive of a sudden, bunching the newspaper with one hand in order to slam his fist on the table. 'Do not speak of the military in my house,' he growled, as the blow rattled plates, cutlery and teacups alike. 'Neither those dunderheads, nor the idiot politicians, nor–'

'Calm yourself, father,' said Roberta mildly.

'I'm going to my study,' said the professor, and he departed the room in a huff, leaving the crumpled newspaper lying across the table.

'I'm sorry, I didn't mean to upset your father,' I said, as his footsteps receded down the hall.

'You weren't to know,' said Roberta quietly. 'He tried to sell the idea once, but a room full of experts laughed him out of the meeting.'

'But surely a practical demonstration must have swayed them?'

'They put it down to trickery. Unfortunately, father has a somewhat colourful past.' Roberta eyed me, unsure how much to share. 'In years past, he convinced investors to fund a number of well-intentioned schemes, but alas they did not come to fruition. People lost their money, and in many circles my father was regarded as a charlatan at best, and a fraud at worst.'

'But that's unfair!' I cried. 'I've witnessed two unexplained mysteries in this house already, and I've been here less than a single day. These people would only have to see–'

'Please, Mr Jones. I will not have my father exposed to ridicule again. He's accepted his lot, and I'll ask you not to upset him.'

She was almost desperate in her pleading with me, and I couldn't very well argue. 'I understand,' I said, but inside I was excited by the possibilities. The professor and his daughter had discovered a fantastic new property in ordinary, everyday metals, and apparently there were many more discoveries to come. I foresaw endless practical applications for this store of unique knowledge, and my brain conjured up balance books overflowing with pounds, shillings and pence. I had an image of the professor and his daughter wealthy beyond measure, and I confess there was a selfish element too, because such riches in their pockets would surely inspire them to raise my own meagre wages.

But it all seemed for naught, because the professor was unwilling to risk his reputation. I noticed Roberta was still looking at me, unconvinced, and I took her hand in both of mine. 'Roberta, I vow to obey your wishes.'

She smiled at that, and I saw her relax. Then she got up to retrieve the letter, which she read quickly.

'Your father mentioned a case...' I began delicately. I didn't mean to pry, but they'd told me nothing about the nature of my job, and I was naturally curious.

She looked at me across the top of the letter. 'Do you believe in spirits? Ghosts and phantasms and the like?'

I laughed. 'I'm a bookkeeper. I believe in neat columns of figures.'

'I see.'

From the tone of her voice, I realised I'd erred in making light of the question. 'In truth, I have an open mind. But why do you ask?'

Slowly, Roberta folded the letter, placing it on the table. 'In order to further our discoveries, my father and I need money. And in order to earn money, we perform certain services for wealthy patrons. Services you might find distasteful.'

My mind leapt to several conclusions, one of them very distasteful indeed. But no, that simply wasn't possible.

Roberta noticed my expression. 'It's nothing illegal or immoral, I assure you.' She hesitated. 'Some folk, especially the elderly, are beset by...worries. We help to soothe their troubles.'

I was completely in the dark, and her skirting around the heart of the matter wasn't helping. 'Perhaps if you started with the letter?' I suggested.

'Here. Read it for yourself.'

My dearest Roberta,

It was such a relief to be free of troubling spirits after your recent visit, but I'm afraid that relief lasted barely a week. Already, the phantasms return, and my household is all on edge once more.

I urgently require your assistance in this matter, and I understand if your bill reflects the rapid attention I require. No amount of money is too much for peace of mind.

Lady Fotherington-Eames

P.S. Although money is no object, I did feel your last bill was excessive.

I read the letter twice, but could make no connection between her ladyship's fancies and the professor's study of metals. Finally, I placed the letter on the table and looked to Roberta for an explanation.

'She is troubled by spirits,' said Roberta.

'So I see.'

'And she will pay to have them removed.'

'I read that also.'

'My father and I, we...' she stopped, and was unable to look me in the eyes. 'We remove troublesome spirits on behalf of our clients.'

In my dream, the professor had appeared as a music-hall magician, complete with top hat, tails and magic wand. Now, it seemed, my dream had a ring of truth to it after all. And what of Roberta? Was this intelligent young woman nothing more than the magician's assistant, twirling around in her undergarments and handing her father his props during his act? Shocked, I sat back in my seat, subconsciously distancing myself from Roberta. 'But only the worst kind of charlatan would play a trick like that! Why, you're deceiving an old lady out of her money!' Then a further thought occurred to me, one even more troubling. 'You're not planning on involving *me* in such parlour games?' I pushed my chair back and stood. 'If that's the case, then the devil take your contract and your fifty pounds a year. I shall walk out this instant!'

She looked up at me. 'Will you sit and listen, you self-righteous idiot?'

The words were cutting, but she spoke with a certain fondness, like a sister chiding a sibling. Feeling a little foolish after my passionate outburst, I retook my seat.

She, in turn, leaned towards me and clasped my hands in hers. 'You must understand this. Whatever we're doing, whatever show we put on for our clients...it works.'

I studied Roberta's face, noting her earnest expression, and I decided that she had to be telling the truth. Either that, or she was the most accomplished liar I had ever met. 'But ghosts and phantasms...' I protested. 'They belong in a Dickens serial, not real life!'

'Septimus, all I ask is that you keep an open mind,' said Roberta.

At that moment I became aware of two things. First, she was still holding my hands, and her slim fingers were warm and strong. And second, she had addressed me by my Christian name for the very first time. I am not a man given to romantic notions and the like, but I confess my heart quickened.

She, perhaps noticing this, withdrew her hands and folded them in her lap. 'In any case, it does not matter,' she said, her manner all of a sudden more formal. 'You were employed in a financial capacity, and the work my father and I perform is neither here nor there. I have already revealed more than I should have, and should you be tempted to speak of our methods to outsiders, I would direct you to the terms of your contract.'

I recalled the document I had signed the day before, of which I had read not a single word. 'I will not share your secrets. You can trust me.'

'I hope that is the case.' Roberta gave me a reassuring smile. 'Over time, as we get to know you, I'm sure father and I will reveal more of the workings of our business. You must be patient though, since others we once thought trustworthy turned out to be anything but.'

This was the first I had heard of any others, and I was about to ask about the fate of my predecessors when Roberta stood. 'Come, I will show you to your office. It's time you made a start on your day.'

She led me to a study on the second floor, smaller than the professor's and illuminated by a single gaslight. There was a modest desk, the surface worn from use, and a small bookcase nearby which contained several dozen ledgers. Piled on top were numerous stacks of paperwork, at least a foot thick from the look of them. On the desk stood an inkwell and a number of quills, along with a blotter. On the wall behind the desk there were two paintings, one depicting a naval battle with tall ships, the other a country scene with cows. Nearby, a high-backed chair completed the furnishings, the leather seat sunken and cracked.

Roberta gestured towards the bookcase. 'For the time being, I'd like you to enter expenses, receipts and invoices into the correct ledgers. It is some weeks since they were updated, and I know there are clients who have yet to pay what they owe.'

'But of course.' After the strange events and revelations of the past twenty-four hours, I relished the opportunity to bury myself in some traditional bookkeeping. 'Until what time should I work?'

'There are no set hours, as long as the accounts are up to date.' She saw me eyeing the stacks of paperwork to be processed, and laughed. 'There is no need for alarm, Mr Jones. We do not expect miracles. Work at a steady pace, and you will be meeting your obligations. Now, I have matters to attend to, so I will leave you to your work.'

After she departed, I transferred the three most recent ledgers to the desk, these covering a period of approximately six months. Then I took a large stack of paperwork and set it alongside. There were pages of all sizes, with notes from merchants requesting payment for goods and services rendered, all mixed up with letters and invoices for the Twickhams' clients. The first dozen pages alone spanned the past week, and lines from several jumped out at me as I leafed through.

Qr cwt Portland cement
10 lb copper
10 lb lead
2 lb tin
Cleansing and inspection, five pounds ten shillings.
Half cwt charcoal

With enough to be going on with for the time being, I sat at the desk and began sorting a large pile of paperwork. Engrossed in my task, I scarcely noticed the passage of time until I reached the final page. Then, with the paperwork ready, I opened the most recent ledger in order to transfer the figures. I was met by neat columns of figures, and I nodded in approval as I saw the careful penmanship. Turning the pages, I discovered that the previous bookkeeper – whoever he or she might have been – had been fastidious and accurate.

The figures continued in this fashion until well into the ledger, but then something strange happened. As I turned the pages, I saw the neatness marred by frequent crossings-out and corrections. The lettering was no longer even and well-ordered, but instead became ragged and spiky, as though the author had suffered cramps in their fingers. Turning more pages, I saw gaps in the numbers, with random markings and symbols I did not recognise.

Then came two pages with hundreds of symbols scrawled one atop the next, forming an indecipherable jumble. And finally, as I turned to the final page, an oath escaped my lips. For there, scrawled across the page in a savage, barely-controlled hand, were the following words:

KILL THEM!
KILL THEM ALL!

I felt a cold sensation creeping over me as I stared at the ragged lettering scrawled on the page, and then I could stand it no more. Closing the ledger with a snap, I pushed it away from me in horror. What tortured soul had poured such vitriol onto the pages? What kind of slow, creeping madness had overtaken them?

For it was obvious from the dates in the ledger that this had not been a sudden transformation, triggered perhaps by an evening of strong liquor or drug-taking. No, this was a slow infusion of horror which had overtaken the bookkeeper day by day, week by week.

I felt a shiver up my spine, and I glanced around the small office. It felt like a malevolent presence was watching me.

Knock knock!

I started, then realised this had not been the taunting of some other-worldly spirit. No, it was merely someone at my door. 'Enter,' I called.

Elsie, the Twickhams' maid, came in carrying a silver platter. 'A letter for you, sir,' she said quietly. 'Came by messenger, it did.'

This was a surprise indeed, for nobody outside the household knew of my current address. 'Are you sure it's not for the professor?'

'I *can* read, sir,' said the girl, with a hint of rebuke in her voice.

'I'm sorry, I didn't mean to question you.' She held out the platter without comment, and I took the letter. 'Thank you, Elsie.'

'Begging your pardon, but Mrs Fairacre will serve luncheon at noon.'

'Excellent. Please tell her I am most grateful.' I spoke absentmindedly, for I was inspecting the envelope, which was indeed addressed to me. Then, as the maid turned to leave, a sudden thought occurred to me. 'Elsie, what do you know of my predecessor?'

She looked confused. 'I'm sorry, sir?'

'The person who kept the accounts before me,' I said, gesturing around the small office. 'The person who worked in here. Did you know of them?'

She looked down at the floor. 'I'm sure I can't say, Mr Jones. It's not my place to speak out.'

'Very well. My thanks once more.'

The door closed behind her, and I turned the envelope over and broke the seal. Inside was a single sheet of paper.

Attend the Crown and Feather after seven p.m., and you will learn something to your advantage.

At the bottom was a drawing of two triangles, entwined, but apart from this curious symbol the note bore no signature, nor any other clue as to the sender's identity. I raised the page to my nose, but there was no discernible scent, and I was just inspecting the envelope once more when I heard a commotion downstairs. I opened the door and heard a clatter of footsteps in the hallway, and then Roberta's distraught voice.

'Elsie, help him to the sitting room!' she cried. 'Quick now, and fetch brandy!'

I dashed from my office and bounded downstairs, leaping the steps two at a time. At the bottom, I saw Roberta and the maid supporting Professor Twickham, who looked as near-death as I've ever seen a man. His face was pallid and his head lolled to one side, his movements feeble and helpless. But then, as he was half-carried through the doorway to the lounge, his eyes met mine, and I drew a shuddering breath. The orbs were entirely black, as though fashioned from the night sky, and at the sight of such horror I let out an involuntary cry.

'Don't just stand there!' shouted Roberta, catching sight of me. 'Come and help him!'

The three of us guided the professor to an armchair, knocking over a side table in our hurry. Knick-knacks and mementos scattered on the rug, and Elsie automatically crouched to pick them up.

'Leave that!' shouted Roberta. 'Brandy.'

'Yes, ma'am,' said Elsie, and she fled the room.

Meanwhile Roberta had knelt before her father, and was feeling his wrist. He'd slumped in the chair, those dark eyes now hidden behind closed eyelids, and with growing horror I feared he might have breathed his last. But when Roberta slapped his cheek, none too gently, he groaned and struggled to sit up. 'Father, can you hear me?'

Elsie returned with a glass brimming with brandy, and Roberta snatched it from the tray and held it to the professor's lips. 'Here, drink deep,' she muttered. 'This will aid you, if nothing else.'

Until this point, I'd been rendered speechless by the professor's appearance, but now I finally gathered my wits. A stiff drink wouldn't be enough to revive the old man, I was sure of that. 'I shall fetch a physician,' I declared.

'No!' Roberta grabbed my arm. 'No earthly medicine will heal this wound. Instead, I will ask you to watch over him while I devise a method of extracting...' Her voice tailed off.

'Extracting what?' I demanded.

'I–I cannot explain right now.'

'But...what happened? What manner of illness *is* this?'

Roberta dashed a lock of hair from her eye. 'A piece of equipment malfunctioned, that is all.'

If the words were meant to be reassuring they failed dismally, for I could see how worried she was. Then the professor coughed, and we turned to see him reaching for the brandy glass. Roberta pressed it into his hands, and the professor drained the glass before coughing once more. Finally, he opened his eyes, and to my surprise there was no sign of the earlier darkness, his eyes now being normal aside from the tears brought on by the brandy. I recalled his earlier appearance, and wondered whether I'd been mistaken. Had it had been a trick of the light, perhaps exaggerated by my experience with the ghastly writing in the ledger upstairs?

'Father?' asked Roberta in concern. 'Do you know where you are?'

The professor was looking wistfully at the empty glass. 'A little more brandy, I think, and then I will remember for certain.'

'Oh, you old goat!' cried Roberta, and she hugged him where he sat. Her face was turned towards me, her eyes closed tight, and I saw tears of relief running down her cheeks. 'I thought you were dead!'

'There there,' said the professor, patting her awkwardly on the head. 'Don't fuss now. Don't fuss.'

I felt entirely out of place witnessing this tender scene, and I turned away, intending to leave them in peace. Then I saw the maid with her tray. 'Come, Elsie. Fetch the professor another glass, if you please.'

She hurried away, and I followed her from the room. Here I encountered Mrs Fairacre, who was coming towards me from the kitchens. 'What's happened now?' she demanded. 'Why all the fuss?'

'An accident, by all accounts, but the professor is recovered,' I said, and I laid a hand on her sleeve as she made to enter the lounge. 'I would leave them be for the time being.'

'Oh, that foolish old dear,' muttered Mrs Fairacre. 'He *will* meddle with things he doesn't understand. I warned him it would lead to no good, I swear I did!'

I was tempted to enquire further, but the housekeeper was almost as upset as Roberta and it would have been unseemly to press her for information in that state. Then Elsie returned with a glass of brandy on her tray, only for Mrs Fairacre to take the tray and send the maid back to the kitchens. 'Go on, back to your work,' she said, and I wasn't sure whether she was addressing Elsie...or me. Before I could say anything, the housekeeper bustled into the lounge room carrying the brandy.

I did not want to return to my office, not after Roberta had indicated I might be needed, and so I waited in the hallway. The three in the lounge were talking in low voices, and I decided to move down the hall a little way to avoid overhearing their conversation. Had I been lacking in morals I would have listened to every word, but I consoled myself with the thought that the truth would come out eventually.

As I neared the front door I noticed a pair of haversacks leaning against the wall. I could see the legs of two metal tripods protruding from the nearest, and I wondered what cache of intriguing equipment was causing the bags to bulge in such an interesting fashion.

'Mr Jones?'

The housekeeper's voice made me jump, even though I had been doing nothing wrong. Reluctantly, I turned away from the haversacks, any chance of exploring further now lost. 'Yes, Mrs Fairacre?'

'Miss Twickham asks if you would mind the professor.'

'Of course.' I hurried down the hall and entered the lounge, where I found the professor much recovered. He was sitting up, he looked brighter and he'd managed to empty the second glass of brandy...a fact which I suspected largely responsible for the ruddy colour now present in his cheeks. 'Sir, how are you feeling?'

'Ver' good, ver' good indeed,' said the professor. 'Take more than a stray ghostie to knock me down, eh?'

I turned to Roberta, concerned that the shock had unhinged the professor's mind, but she merely smiled. 'He's just a little merry,' she said. 'Be a dear and watch him for me, will you? I must go and prepare.'

She got up and left, and after a hurried conversation with Mrs Fairacre in the corridor, I heard both of them departing. As for me, I set the side table back on its legs and gathered the items which had been knocked all over the rug earlier, placing them anyhow on the polished wooden surface. Then I drew up a nearby armchair and sat facing the professor.

The elderly gentleman was showing no signs of his earlier distress. Rather, he was sitting in his chair and smiling at nothing in particular. I decided not to speak with him, preferring to leave him be and not risk agitating him. Instead, I gathered what clues I had and tried to set them in order.

I guessed that the professor and his daughter had paid a visit to the customer who'd written to them that morning. Furthermore, from the professor's obvious malaise, their visit had been less than successful. Were there clues in the haversacks full of equipment? Oh, how I wished I could inspect them more closely!

I glanced at the professor. Dare I leave him, even for a moment? He ought to be safe enough, and this might be my only chance to gain the knowledge I sought before Roberta or Mrs Fairacre packed the equipment away.

I decided to risk it, and within seconds I was on my feet, heading for the hall. I stopped in the doorway, listened carefully for the sound of voices or approaching footsteps, then hurried along the corridor towards the front door.

6

I moved quickly along the hall, making for the shadows at the front door where the bags were still present. I confess my heart was in my mouth as I crouched to inspect the contents, for I am not one given to snooping or sneaking. My usual thrills came from checking the totals in a double-entry ledger to discover my sums were accurate and without error, not poking through someone else's belongings.

Under the circumstances, though, I felt it justified. If nobody would reveal the truth to me, I would uncover it for myself.

Opening the straps on the nearest haversack, I lifted the flap and peered inside. The first item to meet my eyes was a metal cage of around six inches in height, with a screw fitting on the underside. It looked like a lantern, although there was no glass, and instead of a wick I saw a bronze cylinder within, suspended from fine wires like a spider in its web. I recognised the cylinder, for I had seen numerous examples in the professor's study the day before, but unlike those specimens this one had been blasted open at one end. The rounded metal cap was split, with fragments peeled back like a ring of petals, and I could see right inside to the blackened metal interior. Was it an explosive device which had gone off prematurely, leading to the professor's dazed state?

Some of the wires holding the cylinder were broken, snapped apart by the same force that had damaged the device, and as I studied the curious setup I itched to pick it up for a closer look. I glanced down the hallway, but the house was as quiet as the grave and there was no sign of Roberta, the housekeeper, or the maid.

So, I lifted the cage from the haversack and set it aside. Underneath there was a wad of netting, carefully folded. It was cold to the touch, and I realised it was made from metal wire, drawn to an unnatural thinness. I laid this aside also, and beneath that I saw half a dozen metal discs of the type the professor had shown me the day before. I picked one up, turning it over, but there was nothing unusual about it.

There was nothing else, so I replaced the contents and turned my attention to the second bag. Engrossed, I was reaching for the flap when I heard a sharp voice behind me.

'Mr Jones? What are you doing?'

I stood up fast, as though my legs were on springs, and turned a ghastly, guilty look on Mrs Fairacre. 'The professor asked me to fetch his bag,' I said quickly, for it was the first thing that came into my head.

The housekeeper's face softened at the mention of her employer. 'The professor is fast asleep. You would know this, if you were still watching over him.' She eyed the bags at my feet, which were both closed, and I was relieved I'd yet to begin my inspection of the second. 'And in any case, those are Miss Roberta's things.'

'The professor seemed a little confused,' I said lamely. 'I, er...I'll return to him immediately.'

'No, I will mind the professor. You are to join Miss Twickham in the workshop, where she requires your assistance.' Mrs Fairacre pointed down the hall. 'Go past the stairs and take the second door on the right.'

I set off, relieved I'd escaped further questioning. The housekeeper was no fool, and I was certain she'd have interrogated me further if she weren't so concerned for the professor's well-being. I got the impression that Mrs Fairacre was fond of the professor, but there was nothing improper in that. The previous evening, over dinner, Roberta told me her mother had passed some years ago, after a long illness. If Mrs Fairacre sought to become the professor's next wife, it was no business of mine.

As I approached the door I'd been directed to, I felt like one mystery at least had just been solved, for a workshop would explain the overalls Roberta frequently wore as well as the soot liberally sprinkled all over them. Upon opening the door I was met by a wall of heat, such that I took an involuntary step back. If the very gates of hell had opened before me, I couldn't have been more surprised, and my first impression was reinforced by the steep, narrow staircase leading down beyond the door. This was illuminated from below by a deep reddish glow, which flickered and gleamed off the brick walls in a most disturbing fashion. There was also a roaring sound, such as a furnace might make, and the clatter and whirr of machinery.

After closing the door behind me, I started down the steps, and fortunately the heat grew a little less intense as I descended. The noise, on the other hand, increased. I once visited a textile mill, with its steam engines and giant rattling looms, and this sound was eerily similar. It was also the last thing one expected to hear inside a cellar.

I reached a turn in the stairs, and as I rounded the corner the noise grew louder still. I could now see a large fireplace set into the far wall, with grated vents providing fresh air from outside in order to feed the flames. And fed they were, for the flames danced, white-hot, upon a boiler almost large enough to drive a locomotive. A heavy pipe led from the boiler to a smaller receptacle, and from there steam pipes branched out, leading along both walls.

At the bottom of the steps I came to a halt and looked around. The cellar was large, the roof supported by numerous brick columns which cast long shadows across the uneven floor, and I could see workbenches and machinery against the walls, along with racks of tools, spare parts and half-built equipment. There was little time to waste gawking as Roberta was working nearby at a lathe, and even as I watched I saw bright swarf curling away from whatever she was turning. The lathe was driven by a pulley, itself turned by a belt running at enormous speed. The belt ran almost to the arched ceiling, where it looped over a second pulley on a shaft driven by steam from the boiler.

The speeding belt was only a foot or two from Roberta's shoulder, and as I watched it flexing and vibrating I feared the grievous injury she might suffer if it should come free. But she seemed oblivious, the long corkscrews of metal gathering at her feet as she worked. Then, Roberta having finished, she turned and nodded her thanks as she saw me standing nearby. 'I know this isn't your area of expertise, Mr Jones,' she shouted, 'but I really need your help.'

'What are you *doing* down here?' I asked her, raising my voice over the sound of machinery.

Roberta reached for a lever on the wall and pulled it firmly, relaxing the pulley near the ceiling and thereby stopping the frantic spinning of the lathe. The noise lessened immediately, and we were able to converse at a more normal volume. 'There's no time to explain fully,' she told me. 'Suffice to say father has been infected by a particular malaise, and I must draw it out of him.'

'Is it...a malevolent spirit?'

She looked at me, surprised. 'Why, Mr Jones. Just this morning you were scoffing at such notions.'

This was true enough, but at breakfast that morning I'd yet to see the mad scribbling in the ledger, nor the blackness which had briefly flooded the professor's eyes. 'Certain...phenomena...have convinced me to take your claims a little more seriously.'

'Only a little?' She gave me a wry smile. 'Well, it's a beginning at least. But come now, my father suffers while we chatter.'

'Mrs Fairacre told me he was fast asleep.'

'A glass or two of brandy never fails,' said Roberta, with a nod. 'I find it easier to treat him like this. He complains a good deal less whilst sleeping.'

'Are you saying this has happened before?' I asked, scandalised.

'It's a hazard of our work, Mr Jones.'

'But–'

'Please! You shall have your explanations later, if you care to listen. For now, you must do as I ask.' Roberta led me to a manual arbor press, where I saw a small bucket of objects which looked like misshapen bronze pebbles. She took one of these pebbles, placed it on the die, then reached up with both hands and put all her weight behind the press's lever. The ram came down, slowly, and when Roberta released the lever I saw the pebble now flattened into a perfectly round disc. Roberta tapped it out of the die and handed it to me, and I felt the warmth in the newly-shaped metal. It was a twin to those in the haversacks upstairs, but this one had intricate tracings stamped into each side. 'I need a dozen of those,' said Roberta. 'Hurry, please.'

I set to work, and discovered the lever took a lot more effort than

I expected. My arms were more used to the turning of pages in a ledger, and I felt my muscles aching after I'd created no more than two or three of the shaped discs. Then I heard a roar, and I turned to see Roberta near the fire, using a bellows to generate even more heat. She'd placed a small crucible in the flames, the metal glowing cherry-red, and as I watched she plucked the crucible from the fire and carried it to a workbench. Here, I saw a small bronze cylinder propped upright, the open end facing down into a thick metal cup.

Very carefully, Roberta poured a small quantity of molten lead into the cup, where it spattered and hissed. She set the crucible aside, and used the tongs to pick up the cylinder, which now had a domed cap of silvery metal sealing the open end. I recognised the shape, for the cylinder was the same design as those in the professor's study. This one was slightly larger, though, and as I recalled the shattered cylinder I'd spied in the haversack, I understood why Roberta had built one of a heavier design.

I had not paused in my work whilst observing Roberta at hers, and by now I had forged half a dozen of the metal discs. My shoulders were protesting at the labour, and my hands felt like they were about to come apart at the wrists. I stopped to dash the sweat from my brow, and as I moved the latest disc from the press, I noticed something odd. The markings stamped into the surface were arranged in an intricate, swirling pattern, but there were no corresponding ridges on the face of the die. In addition, when I compared the latest pressing to the half-dozen I'd already manufactured, I discovered every single one of them exhibited a different design.

Stunned, I picked up one of the large copper-alloy nuggets I'd been stamping, and I turned it over and over in my hand. It was heavy, as smooth as a beach pebble, and there was no sign of any markings that would explain the whorls in the finished discs. At breakfast, Roberta had told me about the ingredients she'd been experimenting with, and I wondered what manner of other-worldly materials might be present in the metal. Then, realising I was falling behind in my work, I placed the large nugget in the die and applied my protesting arms to the lever once more. A new disc emerged from the die, and I was not surprised to see a distinctive pattern that was unlike any of the others.

I heard a metallic squeal, and turned to see Roberta spinning the cylinder in the lathe, which was rattling and rumbling once more. Curls of swarf flew from the newly-sealed cylinder, and I saw the misshapen end cap become gleaming and smooth under the cutting tool's sharpened bit. I realised Roberta had almost finished, and so I pressed the remaining discs until I had the round dozen she'd asked for.

She completed her work at the same time, and, after stalling the lathe and dousing the cylinder in a bucket of water, she headed for the stairs. 'Bring those,' she called over her shoulder, indicating the discs.

7

We found the professor asleep still, with Mrs Fairacre in attendance. The housekeeper spied the cylinder in Roberta's hands, and shook her head, her lips thinning. 'You're meddling with things you don't understand, Miss Twickham. One day you'll both go too far.' Then she glanced at me. 'And now there's another innocent roped into your schemes. Have you not learned your lesson?'

'Hush, Mrs Fairacre. I promised Septimus a full disclosure after I've seen to my father.'

'If he lasts that long,' said the housekeeper darkly. 'You do what you must, but I will not be made to watch. It's unnatural.'

As she left us, I recalled the frantic scrawl in the ledger. Had my predecessor been asked to help as well? Was that why he'd been driven out of his mind? As I stood there clutching the metal discs, I wondered whether to walk out of that house and never look back – contract be damned. But then I caught Roberta looking at me, her face flushed from the fire, and I realised I could not abandon her. My contribution, no matter how minor, might help to save the professor, and I could not flee from such a responsibility.

'Hold this for me,' murmured Roberta, and she added the newly-fashioned cylinder to my load. It was about five inches long, half as big again as the smaller versions I'd already seen, and heavier than it looked. I still had no idea as to its purpose, but I guessed I would shortly find out.

Roberta left, returning moments later with the two haversacks. She took out the tripods and placed them one at each end of the room, then began unfolding the fine metal netting I'd seen earlier. 'Take this end for me,' she said, holding it out. 'Careful. It's fragile.'

I took the net as requested, and watched as she extended the tripod and fastened her end to a pair of hooks. I copied her, and we moved the tripods apart until the net stretched across the room. The professor was seated on the far side, between the net and the bay window, and as a shaft of sunlight gleamed on the fine wiring I wondered at its purpose. It reached neither floor nor ceiling, so could not be intended to catch anything, and it wasn't strong enough to stop the professor, so it was not meant to trap him either.

Roberta now took the metal discs and began placing them about the room, forming a circle around the professor. I noticed she omitted one disc from the pattern, leaving an opening next to the bay window. Then she took the cage from the haversack and removed the broken cylinder, dropping the latter into the bag. She took the new, larger cylinder from me, and after some fiddling and adjustments she got it mounted in the centre of the lantern-like cage, where it stood like a metal candle. Then she placed the lantern device on a side-table near the professor.

I should add that every step of this process was carried out with practiced ease, as though Roberta had performed the routine numerous times. For my part, I tried to absorb every detail, adding to the abundant questions I was saving for later.

Now Roberta returned to the haversacks, opening the one I had not managed to inspect earlier. She fished around inside, the contents clanking as she did so, then withdrew a tool much like a spanner or wrench. But this device had a round bulge in the middle of the handle, and each end had four prongs rather than the usual two. Hanging the tool from her overalls, Roberta took out a skullcap fashioned from the same fine metal as the net, with a broad metal band to hold it in shape. Finally, she withdrew two glass bottles, one containing amber fluid and the other, clear. These had cut-glass stoppers, and looked like they belonged in a drinks cabinet rather than a tool bag. She set them on a side table, then beckoned me over.

'What do you want me to do?' I asked her.

'Hold the bottles for me, and I beg you not to drop either of them.'

Once I had them in hand, Roberta ducked under the net and approached her father. Without ceremony she placed the metal cap on his head, adjusting it to her liking before turning to me. 'Bring them here, if you please.'

The bottles were cold to the touch, unnaturally so, and I felt my fingers turning numb as I obeyed. Roberta took the bottle containing the amber fluid and, holding the stopper tightly in place, tipped it over and back again several times. Then she pulled the stopper, and I stepped back in alarm as a greenish mist rose from the neck of the bottle. 'Wh-what is that?' I asked.

'It's a highly volatile liquid,' she explained. 'The bottle must be stoppered at all times, for the contents would soon disperse if not.'

That didn't explain why the amber fluid gave off a green gas, but Roberta was busy and I didn't want to interrupt again. She took the stopper, which contained several drops of the liquid, and dabbed them on the metal cap. Then she replaced the stopper and handed me the bottle, taking the other in its place. This one she tipped over far more carefully, and I could see her tensing as she prepared to remove the stopper. 'Whatever happens...' began Roberta, addressing me in a low voice. 'No matter what you see, I ask you not to disturb my preparations, for it might prove fatal.'

Fatal for whom? I wanted to ask, but at that moment Roberta took the stopper from the second bottle. She applied several droplets of the clear liquid to the mesh cap on her father's head, then stoppered the bottle and passed it back to me. I, meanwhile, was studying the professor intently for any change in his condition. Or, indeed, any sign that the two liquids were anything other than dye and plain water respectively. In the back of my mind I still wondered whether this was part of an elaborate hoax, but what would be the point? I was a penniless bookkeeper, not the sole heir to a wealthy estate.

In the next few moments my lingering doubts would be erased for good, and the events I was about to witness would change my life for all time.

It began with tendrils of purplish smoke, which trickled from under the cap on the professor's head and ran down his body like rivulets of blood. The smoke pooled on the rug at his feet, spreading out rapidly. Roberta ignored it, and was soon ankle-deep in the foul-looking fumes, while I, far less daring, backed away rapidly.

'You must stand still!' cried Roberta. 'Do not flee now!'

Standing still was the last thing I wanted to do, but her manner brooked no argument. Unwillingly, I let the smoke roll over my shoes, watching it rise almost to my knees, and at the same time I sensed a cold, unpleasant tingling in my ankles and calves. I wanted to break free of the smoke and leap onto the nearest chair, but my legs felt immobilised and I was no longer certain movement would even be possible. 'I–is this...a spirit?' I whispered, and I was convinced my eyes were as round as saucers.

Roberta shook her head. 'This smoke is merely the result of a chemical reaction.'

I took heart from her casual acceptance of the situation, even though the urge to step out of the rolling waves of purple smoke was strong. As the seconds passed and my legs failed to dissolve, or even vanish into thin air, I grew more accustomed to the smoke, and the feeling of panic subsided.

Meanwhile, the spreading pool of smoke had now reached the circle of metal discs Roberta had laid out. Here, the advancing waves reared up like a living thing, before falling back on themselves. Then, with a flash that seared my vision and a bang that made me jump two feet in the air, a bolt of lightning shot out of the cap on the professor's head. It struck the nearest metal disc, then jumped to the next, and the next after that, until the circle arced with high-powered electricity. Tendrils of pure light crackled and sparked, illuminating the room with the power of a thousand photographic flashes, and through squinting, shielded eyes I saw that all of the circle was joined apart from the one missing disc at the window. Nearby, stray bolts of light jumped out at random, connecting to metal objects all over the room, and I saw candelabra and engraved metal cubes knocked flying by the force of the discharge. The smell was intense, like seared metal, and the noise indescribable. Through all of this, Roberta and I were untouched, but then I remembered the source of this wild, uncontrolled power, and I turned to the professor in concern.

He sat in the chair with his eyes wide open, his jaw clenched, his fingers gripping the armrests as though he were trying to crush the wood with his bare hands. I could see him convulsing, helpless, and I was about to leap forward to help when Roberta raised a hand, stopping me. 'Let it run its course!' she shouted. 'It's the only way.'

'But you're killing him!' I protested.

'You have to trust me,' Roberta shouted back.

Even as she spoke, the writhing bolts of electricity changed colour, turning a deeper shade of blue. They also lessened in intensity, and the professor stopped shaking quite so much. I wondered whether the process was complete, but now Roberta took the odd-looking wrench from her belt and waded through the smoke to the professor, moving closer until she could reach out and touch the tool against the metal cap. Before it got close, I saw a ball of red energy *oozing* from the mesh enclosing the professor's head, as though his very life force were being squeezed through the fine metal. This red energy stretched out towards the tool in Roberta's hand, growing in size and intensity as it fastened onto the prongs. The bulk of the glowing, iridescent shape was already attached to the wrench, but a fine strand remained, connecting the tool to the mesh cap. Then, with a deft motion reminiscent of an angler, Roberta whipped the wrench backwards, drawing the final remnants of glowing red energy from the professor's being. I stared in fascination as the energy writhed and twisted on the device, mere inches from Roberta's hand, the glow bathing both her and the professor in baleful red light. I had no doubt this was the evil energy – the spirit, if you will – that had taken refuge in the professor's body, and I wondered how he'd survived the hosting of such a being.

I watched, heart in mouth, as the baleful red energy struck tendrils out in several directions. In turn it met the sparking electrical current and the metal net Roberta and I had strung across the room, and each of the questing tendrils were forced back to the parent, thwarted in their escape.

I wondered what would happen if it slunk down the tool and transferred itself into Roberta. I would have no chance of helping her, not even if I repeated her steps one by one, and I doubted the professor would be in any state to save her. At least if it came for me, Roberta might be able to banish it once more.

But the restless entity did not try to attack us, and I decided the purple smoke filling the area had to be the reason. It must have imbued us with a defensive screen of sorts, and was sufficient to keep the foul being from our flesh.

While I'd been observing, Roberta hadn't been idle. She was approaching the lantern-style device with the energy still clinging to the very end of the tool. As she got closer, I saw the dense red glow *reaching* for the newly-made cylinder in the lantern, with tendrils seeming to float through the very air. The first of these connected with the cylinder, and then, with an audible *snap*, the entire mass of glowing red light disappeared.

The crackling, spitting lightning ceased immediately, and the professor slumped in his chair, motionless. Roberta hung the tool from her overalls and crouched to pull back one of her father's eyelids. 'That's a good sign,' she said, her face strained and pale. 'He's alive, at least. Now he must rest.'

The purple smoke was rising into the air, slowly dissipating. I coughed as the acrid fumes invaded my lungs, and crossed to the bay windows to let the haze clear. The catch was stiff, but I managed to get one window open, and the smoke drifted into the thick rose bushes outside.

I turned, and was struck by the scene. Roberta was still inspecting her father, both of them half-hidden in the thick, foggy atmosphere. The cap on the professor's head still flickered with occasional sparks, and then I forgot the sight as a rattle from the nearby table caught my attention. The metal cage sat on the side table nearby, and the cylinder inside was shaking purposefully, as though the spirit inside were fighting to get out. The maze of metal wires suspending the cylinder tensed and slackened as they absorbed these violent movements, and to my relief I saw they were holding fast.

'Well, Mr Jones,' said Roberta at last. 'After what you've just seen, do you still believe my father and I are nothing but charlatans?'

For once in my life I was lost for words, and I could only shake my head.

8

Roberta and I unhooked the net together, then folded it and packed it away. She collected the tripods while I went around the room picking up the metal discs. As I collected each one, I discovered to my surprise that the elaborate patterns on both sides had simply...disappeared. Now, they were just smooth, featureless metal.

Roberta saw me inspecting the discs, and explained. 'When forged, they contain certain elemental powers. These are leached out during the extraction process you just witnessed.'

'What...what kind of elemental powers?'

Roberta indicated the cylinder inside the metal cage. It was still moving of its own accord, although much less violently. 'When melting the source materials, we include traces of the captured spirits themselves.'

I looked down at the inert discs in my hand, and my expression must have betrayed my concerns.

'Don't worry,' said Roberta. 'The spirit matter is entirely consumed by the process.'

'But how did you learn of these properties? How did you–?'

She smiled at the professor, who was sleeping peacefully in his chair. 'Father spent many years experimenting, and we learn more with every passing day.'

'But this is immense!' I cried. 'If these malevolent spirits infest our very beings, why is there no outcry in the papers?'

'If you spoke to a reporter about the events you witnessed here today, what would the reaction be?'

I took her point, but I still had objections. 'Your clients, then. Lady...Fotherington-Eames, was it not? Surely people would believe a respected member of the nobility?'

'Mr Jones, members of the nobility would be far less respected if they went around claiming they'd employed my father and I to capture ghosts and phantasms on their behalf. We are bound to strict secrecy, as you can imagine.'

I recalled an invoice I'd seen upstairs, in my office. 'You call it a cleansing, don't you?'

'An accurate description, you must admit.'

Even so, the secrecy astounded me. 'How many of these...ghosts...are there?'

'Nobody can say for certain. As you saw with my father, possession can appear to be an everyday illness, and let me tell you, that was a particularly strong spirit. The lesser entities we encounter cause little trouble, with most of them being entirely harmless. Why, you could be possessed by a mild spirit this very instant, and you would not know it.'

A shiver ran down my spine at the thought, and I wondered whether I was truly infected with an ethereal being. Would I even know it, or would it take over my very thoughts and actions piecemeal, until I was a helpless automaton held in its thrall? All of a sudden I recalled the defaced ledger in my office. What if the bookkeeper who'd scrawled in those pages hadn't been driven mad after all? What if there was another explanation? 'Tell me, what happened to my predecessor?'

Roberta's expression changed. 'Edgar,' she said, in a low voice. 'His name was Edgar.'

I don't know which troubled me more: her obvious distress at the thought of him, or her use of the past tense.

'He was my cousin,' continued Roberta. 'He...died. It was very sudden.'

'I'm sorry, I did not mean to pry.' Despite my words, I very much wanted to know more about this Edgar, and especially his fate. 'Was his demise the result of...' I began delicately, indicating the equipment.

'A contributing factor, perhaps.' Roberta shook herself. 'I'd prefer not to speak of it, if you don't mind. My father is still weak, and I must tend to him.'

'Of course, of course!' I exclaimed. 'Forgive me. I will leave you in peace while I attend to my duties.'

'Thank you, Mr Jones. We both appreciate your help today, and I hope that witnessing the extraction did not overly tax your nerves.'

'I believe I'm made of sterner stuff than that, Roberta.'

'I hope you are, Mr Jones. Believe me, I truly hope you are.'

After a brief lunch, which Roberta did not attend, I retired to my office to continue sorting paperwork. First, though, I excised the ruined pages from the journal, cutting them out with a sharp knife to disguise the fact they were missing. I planned to burn them in the downstairs fireplace at the earliest opportunity, but for now I folded them into quarters and tucked them inside my breast pocket.

With cousin Edgar's handiwork removed, I proceeded to update the ledger, spending a busy few hours entering figures and totalling the results. It was a relief to work on something so mundane and ordinary after the scenes in the sitting room, and I confess I lost track of time completely.

It must have been three o'clock when I heard a knock at the door. It opened, and Roberta looked in. 'Good afternoon, Mr Jones. I'm sorry to trouble you, but–' She broke off as she saw the paperwork covering my desk, and the much-reduced stacks on the bookshelf. 'Goodness, you *have* made a start!'

'It's a beginning,' I said modestly. 'But I hope to catch up soon.'

'Yes, that's why I'm here. I was rude to you in my father's office when I learned that he'd hired you, but your actions earlier today proved that he was right and I was wrong.' Roberta smiled at me. 'I'm not afraid to admit it, and I wanted to apologise for doubting you.'

I could still remember the shouting match between herself and the professor, when she'd accused him of hiring the wrong applicant. I also remembered that they'd conspired to hire me for one quarter of the agreed wages, but that was something I'd raise later, when I was better established. 'Well, er, that is most kind of you.'

'I admired the way you kept your head. Many would have fled, leaving me to cope on my own, and I'm very pleased you stayed.'

I felt a swelling in my chest, for praise was rare in my regular line of work. With bookkeeping, accuracy was expected, not celebrated, and as a rule one did not receive a clap on the back after successfully adding up a column of figures.

'With that in mind...' began Roberta, and then she faltered.

'Yes?' I asked, encouraging her.

'I was due to visit a client this afternoon with my father, but he's in no condition to leave the house. I wonder...would you be willing to accompany me?'

She finished her request with a rush, and I could tell she was nervous about asking me. For my part, I was nervous about accepting. It was one thing to step in during an emergency to assist with her father, but this was entirely different. What if I made a mistake, and a spirit got loose? What manner of a fool would I seem, should the client pepper me with questions? 'Are you certain that's a good idea?' I asked. 'I have no experience in your work.'

'But you were such a help earlier!' exclaimed Roberta. 'And by all accounts, we will have a much easier time of it. The note from Lady Snetton mentioned a minor disturbance, nothing more. Father and I have dealt with such matters countless times.'

Her entreaties were so earnest I had no choice but to accept. 'Very well, I shall accompany you to Lady Snetton's, but I hope you do not live to regret it.'

She gave me a grateful smile. 'I knew you would agree. Come, my equipment is already at the front door. Let us catch a cab, and I'll explain the nature of our work on the way to the station.'

I doused the gaslight and followed Roberta downstairs, where I slung one of the haversacks across my shoulder. She took the other, and together we emerged into the afternoon sunshine. It was a warm spring day, and I felt the sun through my coat as we took the short path to the wrought iron gates separating the front garden from the street. There was abundant greenery, with the garden having been allowed to grow wild, and I ducked my head to avoid the twisted bough of an ancient tree.

Roberta opened the gate, and we emerged into the busy street. Here, goods wagons moved steadily in both directions, while hawkers with their wares threaded between the slow-moving vehicles, calling to passersby. Others carried goods on their backs, while the occasional delivery boy pushed past wheeling a barrow. A smoky haze filled the air, almost as heavy as fog, and the mingled stink of sweat, and soot, and waste was omnipresent and unavoidable.

A hansom cab approached, steering nimbly between the heavy vehicles, and Roberta signalled the driver. He brought the cab to a halt, and I placed the bags inside before turning to offer Roberta my hand. Instead, she clambered in unaided, leaving me to follow.

'Where to, guv?' called the driver, an older man with sideburns and a drooping moustache.

'South Kensington station,' replied Roberta, and she took hold of a strap as the cab set off. We passed between lumbering goods wagons hauled by huge horses that dwarfed our own, their teetering loads seemingly on the point of tumbling into the road. With the rumbling of wheels, the sounds of horses and the cries from the crowded streets it would be impossible for anyone to overhear us, and so Roberta leaned closer and raised her voice to tell me about Lady Snetton. 'She will make for a valuable client, her husband being someone important in naval circles. A friend referred her to us, but father says Lady Snetton is highly sceptical about the services we offer.' She turned to me. 'The friend persuaded Lady Snetton to employ us, but only after much argument wore down her protestations. I cannot be certain, but we may face outright hostility.'

My heart sank at this news, for despite the strange events I'd witnessed with my own eyes, I could not imagine myself describing them to an incredulous aristocrat. We would be treated like explorers with news of the discovery of a solid gold mountain. *I swear it's true ma'am, and the treasure map can be yours for no more than five guineas.*

'Come now, it won't be that bad,' said Roberta, smiling at my pensive expression. 'After all, how long did it take me to convince the sceptic in you?'

I knew she was right, but at the same time I felt like a child wading into deep waters for the first time, while a well-meaning parent stood safely on the shore and assured them that swimming was easy. I felt a deep sense of unease and foreboding, and no amount of honeyed words were going to dispel my fears.

We reached the station, where we boarded the underground train. This was a new experience for me, sitting in a rattling carriage with its own gas lanterns as we plunged into the tunnel that passed beneath the very streets of the city. Immediately, we were beset by cinders and smoke from the engine, and the air was unbearably foul despite the ventilation shafts that I knew rose to the surface above. The walls of the tunnel sped past, faster than a man could run, the soot-stained brickwork close enough that I could have reached out and touched it. Above, crowds would be thronging the streets of the city, clogging the thoroughfares, and I marvelled at the ingenuity that had placed an entire railway underground.

The train slowed soon after departing the station, and we reached a new tunnel under construction. Labourers were working in dim, hellish conditions, while ragged-looking children hauled away rubble in wooden carts. The air rang with the sound of picks and shovels, drowning even the regular chuffing of the steam train and the rattle of the carriages. As we passed the area, I happened to glance into the dark, cavernous mouth of the new tunnel, still half-built and shored up with dozens of planks. In the far distance I thought I saw a flicker, as if lightning had somehow managed to enter the tunnels, but when I blinked it was gone. I put it down to a trick of the light, and did not mention it to Roberta.

Once past the workings our train sped up again, and we soon alighted at the end of the line. Here, we emerged at Westminster Bridge station, and we strolled to Bridge Street to obtain a cab. On the way I dusted at my coat with a handkerchief in a vain attempt to shift the soot from the train. Alas, I only succeeded in distributing the substance around my person. I glanced at Roberta, who wore the garb of a labourer, and gave a rueful smile.

The cab bore us past the busy vegetable markets and on to a street in Covent Garden, where it drew up outside a row of impressive Georgian residences. They were the sort of houses where a liveried butler met important visitors at the front, perhaps with a footman or two to help guests out of their carriages, while everyone else gained access via the rear.

Roberta paid our driver, and we carried our haversacks down a narrow alley between two of the houses. At the rear we found a yard, where a scullery maid was emptying a bucket down a drain. She glanced at us, startled, and then her face cleared. 'You're the rat catchers, aren't ya?'

'That's right,' said Roberta, giving me a warning glance.

'If you'll follow me, Miss, I'll show ya both indoors.'

9

'Rat catchers?' I whispered to Roberta, as we followed the maid.

'Do you think Lady Snetton would tell her staff the real reason we're here?' hissed Roberta. 'An article in the Gazette with that manner of gossip would ruin her reputation.'

I saw her point. Staff were loyal to a certain extent, but a newspaper reporter with a spare shilling could extract juicy titbits at will. The daily papers were full of gossip, with only the most cursory effort at concealing the identity of those in the firing line.

We entered through the kitchens, where preparations for the evening meal were in full swing. A portly cook was tending pots and pans bubbling on a large stove, and as she noticed our presence she turned her ruddy face to us, eyes gleaming with suspicion. 'What do you want?' she demanded. 'Annie? What you doing bringin' these people into my kitchen?'

Annie bobbed her head. 'Beg pardon, Mrs Watson. They're here about the rats.'

The cook sniffed. 'They don't look like no rat catchers to me.'

'Nevertheless, we do have an appointment with Lady Snetton,' said Roberta. 'Would you have someone show us up?'

'Why would her ladyship deal with the likes of you?' demanded the cook. 'Be about your business, and then be off with you.'

'We come recommended by one of Lady Snetton's closest friends,' said Roberta, persisting despite the cook's brusque manner. 'We were specifically told to report to–'

'There's no stoppin' you, is there?' Mrs Watson gestured impatiently with her ladle. 'Annie, take 'em up, but on your head be it.' Then, having divested herself of all responsibility, she turned her full attention to the stove. 'Bloomin' trades and their bloomin' airs,' she muttered, loud enough for all to hear. 'What's the world comin' to?'

'If you'll follow me,' said Annie, keeping her voice low. As we left the kitchen, she offered further explanation. 'Mrs Watson's put out, see? She's lost two helpers this week, and she's having to mind everything herself.'

'Lost two helpers?' I repeated. 'Whatever happened to them?'

Annie snorted. 'They believed they saw ghosts, sir, and ran off without giving notice. Too fanciful by half, if you ask me.'

The maid seemed like a solid, dependable sort, and the scorn in her voice was obvious. I wondered whether she'd be so sceptical had she seen a malevolent spirit being drawn from a living being, as I had with the professor. Roberta made no move to correct her, though, and I was reminded once more that her business was forced to operate under a veil of secrecy.

The maid led us out of the kitchens, and as we left the servants' areas and entered the main house I was struck by the furnishings and ornaments. Some of the pieces wouldn't have looked out of place in the fabulous collections of the South Kensington Museum, and I wondered at the wealth required to maintain such a household.

I began to visualise our host, who'd be a severe-looking dowager with elaborate clothes from a bygone era. She would look down her nose at us with gooseberry eyes, pale and slightly bulging. There would be no warmth in her manner, which would be haughty and disdainful, and as I pictured the formidable client awaiting us, I brushed again at my soot-streaked coat.

Our footsteps echoed off the parquet flooring, and we passed several rooms before the maid stopped before an ornate pair of doors. Here she paused to straighten her uniform, before giving us an appraising look. Roberta ignored her, but I adjusted my tie and tried in vain to brush traces of soot from my jacket. Having received a nod from the maid, I watched as she knocked twice before awaiting a reply.

'Come!' said a voice, muffled by the heavy woodwork.

Annie pushed the doors open, revealing a large, well-lit sitting room. There was only one occupant, a woman of my own age who was sitting in an armchair with an open book in her lap. I took her to be the daughter of Lady Snetton, given her age, but as soon as Roberta greeted the woman I realised my mistake.

'Lady Snetton,' said Roberta, advancing into the room. 'I trust we find you well?'

'As well as can be expected.' The woman closed her book with a snap, placing it on a side table. Then she signalled to the maid to leave, and rose to greet us. I saw a hint of amusement as she looked me up and down. 'I have heard great things about your father, Roberta, but I did not expect the professor to look this young. If he's invented a youth potion, my husband will be first in line for a dose.'

I was still trying to reconcile this young woman with the dour matronly type I'd imagined to be waiting for us, and so it was left to Roberta to introduce me.

'This is Septimus Jones, my assistant,' said Roberta quickly. 'Father has been laid low by a fever, else he would have attended in person.'

'He is not, perhaps, providing his services to a more valued client?'

'You have my word, but if you prefer, I can postpone our appointment until he is well enough to–'

'No! I must be free of this devilish spirit today.'

Until this moment Lady Snetton's tone had been light and bantering, but now, for the first time, I saw a hint of the strain she was under. I also happened to notice the title of the book she had been reading, which was a treatise on the various types of ghosts and apparitions one might encounter. I'd heard of the publication, for it had raised a stir on first release. Now, after my own recent experiences, I realised it might not be as fanciful as everyone declared it to be, and I smiled grimly at the thought.

'You must take me for a fool,' said Lady Snetton in a low voice, having noticed my expression. 'But if you lived in this miserable house for a single day, you would see and hear things that would turn your hair white.'

Roberta hurried forward, guiding the unhappy young woman towards the armchair. 'Lady Snetton, please make yourself comfortable. Should I ring for your maid? Brandy, perhaps?'

'There are spirits enough in this household,' said Lady Snetton, with a wintry smile, but she took her seat all the same. 'Please sit with me, and I shall reveal the troubles with which I am plagued.'

I was eager to set up the equipment in order to catch the wayward phantasm, but Roberta seemed to be in no hurry. As she sat down, I realised there was more to her profession than I'd first thought. Apparently, our services included listening to our clients unburdening themselves of their worries and discussing details of their private lives.

'My husband's first wife died two years ago,' began Lady Snetton. 'Theirs was not a happy marriage, but my dearest David – that's Admiral Lord Snetton – was at sea for months on end, and they got by during those brief intervals when they were forced to live under the same roof. Fortunately there were no children, and–'

I would sooner have faced ten glowing red phantasms than endured one intimate conversation of this sort with a stranger, and thus I was perched on the edge of my chair, feeling most uncomfortable. 'Lady Snetton, would you prefer me to leave the room?'

'Why? Are you feeling unwell?'

'No, but–'

My face must have been flushed with embarrassment, because she laughed. 'Oh, have no fear. I will not share anything you wouldn't read in the Gazette, should you have a mind to. Please, sit back and allow me to finish, for I must pour out this sorry tale.'

I obeyed, striving to keep my soot-marked clothes off the pristine upholstery.

'I knew David through an acquaintance of my father's,' continued Lady Snetton. 'We grew close after the death of his wife, and were married before too long. Our lives were very happy for some eight months or so.' Her face, which had been glowing as she recounted the tale, now fell. 'Then the hauntings began,' she continued, in a low voice. 'David hasn't noticed a thing, bless him, but I am slowly being driven mad. I will wake in the middle of the night for no reason, and a cold chill will come over me, even though the fire in the grate has not yet died. Sometimes I smell the perfume David's first wife preferred, even though there is none in the entire house. At other times, things will...move...of their own accord.' She eyed us anxiously, looking much younger than her years. 'You do believe me, don't you? More than anything I fear I shall be mocked for these fancies.'

'We believe you,' said Roberta firmly. 'I think, too, that you know whose spirit this might be.'

'David's first wife,' whispered Lady Snetton.

CRASH!

We all spun round, shocked by the sudden noise. A painting which had been hanging above the fireplace had just plunged to the ground, splintering the frame and splitting the canvas. I could still see the remains of the picture, which was a portrait of the lady sitting before us. Even now, flames from the fire were licking at the ruined portrait, and I leapt from my seat to beat them out.

'Oh, do you *see*?' cried lady Snetton. 'If you can't banish this hateful spirit, I swear I'll be forced from my own house!'

I inspected the back of the ruined painting, where the hanging-cord had parted to leave two frayed ends. The sudden fall *could* have been a coincidence, especially as the frame was an older one which had been reused, but the timing had been impeccable. I shifted my investigation to the wall, and was just inspecting the area around the brass hook set deep into the plaster when Roberta called out to me.

'Mr Jones, would you see if you can find a small glass vial in our things?'

I hastened to obey, and I confess my hands were unsteady as I searched in the haversacks. I was still shaken by the falling painting, which had given me much to think about. It seemed that spirits could appear in different guises, and it shocked me that they could also interact with physical objects. If this were the case, then what could possibly prevent a ghost from placing its hand over a sleeping person's mouth, choking them to death? After all, whether flesh or wood or metal, matter was matter, and the force required to snap a strong piece of hanging-cord could be applied just as effectively to someone's throat. A shiver ran up my spine at the thought, for there is nothing I find more terrifying than the idea of being attacked in my sleep, when I am completely unable to defend myself. With an ordinary intruder, locked doors and windows served as a warning, for they had to be broken down to gain access. But what of a spirit that could slip beneath the door, or slither down the chimney despite a fire burning in the hearth?

I checked those haversacks three times over, but in spite of my troubled thoughts I was certain there was no glass vial. 'I'm sorry, Miss Twickham. I can't find the item you need.'

'No matter. It's not important.' While I'd been searching the bags, Roberta had been comforting Lady Snetton, reassuring her that we would do our very best to free the house of the malevolent presence. Now, she offered a suggestion. 'Your ladyship, why don't you take afternoon tea with a friend, so we might work in peace?'

'But I thought I might watch as you–'

'I advise against it,' said Roberta briskly, laying a hand on her ladyship's sleeve. 'In my experience, phantoms are most unwilling to depart, and many put up a very good fight indeed. I would not want you to witness the spectacle, for it can be most distressing.'

'Are you sure? If I do not witness this...capture...with my own eyes, how will I know you've succeeded?'

'I assure you, once the phantom has departed you will feel a difference in this house.'

'Oh, my dear. You are a great comfort,' said Lady Snetton, squeezing Roberta's hand. 'Succeed in banishing this spirit, and you can name your own price.'

'For a difficult case such as this, twenty pounds is our usual rate,' said Roberta smoothly.

Lady Snetton blinked, and I wasn't surprised. Twenty pounds was an immense sum, and easily four times the largest invoice I'd processed that morning. Why, I would scarcely earn that much in the next six months!

'Of course, I would never charge a friend of Lady Fotherington-Eames such a large amount,' continued Roberta. 'Therefore, as long as today's extraction proceeds as planned, I would expect to invoice you no more than ten pounds.'

'Done, and I'll be glad to pay it,' said Lady Snetton, looking relieved.

I admired Roberta's tactics, for despite the substantial discount, she'd still managed to obtain promise of twice the usual rate. This gave me pause, because I now wondered whether she expected the banishing to be twice as difficult also. That was not something I wished to contemplate, not with the professor lying abed half a city away, and only my inexperienced help to catch this wayward spirit.

Lady Snetton rang for a maid, and together they departed for the upper reaches of the house. 'We'll wait until she's gone out,' Roberta murmured to me. 'I don't like them witnessing our methods.'

'Are you afraid she won't see ten pounds of value?'

'She can afford it,' said Roberta, unmoved. 'But I'd rather she didn't reveal all to her friends. A little mystery goes a long way.'

And it doesn't harm your income any, I wanted to say. Instead, I raised a point that had been troubling me. 'You told me Lady Snetton was sceptical of your services, and yet she employed you without protest.'

'No doubt she expressed reservations to her friends, but in reality she knew I was her only hope.' Roberta smiled. 'That's why father leaves this side of the business to me. He can be prickly, as I'm sure you've noticed.'

I said nothing to this, and instead looked around the room. 'Is the spirit of his Lordship's first wife truly present in this room with us?'

'We'll find out soon enough, Mr Jones. Now, will you help me with the equipment? There is lots to do, and I'd like to be off the streets before evening. Tinkering with the spirit world as I do, I sometimes feel they might single me out for special attention, and I have no wish to be cornered in a darkened alleyway by a vengeful phantom.'

I too wished to be home by evening, for I had not forgotten the note in my pocket inviting me to the Crown and Feather for a clandestine meeting.

10

I thought we would be setting up the equipment in the sitting room, but Roberta shouldered her haversack and led me into the hall. Here, we encountered our host coming downstairs with a maid. Lady Snetton had donned a fancy hat and coat, and the maid was carrying her bag.

'Lady Snetton,' said Roberta. 'Would it be possible to perform our work upstairs, in the main bedroom?'

'Is that really necessary?'

'In my experience, yes. Sleeping areas are usually a focal point for–'

'I understand, and I give my permission,' said Lady Snetton quickly. She gestured at the maid. 'Run and find Annie, and tell her to show our guests to my bedroom.'

'Yes ma'am.'

The maid hurried off, and there was an awkward silence as we waited in the hall with Lady Snetton. Finally, both maids returned, and Annie promptly led us upstairs to the sleeping quarters while Lady Snetton's personal maid accompanied her to the front door. As we reached the landing I glanced back down the stairs, and I saw Lady Snetton at the far end of the hall, looking anxiously up at me. She gave me a small, hopeful smile just before the door closed, hiding her from view. With that look she'd bared her soul to me, revealing a scared, vulnerable young woman, and I resolved to do everything in my power to rid this house of the malevolent spirit. This, even though I was feeling somewhat vulnerable and scared myself, loath though I was to admit it.

We reached the upper floor, where Annie showed us into a sumptuous room with a four-poster bed, expensive furnishings and a large bay window that looked out on the smoky haze blanketing the city. A tree in the road outside stuck its twisted branches into the sky, with its sparse spring growth struggling for life in the heavy, polluted air, and I saw a mangy-looking dog darting through the foot traffic, bound for who-knew-where. Below, Lady Snetton's carriage was drawing away from the house, pulled by two magnificent horses. The driver flicked his reins, and the carriage vanished down the road, lost in the thronging crowds and the late-afternoon gloom.

'Mr Jones, would you assist me please?'

I turned to see Roberta near the bedroom door, which she'd just closed. The maid had already left, and the two of us could now speak freely. 'What caused the painting to fall?' I asked her.

'Some spirits have influence in the physical world, although it's rare.'

I recalled the shattered equipment from her previous cleansing, and also the ill-effects that phantasm had inflicted on the professor. 'Is this one of the...stronger kind?' I asked nervously.

'Fear not, Mr Jones. Together, we will cope.'

I admired her confidence, even though my own was sorely lacking. There was little time to dwell on the dangers though, because Roberta had me unpacking the equipment and setting it up in every nook and cranny of the room. I placed the metal discs where she directed, this batch once again marked with fine tracings. 'What is the purpose of these designs?' I asked, as I laid a disc on the windowsill. No sooner had I let go than it gleamed briefly in the light, the pattern seeming to pulse with energy.

Roberta hesitated, and I guessed she was debating how much information to share with me. 'As I already explained, we infuse the metal with traces of the spirits we capture. There are many different kinds, and when we blend them it leaves a distinctive pattern.'

I finished placing the discs and took up a tripod, setting it up where she indicated. 'What kinds of spirits are there?' I asked, as I adjusted the legs and tightened the brass thumbscrews to hold them in place.

'We have catalogued more than a dozen to date. Some are lost souls, unable to find their way to the next world. Others are vengeful spirits out to cause harm to those who wronged them.' Roberta indicated the bedroom with a sweeping gesture. 'And some are jealous of a rival.'

I half-expected another painting to topple from the wall, but the room was still. 'And the one which...attacked the professor?'

Roberta's face darkened. 'That was a being the likes of which we've never encountered. It had enough power to shatter the trap, and my father happened to be holding the device at the time. It flowed up his arm and entered his very being.'

I swallowed. 'That's...that's not likely to happen here, is it?' I lamented the stammer in my voice, for I knew I sounded like a nervous child. But surely I had an excuse!

'Oh no,' said Roberta calmly. 'This may be far worse.' Then, noting my expression, she gave a peal of laughter. 'Oh Mr Jones, if you could only see your face.'

'I don't see anything remotely amusing in this situation,' I snapped, irritated by her casual attitude towards a very real danger. 'You hired me to look after your accounts, and traipsing around the city after perilous ghosts was not included in my duties!'

She was immediately contrite, and she left the device she'd been setting to come over and comfort me. 'Septimus, I'm sorry,' she said, her tone genuinely apologetic. 'Sometimes my sense of humour–'

'I'm sure I'll get used to it eventually,' I said stiffly. Then, seeing she'd just laid her hand on my sleeve, I managed a smile. 'Assuming I live that long, of course.'

'That's the spirit!'

'Where? Where?' I demanded, looking around in panic.

'No, I meant...I was just...' Roberta took one look at me and doubled up, this time fairly cackling with laughter. I too saw the funny side, and moments later we were both shaking with mirth. If one could banish ghosts with happiness alone, at that moment the entire city would have been cleansed of their foul presence. Unfortunately, the power of laughter wouldn't suffice, and so we returned to our work. The mood was noticeably lighter though, and I had a spring in my step as I helped to set up the equipment.

The procedure was similar to that used when banishing the professor's unwanted passenger, and once the net was in position and the lantern – or rather, trap – was installed near the centre of the room, Roberta took out the same tool she'd used on her father. I watched, curious, because unlike earlier, this time there was no knowing where the spirit might be hiding. So how, then, was she going to trap it?

Roberta donned the curious spectacles with their mismatched lenses, and, standing with her back to the door, she traversed the room with an unblinking gaze. Once or twice she paused, seeming to study a piece of furniture, and each time I held my breath. Would the spirit launch from hiding, intent on causing as much harm as possible before it was caught? Or would it slide from one hiding place to the next, trying not to reveal itself?

The tension was unbearable, and I almost prayed for the phantasm to break cover. It would mean facing genuine danger, but anything would be better than this silent anticipation.

'There,' murmured Roberta, her voice all but inaudible.

She'd frozen where she stood, and appeared to be looking at the nightstand on the far side of the large bed, where a pitcher of water sat next to an enamelled mug and a silver-backed hand mirror. I stared at the same location, and I fancied I saw a faint shimmering in the air. I could have been imagining things, but even so I felt my hackles rising.

Roberta took a step forward, holding the tool in front of her in the manner of St George approaching the fabled dragon. Then she took another step, and my eyes felt like they were standing proud from my head as I strove to identify the focus of her attention. My hands were clenched, my breathing shallow, and at that moment I had little doubt that the slightest unexpected noise would have stilled the heart pounding in my chest.

Seemingly immune to such fancies, Roberta continued to advance on the nightstand, skirting the bed with the tool held in both hands. There was a faint keening noise, as if the wind were suddenly blowing through a gap in the windows, and it grew louder the closer Roberta got.

Crash!

The nightstand shook from a sudden impact, and the jug sitting on the polished wooden surface toppled to the floor, where it shattered into a dozen pieces. Water sprayed out, hitting the curtains and splashing on the bedspread, and for a brief moment I fancied I saw the outline of a figure inside the welter of flying droplets. Then it was gone, and I saw Roberta leap backwards, brandishing the tool as though warding off an invisible attacker. The end gleamed a dull red, and in the baleful illumination I saw a shadow pursuing her.

'What should I do?' I cried desperately.

'Stay back,' she commanded me. 'Stay back, and do not approach.'

I noticed Roberta was retreating towards the trap in the middle of the bedroom, and as she got closer the keening wail got louder and louder, until I was forced to cover my ears. The window panes shook, rattled by an invisible hand, and then, without warning, a lightning bolt flashed around the room, leaping from one patterned disc to the next. Through half-closed eyes I saw an other-worldly being framed in the circular flash of light, a figure in a tattered nightdress with outstretched arms, its hands like grasping claws.

Then the light winked out, leaving the room in comparative darkness. All I could see was the glow of the tool in Roberta's hand, and a vivid after-image of the lightning flash. Slowly, my eyes began to adjust, and that's when I saw the fine copper netting bulging in the centre. It was as though a heavy body were pushing against the net, and I could see the tripods leaning as they took up the strain.

Roberta was turning her head this way and that, trying to find the spirit, and she hadn't noticed the distorted net. Gritting my teeth, I darted forwards and gripped the net in both hands, right at the bulge, and I started to push against it with all my might.

'What are you doing?' shouted Roberta. 'Mr Jones, no! Don't touch that!'

Too late. I felt a chill run up my arms, as though they'd been doused in freezing water. As the cold reached my chest I found I could not breathe, and as my vision dimmed I felt a rising panic. Frantically, I waved at the air in front of me, trying to ward off my unseen assailant, but I was fighting fog and my wild swinging hands achieved nothing.

Roberta was not idle while I struggled. She leapt towards me, brandishing the tool, and the closer she got the more the tip glowed. I was suffering from tunnel vision now, and could barely feel my arms, but I was all too aware of the furnace-like heat emanating from that device in her hands. I felt the spirit release me all of a sudden, and then the net parted in two with a ripping, rending noise.

Roberta cried out in alarm, and she was past me and heading for the bedroom door before I knew what was happening. She stood there with the glowing device held high, and I realised she was trying to herd the spirit back into the centre of the room.

I turned wildly, looking around for any hint of the phantasm, fearing it might assail me from any direction without the slightest warning. Each time I turned I imagined it right behind me, ready to set upon me with those freezing claws, and I spun again and again to confront it…only to meet thin air. Shivers ran up my spine, and my heart pounded with terror. I wanted to flee the room, run down the stairs and leave this madhouse for the sanity of the busy afternoon street, and had Roberta not been standing directly in my way I would have done so.

But the sight of her standing firm, her expression determined, with the glowing tool at the ready, calmed my nerves. If the spirit did happen to fasten on me once more, it would not be the end. Indeed, it would probably give Roberta the opportunity to snare it. All of a sudden I realised what I had to do, and, swallowing my fear, I stepped into the middle of the room and raised my arms. In effect, I had just presented myself as the bait in a trap.

Roberta shouted a warning, but I ignored her and stood my ground. I could sense the spirit approaching from behind, but unlike before I did not turn to look for it, nor wave my arms to drive it away. I felt a steely calm, a determination to play my part whatever the cost. 'Come, you foul being!' I shouted, my voice filling the bedroom. 'Feast on my living flesh! Consume my very life force! *Do with me what you must!*'

A chill circled my legs and began climbing my spine, and I gritted my teeth as the cold threatened to overwhelm me. I pictured the clammy horror that was even now fastening itself to my back, and I battled the strong urge to run.

As I stood there, enveloped by the spirit, I heard Roberta spring towards me. There was an electric crackle, and I felt the hair on my head stand on end. Then, with a rush of relief, I felt the cold ripped from my back. I turned to see Roberta stepping over the ruins of the net, heading for the trap with the indistinct shape of the spirit coalescing around the tool gripped in her hands.

She was having trouble with the thing, for it jerked this way and that as it tried to get free, and I could see from her expression that it was a hard-fought battle. She made it though, and there was a tremendous gust of wind as the tool contacted the cylinder suspended in the trap. Curtains were torn from the windows, books and vases tumbled to the floor, and paintings rattled on the walls as though the subjects of the portraits were trying to break free of their canvas bonds.

Then, all was still.

I barely had time to relax, because Roberta strode up to me, her face working furiously. 'You foolish, foolish man!' she cried, pushing me in the chest with both hands. 'Do you have any idea of the danger you placed yourself in?'

'I–it seemed the only way,' I mumbled, looking at the ground.

'Idiot!' She went to push me once more, but to my relief she lowered her hands instead, her anger having dissipated as quickly as it had arisen. ''Consume my very life force?'' she growled, giving me an arch look. 'Which penny-dreadful did you plumb for that particular turn of phrase?'

'I was determined to attract the spirit,' I said earnestly.

'And what gave you the idea an otherworldly phantasm might *hear* your impassioned pleas? Do you think they have ears, and eyes, and mouths to bite you with?'

'I confess, in the heat of the moment I did not stop to inspect the spirit's physical features.' I hesitated, for I was unwilling to provoke her anger once more. 'But it seemed the thing to do. And it worked,' I pointed out.

'It was remarkably stupid.' Then she lowered her voice. 'But even so I–I must commend you, for your actions were brave indeed.' Before I could say any more, Roberta turned from me, and together we surveyed the wreckage of the bedroom. Two pictures had fallen, the curtains were lying in a heap on the floor and the puddle of water from the broken jug had spread to an expensive-looking rug.

Behind us, the copper netting was torn asunder, the metal tripods lying on their sides all twisted and bent. Only the trap looked intact, and I could see the metal cylinder within shaking and twisting as the captured spirit fought for its freedom. 'It's just as well I settled on a fee of ten pounds,' muttered Roberta. 'Once Lady Snetton accounts for damages, I'll be lucky to see five.'

'She will make you pay for damages?' I asked in surprise.

'You can place a substantial wager on that, Mr Jones.' Roberta picked up a painting and hung it on the wall, straightening it. 'Once they gain a modicum of wealth, clients like Lady Snetton strive to maintain a deathly grip on it.'

I knew what she meant, for I'd noticed many invoices for cleansings whilst I was updating the ledgers earlier that day, and a fair number had yet to be paid. I was about to reassure her that I would soon bring the accounts up to date when I felt the floor moving underfoot, as though something large and heavy were shaking the very foundations of the house. Furniture creaked, a wardrobe door swung open, and one of the paintings Roberta had just replaced fell down again. 'What manner of–' I began, but Roberta silenced me with a gesture.

She donned those curious eyeglasses and hurried to the haversack, digging inside until she found what she was looking for: a device which looked just like a metronome. It was only when she set it upon a nearby table that I realised it had three pendulums. Each was tipped with a different colour, the largest being carmine red, the smallest a dull copper and the middle pendulum a ghostly white.

The floorboards were still groaning and creaking underfoot, and to me it felt like the entire house was swaying. I'd read hair-raising tales of earthquakes as a boy, but even though they were unheard of in this fair land I could think of no other reason for the violent movements.

Roberta wound the device with a small key protruding from one side, then set the smallest of the three pendulums in motion. She seemed oblivious to the commotion all round us, as furniture rattled and the very walls threatened to fall in. 'What's causing this?' I shouted over the noise. 'Was it something we did?'

'Please! Let me calibrate the detector.'

I held my tongue even though I had a dozen more questions begging to be asked. Instead, I supported myself by gripping one upright of the four-poster bed, and then I watched Roberta at work. The second pendulum on the device was now in motion, moving in counterpoint to the first, and she adjusted the angle of the metronome before starting the third and largest pendulum. This one swung to one side, hesitated several seconds, then swept quickly to the opposite side. Along the way it disturbed the motion of the two smaller hands.

The floor trembled again, fiercely this time, and I heard a distant crash. I guessed one or more tiles had slipped from the roof to smash on the ground below, and I hoped nobody had been in their path. That gave me pause for thought, and I struggled to the window, using furniture to help with my balance. When I got there I looked out on the street, where I saw scenes of total chaos. People were running in every direction, trying to avoid the terrified horses that were bucking and rearing in the traces of their laden carts. Several large vehicles had overturned, and I saw gangs of men bearing the scattered cargo away while the drivers were occupied with the frightened beasts. I saw three or four huddled forms lying still in the middle of the road, whether struck by carts or crushed in the panic, I had no way of telling. Even as I watched, an urchin ran to one of the wounded and helped himself to the man's pocketbook, before fleeing down an alleyway. Moments later a pair of constables appeared on the scene, blowing their whistles before setting off in pursuit.

'It's about eighty feet below us!' called Roberta.

I turned to see her studying the metronome device, whose pendulums had all ceased moving.

Roberta gestured towards the window. 'The source is somewhere between here and South Kensington.'

I saw the worried look on her face, and I understood the reason. Her home, her father...South Kensington was precisely where they were located. I glanced to my right, where the bulk of the city was hidden behind rows of houses, and then at the nearby trap with its gleaming bronze cylinder. The device was still shaking, but whether it was the movement underfoot or the angry spirit I had no way of knowing. 'This tremor...could it be connected to the phantasm?'

'How could it be? Nothing like this has ever happened before!' declared Roberta.

'Your father was possessed by a spirit earlier in the day,' I said. 'You told me that never happened before either. What if...what if there are far more powerful phantoms than you've encountered before?' I gestured at the trap. 'What if these are merely supporting players, and the protagonist has yet to reveal itself?'

'Mr Jones, you have an overactive imagination,' said Roberta, but for once her air of confidence had deserted her.

Then, without warning, the tremors died away. In the sudden silence I heard the frantic tick-tock of the metronome device, until Roberta stilled the pendulums. There were cries from the street still, but they were lessening now that the upheaval had ceased.

'Thank goodness that's over,' said Roberta. 'Would you help me with the equipment?'

It took a good half an hour to pack everything away, after which we tidied the room as best we could. Then, following a last look around, we shouldered our haversacks and headed downstairs.

We met Annie near the kitchens, where the cook was keeping up a non-stop monologue as she dealt with the aftermath of the tremors. There were several overturned pots and pans, and steaming liquid formed pools on the tiled floor. 'What's the world coming to?' demanded the cook. 'Shakes and quakes and convulsions like I've never seen, the Lord be my witness. A body can't even cook dinner without the walls come tumbling down around their ears. If you ask me...'

The maid led us out, and as we left the house the cook's stream of protests faded into the distance. We took the alley to the main road, where workmen were setting carts back on their wheels and helping to reload the cargo. The police constables I'd seen earlier were overseeing events, and calm of a sort had returned to the scene.

It was five minutes before we could hail a cab, but eventually we were on our way to the station, the haversacks at our feet. I could see the square bulge of the trap inside Roberta's bag, its victim still inside, and I wondered how the crowd would react if they knew what moved amongst them. Sheer panic, I suspected.

The hansom cab stopped outside the station, where we alighted and purchased our tickets. Then we took the stairs to the underground, boarding the cramped carriage as quickly as possible to avoid the thick haze, the noise and the smell. Before long we were under way, the train rattling and groaning as it navigated the tracks in the tunnel. The gaslights in the carriage cast hardly any light, and the thick smoke seeping through the windows dimmed the interior even further. I closed my eyes against the fumes, for just a moment, and let the day's events wash over me.

I was in the habit of writing a letter home to my parents once weekly, letters in which I disguised my true situation. Now, I wondered exactly what I was going to write in the next letter. I could not tell them about the professor, nor Roberta, nor the work I was engaged in, and so I decided to continue the web of lies I'd been spinning for some time now.

Over the past few weeks I'd led my parents to believe that I was working at a small accounting firm, earning a modest wage and living out of decent lodgings. I was careful not to share too many details, lest I be caught in a lie, but even so I found it prudent to keep a diary containing these invented facts and figures. To date I'd fabricated my employment, the quantity and quality of food I was eating, several close friends, details of my daily life and snippets of news and gossip gleaned from the papers.

Now that I *did* have a job, and lodgings, and new acquaintances – if not yet friends – I realised I would not be able to share any of this with my parents. I would have to continue fabricating details of my life as before, spinning my web of lies in the weekly letters. To simplify things, I decided I would draw up a table, mapping each truth with a matching lie. For example, Roberta would become Robert, a fellow accountant. The professor would become my employer, the head of the firm. Any odd happenings would be explained away as visits from clients, with their pets or wayward children representing the spirits. The traps and other equipment could be referred to in bookkeeping terms. In this fashion I would be able to write to my parents without tripping over myself.

With the tricky matter of keeping my parents abreast of my news now resolved, I felt a lessening of the tension within me. I would not be telling them anything of import, and they in turn would not worry needlessly on my behalf. In addition, I looked forward to fabricating my weekly letters, and I resolved to write to my parents that very evening.

'Why do you smile?'

I opened my eyes, and in the dim, smoky carriage I saw Roberta looking at me. There was a smudge of soot on her cheek, and as I studied her face, and the genuine concern it carried for my well-being, I felt a glow at the very core of my being. 'I must write to my parents this evening, and I was imagining their reaction should I reveal the things I've witnessed recently.'

She looked thoughtful. 'I trust you will not share the truth?'

'You may soothe your concerns in that regard,' I declared. 'Why, they would take the next train to London, and I would be dragged home by my necktie.'

'You must not speak to anyone about our business,' said Roberta, with a frown. 'The merest whisper might cause ridicule to be heaped on my father, and I would never forgive you for that. Never!'

She kept her voice low, but her tone was fierce. 'Roberta, I wouldn't dream of such a thing,' I declared, hoping to persuade her with my earnest tone. At that moment I was tempted to tell her about the note tucked into my pocket, but decided against it. There was no harm in meeting this mysterious person at the Crown and Feather that evening, and if they attempted to question me about the professor's business, I would keep my promise to Roberta and say nothing.

12

When we emerged from the underground station it was already evening. The occasional streetlight barely lit an area five feet across, leaving sixty feet of near-total darkness in between the lampposts. There was no sign of damage from the tremor, and I wondered whether it had been localised to an area immediately surrounding the Snetton house. This gave me pause, for I did not want to believe that the earthquake and subsequent scenes of chaos had been caused by the spirit Roberta and I had captured.

We managed to find a cab, the riding lights barely enough to illuminate the weary horse in its traces, never mind the pedestrians who darted across the road in front of us. To make things worse, a thick fog had rolled in from the river, and aside from a lack of visibility this also served to muffle the regular noises of the city. Sitting in the open cab, chilled by the cold, it was like being transported through some ghostly tunnel cut through the dirty yellow smog.

As our driver picked his way along the ill-lit roads I saw many pedestrians on either side, some carrying lanterns while others carted goods and belongings. Most were exhausted from a full day's work, but I knew it would be near midnight before the streets were finally still.

We arrived at the Mews without incident, and after paying the driver we carried the haversacks through the wrought iron gates and up the path to the professor's front door. Mrs Fairacre opened it before we got there, somehow forewarned to our presence, and I saw her giving Roberta an enquiring look as we passed into the house.

'I'm happy to report smooth sailing this time,' said Roberta, which seemed to satisfy the housekeeper. 'Tell me, how is my father?'

Mrs Fairacre sniffed. 'Much as you'd expect him to be, after quaffing half a bottle of brandy.'

'Surely it was no more than a quarter?'

'It was, until he recovered enough to venture forth from his room. At that point he located the rest, and now he's sleeping off the effects.'

'Thank you, Mrs Fairacre.'

'Will you be wanting supper?'

'If you wouldn't mind.'

'I'll serve something directly.'

Mrs Fairacre bustled off, and Roberta asked me to follow her with my haversack. We took the stairs to the first floor, where she opened a door leading to a large, untidy bedroom. The furnishings were similar to those in my room at the top of the house, apart from a large workbench situated along one wall. This was crammed with small hand-tools, odds and ends of metal and many items of half-built equipment. Roberta carried her bag inside, placing it against one leg of the workbench, while I hesitated in the doorway with my own. I watched as she took the trap from her bag and freed the cylinder inside, depositing it on a small metal tripod above a

Bunsen burner. Then she glanced at me. 'Come in, Mr Jones, and bring that bag with you. I have work to do and very little time to complete it.'

I remembered the damaged netting and the tripods which had been bent almost double at Lady Snetton's. 'Can I help in any way?' I asked, as I put the haversack beside hers.

'No, this will require a certain amount of skill.' She took a seat at the workbench and cleared the space in front of her. Then she removed the ripped netting from the bag, laid it on the workbench and reached for a spool of wire. 'Would you send the maid up when supper is served?'

'Yes, of course.' I took the hint and left the room, closing the door behind myself. I decided to change my coat, for the one I was wearing had endured much ill-treatment throughout the day and was sorely in need of a good brushing. It was still my intention to visit the Crown and Feather that evening, and I did not wish to appear as a chimney sweep's assistant.

While changing my coat I discovered the pages I'd removed from the journal earlier. I looked around my room, but there was no fire in which to dispose of them, and I didn't want to leave them lying around for the servants to find. So, I tucked them into my pocket and resolved to dispose of them at the earliest opportunity.

When I came down for supper I discovered to my surprise that the professor was also present. He was seated at the table with a plate of cold ham, sliced boiled eggs and fresh buttered bread before him, and he looked little the worse for wear. Mrs Fairacre had laid on quite a spread, and Roberta was at the sideboard behind her father, transferring food to her own plate.

'Well, my boy?' said the professor, in his reedy voice. 'How was your day?'

'Very interesting, sir. Miss Twickham and I paid a visit to Lady Snetton's residence, where we successfully captured a wayward spirit.'

All too late, I saw Roberta gesturing at me wildly from behind her father, and as I caught sight of the professor's changing expression I realised I'd erred most grievously. His genial air of bonhomie vanished, and he pushed back his chair and leapt up, turning to confront his daughter. 'You took our *bookkeeper* on a *cleansing*?' he roared. 'Have you quite lost your *mind*?'

'You were hardly in a position to help,' said Roberta mildly. She seemed unperturbed by her father's rage, and it dawned on me that these angry clashes of theirs must be frequent occurrences.

'Taking an untrained amateur along is the height of stupidity,' shouted the professor. 'You should have postponed until the morrow!'

'Everything proceeded to plan, father. And in addition, Lady Snetton agreed to pay us ten pounds.'

'I don't care what...' The professor's voice tailed off, and I saw a gleam in his eye. 'Wait. Did you say she agreed to ten pounds?'

'Indeed.'

'I see.' The professor glanced at me. 'And what is your opinion? Did things go as smoothly as my daughter claims?'

I recalled the torn netting, the bent stands, and the clammy feel of the spirit as it fastened itself to my spine. Those, and the severe tremors which had shaken Lady Snetton's house to its very foundations. 'Er, very smoothly indeed sir. No trouble at all.'

'Ah-hmm.'

The wind had completely gone out of the professor's sails, whether at the mention of money, or due to the lingering after-effects of the brandy. He gave his daughter a stern look, then retook his seat and transferred his attention to a thick slice of ham, carving a bite-sized piece before gazing upon me once more. 'You seem remarkably sanguine under the circumstances. Many would have run for the hills at the very mention of wild phantasms and vengeful spirits, never mind witnessing them with their own eyes.'

'I did what I had to, sir.'

'Stout fellow,' he said, with a nod.

Roberta gave me a grateful smile as she took her seat at the table. I left the pair of them to fill my own plate with eggs and ham, for I had not eaten for some hours and was feeling the lack of food. In addition, I still had an errand to run that night, and I did not know how late I would be back. 'An acquaintance of mine mentioned a tavern in the area,' I said casually. 'Would either of you know of the Crown and Feather?'

Roberta shook her head, but the professor glanced up. 'A low establishment indeed,' he said, eyeing me in concern. 'I would avoid the place if you know what's good for you, since it's plagued with cut-purses and burglars and women of ill repute. In fact, I'm surprised you admit to the acquaintance of any who might be likely to frequent such an establishment.'

'It was mentioned to me in passing,' I said hurriedly, fearing he might believe I was seeking female companionship of *that* kind...and that I was crass enough to ask my hosts at their own dinner table where I might find such an establishment. 'I was merely curious as to the location.'

'Curiosity is a noble virtue,' said the professor loftily, 'but one must be careful to channel the pursuit of knowledge into worthwhile areas.'

Roberta snorted at this. 'Father, you speak as though you've never once visited a tavern. Mr Jones is not a child of ten, and we have no call on his time of an evening. Why, for all you know he is betrothed to an innkeeper's daughter!'

'I assure you I am not betrothed to anyone,' I said quickly. Rather too quickly, I fear, for both father and daughter looked at me in some amusement. I ignored their questioning looks and concentrated on my plate, and thankfully they were too polite to press me further. It was true that I was not betrothed, but my parents had hoped to make a match for me with the daughter of a local textile merchant. This merchant was moderately wealthy, as I well knew, having worked part-time keeping his books, and his daughter was a pleasant, kindly girl. Unfortunately, she was also as dull as ditchwater, and only by fleeing to London had I avoided my parents' non-stop entreaties to 'settle down'. Instead, my mother wrote me weekly letters asking whether I'd met anyone suitable.

Roberta finished her meal, and stood. 'I must go to my room, for there is lots to accomplish before the morning. Goodnight father, and I trust you sleep well. Goodnight, Mr Jones.'

We both stood as she left the room, then resumed our seats. There was silence as we finished our own repasts, and then the professor laid down his knife and fork before clearing his throat. 'Would you like a little port?' he asked me.

I was conscious of the time, but it would have been rude to refuse. Also, I could hardly leave the house while the professor was seated within earshot of the front door, and I did not know the layout well enough to seek the rear entrance. 'Thank you, sir. That would be most welcome.'

The professor fetched a decanter and a pair of glasses, and poured us each a generous measure. 'You must have questions aplenty,' he said quietly. 'In your position, I know I would.'

'Roberta explained a little,' I said, 'but she was reluctant to give away your secrets.'

He nodded his approval and took a sip of port. 'Is there anything in particular you'd like to know?'

A dozen questions sprang to mind, all clamouring to be asked. The professor's background, the odd machinery he and Roberta had designed, the very existence of spirits and phantasms...those and many more. But there was one question which I'd been asking myself for some time, and this was my opportunity to seek an answer. 'Sir, given that these spirits really do exist...why is there no mention of them in the newspapers? Why aren't ordinary people demanding the government do something to protect them?'

'Or, in other words,' said the professor, taking another sip of port, 'why is there no hue and cry? No clamour?'

'Precisely!'

'To understand that, you must first understand the very nature of humanity. Only a decade ago, in a farming village in Essex, an elderly man was accused of witchcraft, beaten by the locals and thrown into a river. It takes very little to rile up a mob, even in these enlightened times, and once they're baying for blood there's no stopping them. You can understand, therefore, a certain reluctance to admitting the ghost of an ancestor is inhabiting your parlour.'

I took his point.

'The nobility do not want to be forsaken by their peers, if you'll excuse the pun, and as for the poor…well, they're too busy trying to eke out a meagre existence.' The professor gestured with his glass. 'The newspapers have enough to report on, what with murders and wars and the like, and stories of ghosts and hauntings are barely mentioned in passing, if at all. No, believe you me, the subject is usually confined to stories and serials and the like, where it serves to amuse those of dull wits and feeble minds.'

I had no rejoinder to the professor's observations, and I watched idly as he drained his glass. Then he stood, and declared his intention to retire for the night. 'Sleep well, Mr Jones, for I'm certain we will have need of your services tomorrow!'

'I'll be ready, sir.'

The professor hesitated, then dug in his pocket and withdrew a key. 'This is for the front door,' he said, with a roguish wink. 'We don't want you waking the entire household when you return from your dalliances, do we?'

'Er…no sir. But I have no intention of…'

'Oh no, of course you don't.' He approached, placed the key in my hand, and clasped my shoulder. 'We all have needs, my boy. It's nothing to be ashamed of.'

'Sir, I assure you–'

'You'll find the Crown and Feather a few hundred yards down the high street, on the left. Just be sure not to bring company back to my house, eh? Keep such things where they belong.'

'Professor, I was merely asking as to the whereabouts of the tavern. I have no intention of–'

'Of course you don't. Of course. And if I were a younger man I'd come with you.' The professor gave me another knowing wink and left the dining room, swaying slightly as he negotiated the doorway.

Then I was alone, writhing with embarrassment after the

excruciating conversation. My embarrassment grew further still as I imagined the professor telling Roberta I was going to the tavern to sow my wild oats, and I prayed he would keep his erroneous conclusions to himself.

I pushed the key into my pocket, and my fingers encountered the note I'd been carrying around for most of the day. For a brief moment I wondered whether to ignore it, since the others could not think me capable of immoral behaviour if I did not visit the tavern in the first place. In addition, the professor and Roberta had welcomed me into their home, answering my questions and dealing with me fairly. What possible benefit could arise from meeting this mysterious stranger? What could he tell me that would alter my view of the Twickhams?

I took the note out and inspected the handwriting. It was neatly lettered, the work of an educated man, but it was the curious symbol beneath that drew my attention. Those interlocking triangles were drawn where the signature might be, and they intrigued me enough to make up my mind.

I would find the tavern, speak with this stranger, and discover what he had to say. After all, I had nothing to lose.

13

After locking the front door behind myself I took the short path to the street, narrowly avoiding the low-hanging branch in the front garden. It was truly dark now, and the fog was thicker than ever. I realised I should have brought a lantern with me, but fortunately the occasional streetlight cast a dull gleam through the fog, and it was enough to find my way.

Soon after, I was wishing for not only a lantern but also a pistol. I'd noticed three shapeless figures dogging my footsteps, keeping to the shadows to avoid being seen, and generally acting like a group of thieves about to set upon my person. It didn't help that I carried little in the way of valuables or money, because they would likely be so upset at the lack of loot as to cut my throat without a second thought. A florin or two in my pocketbook wouldn't save me, and I shuddered as I pictured my lifeless body tumbling into the Thames, to be found the next day by a scavenger or a boatman. If anything, I was more scared in that moment than I had been at Lady Snetton's house, when I'd been standing still and waiting for the spirit to attack me.

I was tempted to stop, to see whether the men continued past me, but if they were bent on mischief that would only bring matters to a head even sooner. Instead, I increased my pace, despite the darkness, and so it was that I happened to slip on a patch of mud and end up flat on my back in the road. Winded, I drew in lungfuls of breath and stared helplessly at the yellow fog swirling overhead. Then three faces appeared, looking down at me. They were rough sorts with whiskers and soot-streaked cheeks, and I braced myself for the attack.

''Ere, mister. Give us your 'and.'

Dazed, it took me a moment to process the request, and then, cautiously, I extended one hand towards the newcomers. One of them took my wrist in a firm grip and hauled me to my feet, while the others brushed me down vigorously with their bare hands, removing the worst of the mud.

'You want ter be careful out 'ere, mate. Pitch dark an' 'orse shit everywhere.'

The others nodded in agreement, and I gazed at them in surprise. Far from attacking me, they seemed eager to help. Even so, a small part of me still feared a confrontation, and I decided to be as generous as I could. 'Thank you all, kind sirs,' I said, reaching for my pocketbook. 'Would you please accept a small token of my gratitude?'

'Nah, that's orl right, mister. You walk more carefully, you 'ear?'

The men melted away before my fingers located my wallet, and as I fished inside my empty coat I realised why. During the vigorous brushing-down, they'd relieved me of it with expert precision. I examined the area where I'd fallen, just in case, but was not surprised to find sign of neither wallet nor money.

I checked my other pockets and discovered the pages from the journal and the note inviting me to the tavern had disappeared also. In the darkness the men probably mistook them for five pound notes, and on that troubling thought I left the area in some haste. For, when the footpads discovered they held worthless paper instead of a fortune in currency, they might return with a lot less of their good-natured cheer.

As I approached the high street I passed an alleyway, and here I saw a sheet of paper flapping gently in the wind. It had been discarded, and was now half-glued to the damp, muddy road. I took it up, and in the dull gleam from a nearby streetlamp I discovered it was a single page from the journal. I cast around further, and soon located the somewhat crumpled note from the mysterious stranger.

Of the other pages, and the robbers, there was no sign at all.

Having folded the tattered pages, I tucked them away and crossed the high street, avoiding a lumbering horse and cart. There were many more pedestrians here, and I relaxed a little as I sought the tavern. It was not hard to find, despite the fog, as the rowdy patrons were singing a bawdy song which carried the length of the main road. As I got closer I saw light spilling from the crowded interior, with a dozen or more drunkards lying in the street outside. There were urchins with filthy faces amongst them, one of whom ran up as I approached.

'Spare a few coppers for a tot, sir? It's a cold night, it is.'

'I'm sorry, but I've just been robbed,' I said gently.

'Stingy bleedin' toff,' muttered the boy, and he ran back to join the others. He made a comment, gesturing in my direction, and the rest jeered at me with their high-pitched voices.

I entered the tavern, where I was met by a blast of warm air and noise from the crowd. The place was packed, and there was barely room to move. Somehow, serving girls managed to push their way through the patrons with trays full of tankards, and when one of them passed me on her way to the bar at the rear of the establishment, I followed in her wake.

On the way I kept an eye out for the stranger I was supposed to meet. Most in the tavern were clearly workers of one sort or another, and I must have stood out like a gold buckle on a cart horse in my relatively fancy attire. I attracted some attention, along with the occasional comment, but luckily most were deep in conversation and ignored me. I was hoping to find someone dressed in a similar fashion, so that I might introduce myself, but when I reached the bar and turned back to the entrance, I found I was looking across a sea of muddy brown. That's when it occurred to me that my contact might have been smart enough to wear something similar to these labourers, and I cursed my stupidity. Had I been similarly dressed, I probably wouldn't have lost my pocketbook to the thieves.

I needn't have worried about identifying the man I'd come to meet, for at that moment a strong hand gripped my elbow.

'Septimus Jones, I'm guessing,' said a low voice in my ear, easily heard despite the rowdy tavern. 'Why don't you come along where it's nice and quiet?'

I turned to look at the man standing beside me, and recoiled in shock. He was about my height, which was unusual, and he wore a rough working-man's outfit with a battered old cap, the peak pulled down to his eyebrows. It was his face that gave me pause, though, for it was heavily scarred, with a faded red line running from temple to chin, the lower portion barely covered by a growth of whiskers. The man's nose was misshapen, as though it had been broken and reset on several occasions, but all of this was trumped by his eyes. These were as stark grey as fresh-hewn flint, and they gleamed with an intensity that had me wishing I'd never left the professor's house. 'What is your name, sir?' I asked, and I hoped he hadn't noticed the slight quaver in my voice. 'What do you want with me?'

'Not here.' He nodded towards the exit. 'Outside.'

I was unwilling to leave the safety of the tavern, but the grip on my elbow was painful and the man showed no signs of letting go. Also, I'd heard of people being knifed in crowds, with none the wiser until the unfortunate victim sank to the floor and breathed his last. Any safety I felt in the tavern was merely wishful thinking, for this man seemed capable of ending me where I stood. Nevertheless, I tried one last time. 'Can you tell me the nature of your business? Why did you send me a note?'

The man's jaw tightened, and before I knew what was happening he was directing me towards the door. The crowd parted before him as though pushed aside by an invisible force, and I saw many surprised looks as annoyed patrons turned to see who'd shoved them, only to find there was nobody directly behind them.

The man ignored them all, and I was hauled unceremoniously from the tavern like a reluctant winkle from its shell. Outside, we skirted the drunks, and even the boys begging pennies from passersby held their tongues as the man swept by with me in tow. Then the hubbub and light from the tavern were dimmed by the thickening fog, and we were alone in the darkness.

'Down here,' said the man, indicating an alley.

I was truly frightened now, for I was certain my end was near. The man looked like a killer, there was no two ways about it, and he was leading me into a dark alley away from all prying eyes. 'I–I have no money,' I stammered. 'I was robbed on my way to the tavern.' My voice sounded high, nervous, and I cursed my timidity. Why hadn't I stood my ground? Why hadn't I demanded answers in the Crown and Feather? And why oh why hadn't I thrown the note away instead of putting my very life in danger?

'I don't want your money,' growled the man. 'Here. Sit.'

He indicated a packing crate, barely visible in the gloom, and I sat down as ordered. This gave me some little comfort, as it seemed unlikely the man would be able to slit my throat from ear to ear while I had the wall at my back.

'What are the terms of your employment?' the man asked me. 'Quick now, and no lies!'

Of all the questions he might have asked, I would not have guessed at this one. 'I–I serve as a bookkeeper, maintaining the accounts. Fifty pounds a year, plus room and board.'

'You think me a fool?' snapped the man. There was a rasp as he took out a dagger, and as he held the tip under my nose the weapon looked as long as a sword. 'I'm warning you. The truth now!'

'I swear! Cut me if you will, but I'm telling the truth!'

Something in my voice persuaded him, because he lowered the tip of the fearsome weapon an inch or so. 'You have not been involved in the professor's business? You have not witnessed the capturing of spirits?'

Now I faced a dilemma, because I'd promised Roberta my complete silence on the subject. However, for her part she'd neglected to mention the possibility of evil-looking men dragging me into dark alleys, and the likelihood that I might be dismembered with a dagger the size of a seaman's cutlass. Had she but raised the subject, even in passing, I might not have made so free with my promises.

'Before you answer,' said the man, 'you should know that I followed both you and the professor's daughter to Lady Snetton's house this afternoon. I was also present on the train for your return journey.' He reached into his filthy jacket and took out a folded piece of paper. 'In addition, I would like you to inspect this and tell me whether it's familiar in any way.'

I took the paper, unfolded it, and angled it this way and that. It was near-impossible to make out in the gloom, but from what I could see it appeared to be a letter of some kind. The writing, though indistinct, seemed familiar, and then, with a jolt that shook me to the core, I recognised the thing. 'This is a letter I mailed to my parents!' I exclaimed. 'How the devil did you get your hands on it?'

'Why, I took it from their house, of course.' He grinned wolfishly, the scar down the side of his face crinkling in a most distasteful fashion. 'Don't fret, Mr Jones. They are blissfully unaware of the theft, and both are in perfect health...for the time being. However, if you continue to dissemble in this fashion I promise they will not survive my next visit.'

My resistance, such as it was, crumbled in the face of this terrible threat. 'What do you want from me?' I asked, in a low voice.

'Engineering diagrams, information on the professor's methods, and any equipment you can deliver to me,' he said promptly.

'But–'

'In return for your ongoing cooperation, my organisation will send five pounds a month to your parents. In your name, naturally.'

Having threatened me with the stick, here now was the carrot.

But, dazed though I was, my ears pricked at the mention of an organisation. It was the first clue I'd had that this man was not working alone, and I wondered whether it was intentional or merely a slip of the tongue. I decided not to press him on the subject, but instead asked him a question of my own. 'There was someone before me at the professor's, a man by the name of Edgar. Was he working for you also?'

'Why don't you ask Roberta about him?'

'I did exactly that, and she informed me that he'd died.'

'Did she now?' asked the man. 'That's interesting.'

'How so?'

'Edgar is not dead. Far from it.'

'What!'

'He's confined to the mental ward in Bethlem Royal Hospital. Quite viciously mad, they tell me, and unlikely to ever recover his wits.' The man looked at me, then revealed further news just as shocking. 'The professor's wife spent her final years in the same hospital, until her eventual demise. Did Roberta mention that, perchance?'

'I only knew that her mother had died,' I said slowly. Two persons driven insane under the same roof? It could be no coincidence, and I wondered whether the professor's interactions with the spirit world might be the root cause. Did that mean both he and Roberta were also in danger? Was I?

'Now that you're apprised of the true situation, will you not help me? The professor is meddling with forces beyond his understanding, and one wrong move on his part could unleash a hellish danger on this nation the likes of which has not been seen for centuries.' The man spoke earnestly, gesturing with the dagger so animatedly that I was forced to draw back, lest he gift me a scar the twin of his own. 'If his amateur fumbling mistakenly opens a rift...' Here, the man's voice tailed off, as though he'd said too much. 'Well, it would be a true disaster,' he finished lamely. 'That, sir, is why we need your help. We must learn of his methods, to determine from whence the danger might come. We must know how far his research has progressed before it is too late.'

'If the professor is putting lives in danger, why do you not speak with him? He seems a reasonable man.'

'Reasonable, you say?' cried my captor, and the dagger swished through the air as he made his point. 'Oh, we have tried speaking with that man, but he's stubborn, and wilful, and as obstinate as a mule. But he is also brilliant, and gifted, and likely to uncover answers that others may not stumble upon for decades. Do you see our dilemma, Mr Jones?'

I had my eyes on that dagger, and chose not to move my head in the slightest.

'Of course you do. You understand that we must let him work freely, to a point. We must let him uncover mystery after mystery, but when the time is right we must step in and prevent a calamity.' The man gestured at me. 'That is where you come in, sir. You are my eyes and ears, and you will tell me what I need to know. With the information you gather, and minor pieces of equipment purloined at the right moment, you will keep me informed as to the professor's progress. With your help, we can avoid blighting every soul in the nation...and perhaps the whole world!'

Without warning, the man dug into his pocket and took out a crumpled page, which he brandished in my face. Despite the darkness I could just make out the ragged scrawl across the paper, and I saw it was the last sheet from the journal, the one with Edgar's final entry:

Kill them! Kill them all!

As I stared upon the page, it dawned on me that the robbery had been staged by this man. I'd been harbouring a faint hope that he'd come across the letter to my parents by innocent means, but now it seemed he had several others in his employ. I knew then that I had no choice but to comply with his demands, for I was completely outmatched. 'Very well,' I said in a low voice. 'I will do as you ask.'

'Good man. Gather what information you can, and I will arrange a meeting in a day or two.' He held the dagger up, sighting along the blade. 'Not a word to anyone else. Understood?'

'Yes.' I hesitated. 'Tell me, by what name should I call you?'

'I think not, Mr Jones.'

'But–'

'You will know it is I by the symbol on my note.' He stepped back, sheathing the long, gleaming dagger. 'Now, I shall bid you good evening. Until we next meet, sir!'

He turned and left the alley, a fast-moving shadow that vanished into the night. For myself, I stood up and followed almost as quickly, braving the darkness and fog at a breakneck pace, and not slowing until I reached the iron railings outside the professor's house. My heart pounded like a steam hammer after running so far, and as I gazed up at the unlit windows, the enormity of the situation dawned on me. I would have to lie and sneak and steal, and all the while I would have to maintain the professor and Roberta's trust in me.

Was I capable of such duplicity, or would they uncover my betrayal and throw me out of their home?

14

I cannot say how many hours I managed to sleep, if any, but I awoke the next morning feeling as wrung-out as Pheidippides must have done after his twenty-five miles. To say my dreams had been troubling would be an understatement of the worst kind.

After arriving home the night before I'd gone straight to my room, where I'd paced to and fro for the best part of an hour. As the floorboards creaked repeatedly underfoot, I'd sought an exit from the situation I'd found myself in. My first thought was to quit the professor's employ and take the next train home, but I discarded the idea immediately. I'd discovered that the scar-faced man was part of a larger organisation, and I could not hope to defend my parents against brigands and armed ruffians.

My next idea was to warn my parents of the danger, but this too was impractical. First, my letter might be intercepted, warning the enemy of my betrayal. And second, I knew my parents would not flee their lifelong home. After all, where would they go? And how long would they have to remain there, hidden from the world?

Finally, I debated revealing all to the professor and Roberta. The professor's word carried more weight than my own, and if I told him of the scar-faced man and his desire for the professor's secrets, would the authorities not be stirred into action? But again, I imagined the reprisals against my parents should I take this course of action.

My last two thoughts were somewhat impractical. The first was to flee for my life, but that would take money I did not have, and in any case it would not help my parents.

The second was the stuff of fiction. In this plan, I would arrange a clandestine meeting with the scar-faced man and his entire gang, then blaze away with a pistol until all were dead. As a young man I'd heard stories of gunfights and gold and outlaws in the Wild West from my father, but alas, I suspected that Wild Bill Hickok himself could not have carried out this plan. I was merely a bookkeeper, and in any case I did not possess a revolver.

And so it was that I retired to my bed, my mind still worrying at the awful bind I found myself in.

During my brief moments of sleep I was assailed by terrible visions. The first involved my parents, relaxing in their sitting room of an evening. As I walked in they turned their faces to me, but instead of their friendly countenances I saw nothing but black, featureless voids. In another dream I saw Roberta and the professor hacked to pieces by a maniac wielding a pair of cutlasses, chopping and chopping at their bodies even though they were clearly dead. And in another, I walked the streets of London in complete silence, with not a soul to be seen. The sky was blue and the sun shone gaily, but all life had been spirited away. Hansom cabs stood empty, with driver and horse missing. Goods wagons had rolled to a gentle halt, stopping where they may. Pages from newspapers blew down the streets, tumbling over and over like autumn leaves. And underfoot, repeated tremors shook the ground, until a broad fissure split the city in two, swallowing rows of buildings whole.

Disturbed by my dreams, I was lost in thought as I dressed myself.

I'd been supplied with a small shaving mirror, and the eyes that stared back at me were dark with shadows, the face haggard and drawn. It was the face of a condemned man, and I finished my morning ablutions in some haste so as to avoid gazing upon myself at length.

I felt a growing apprehension as I negotiated the staircase to the hallway below. I was in thrall to the man with the scar, with no choice but to follow his orders, and I suspected the expression on my face might betray my nefarious intentions to Roberta and the professor. They could not fail to notice my appearance, and I feared they might subject me to robust questioning as to the reason. I could only imagine the reaction if they learned of my meeting with the stranger, or the shocking news that I was to spy on them both. Instant dismissal was a given, and if the professor felt betrayed enough he might also involve the police.

I took the hallway to the dining room, and on the way one question repeated itself over and over: Could I face the professor and Roberta, and still keep my secret safe?

I entered the dining room to find the professor and Roberta already seated at the table. The professor was engrossed in his newspaper, as was his custom, and he ignored me completely. Roberta looked up from her repast to give me a quick smile, and I noticed that she too looked tired. 'Good morning, Miss Twickham. Did you sleep well?' I asked her.

'Hardly,' she replied. 'I worked late, and I believe daybreak was approaching before I finally turned in.'

I took up a plate and approached the sideboard, which was groaning under the laden dishes of hot food, but as I prepared to help myself I discovered my appetite had quite deserted me. There was a painful knot in my stomach, and the sight of sausages, eggs and bacon made me feel physically ill. To give the appearance all was well, I took two slices of bread, adding a curl of butter and a spoonful of fruit preserve. Then, with a teacup in my free hand, I returned to the table and took my place.

'Are you not hungry, Mr Jones? I have seen sparrows eat heartier meals.'

Before I could reply there was a rustle from the head of the table. The professor had folded his paper, and was tapping his finger on a column of newsprint. 'It says here there was a collapse in the new diggings for the underground railway.' He gave Roberta a look. 'You persist in using the underground, do you not?'

'I do indeed,' said Roberta. 'It saves a tremendous amount of time.'

'It'll never catch on,' growled the professor. 'Trains going here and there beneath the dirt. It's not natural!'

I almost laughed at that, given his work with the supernatural.

'Father, you can't expect me to take a cab halfway across the city,' replied Roberta. 'Think of the expense!'

'You should use the omnibus service, as I do.' The professor peered at the news. 'Five workers dead, and two injured children amongst them, the poor souls. Dear me! What is the world coming to?'

I felt sick to my stomach. 'Sir,' I began, 'Do they say what caused the collapse?'

'A tunneling shield failed, and the roof came down. They suspect an earlier tremor weakened the structure.'

Roberta and I exchanged a glance, and I knew instantly what she was thinking, for I felt the same dreadful apprehension. Had we not caused the tremor ourselves? Did we now bear the blood of the unfortunate victims on our hands? I turned to the professor, intending to confess, but just before I did so Roberta gave a quick shake of the head.

'Later,' she whispered.

'Eh? What was that?' demanded the professor. Then he saw something of interest in the paper, and he leaned closer to peer at the newsprint. 'Roberta,' he said mildly, 'I don't suppose you happened to murder Lady Snetton while you were attending her house, did you?'

'Father!' exclaimed Roberta, thoroughly shocked. 'Why would you ask such a dreadful thing?'

The professor lowered his paper. 'A servant found her this morning. She's dead.'

Dead! I recalled our meeting with Lady Snetton the day before, and had trouble taking the news in. She'd been young and full of vitality, and I could not believe she'd simply passed away. 'Sir, was there foul play involved?'

'It seems not. Her husband was away, and the servants reported no disturbances. According to reports, the lady appears to have died in her sleep.'

'But she was so young!' exclaimed Roberta.

'That does not grant immunity from an untimely end,' said the professor, somewhat pompously. 'You'd do well to remember that the next time you travel on that infernal underground train.' Then something occurred to him, and he stared at her, eyes wide. 'The fee! You did collect the ten pounds before departing her premises yesterday?'

'How can you think of money at a time like this!' exclaimed Roberta. 'It's unseemly!'

'No, my dear. It's business.' The professor folded his paper and stood, tucking it under his arm. 'You should have Mr Jones draw up an invoice immediately. There is plenty of time to catch the afternoon post. As for myself, I must attend to my work.' With that he departed, leaving me alone with Roberta. We were both shocked by the news stories, and there was a lengthy silence as we dwelt on the twin tragedies.

'The tremors were no fault of ours,' Roberta said eventually, in a low voice. 'They were a coincidence, nothing more.'

'And Lady Snetton's demise?' I recalled the chill hand of death that the spirit had laid upon me, and I had no trouble imagining a similar deathly touch ending our unfortunate client's life as she slept.

'We captured the spirit from her room, did we not?' Roberta leaned across the table. 'I beseech you, do not trouble my father with your wild suppositions. I'm sure there are innocent explanations for these events, and I would not have him worry over them.'

'He seemed more worried about the ten pounds,' I pointed out.

'Have you ever wondered where your next meal is coming from, Mr Jones?' demanded Roberta, her voice rising with her temper. 'Have you ever been so short of money you could not afford a roof over your head? Well, I should tell you that my father endured hard times in his early years, and he has no intention of experiencing them again.'

Little did she know, for without my current employment I would have been destitute, hungry and homeless. But I decided not to mention this, lest it lowered her opinion of me even further. 'I'm sorry,' I said quietly. 'I spoke poorly, and for that I must apologise.'

'Very well,' said Roberta, calm once more. 'Now do please eat a proper breakfast before you faint from hunger.'

I spread butter and conserve on my bread and took a bite. It tasted divine, and as I ate more my protesting stomach grudgingly conceded the battle. In fact, the slice of bread helped to restore my appetite, and I took my plate to the sideboard for a more substantial helping. As I loaded my plate, I saw Roberta smiling with pleasure, but whether it was due to my acquiescence or my healthy appetite, I could not say.

I was just returning to the table when I heard a loud hammering from the front door. Moments later, Mrs Fairacre hurried by, protesting under her breath. 'I don't know, I really don't,' muttered that worthy, loud enough for all to hear. 'Calling at this hour? Inconsiderate, I call it, and never mind trying to knock the front door clean off its hinges.'

There was a delay as she unlocked the door, and then I heard a cry of astonishment. I feared the worst, and I set my plate on the table and took up a poker from the fireplace before hurrying into the hall to lend assistance. What I saw stopped me in my tracks, for there at the front door were two uniformed policemen, the buttons on their coats gleaming in the morning sun. They towered over Mrs Fairacre, and with their severe expressions, tall helmets and mutton-chop whiskers they were a formidable presence.

'Good morning, ma'am,' said one of the policemen, in a deep, authoritative voice. 'Professor Twickham here, is he?'

I whipped the poker behind my back as Mrs Fairacre replied to their query, and backed quickly into the dining room. 'It's the police,' I hissed to Roberta. 'They're looking for your father!'

'Whatever for?'

'I don't know! They're talking to Mrs Fairacre.'

Roberta eyed the poker. 'Do you fear for your life, Mr Jones? Did you think a chimney sweep or a brush salesman intended you harm, perhaps?'

I was still gripping the poker in one hand, my knuckles white on the handle, and belatedly I realised that springing from the breakfast table and gathering up a weapon had not been the actions of an innocent man. 'I don't know what I was expecting,' I said quickly. 'With so many strange happenings recently, I–' I broke off as I heard footsteps approaching. It was not Mrs Fairacre, who barely made a sound, but the heavy tread of the two policemen. Hurriedly, I replaced the poker, and then I took a seat at the table and busied myself with my plate.

'Miss Twickham,' said the housekeeper, 'I'm sorry to interrupt your breakfast, but these gentlemen from the police would like to interview you.'

I glanced up to see the two policemen standing behind Mrs Fairacre. Both had removed their helmets, which were now tucked under their arms, and I felt a stab of alarm at their businesslike manner. One of the men was in his mid-fifties, his face weathered and his sideburns laced with grey, while the other was a ginger-haired man in his late thirties. The older man bore the uniform of a sergeant, while the younger man's dark blue coat was devoid of insignia. In the brief moment I was looking at the new arrivals, the ginger-haired policeman met my gaze, but his expression altered not a whit.

'Me? But of course!' Roberta indicated the table. 'Will you take a seat, gentlemen?'

'Thank you, Miss,' said the sergeant. 'We'll stand, if you don't mind.' He cleared his throat with a loud noise, then reached into his coat for a well-worn leather notebook. 'I'm Sergeant Parkes, and this 'ere is Constable, er, Smith.'

'Good morning,' said the constable, with a nod.

The sergeant took a moment to study the sideboard, his gaze running over the plates laden with bacon and sausages. 'Sorry to interrupt your breakfast, Miss. This won't take long, I'm sure.' Despite the courteous words, his expression said it would take as long as necessary.

'Sergeant, there's no need to be so formal,' said Roberta. 'Why don't you help yourself to breakfast, and then we can answer your questions at the table in a civilised manner.'

The sergeant glanced at Smith, who gave an almost imperceptible shake of his head. At that point I realised 'Smith' was no more a constable than I was, and I knew instantly we were in more trouble than I'd suspected. This was someone with real authority, and I guessed he was pretending to be a lowly constable to set us at ease.

'Thank you, Miss, but rules are rules.' The sergeant opened his notebook, licked his thumb and leafed through the pages. 'Now tell me,' he said, 'what was your reason for visiting Lady Snetton yesterday afternoon?'

15

I expected Roberta to quail at the sergeant's question, but instead she drew herself up, confronting him. 'Lady Snetton invited me to high tea.'

The sergeant eyed his notebook. 'They say you used the servant's entrance.'

'The front door was unattended,' replied Roberta promptly.

'You informed the maid, Annie, that you was there to catch rats.' The sergeant looked Roberta up and down, beset not so much by doubt as complete disbelief. 'And you was accompanied by a tall young man of...' he peered at the notebook, then looked at me, '...bookish appearance.'

The constable now spoke, indicating the poker in the grate before addressing me. 'Is that your weapon of choice when hunting rats? Or do you only take it up when the police come knocking?'

I swallowed.

'Your name, sir?' the sergeant asked me.

'S–Septimus Jones,' I whispered.

'I'm sorry, would you repeat that?'

'His name is Septimus Jones, and he is my father's bookkeeper,' said Roberta sharply. 'Why do you question him?'

Constable 'Smith' strolled to the table and sat down, resting his elbows on the polished surface. He steepled his fingers, tilting his head forward until the tips were brushing his moustache, and then he regarded us both coolly, without emotion. 'Let us dispense with this charade,' he declared at last, and I could not say whether he spoke to the sergeant, or to us. His next words, though, made it clear enough. 'My name is Inspector Cox from F division, Kensington. I'm investigating the murder of Lady Snetton, and when you've both finished playing verbal games you will tell me the true reason why you paid her a visit yesterday.'

I gaped at him in shock. *Murder?*

'But the newspaper–' began Roberta. 'The story said she died in her sleep!'

'Indeed she did, but not of natural causes.' The inspector regarded her. 'There were signs of struggle in the lady's bedroom, with the furniture in disarray, paintings damaged, and the curtains torn from the very walls. The maid informed us that you left the room in that state.'

'But Lady Snetton was not home at the time! The maid surely told you that.'

'So you felt the need to destroy her property in her absence? Tell me, Miss Twickham, have you been feuding with Lady Snetton?'

'No, far from it!' Roberta hesitated, and I perceived her internal struggle. She could not tell the policemen about capturing spirits and phantasms, even if she felt she could share her father's secrets, for these staid, ordinary men would not believe a word of her story. How, then, would she avert their suspicion? 'Might I ask one question?'

'Proceed.'

'Do you believe Mr Jones or I...do you think we killed Lady Snetton?'

'Miss Twickham, my investigation is only just begun. I merely seek facts, so that I might order them and gain clarity.' Cox leaned back in his chair. 'Let me be frank. The more trouble I have obtaining straight answers, the more I'm going to suspect your motives.'

'It was a seance,' declared Roberta suddenly. 'There! The secret has been revealed, and you may laugh at her Ladyship's folly.'

'A seance?'

'Indeed! Poor Lady Snetton lived in the jealous shadow of her husband's former wife, and she engaged me to facilitate communication with the spirit. I was to convey Lady Snetton's desire for harmony.'

I sat there in silence, marvelling at Roberta's composure in the face of such questioning. Almost every word she uttered was false, and yet she wove in enough truths to make the whole seem conceivable. What skill! What poise!

'What rot,' said the inspector. 'Are you telling me this vengeful spirit tore down the curtains, smashed vases and destroyed paintings?'

Right on the nose, I thought, but I held my tongue.

'Of course not! We closed the curtains for complete darkness, which is required when contacting wayward spirits, but fool that I am, I neglected to light the gas beforehand.' Roberta indicated me with a gesture. 'Mr Jones here, who is a gangling, clumsy sort, tripped on the carpet and knocked the jug clean off the nightstand. When I attempted to open the curtains, the rail came away all of a sudden, burying me in the fabric, and Mr Jones knocked a painting from the wall as he sprang to my aid.' Roberta lowered her gaze.

'So embarrassed were we at the damage, we left the house before Lady Snetton returned.'

I'd been holding my breath as she fabricated this web of lies, but now I let it out with a gasp.

'I'm sorry, Mr Jones,' said Roberta, patting my hand, 'but you are indeed clumsy.'

'Indeed I am,' I said, and I gave an apologetic smile for the benefit of the police.

'What's all this?' demanded a reedy voice from the doorway. 'Why do I have policemen in my house?'

I turned to see the professor marching in, and my heart sank. If they questioned him about Roberta's seance, he would let the cat out of the bag.

'Father,' called Roberta. 'I was just telling these good gentlemen about my seance with Lady Snetton yesterday. Did you know she was murdered in her sleep? They're interviewing us as suspects!'

As usual, Roberta was thinking six steps ahead of me, and I experienced a flash of admiration at the way she'd outmanoeuvred the inspector. Before Cox could stop her, she'd given her father enough information for him to back up her story.

'Not another seance,' said the professor, feigning exasperation. 'Roberta, my dear. When will you give up these foolish fancies?'

Inspector Cox looked from one to the other, his eyes sharp. Then he turned to me. 'What is your role in this seance business?'

'He fetches and carries on my behalf,' said Roberta.

'I'd like Mr Jones to answer for himself,' said Cox.

'I fetch and carry for Roberta,' I said dutifully.

'But you keep the books for her father?'

'Indeed, sir.' I felt myself growing uncomfortable under the inspector's gaze, and I looked down at the table, my face reddening.

Then, all of a sudden, I realised I could turn my self-consciousness to my advantage. Roberta was not the only one who could fool the police! 'I always do as Roberta asks,' I mumbled. 'I think the world of her, you see, and...' Here, I allowed my voice to tail off, as though embarrassed beyond words.

The sergeant suppressed a laugh, and I guessed he was exchanging an amused glance with the inspector. Then I pictured Roberta and the professor exchanging an entirely different sort of glance, and I was instantly mortified. I was living under the man's roof, and I had just admitted feelings for his daughter! I wanted to apologise, to tell them it was all part of the ruse, but the police were sitting opposite and I was forced to hold my tongue.

'Very well,' said the inspector at last, and his chair scraped as he stood up. 'Apologies once more for disturbing your breakfast, and I hope we won't need to bother you all again.'

'But the murder?' asked Roberta. 'Who could possibly have killed that poor woman?'

'The truth will come out,' said the inspector loftily. 'We'll get our man, you see if we don't.'

I raised my head cautiously, my cheeks still flaming with embarrassment. Nobody was looking at me, but I was particularly careful not to meet Roberta's eyes. Then I saw the sergeant fold his notebook and tuck it away, and to my enormous relief I realised the interview was truly over.

'Come,' said the professor. 'All this food is going to waste. Sergeant, will you take some sausages back to the station for your lunch? They're fresh cooked, and I can have Mrs Fairacre wrap them in grease-proof for you.'

'Thank you, sir. That's most kind.'

'And you, inspector? I have an unopened bottle of whisky in my office, and I never touch the stuff. Will you take it off my hands?'

'Well, if you insist,' said the inspector, and the three of them left the dining room together. Moments later Elsie, the maid, came in, gathering the breakfast things on a large tray before departing.

'Well done, Mr Jones,' murmured Roberta. 'That declaration of your undying love for me was the icing on the penny loaf, and no mistake.'

'I'm most dreadfully sorry about that,' I replied earnestly. 'It was a complete fabrication of course. I would never presume to, er...'

She raised one eyebrow. 'You do not find me appealing in any way?'

'No! I mean, yes! I mean...'

Roberta took my hand. 'Do not torment yourself, Septimus, for I fear there is no answer you can give that will not lead to further embarrassment.'

I nodded dumbly.

'But come, for we have work to do.'

'We do?'

'Indeed! Someone murdered my client, and I must find out who...or rather, what.'

I realised what she was hinting at. 'You think a *spirit* did this?' I whispered, aghast.

'It's likely it was Lord Snetton's first wife.'

'But– but we captured her!'

'We captured something, Mr Jones. What if we took a wandering spirit and left the far more dangerous one behind?' Roberta looked serious. 'If it was a ghost that ended Lady Snetton's life, we're duty-bound to capture the foul being before it harms anyone else.'

'But the police–'

Roberta snorted. 'Do you imagine the police will be any use in this matter?'

They might not be any use when it came to catching spirits, but I could just imagine Inspector Cox's reaction if he discovered Roberta snooping around Lady Snetton's house in my company, complete with traps and nets and discs inlaid with arcane patterns. And quite aside from the police, there was the horrifying notion of tracking down and capturing a spirit which might already have murdered one perfectly healthy young woman.

What if this demon decided to add Roberta and myself to its tally of victims?

At that moment the professor strode into the room, gesticulating with the folded newspaper. 'They found his body in the river!' he exclaimed. 'Yet another tragedy!'

Roberta and I both spoke as one. 'Whose body?'

'That young buffoon you wanted me to employ, my dear. The unsuitable one.'

'You cannot mean Jules Hartlow?' cried Roberta.

'Indeed. They say he'd been lost to the river for a day or more.'

I shivered as I recalled the applicant in question. Mr Hartlow's interview had occurred immediately prior to my own, and but for the professor having selected me for the position, the unfortunate young man would have been sitting in my position at that very moment. But had he thrown himself into the river in despair? Had I been the ultimate cause of his demise? 'Sir, was there foul play?'

'I should say so. His throat was slashed from ear to ear.'

There was a lengthy silence as we digested this gruesome news. 'At least...' began Roberta.

We turned to look at her.

'At least we can be certain a malevolent spirit did not cause this,' she finished. 'It sounds like the bloody deed of a human murderer. An argument over debts, perhaps, or a card game gone wrong.'

'So you don't believe the police will come knocking once more?' asked the professor.

'I very much doubt it. Think of all the people this young man must have encountered recently. The police have no reason to single us out for questioning.'

'Good,' said the professor, with feeling. 'This mess has already cost me one good bottle of Scotch for the inspector, and–'

'Father!'

'What?' retorted the professor. 'I'll have you know it wasn't cheap.'

'And if a second applicant is found horribly murdered?' demanded Roberta. 'Will you then complain about the price of sausages?'

'They're not cheap either,' muttered the professor, with a glance at the empty sideboard. 'And I was very much looking forward to those for my lunch.'

16

As the professor and his daughter wrangled back and forth, I recalled my encounter in the alley the night before, and I felt cold to my very stomach. I still had nightmares of the scar-faced man holding his long, pointed dagger to my throat, and I wondered whether he'd been responsible for the applicant's death. Had he approached Jules Hartlow before the interview in an attempt to inveigle the man into his schemes? And after Hartlow failed to secure the position which I now held, had the scar-faced man cut his throat and tipped him into the river out of pure spite?

'Father,' said Roberta suddenly. 'Mr Jones and I have decided to investigate the murder of Lady Snetton. Will you join us in our endeavours?'

'Are you quite mad?' demanded the professor, giving her a hard stare. 'I have just escorted one lot of police from my house, and now you want them to return in ever-greater numbers?' He shook the newspaper at her, working himself into a fine old temper. 'A second person with connections to my household has been found dead, and I cannot believe the pair of you now want to upset the apple-cart by poking your noses where they don't belong!'

'If Lady Snetton died of unnatural means–' began Roberta.

'I don't give two hoots if she was choked by a dozen feral spirits!' shouted the professor. 'You will not visit Lady Snetton's residence and you will not trouble the police. I order you to abandon all thoughts of investigations and sleuthing and suchlike. Do I make myself clear?'

'Yes father,' said Roberta meekly. 'I shall do as you ask.'

'Then the matter is settled,' declared the professor. He turned to me, lowering his voice to a conversational tone. 'Mr Jones, I would ask you to attend to your work this afternoon, for I must know the state of my accounts. You will work diligently and without interruption.'

'Yes sir.'

'If my daughter comes to you with her foolish notions you will report to me immediately. Immediately!'

I glanced at Roberta, hoping to divine her reaction to these orders, but her face was expressionless. So, I turned to the professor and gave him a nod. 'I will do as you ask, sir.'

'Excellent. And now I must retire to my study, for there is much to do. I believe a breakthrough is imminent, and I can delay no longer.'

'Father,' began Roberta. 'There has not been time to draw up the invoice for Lady Snetton, and I fear we might have missed the post.'

A shadow crossed the professor's face at the reminder of the ten pounds he might never lay eyes on. 'It's not surprising Mr Jones has yet to attend to the matter, what with the police traipsing all over my house,' he said testily.

'I intend to visit a friend in Westminster this afternoon. Her residence is not far from Lady Snetton's, and I could place the invoice into the right hands if you allowed me to.'

'I ordered you to steer clear of the Snetton house,' snapped the professor.

'But a bill arriving at the household by mail will not be dealt with for weeks, if at all,' said Roberta, in a coaxing tone. 'It will lay unopened in the butler's pantry, along with many others. However, an invoice hand-delivered, with a word or two of explanation...' Her voice tailed away to silence, leaving the suggestion hanging.

I could see a titanic struggle playing out in the professor's expression. He'd ordered his daughter to stay away from Lady Snetton's, and did not want to seem weak by now allowing her a visit. On the other hand, he was not one to waste a penny, and the lure of ten whole pounds was strong. It did not seem to occur to him that he would need that ten pounds, and more, in order to pay for all the sausages and whisky required to bribe the fresh waves of policemen. For I was sure they'd return in force if Roberta put in an appearance at the unfortunate Lady Snetton's dwelling.

'Oh, very well,' said the professor with some asperity. 'But do not tarry. And do not question the household about their mistress's death, for they will be in mourning, and you will be unwelcome in the extreme.'

'Of course, father.'

'And now I shall retire to my office.'

'There is one more thing I must ask.'

'Oh for heaven's sake!' cried the professor. 'Have I not given in to your wishes? What else do you torment me with?'

'It would appear a murderer is at large, and I would not like to become his next victim. Therefore, I would ask that Mr Jones accompany me as a bodyguard.'

The professor stared at her, then turned to look at me in disbelief.

'Him? But he has the physical presence of a sapling, and I swear a waved feather would be more deadly!'

'He will give an attacker pause for thought,' said Roberta stoutly.

'He will give an attacker a laughing fit,' replied her father.

'Sir,' I said. 'I would place my body in harm's way to defend your daughter.'

'Mr Jones, a stiff breeze would lift your body and place it in the Thames,' said the professor tartly. 'And in any case, I ordered you to work on my accounts.'

'I can tend to my bookkeeping duties later this evening, when the household is asleep.'

'As you did last night, when you paced up and down directly over my head?' demanded the professor. 'I barely got a wink all night!'

'Oh father, how you exaggerate,' sighed Roberta. 'I heard your snores for a good eight hours. Anyway, I refuse to place myself in danger by travelling the city on my own, so you simply must allow Mr Jones to accompany me.'

Trapped, the professor could only throw his hands up in disgust. 'Oh, do as you will!' he cried. 'It appears I have no say under my very own roof, so take the thrice-cursed invoice and your ineffectual bodyguard and do your best to stir up every policeman in London. Let them arrest the pair of you, but don't expect me to waste time pleading at your trial!'

After this rather theatrical outburst, he turned on his heel and marched from the dining room. The exit was dramatic indeed, but he spoiled the effect by returning for his newspaper, which he'd left on the table. Then, with a final glare at the both of us, he stormed off a second time.

'Ah, my dearest father,' said Roberta softly. 'He protests and blusters, but he has a good heart.'

I certainly hoped so, because his daughter seemed to delight in putting an immense strain on it. She had the ability to not only wrap him around her little finger, but also to persuade him to hold the knot while she put a bow on top. Then I remembered the argument she'd used to sway her father's decision. 'Do you truly intend to visit a friend in Westminster?'

'Don't be obtuse, Septimus.'

'And the bodyguard business? I confess I am not much given to brawling, and I do not possess a weapon.'

She looked me up and down, then gave me a warm smile. 'As far as I am concerned, Mr Jones, you will serve the purpose admirably. Now, let us prepare our things for the investigation. We must inspect Lady Snetton's room at the very least, and there are servants to be interviewed.'

I was still experiencing a heady glow after her smile and her compliment, and it was a moment or two before the rest of her words sank in. As I realised the import of what she was saying, the glow faded and I stared at her, appalled. 'But– but–'

'I intend to leave this house at three p.m., so that we have time to investigate properly. I suggest you attend to some bookwork in the meantime. If nothing else, that will help to soothe father's anger.'

Thus dismissed, I left the dining room and took the stairs to my office. I sat behind my desk for several minutes, contemplating Roberta's plans, and then I placed my elbows on the scarred wooden surface and buried my head in my hands.

It was some time before I managed to fight off the overwhelming fugue of despair and hopelessness. I felt as though I was being hounded from all sides, what with the scar-faced man, the police investigation and now Roberta's intention to track a murderer, and I knew that before long I would shatter like a china vase under the repeated hammer-blows.

When I was finally able to remove my head from my hands, straightening in my chair, I came face to face with the pile of bookkeeping work awaiting me. A groan escaped my lips, for I would sooner have thrown myself from the nearest window than spent the next three or four hours engaged in laborious calculations.

To delay the inevitable, I convinced myself I needed a new quill, and I opened the drawers in my desk one by one, inspecting the contents. The first two drawers slid open easily, and I discovered a pair of eyeglasses, a few sheets of parchment and a broken piece of India rubber within. The larger drawer at the bottom resisted my efforts, and so I let it be, fearing I might wrench the handle clean off if I persisted. I doubted it contained anything of interest, although I promised myself I would investigate further when I had the opportunity.

The paper gave me an idea, so I took a sheet of parchment, sharpened a quill and began a letter to my parents. I was not due to write for two or three days, but the threats to my person were mounting and I wasn't entirely certain I would survive that long. If the scar-faced man didn't kill me and throw my corpse in the river, one of Roberta's assorted spirits would most likely do the job. And if neither ended my life, it was likely the police would find some reason to arrest me over the recent deaths, and I'd probably hang.

Or worse, face transportation to Australia.

My dearest mother and father,

I trust this missive finds you well. I myself am in good health, and–

There I stopped. Ill-at-ease though I was, I could not find it within myself to deliver a cheery letter full of inane witterings about the city and her inhabitants. Nor could I reveal that my parents might never see me again, for that would cause great concern for my well-being.

I decided there had to be a middle ground, wherein I said my goodbyes but also gave them no cause for concern. Unfortunately, I did not believe this possible, even if the great Mr Dickens himself were to rise from the dead and pen the letter on my behalf. Something had to be written, though, so I took up the quill and tried once more.

I myself am in good health, and working hard at my new place of employment. My colleague Robert has been most helpful in showing me the ropes, and I am settling in well to my new position. The owner, a man by the name of Twickham, is occasionally short-tempered, but he has a good heart.

The work is refreshing, and I am paid enough to send you a portion of my wages every month. I hope these funds prove useful, and know that they are small recompense for the years of care and attention you lavished upon me.

I paused, worried I'd taken the syrupy prose a little too far. I decided I had not, for my parents would try to send the money back if I did not give them good reason to keep it.

As I sat back in my chair to consider an ending to the letter, I happened to glance down at that stubborn drawer. It had been nagging at me since the discovery, for I knew it might contain effects belonging to Edgar, my predecessor. Failing that, there might be long-forgotten information I could take to the scar-faced man, or perhaps some outlandish device discarded by the professor some years earlier. The former would not be aware that the items I delivered into his possession were old and possibly useless, while the professor would never miss them. In this way, I could maintain my standing with the scar-faced man without the professor accusing me of theft.

Unfortunately, this fabulous dream castle I was building for myself still had a foundation of fog and smoke. For if the drawer was empty, the edifice would crumble like sand before the ocean wave.

I pushed my chair back and dropped to my knees, so as to inspect the stubborn drawer more closely. There was no keyhole, and yet when I tried to open the drawer it gave very slightly before stopping, as though it were secured by some obstruction. The behaviour was that of a locked drawer, keyhole or not, and so I began to search for a hidden latch. I felt along both sides, but apart from a splinter or two I encountered nothing of interest. No concealed buttons or sliding mechanisms, and no protrusions or recesses.

I rested on my haunches and eyed the drawer critically. The desk sat flush with the floor, and I could not imagine the secret to opening the drawer lay underneath, for the casual user would not wish to stand the entire desk on end every time they wished to access the contents. Neither could I imagine an elderly matron scrabbling around on hands and knees to reach a remote locking device, which meant the catch had to be within arms-reach whilst seated.

I turned my attention to the handle, which to my eye was ordinary to a fault. Fashioned from brass, it consisted of a square metal ring threaded through two small pegs. There was a circular backplate to protect the varnished wood, scuffed and worn with age, but this was fixed firmly in place. The pegs were securely fastened also, and in any case they could not be rotated as the handle passed right through both of them, locking them in place.

That left the handle, which was a squarish ring of brass, much like a belt buckle. I tried twisting it to and fro, then lifted it until the metal was pressing against the wooden face of the drawer. It was at this point that I noticed the ring was slightly thicker than the handles of the two upper drawers. The lower drawer was larger than the first two, and therefore likely to be heavier when full, but did that really require the handle to be so much stronger? I looked closer, and noticed the right-hand side of the handle had a join top and bottom, just before the metal curved to form the side. So fine was this join that it was no surprise I had not seen it earlier, but now, as I ran my finger over the smooth brass, I could feel the edges clearly. Gently, I tried easing the handle apart, and to my surprise the right-hand segment came away in my hand, leaving a U-shaped piece hanging from the pegs.

At first I thought I'd broken the handle, until I inspected the detached piece. There were holes top and bottom, matching protrusions on the larger piece still attached to the desk, and when I pressed the pieces together they formed a whole once more. I was about to leave well alone when I decided to check the handles on the upper drawers. These were solid, and could not be separated, and this told me there was a reason for the novel construction of the lower handle. And that reason had to be connected with opening the drawer.

I pulled the handle apart once more, setting aside the smaller piece. Then I slid the larger piece to the left, so that it came free of the pegs. Once again I pushed and pulled at them, thinking the stubborn drawer must finally yield to my mechanical prowess, but alas, I was destined for disappointment once more.

As I squatted on the floor, eyeing my venerable foe, I hit upon a fresh idea. Taking up the U-shaped handle, I fed it through one peg only, then attempted to twist it.

Snick!

A broad smile lit my countenance as the drawer popped open, and I leaned forward eagerly to discover what treasures it might hold.

17

As the drawer slid open my first reaction was disappointment, for it appeared to be empty. Then I realised there was a large metal box sitting inside, similar to a valise or a travelling case, but laid on one side. The tarnished bronze lid was easily mistaken for polished timber, which is why I'd missed it at first glance. The box had the same dimensions as the drawer it occupied, with two recessed handles in the lid, one at each end. As I began to lift the metal case clear of the drawer I discovered it was surprisingly heavy, and it took some effort to regain my feet and place the box on the desk.

I had barely done so when I glanced towards the door. If anyone should enter, I would be caught snooping in another man's effects, and my hopes of placating the scar-faced man with a purloined treasure or two would be dashed. So, I rearranged the ledgers and paperwork to form a sort of wall across my desk, a barrier almost a foot high that would suffice to conceal the box from anyone standing in the doorway.

Next, I flanked the box with a pair of ledgers. These were additional insurance, for the instant someone knocked upon my door I'd have only to place the ledgers on top of the container to conceal it completely.

Now, fully prepared against discovery, I turned my attention to the box itself. The surface was absent any features aside from the two handles, although it did have finely engraved lines that gleamed dully in the gaslight. They formed curls and whorls like the markings on a five pound note, but did not appear to serve any useful purpose. I was reminded of the cube in the sitting room which I had inspected on my first visit to the house, and I suspected the case was of similar origin.

Next, I turned my attention to the front, where I found two dozen inlaid squares arranged in a single line that stretched almost the entire width of the surface. Each square was approximately half an inch to a side, identical in appearance and shading. All except the last, to the far right, which had been engraved with an 'X'.

I tried opening the lid, and was not surprised to find it tightly sealed. The squares had the look of buttons, and when I tried pressing a few they emitted a faint click and remained pushed-in. Pressing them again had no effect, but pushing the button marked with the 'X' forced all the others to pop out once more with a series of loud clacking noises.

I held my breath and glanced towards the door, fearful the strange rattle would attract unwanted attention. I took up a ledger in each hand, ready to cover the case the instant I heard footsteps, but a minute passed and the house remained silent. With no immediate signs of discovery, I replaced the ledgers and resumed my inspection of the case. I decided the buttons had to be the key, so to speak, but without markings there was no clue as to the sequence or pattern required to open the case. I tried several combinations, but each time I was forced to use the reset on the indented buttons. After the rattling sound of failure echoed around my small office for the third time in a row, I shrugged off my coat and laid it over the case to muffle further noises.

On a whim I tried the digits from Pi, pressing in the third, fourteenth and fifteenth buttons, counting carefully so as not to make any mistakes. Unfortunately, nothing happened. Then I discovered the buttons could also be moved vertically, albeit only a fraction of an inch. That meant they could be up, down or centered *and* pressed-in or flush with the surface, which multiplied the possible combinations exponentially. My heart sank at the realisation, for this combination would not be easily guessed, nor chanced upon by happy coincidence.

After the threats and terrors I'd faced in the recent past, both mental and physical, it was galling to be defeated by a handful of buttons. But, short of applying a crow-bar, I could see no easy way to open the metal case, and so I placed the box in its former home and secured the drawer with its two-piece handle. I would continue thinking on the lock when I had the opportunity, but in the meantime the box was best left alone.

As I tidied my desk I consoled myself with the thought that, failing all other options, I could hand the unopened box to the scar-faced man. Let him puzzle over the combination, and perhaps he might leave me alone whilst he did so!

It took me a good half-hour to finish the letter to my parents, and when it was done I blotted it, folded it in three, and sealed it for delivery. I had finished the missive with a few sentences about the city, including my journey on the underground railroad and the ever-present smog from coal fires and furnaces. I did not mention a single one of the dangers I faced.

After a glance at the desk drawer and its mysterious contents, I turned my attention to the bookwork. It was some time yet before Roberta and I would be leaving for the Snetton residence, and I decided to calm my nerves by applying myself to the staid, comforting matter of the professor's finances.

It was some hours later, and I was making excellent progress on the bookwork when I was interrupted by a knock at the door. It was Roberta, and I placed my quill in the inkpot and pushed my chair back.

'Do not rise on my account, Mr Jones,' she said quickly. 'I came to say that you may not be needed for my investigation, as my father has decided to accompany me to Lady Snetton's after all.'

My first reaction was surprise, for the professor had been adamant he'd have nothing to do with the Snetton case, and I wondered what might have altered his thinking on the matter. My second reaction was relief, for I was in no hurry to face the phantasm that might have killed the poor woman. It had to be a powerful spirit indeed to end her life, and I, as a complete newcomer to the hunting of evil spirits, was more likely to become its next victim than its captor. My third reaction was regret, as I would not have the opportunity to enjoy Roberta's company for the afternoon. 'I understand,' I said, with a brief nod. 'It is for the best.'

'Septimus, do not look so downcast,' said Roberta, approaching my desk. 'There will be plenty of chances in the future for you to grapple with the spirit world, and you still have much to learn.'

'Indeed I do.' I gestured at the ledgers piled on my desk. 'In any case, this was the work for which I was employed.'

Roberta gave me a curious look, and seemed on the point of saying something.

'What is it?' I asked. 'You know you can trust me.' Even as the words left my mouth, I felt like a cad of the highest order, for my statement could not have been further from the truth. 'You don't have to say, of course,' I added quickly, in a vain attempt to salve my conscience.

'It is something best demonstrated, rather than discussed.'

My heart quickened, both at her secretive manner, and at the idea that some magnificent secret was to be revealed to me. 'Please demonstrate, I beg you, for my nerves will not take the suspense much longer.'

She laughed at my overzealous response, and bade me follow her from the study. We took the stairs down to the next floor, where she led me to her bedroom. If possible, the interior was even more disordered than the first time I'd laid eyes on it, with equipment strewn hither and thither with no regard for order or propriety. To my horror I beheld a chemise, petticoats and corsets scattered upon the bed, and I averted my eyes from the display, my face reddening with embarrassment.

Roberta was unaware of my discomfort, for she was seeking something amongst the piles of clutter on her workbench. 'I know I left them somewhere around here,' she muttered, as she sought whatever it was beneath tangles of wire, small plates of metal and sheets and sheets of intricate drawings.

As she ferreted out her prize, muttering to herself at intervals, my gaze was firmly affixed on those diagrams. The professor and Roberta would be absent for the afternoon, leaving me alone with the servants, and one or two of those pages could be secreted easily about my person. There were so many of them, and in such disarray, that a page or two would surely not be missed? Also, Roberta was treating them with disdain, throwing them around like refuse, and while they might hold no value for her, the scar-faced man would surely give his front teeth for a sight of these drawings and diagrams.

Then I had a fresh idea, one that excited me to such a degree that I struggled for breath. It was the answer to all of my problems, and I cursed myself for not seeing it sooner. I would not steal drawings and devices from Roberta and the professor...I would make crude copies of their work in my own hand, and pass *those* to my blackmailer! His organisation might spend weeks attempting to build devices that had no earthly function, and for my part I would continue to serve up sheet after sheet of useless diagrams and made-up observations.

All of a sudden, the weight that had been bearing down on my shoulders was lifted, and I felt a lightness of spirit which had been sorely lacking these past few days. My plan was genius, sheer genius, and I beamed with delight at the thought of the scar-faced man and his cronies wasting their time, effort and money on my idiotic creations. I would have my revenge upon them, and they would never know it! My parents would not be made to suffer, and in addition I would be betraying neither Roberta nor the professor.

At that moment Roberta gave a satisfied cry and turned to me. She was holding up an old-fashioned pair of spectacles, but when she saw the huge, foolish grin on my countenance her own expression faltered somewhat. 'Why, Mr Jones,' she said uncertainly. 'Whatever are you so happy about?'

'It's nothing,' I said quickly. 'My mind was wandering, I assure you.'

Roberta must have suspected I was amused by her lack of tidiness, and she gestured at her workbench. 'I am well aware of the state of my things, Mr Jones, but I know the precise location of every item.' Then she glanced down at the spectacles, which had taken a good five minutes to locate. 'Well, *almost* every item.'

'Do you need those to see by?' I asked her, for I'd not noticed Roberta wearing eyeglasses before. Aside from the curious pair of lenses she'd used at the Snettons', of course.

'In a fashion, yes.' Roberta held them out to me. 'Please...try them on.'

'My vision does not require correction,' I said. 'No doubt it will falter as I age, particularly in my chosen line of work, but–'

Ignoring my protests, Roberta stepped close and reached up with the glasses, placing the earpieces either side of my head and easing the frame backwards until the spectacles rested upon the bridge of my nose. She stood barely a hand-span away, directly in front of me, and I held my breath as I beheld her shapely figure and felt the warmth of her body. Then I gave a great exclamation of surprise and staggered back in shock, for her face, so dear to me already, was entirely aflame!

I wrenched the spectacles from my nose, and was relieved to see Roberta standing before me, quite unharmed. She gave a peal of laughter as she saw my stunned expression, before stepping closer to reassure me. 'Do not fret, Septimus,' she said, placing her hands on my shoulders and smiling at me like a mother comforting a frightened child. 'The visions you see will not harm you!'

'B–but you had flames rising from your hair!' I looked down at the spectacles, turning them in my hands. The lenses were scratched in places, the frame worn with age, but they looked ordinary enough. 'Is this a parlour trick? Do you make fun of me?'

'Place them on your nose once more, and I shall explain.'

Rather than wearing them again, I wanted to hand them straight back to her, but even though the glasses had toyed with my vision, they had not harmed me in any way. So, reluctantly, I obeyed. Immediately, Roberta's entire face was surrounded by a fluttering curtain of red and yellow, but now that I was expecting it, I realised it did not look so much like flames as shimmering light. I reached out a hand to see whether the strange effect was tactile as well as visual, but my fingers merely brushed Roberta's cheek. Ordinarily this would have distracted me, if it had not been for a singular observation. When viewed through the glasses, my own pale skin was a deep navy blue! 'Wh–what is it?' I demanded. 'What am I seeing?'

'Those glasses belonged to my father's father,' said Roberta, side-stepping my question. 'They've been in the family for years, and their origin is unknown. What I can tell you is that they reveal the extent to which a person is in tune with the spirit world.'

As she spoke, I moved my hand before my face, and the aura emanating from my skin transitioned from navy blue to a virulent purple. 'What do the different colours signify?'

'Nobody knows,' said Roberta. 'But many people, if not most, exhibit no aura at all. Were you to look at Mrs Fairacre, or Elsie, or even those policemen who called on us this morning, I suspect they would be as ordinary when viewed through the spectacles as they are without them.'

'I wouldn't call Mrs Fairacre ordinary,' I muttered. 'Why, she moves around the house like a ghost, making no discernible sound.'

Roberta laughed. 'She does pride herself in being unobtrusive.'

A thought occurred to me, and I removed the eyeglasses to study Roberta's face. 'Were you aware of this when you employed me?'

'Aware of what, Mr Jones?'

'Did you know that I possessed this...aura?'

Roberta looked askance. 'Father may have taken it into account.'

'That's impossible! Why, I did not meet your father until the interview.'

Now Roberta looked even more uncomfortable. 'If you must know, father viewed all the applicants through a spyhole in the sitting room wall, using these very eyeglasses. That was the method he used to arrive at his final choice.'

Shocked at the professor's nefarious behaviour, I could only stare. Then I remembered the circumstances of my interview. 'Is that how he happened to have a contract drawn up with my name already present?'

Roberta nodded.

'And your argument with the professor over my employment? My reduced wages?'

She had the good grace to look embarrassed. 'Money is not plentiful in this house, Mr Jones. Our expenses are high, and clients frequently neglect to pay for our services.'

I knew that to be true, for I'd seen it time and again in the accounts. 'But why, for heaven's sake? Why did you seek someone with this aura...this special connection to the spirit world? I am only here to manage your books!'

Roberta hesitated, then sighed, lowering her gaze. 'I suppose there's no harm in revealing the truth of the matter,' she said quietly.

'My father is not a young man, and he worries about the future of our enterprise. That, and my own future along with it.'

'But you are more than capable of taking his place!' I declared stoutly. 'I have seen you at work, and I am certain you are his equal!'

She smiled at the compliment. 'That is likely the case, but the unnatural forces confronting us cannot be tamed by one person working alone.'

All of a sudden, the truth of the situation dawned on me. 'You were seeking–'

'Yes, Mr Jones. We needed someone who could learn the ins and outs of this business alongside us, while my father is yet able to teach them.' Roberta raised her head, looking directly into my eyes. 'We needed an apprentice, not a bookkeeper. And we chose you.'

18

'But that cannot be true!' I protested. 'If you sought help with the catching of spirits, why advertise for a bookkeeper?'

Roberta's lips twisted into a smile. 'My father is careful with money, as I'm sure you've noticed, but he has no patience for accounts. I myself have a flair for the mechanical, but I regard numbers and sums with loathing. Thus, by hiring a bookkeeper who could also train in the business, we are paying one wage and filling two positions.'

I was taken aback by her blunt honesty, but could see the merit in their thinking. It had already occurred to me that organising the professor's accounts involved a few days work at most, and I had been wondering why they had employed me on a yearly wage when they could have paid a bookkeeper on a piece rate. But no, of course they couldn't! Fool that I was, I suddenly realised that any bookkeeper worth his salt would have deduced the nature of the professor's business inside the first hour. A disreputable sort, of which there were many, would have sold his tale to a reporter. A more honest man might have gone to the nearest police station, there to report the professor and Roberta as charlatans who were cheating innocents out of their savings.

And me? I was just beginning to accept the notion that I might one day replace the professor. That Roberta and I might work together for years to come. That perhaps, one day, she and I–

'Septimus, will you please say something?' demanded Roberta. 'I cannot read your mind, and I do not know whether you will remain here to help us, or walk out at the first opportunity!'

I was about to declare my intention to stay, even though I was far less certain of my worth than the professor and Roberta appeared to be. But then I remembered the scar-faced man, and my mood soured instantly. How could I dedicate myself to the pair of them, when I might be forced to betray them at any moment? I could not give my answer, at least not until I'd dealt with my antagonist.

'Septimus?' said Roberta, in a small voice.

'I will have to think it over,' I said, and my insides turned cold as I saw the disappointment in her face. 'I'm sorry, but you've given me a lot to consider.'

'Yes, of course.' She turned away, fiddling aimlessly with something on the workbench. 'Don't let me keep you from your work.'

Her manner was brusque, and as I left her room she closed the door firmly behind me. I felt wretched, but I knew I had no choice. In that instant I felt a surge of anger towards the scar-faced man, such that I'd never experienced in my entire life. But for his cruel demands, I would have given Roberta an affirmative answer, and my future would have been secure! Now, I imagined the professor reconsidering the other applicants, and I knew I might soon lose the very position I'd been so happy to acquire.

After leaving Roberta's room, I returned to my office to collect the letter I'd written to my parents. My appetite had returned with a vengeance, thanks to my light breakfast, and I intended to seek out Mrs Fairacre to enquire about lunch. The letter, I felt, would be a suitable excuse for a chance encounter.

I descended the stairs once more, where I met the maid, Elsie, in the corridor. 'Beg pardon, sir,' she said, pausing at the lower step. 'Mrs Fairacre's regards, and she's prepared lunch for you in the dining room.'

'Thank you, Elsie. That is welcome news indeed.' I held up my letter. 'Who should I speak to about mailing this?'

'I can take it for you, sir.'

I gave it to her, but instead of leaving, she waited patiently. 'Is there anything else?' I enquired.

'The postage, sir. For the stamp.'

'Oh, of course!' I took out a penny and handed it to her. 'Thank you, Elsie.'

She bobbed her head and left with my letter, and I turned in the opposite direction and made my way to the dining room. Roberta was absent, but the professor was seated in his usual place, buried in his newspaper as always. At the far end of the table there sat a plate containing thick sandwiches, with a tall glass of ale alongside. I made for the place setting and sat down, and my stomach rumbled as the delicious aroma of fresh bread, sliced ham and mustard rose to meet me.

'There should have been sausages,' declared the professor, from behind his newspaper. 'Such a pity I had to give them all to the police, for I am partial to cold sausages with pickle.'

I felt the professor's complaints were misdirected, and said nothing. Instead, I picked up a sandwich and prepared to bite into the tempting fare.

'Did you say something to upset my daughter?' enquired the professor, peering at me over the top of his newspaper. 'She is in quite a huff. Worse, she refused lunch, and that is almost unheard of.'

I lowered my sandwich. 'Roberta spoke of the duties you wish me to engage in. Not the bookkeeping, but the other.'

'Hmph.' The professor eyed me with disfavour. 'Do you consider my work too much of a challenge? If so, you are half the man I took you to be.'

'Sir, I–I merely asked for time to consider.'

'What's to consider?' demanded the professor. 'You are penniless and have no prospects. Your qualifications are laughable, and you'll find a hundred more favourable applicants for every position you might apply for. And yet Roberta and I offer you the comfort of our home, the opportunity to learn and grow, and, with time, perhaps an equal share in the business.'

And the chance to die in a most horrible fashion, I thought to myself, but that was not the reason for my reluctance. 'I am placed in an awkward position, sir, and I must resolve a certain situation before I may commit to your generous and kindly offer.'

'Is it a debt?' demanded the professor. 'A woman, perhaps?'

'I cannot reveal the true nature of–'

'Have you been promised employment elsewhere?' The professor's voice rose. 'You have taken a new position? Is that it?'

A prisoner in the Old Bailey would have been questioned less searchingly, and I was becoming tongue-tied as the professor's interrogation proceeded apace.

'Do you doubt yourself?' he cried, working himself up. 'Are you not up to the work? Are you *afraid?*'

'Sir, none of the things you mention are the true reason. If you'll just allow me a week to–'

The professor snorted and raised his newspaper once more. 'I would be surprised if you were still here a week from now,' he muttered, before drinking noisily from his teacup.

I ate my sandwiches in silence, but after the heated conversation the fresh bread, ham and mustard tasted like ashes in my mouth. The beer was refreshing enough, but Roberta's disappointment in me weighed heavily on my mind. 'Sir,' I began, 'to make amends, would you allow me to accompany both you and your daughter to the Snetton residence? Perhaps if I demonstrate my eagerness to help you both...' I left the question hanging.

Slowly, the professor lowered his paper. His eyes met mine, and I could see from his expression that he was not dismissing the idea out of hand. Then, abruptly, he nodded. 'Very well. I shall permit it.'

The professor returned to his newspaper, and it dawned on me that he'd accepted my suggestion with remarkable speed. As a consequence, rather than my being dragged to the Snetton house by Roberta, protesting all the way about the folly of her investigation, I had willingly offered my services. In effect, I had just volunteered for a rather dangerous task, and on top of that I had promised to do my utmost to aid the professor and his daughter in the capture of a murderous spirit.

All of which gave me pause for thought, for I suspected the pair of them had just manipulated me once more.

I finished my glass of ale, pushing my chair back as I prepared to stand, and the professor cleared his throat. 'Three p.m. at the front door, and not a minute later.'

'Yes, sir.'

'Good man.'

I left the dining room and strode along the corridor towards the stairs, intending to continue working in my study. I reached the door to the sitting room, which stood open, and on my way past I happened to glance inside. One of the metal cubes was sitting on the side table near the bay window, illuminated by a shaft of sunlight just as it had been on my first day with the professor.

At the sight of it, I came to a halt. Dare I look around, just for a moment?

I glanced over my shoulder, but there was no sign of the professor. I peered towards the far end of the corridor, where the kitchen and the servants' quarters lay, but there was no sign of Mrs Fairacre or the maid. I listened carefully, but there was no sound of footsteps from the floor above.

It occurred to me that I was being foolish, for I was a guest in the professor's house, and as such I had every right to use the sitting room. But deep down I knew that any time I spent therein would be in the service of the scar-faced man...hence my furtiveness.

Having assured myself that I was not being observed, I entered the sitting room. It was just as it had been on the day of my interview, minus the other applicants and the unfortunate Jules Hartlow. Metal cubes occupied positions all over the room, sitting on the mantlepiece, the windowsill, on side tables and bookcases. They varied in size, from large devices the size of my head to small boxes no bigger than my fist, and as I took stock I decided that, should all else fail, one of the smaller cubes was unlikely to be missed.

With my parents' safety in the balance, I knew I would not hesitate.

I did not want to be observed inspecting the cubes, and so I left the room and took the stairs to my study. On the way I glanced towards Roberta's door, but it was firmly closed and there was no sign of her. So, I kept climbing until my own floor, where I sat in my chair and opened the accounting ledger to the latest page. There was only an hour until three p.m., and I resolved to wade through one more stack of bills.

I had barely completed a dozen entries when I heard footsteps outside my door, and then the professor burst in without stopping to knock. 'Septimus, my boy!' he cried, in his reedy voice. 'I must speak with you immediately!'

He was gesturing with a folded sheet of parchment, and when I looked closer I saw it was the letter I'd written to my parents. The seal was broken, and my blood ran cold as I realised the professor must have read every word. My mind all but froze as I struggled to recall the contents, for while I was certain I had not revealed any of the professor's precious secrets, something contained within my missive had riled him up. 'I–Is that my letter?' I asked, playing for time.

'Do you deny it?'

'No, but how–'

'Mrs Fairacre brought it to me.' The professor crossed to my desk, slapping the letter down on a pile of paperwork. 'This is a masterpiece of fabrication,' he cried. 'It's a tissue of lies!'

'I suppose it is, but–'

'Well done, my boy. Well done indeed!' The professor leaned across my desk, and for one horrible moment I feared he was going to hug me. Instead, he clapped me on the shoulders with both hands. 'Capital work, Mr Jones. I knew I could trust you!'

Dazed, I could only stare at the elderly gentleman. The fact he'd intercepted my mail – had opened it and read the contents – was something I'd worry about later, for at that moment I was utterly confused by his reaction.

The professor saw my confusion, and elaborated. 'A lesser man might have been tempted to reveal a whisper of the truth to their family,' he explained, lowering his voice to something less than his previous bellow. 'But not you. No! You, Mr Jones, used wit and cunning and subterfuge when communicating with your parents, and for that I thank you from the bottom of my heart.' He waved the letter at me again. 'Calling my daughter Robert? Admirable! Describing my business as though it were an accounting firm. Ingenious! But above all, you did not once mention ghosts, nor spirits, nor phantasms, and thus you have my undying gratitude.'

'Thank you sir, but–'

'Say no more about it!' The professor pressed the letter into my hands. 'Seal it again, and this time I will ensure it is mailed. Until later, my boy!'

He whirled around and was gone the next instant, leaving me with ringing ears and the somewhat crumpled letter. At that moment I decided to post any future letters by my own hand, for it was apparent I would have no secrecy while under the professor's roof. I was also struck by his complete lack of shame in reading my letter, and his willingness to reveal that he had done so.

I thought of my room at the top of the stairs, and the belongings of mine stored within. Had the professor searched those too? Why, just the previous day I'd been absent throughout the afternoon, giving him plenty of time to inspect every nook and cranny. And never mind yesterday...what if it turned into a regular occurrence, him poking through my things? I'd planned on hiding purloined drawings or equipment beneath my bed, or perhaps atop the wardrobe, but I would have to be far more cunning than that if I meant to avoid discovery.

The intercepted letter had served as a timely warning, and I resolved to take every precaution in future. From now on it would be a game of wits, and I was not entirely confident I could hold my own against the professor.

19

At one minute to three, just a fraction earlier than ordered, I was ready and waiting near the front door. The others had yet to appear, but I could hear metallic noises from the first floor, and I assumed Roberta was still packing detectors and traps and other devices into the haversacks. I could also hear the professor tinkering in his office nearby, which shared a common wall with the sitting room.

At three past the hour there was still no sign of the professor nor Roberta, and if anything the noises they were making were even more pronounced. I could hear muttered exclamations from the professor, sometimes delight and sometimes displeasure, while Roberta appeared to be chasing around her bedroom in heavy boots, pausing now and then to hurl a tea tray at the wall.

I'm sure I exaggerate, but that is what it sounded like to me as I stood there waiting for them both. There was little to occupy my mind, and I did not want to leave my post in case I was then accused of tardiness. Vacate the hall for but an instant, and the professor and Roberta would inevitably choose that very moment to put in an appearance.

At ten past the hour I began to suspect that both of them might have forgotten our plans entirely, and I decided to approach the professor's study in the hope that my sudden appearance would provoke a response.

That, it most certainly did.

I looked into the professor's office to see him dressed from head to toe in white, with a metal grill covering the lower half of his face. He was holding a weapon which looked like a fencing sword, except it had a forked tip and the guard was square rather than the more usual rounded shape. He also bore the spectacles with the ruby and black eyeglasses.

The professor stood in a crouch, with his legs apart and his weapon raised as though he were preparing to defend himself from an assailant. The forked tip of the weapon crackled and sparked with power, and I looked around in vain for the professor's opponent. There was none to be seen, and the professor appeared to be facing an empty room. Empty, that is, aside from the workbench pushed against the far wall. This held a small brass cylinder nestled in a wooden stand, and I recognised the device as one of those used to contain spirits. As I studied the cylinder I saw the top had been shattered, and even as the significance dawned on me, the professor gave a great cry and sprang forward, sweeping his weapon wildly from side to side. He jabbed, he cut, he thrust upwards, and all the time he grew ever closer to the cylinder standing on the workbench.

I realised that he was duelling with a spirit that only he could see, and I held my breath as the professor fought valiantly. Now attacking, now retreating, and all the while conserving his energy for the final flurry that would drive the spirit into captivity once more. It was an impressive display, and I'm sure it would have ended well had the professor not seen me standing in the doorway. 'Ah, Mr Jones!' he cried. 'Do you see this newly-fashioned weapon of mine? With this to hand, those wayward spirits will stand no chance!'

He was distracted for no more than a second or two, but that was time enough for the spirit. I saw a baleful red glow attach itself to the professor's arm, and he shook himself wildly, trying to dislodge the creeping red stain. 'Back, you foul fiend!' he cried. 'Unhand me this instant, or it will go badly for you!'

Unfortunately, the spirit ignored the professor's threats and physical efforts alike, and the stain continued to move towards his shoulder.

At this point the professor employed a tactic which was both brave and foolhardy. With barely a moment's hesitation, he took the weapon in his left hand and applied the forked tip to his right arm, directly above the gleaming red stain. There was a flash of light as the sparking tip made contact, followed by a tremendous bang. I saw the professor hurled backwards across the room, the weapon flying this way, the mismatched eyeglasses the other. As for the professor, he was thrown against the glass-fronted shelving, shattering the panes, collapsing the shelves and scattering brass cylinders, books and trinkets all over the floor.

The professor moved feebly amongst the remains of his bookcase, with cylinders rolling around and multicoloured liquids forming pools on the floor. He struggled to raise one arm, attempting to signal to me, but after the shock he seemed unable to speak. I rushed forward to help, and as I did so I felt a familiar chill running down my spine. I had seen already that the red stain had departed the professor's person, and somewhere in this room, somewhere close, the phantasm now roamed free.

I saw the professor trying to point at the weapon lying nearby. He was far too weak to wield the thing, and so I sprang forward and snatched it up, discovering as I did so that the grip had a trigger mechanism. The tines at the end of the sword were buckled from its heavy landing, but when I squeezed the trigger a healthy spark crackled at the forked tip.

I whirled around, brandishing the sword like a sailor repelling boarders, but of course there was no enemy to be seen.

'Glasses,' wheezed the professor. 'Need glasses.'

I saw them near the workbench, and I skirted the area I imagined the spirit was occupying, waving the sword ahead of me for all I was worth. Then, with a rapid crouching motion, I swept up the glasses and pressed them into place.

Immediately, my world turned inside-out. Through the ruby lens I could see the professor's prostrate form, only now it flickered and wavered with energy. Through the midnight lens I saw only darkness...total, all-encompassing darkness. Then, without warning, two ghostly hands loomed before my very face, with greenish, transparent fingers, flayed skin and tatters of cloth. It was as though I were looking into a deep, dark pool, and someone within had just pushed their hands through the surface.

I barely had time to jump back, and the grasping hands missed me by the merest fraction of an inch. I felt an icy breath on my face as the clawed fingers swept by, and they were coming back for a second attempt when I remembered the sword. I raised it quickly, jabbing at the phantasm, and there was a crackle of power as the tip made contact. A foul, distorted face loomed towards me, with blank holes for eyes, the mouth wide open in a soundless scream, and I jabbed again and again as I tried to drive the horror back.

As the dark cloud retreated towards the professor, I realised he was in danger once more. I had to herd the spirit away from him, and quickly.

I circled the pulsating, pitch-black cloud, sliding my shoes across the floorboards instead of raising them, to avoid treading on the metal cylinders. All the while I kept the sword raised, and to my relief the occasional jabbing motion was enough to keep the spirit at bay.

But how was I to trap it?

I kept my sword up, feinting this way and that as the spirit tried to find a gap in my defences. Unfortunately, the glasses only showed me the closest portion of the phantasm, for anything further away than a pace or two was hidden inside the dark cloud. Thus, its hands would dart towards me out of thin air, attacking from all sides, and it was all I could do to ward them off. I knew the professor would be no help if the spirit took hold of me, and once it had drained my life force I imagined it would take his next. So, two lives lay in my hands, and my sword-arm was beginning to ache from the effort.

I should have cried out for help, bringing Roberta downstairs with a trap or a weapon of her own, but I feared she would be distracted by the sight of her injured father. If I had to protect the two of them, as well as myself, the ghostly apparition would likely feast on three souls rather than two.

I jabbed at the ghostly face, and as it retreated once more I took a second to glance about me. There! Through the red portion of the glasses I saw the outline of the workbench, and upon it the open cylinder. The professor had been driving the spirit in that direction, and I decided there must have been reason behind his efforts. I did likewise, advancing on the phantasm step by step, jabbing at it repeatedly with the forked tip of my sword.

As it backed away from me, getting closer and closer to the open cylinder, I became aware of a new vision in my right eye. There was a faint conical shape, like a large funnel spun from the clearest glass, the open end facing me and the neck directly above the cylinder. It was turning gently, in the manner of a whirlpool, and through the jet-black lens I saw a wisp of the phantasm's ghostly form drawn out from its body like a strand of wool. It quivered and struggled, but slowly it was sucked into the mouth of the funnel, and gradually the rest of the spirit's body was pulled in after it. I had one final view of its tortured face, the eye sockets wide and pleading, the hands like the desperate grasping claws of a drowning man.

Then it was gone.

Shaken to my core, I ripped off the spectacles, tossed the weapon aside and leapt towards the bench. Here I found a sharp fragment of bronze that matched the jagged hole in the cylinder, and I took the piece up and plugged the hole as quickly as I could. A lit green candle stood on the workbench, the wick swimming in wax, and I took the candle and poured molten wax over the end of the cylinder, sealing it. Then, at last, I took a ragged, drawn-out breath.

I was still filling my lungs when I heard a thunder of footsteps in the hall. I spun, expecting to see some new horror, but instead it was Roberta arriving at speed. She was in her work clothes, and she spared me the briefest of glances before crossing the room to crouch beside the professor. 'Father, what happened?'

He mumbled something inaudible, struggling to sit up. Roberta helped him, and the professor leaned back against the broken shelves, running a hand over his face before slowly surveying the wreckage of his study. Then he looked at me. 'Did it work?' he asked. 'Did you drive it into the receptacle?'

I guessed he meant the cylinder. 'Yes sir. And once inside, I sealed the end with wax.'

'Good work, my lad.'

'Father, what were you doing?' asked Roberta, with an edge to her voice. 'Do not tell me you released a phantasm inside our own home!'

The professor was silent.

'I can scarcely believe your idiocy!' growled Roberta. She turned the professor's head, inspecting his face for wounds, then ran her hands quickly over his arms and legs. From the winces on her father's face, I guessed this inspection was none too gentle. 'Are you hurt?' she demanded. 'Have you broken any bones?'

'I am a little bruised and battered,' admitted the professor. 'But thanks to the quick-thinking Mr Jones, I suffered no long-lasting effects.'

'Aside from rattling your defective brain,' muttered Roberta, but there was a certain kindness behind the insult. 'And just look at the state of your things!'

The professor eyed the wreckage strewn all about him. 'Nothing broken that can't be repaired,' he remarked. Then he looked up at her hopefully. 'Roberta, dearest, I believe I could take a little fortification. Just for the nerves, you understand.'

His daughter's eyes narrowed. 'Brandy? But we're due at Lord Snetton's!'

'Just a sip or two. It will clear my head.'

He looked at her so beseechingly that I, in her place, would have run for the bottle immediately. Roberta, however, was made of sterner stuff. Instead of trotting off to do her father's bidding, she merely raised her voice to a cattle-drover's shout. 'Mrs Fairacre, do you hear me? Brandy for the professor, if you please!'

Less than ten seconds passed before the good housekeeper appeared in the doorway, silver tray in hand. She'd arrived with no discernible sound, as was her way, but I did hear breaking glass underfoot as she crossed the office to the professor. Here, she offered him the tray, upon which stood a single glass containing half an inch of amber fluid.

The professor took the glass, eyed the diminutive dose with disfavour, then downed it in a single gulp. 'Mrs Fairacre, that miniscule droplet achieved nothing at all.'

The housekeeper placed the empty glass on her tray, sniffed loudly at the mess, and departed before the professor could ask for more brandy.

'Oh well, I suppose it will have to do,' said the professor, struggling to his feet. There was a tinkle of glass as fragments fell from his clothes. 'Time flies, and we must be away.'

'You cannot possibly attend Lord Snetton's in that state!' protested Roberta.

'It was barely a mouthful!'

'I meant your appearance, father. You look like the worst kind of tramp.'

She spoke truly, for the professor's hair was awry, his clothes were crumpled and stained with fluids from the cabinet, and a substantial dusting of glass and wood fragments were distributed about his person.

'If you give me but a few minutes–' began the professor.

I glanced at a nearby clock. It had just gone thirty past three, and I guessed it would be well after four by the time the professor was ready. Allowing for time at the Snetton's, it would be late evening before we could hope to return.

Roberta, however, seemed unconcerned, and she ordered him about like a mother with a dishevelled child. 'Very well. Change your things, tidy your hair, and we will depart the instant you are ready.'

The professor left, still shedding stray fragments, and then Roberta turned to me. 'While he prepares himself, you and I will put his study in order.'

I surveyed the wreckage, and it occurred to me that a carpenter and a glazier would be more suited to the job. Still, Roberta and I did our best, and within ten minutes we'd righted the shelves, replaced most of the contents and swept up the broken glass. I collected the scattered bronze cylinders, and as I did so I noted the writing on the labels, much of it faded and hard to read. There were names and dates, and I realised the professor's capturing days had spanned a decade or more. Indeed, one of the oldest cylinders, labelled 'C. Dickens', was dated December 1841, some thirty years earlier.

'Ah yes,' said Roberta, as she saw me inspecting the faint handwriting. 'Father calls that one the spirit of Christmas past.'

I was still staring at the name. 'Is this–'

'Indeed. Father claims to have caught that particular phantasm in the great man's study, but he's been known to embellish a tale.'

I handled the cylinder with reverence, placing it on a varnished wooden rack with a dozen others. Was it possible the spirit trapped within had been the inspiration for the author's famous tale? A shiver ran up my spine at the thought. Imagine if that phantasm were now freed after so many years. Imagine the fury, the chaos, the destruction wreaked upon man, beast and property alike!

'Do not fret, Septimus,' said Roberta. 'The spirits within these capsules are secure, and cannot escape.'

'Unless your father decides to release them, so that he might practice his swordplay.'

She glanced towards the weapon, which now lay on the professor's desk. 'He can be impetuous at times,' she admitted, 'but you must admit, it was wise of him to test the new device on a weaker spirit. After all, it is likely we shall face a more powerful adversary at the Snetton residence, and if the weapon did not work here, in the safety of his study, then what use would it be against a deadlier foe?'

I shuddered as I recalled the distorted, terrifying visage of the phantom I'd barely succeeded in subduing. 'The weapon drove it back, but the professor's glasses only showed the foul being when it was directly before me, and I almost within its grasp. Had it moved any faster, I would have had no chance at all!'

'Father is working to improve the lenses, but the process is slow, and the materials are costly to obtain.' Roberta glanced towards the door. 'Here is father now. Let me fetch the equipment, and we shall be on our way.'

20

We left the house together, with the professor sporting a top hat and walking stick, Roberta in her work overalls with her long hair concealed under a cap, and myself wearing my best coat and trousers. Roberta and I carried a haversack each, while the professor, unburdened, strolled ahead. He showed no ill-effects from his most recent catastrophe, and I assumed his remarkable recovery owed more to the restorative power of brandy than to his ablutions.

Upon reaching the street, Roberta raised her arm to signal a passing cab, but the professor waved it by. 'We are not wasting money on hansom cabs,' he proclaimed, 'and furthermore, I will not travel on the underground. Come! The high street is but a few moments walk, and there we shall catch the omnibus.'

He set off without waiting to discuss the matter, stepping into the road directly in the path of a horse and cart. The driver hauled on his reins, bringing the heavy vehicle to a sudden halt, then proceeded to curse the professor loudly, creatively and at great length.

The professor tipped his hat in apology before forging ahead, this time stepping in front of a speeding cab travelling in the opposite direction. The cabbie swerved at the last second, and we lost sight of the professor behind the towering horse and shoulder-high wheels.

Once the driver had regained control, he stood in his seat and shouted uncouth epithets over his shoulder at the professor, who appeared oblivious to the commotion.

'Come quickly, before he is run down,' muttered Roberta, and she took my hand and pulled me into the road. We crossed more carefully than the professor, but the street was so busy we were forced to dart between moving vehicles with little care for our own safety.

Upon reaching the other side, we found the professor waiting to chide us. 'You must keep a faster pace!' he said impatiently. 'I have no wish to waste an entire afternoon on this expedition.'

I felt this was a trifle rich, as it was his last-minute experiment with the forked weapon that had delayed us in the first place. Then, after eyeing Roberta's knapsack and inspecting my own, I realised the device was nowhere in sight. Had he forgotten to pack the thing? 'Professor, where is the new weapon?' I asked him, already fearing the response.

'Did you not bring it?' he enquired.

'No! I thought you had picked it up!' I exclaimed, my voice anguished.

We turned as one to look across the busy road, and at the professor's house beyond. A stream of carts and riders and cabs moved in both directions, and the thought of crossing that hellish stretch once more left me cold. Why, just last week a pedestrian had been grievously injured on a nearby street!

'Well, I dare say we won't be needing it,' said the professor at last. 'After all, there is no evidence Lady Snetton was killed by a phantasm.'

Roberta and I exchanged a glance, and I knew we shared the same opinion. 'I shall fetch the weapon,' I declared. 'It will take but a moment.'

'If you must,' said the professor, with an airy gesture. 'Roberta and I will proceed to the high street. If you cannot find us, it is because we have caught the omnibus and gone ahead of you.'

The professor departed without waiting for my response, swinging his cane in time to his paces, his top hat at a jaunty angle. Roberta remained long enough to squeeze my hand and whisper 'I had better get after him' before hurrying after her father.

I confess I was taken aback by the speed with which my fellow travellers abandoned me, but consoled myself with the thought that I could find the Snetton house without too much trouble. Moreover, if they reached the residence and encountered trouble of a most unnatural kind, I would arrive soon after with the professor's new weapon, giving me the opportunity to prove my worth by saving the day.

I hurried across the road, avoiding the worst of the traffic, and let myself into the relative calm of the Twickhams' house. It took me but a moment to reach the professor's study, where I found the weapon atop the desk. I took it up, fastening it to my pack, and was just turning to leave when a thought occurred to me. With the professor and Roberta absent, could I not use this opportunity to look around a little?

'Mr Jones, whatever are you doing?'

At the sound of Mrs Fairacre's voice I leapt fully twelve inches into the air. The housekeeper was standing in the doorway, regarding me with the sort of expression reserved for brush salesmen, thieves and wayward children. 'Th–the professor s–sent me back for his w-weapon,' I stammered, as my heart threatened to burst from my chest. It was pounding nineteen to the dozen from the shock, and I wasn't sure it would ever slow to normal pace again.

'And you have it?'

'Yes ma'am.'

'Then why do you tarry in his study?' she demanded, in a sharp tone of voice. 'Come, out with you this instant!'

As she ushered me from the room, closing the door firmly behind us, it occurred to me that Mrs Fairacre was more terrifying than any phantasm I had encountered to date. She was implacable and unshakeable, and, should I happen to fall on the wrong side of her, I had no doubt my life would become the worse for it. 'I must take this to the professor,' I said, indicating the weapon attached to my pack.

'Tell him dinner will be set for seven,' said Mrs Fairacre, her severe expression softening at the mention of the professor.

'We may be later than that.'

The hint of humanity vanished. 'In that case,' said the housekeeper brusquely, 'he shall have a cold supper instead.'

I departed the house at speed, partly at Mrs Fairacre's urging, and partly due to the fact the professor and Roberta were currently *en-route* to the Snetton residence without me. At that moment a hansom cab hove into view, and I came to a rapid decision. While the professor and Roberta negotiated the route by public omnibus, moving slowly through the late afternoon traffic, I myself would take the underground train! In this way I would arrive at the same time, if not sooner, and I would be on hand with the newly-retrieved weapon before they commenced the investigation into Lady Snetton's murder.

Fortunately, I had funds enough for the journey, and as I gave the driver my destination and settled back in my seat, I decided *this* was the way to travel.

I bought a ticket at Kensington Station and took the underground to Westminster. During my journey I marvelled at the engineering prowess involved in the construction, which seemed new to me even though I had travelled the same route the previous day. This time, without Roberta in close proximity, I found I had more time to inspect the tunnel, and the design of the carriages, and the method by which the lights were fed from bags of coal gas installed atop the roof.

But before long my thoughts turned to my travelling companions once more. Somewhere above me, I knew, Roberta and the professor would be making their own progress across the city. At least, I hoped they were, for it would be unfortunate indeed if they had decided to wait for me in the high street near the Crown and Feather. Even now, they might be glancing impatiently down the road, expecting me to appear at any moment, and instead I was travelling at speed in the opposite direction.

I resolved to wait for no more than one hour at the Snettons', and if the pair of them did not arrive by then, I would abandon the errand and take the underground home once more. No doubt we would laugh at the unfortunate mix-up, and postpone our investigation until the morrow. After all, the unfortunate Lady Snetton was already deceased, and I did not think she would be unduly troubled if we delayed our investigation into her demise for a day.

Once the train reached its destination, I climbed the stairs and emerged in the street. After looking in vain for a cab, I decided instead to walk the short distance to Lady Snetton's. It was a sunny afternoon, my haversack was not excessively heavy, and, of more significant import, I did not wish to spend any more of my own funds.

The streets in this area of London were much quieter than those surrounding the professor's residence, and many of the carriages were elaborate, highly-polished affairs that might have suited Queen Victoria herself. I felt out of place despite my tailored coat, and the haversack on my back did little to dispel the impression of a wandering salesman. I had every right to be there, but even so, I felt the gaze of the fine ladies and gentlemen in their carriages, who no doubt feared I would lower the tone with my very presence.

As I approached the Snetton residence I saw the windows had been shuttered. Whether it was due to mourning or the rest of the family having departed, I could not tell, but in either case the forlorn sight gave me pause. I could not very well knock upon the door, and so I decided to wait nearby, in the street. I had passed a fashionable tea-room on my way from the station, and I was tempted to return and take a table. However, barely had I taken two steps when I realised my idea was unsound. Who knew where the professor and Roberta might disembark from their omnibus? How could I tell which route they might take to reach my current location? No, I would have to wait within sight of the Snetton house, closed shutters and all. It was the only way I could be sure to encounter Roberta and the professor.

There were trees lining the street, and bedraggled and ill-looking though they might be they still afforded a little shade. I stepped under the nearest and turned towards the house, keen to observe any signs of life. As I stood there I pulled out my pocket watch, discovering it was still twenty minutes until five o'clock. The sun would not set for two or three hours yet, and I relaxed a little as I realised there was plenty of time until nightfall. I tucked my watch away, and that's when I saw a small procession walking towards me. At the head was a large woman carrying a basket at her hip. She wore a frilled cap and well-used workclothes, and I realised she must be a washerwoman. Behind her trailed three small children, each struggling with their own basket, which in the case of the youngest child was almost as big as she was.

I stepped back as the group approached, but the woman stopped under the tree and set her basket down, clearly intending to rest. She wiped the back of her hand across her forehead, glanced at me, then nodded towards the house. 'Terrible thing, that was. Couldn't walk down the road yesterday without there was so many people gawkin'.'

Terrible it might have been, but she spoke with some relish, and I guessed the death had been the talk of the area. 'A tragedy indeed,' I intoned gravely. 'Tell me, do you know what happened? I only heard that the poor lady passed in her sleep.'

'You a blue devil?'

'I'm sorry?'

'A rozzer.' She spat in the gutter. 'Police.'

'Oh no, most certainly not.'

'You wiv' the newspapers?'

'I work with papers,' I said, skirting the truth.

She spat in the gutter again. 'Load of hoity-toity trash.'

'I cover financial matters.'

'Pity.'

'Why's that?'

'Our Mavis, she had a tanner from a newspaper feller once. Said 'e wanted a story from her.' She looked at me shrewdly. 'What will you give *me* for answerin' questions?'

I thought of the dwindling supply of coins in my pocket, and decided I could spare a penny or two. Then I happened to notice the woman's children. Their clothes were old and oft-mended, although clean enough, but as to footwear I saw that two of the children lacked shoes, while the other sported a pair of tatty boots which were far too large for her feet. All three looked tired from carrying the washing, and my heart went out to them. 'Here,' I said, pushing a handful of coins at the woman.

'What's this, then?' she demanded, her voice laden with suspicion. 'I ain't doing nothin' more than answer questions, and if you have a mind to anythin' else I'll yell for a constable, so 'elp me.'

'No, no,' I said, trying to placate her. 'The money is for you. My, er, editor will reimburse me.'

'Well, I don't know that I 'ave that many answers,' said the woman doubtfully. Despite that, the coins disappeared inside her dress remarkably quickly. 'But you ask away, sir. Ask away!'

'What have you heard about the death? Was there any foul play involved?'

The woman lowered her voice. 'Some say the 'usband did it. Naval gentleman, he is, and they're used to all that killin', ain't they?'

'I thought he was posted overseas?'

'Nah, 'e's a big nob at the Admiralty. Lord something-or-other.' She gestured. 'Gentlemen like 'im, they sleep at their clubs instead o' coming home late. Afeared of robbers and the like. Or maybe afraid of wakin' their wives, what with the whisky and cigars on their breath.'

'So his Lordship was not at home yesterday?'

'I ain't his housekeeper.'

'Of course, of course.'

'But I heard tell 'e was terrible upset this morning. Wailing and shouting and the like. Linda's boy what does deliveries, he heard the fuss and said the language was shocking.'

I began to think my money had been ill-spent, but consoled myself with the thought that some of it might make its way to the children. Also, I had nothing better to do until the professor and Roberta appeared, and I was far less a suspicious figure in conversation with the washerwoman than I would have been standing under the tree by myself.

There was one question I desperately wanted the answer to, but I was afraid the asking would mark me as a madman. I could only imagine the washerwoman's reaction if I enquired as to any sightings of ghosts in the vicinity. Most likely she would draw up her skirts and leave post-haste, with the children following in her wake like over-burdened ducklings. But forewarned is forearmed, as they say, and the confirmed presence of a spirit would be useful news indeed to the professor. Roberta, too, might view me favourably.

Also, assuming the woman had no further titbits to impart, was there truly any loss in asking my question? She might huff a little, and withdraw from my company, but that was all. But then, before I could ask, I saw the familiar figures of the professor and his daughter approaching along the road. 'Thank you ma'am, for your patient replies to my query. Do please have a pleasant afternoon.'

'Pleasant afternoon, is it?' She took up the large basket of washing, then gave me a look. '*Some* of us 'ave to work for a crust,' she said tightly, and then, after an impatient gesture at the children, she departed.

As the professor and Roberta drew closer, I noticed they were walking some distance apart. Was this the result of some argument? Had they fallen out during the omnibus ride? Then they got closer still, and I was overwhelmed by the smell of fish. Plucking a handkerchief from my breast pocket, I pressed it to my nose in an attempt to block the stench. 'Whadever happered?' I managed, speaking indistinctly through the wadded cloth.

'Septimus!' cried Roberta. 'However did you get here first?'

'I took the underground train,' I replied, removing the handkerchief so as to speak more clearly.

Roberta gave her father a meaningful look. 'You see, father? Even Septimus, with limited means at his disposal, saw fit to spend a little extra so as to avoid the omnibus.'

The professor grunted in reply, and at this point I realised that it was he who stank of fish. Indeed, I could see silvery traces all over his coat. Some traces had deposited themselves on his top hat, and while I couldn't be certain, I thought I spied a patch on his cheek.

Roberta, meanwhile, was struggling not to laugh. 'Unfortunately, the omnibus was rather crowded, and a lady carrying a parcel of fish lost her footing as the carriage moved off. My father, bless him, managed to save most of her catch before they landed on the floor.'

'Not intentionally!' snapped the professor. 'That blasted woman threw them all over me!'

'You did complain to her about the smell,' said Roberta mildly.

'Gah!' snarled the professor, and he whirled around to look at the house. 'Is that the residence?' he demanded, pointing at it with his walking stick.

'Indeed, sir.'

'Then let us proceed.'

Privately, I suspected the fish-scented professor would be about as welcome as a brick through the front window, but he was already striding across the road and it was too late to say anything. A passing carriage almost ran him down, and as it sped by the driver turned to give the professor a piece of his mind. The man's angry diatribe faded into the distance as the carriage continued on its way, and I noted that even the cursing had a genteel ring to it in this part of the city.

Then, with the road clear, Roberta and I hurried after the professor, haversacks on our shoulders. I did not know what we would find inside that shuttered-up house, but a large part of me was hoping it was locked up and completely empty.

21

The three of us took the alley to the rear of the house, where the side gate to the yard stood open. There was no sign of the scullery-maid, nor anyone else, and the professor was not inclined to wait for permission before approaching the back door. This stood ajar, and the hinges creaked loudly as the professor eased it open further.

'Would it not be wise to advertise our presence?' I whispered.

The professor ignored me and passed into the house. Roberta followed, the haversack slung over one shoulder, and I, after a brief moment of indecision, brought up the rear. The kitchen was chill and cold, and just for a moment I fancied something terrifying and ancient and deadly lay hidden within this mournful house. I shook myself, dispelling the notion, and looked around for the cook.

'There's nobody here!' exclaimed Roberta. 'Wherever have the servants got to?'

I was still feeling uncomfortable at our intrusion, and I gestured nervously towards the door. 'I think perhaps we should leave.'

'Nonsense!' declared the professor. 'I invested a great deal of my valuable time in order to visit this place, not to mention the expense.'

I felt this was a monstrous exaggeration, since his 'expense' consisted of two sixpenny fares on the omnibus, and that journey had taken no more than thirty minutes.

'And,' continued the professor without pause, 'now that I am here, I am determined to proceed with the investigation.'

'But there's nobody home!' I protested.

'If that is true, it will be all the easier to take a proper look around.'

It seemed he was entirely set on trespass, and I knew any further objections on my part would be pointless. So, I held my tongue as the professor opened the scullery door and passed into the house proper. Before following, Roberta unslung her haversack, placing it against the wall. She indicated I should do likewise, and I saw her point. With the bulging satchels over our shoulders we would look like a pair of housebreakers, and were at risk of being shot dead by a startled homeowner.

With the shutters closed, the house was in near-total darkness, and the three of us made our way cautiously along the spacious hall. Our shoes clattered on the polished wooden flooring, and I knew that anyone within the house would not remain unaware of our presence for long. Indeed, as we approached the sitting room a voice called out to us.

'Are you here to strip the belongings from a suffering man, you accursed thieves?' came a stentorian roar. 'You think me struck down by sorrow to such an extent that I will not defend my property?'

A tall, white-whiskered officer in a splendid naval uniform appeared at the far end of the hallway, his form illuminated by the scant sunlight gleaming through gaps in the shutters. He carried a bottle in one hand, gripped around the neck, and he bore a pistol in the other. As soon as he spied us, he raised the gun and fired without hesitation, blazing away at us five or six times. The sound was deafening, and strips of wood were torn from the panelling as the wild gunfire rang out. A nearby vase shattered, hurling fragments across the floor, and a portrait was almost cut in two by a stray shot.

Fortunately, the man's aim was as wild as his words, and none of us were hit. I guessed he'd downed most of the bottle to drown his sorrows, which also explained his unsteady, swaying gait. Even as I watched, he tried to set the bottle on a side table, only to miss by a foot or more. Eventually he managed to place it, and then, to my dismay, he began to reload the pistol, muttering all the while.

'Your Lordship,' I cried, for I guessed this was the unfortunate Lady Snetton's husband. 'We are not thieves, but friends of your late wife!'

He looked up, squinting at me. 'You knew my darling Hattie?'

'Indeed, sir. Why, we paid her a visit only yesterday.'

At that, Roberta pushed past me and made for the distraught gentleman, taking him by the elbow and relieving him of the pistol before he had a chance to use it. A handful of cartridges fell from his grasp, rattling on the floor, and he was still peering around for them when Roberta took charge. 'Come, sir. Come sit in the lounge and unburden yourself upon me, for I am an excellent listener.'

He looked at her doubtfully, for Roberta was dressed in her working clothes, not the full-bodied skirt with bodice one would expect a friend of his wife's to be wearing. 'I apologise for my attire, Your Lordship,' she said quickly, 'but I was tending the horses in my stables.'

Roberta told this lie without a trace of shame, and Lord Snetton appeared to take her at her word. Together, they retired to the sitting room, while I collected the fallen cartridges and the professor ruefully inspected a hole shot clean through his top hat. 'These people are going to be the ruin of me,' he muttered.

The professor and I joined Roberta in the sitting room, where she'd thrown open the shutters and was now stoking the meagre fire in the grate. Lord Snetton had taken to the settee, and was sitting ramrod-straight as he smoothed his wayward hair and whiskers. In the daylight it was easy to see the years he'd spent travelling the oceans, for his cheeks were leathery and tanned, and his piercing blue eyes were clear and far-seeing.

'Sir, I must apologise for this intrusion,' said the professor, hurrying forward with outstretched hand. 'My daughter was a confidant of your wife's, and she insisted we come to pay our respects. I am most dreadfully sorry for the cruel blow fate has dealt your family.'

'That's very decent of you, sir,' said Lord Snetton.

The fire crackled gaily, but despite the leaping flames there was a deathly chill upon the room. Roberta left the fireplace and returned to the sofa, sitting alongside our host. She took the elderly gentleman's hand in both of hers, and as he turned to look at her in surprise, she gave him a warm smile. I myself had been on the receiving end of a similar gesture a day or two earlier, a gesture that had moved me greatly. Now, I realised it was just her way of setting people at ease, and had no special significance. A small part of me was saddened by that realisation, but at this moment I had more important things to consider.

The admiral, for that was his rank, was slowly unbending as Roberta encouraged him to speak of his wife. 'After my years in the navy I'm used to loss, have no doubt of that,' he was saying. 'But a loss this close to home? Now that is something terrible for a man to deal with.' He looked at Roberta, his expression beseeching. 'My dear, you spoke with Hattie before her death. Tell me, was she content? I was away so often, you see, and one fears that this was no life for a woman of her tender years.'

'Sir, she was happy indeed. She spoke of you with great affection.'

'She was not troubled by any curious, er, fancies?'

'I'm not sure to what you refer, my Lord.'

'Oh, I may as well lay this out before you!' cried the elderly gentleman. 'After my first wife passed, I chose the life of a bachelor. It's the best course for a naval officer, especially an aging specimen like myself, tied as I am to a desk in the Admiralty.' His face took on a distant expression. 'But then came the gala ball, and Hattie was kind, and attentive, and so charming...' He broke off, swallowing fitfully. 'I'm afraid she quite stole my heart, notwithstanding my advancing years.'

'Sir, you do yourself a disservice. Any girl would be happy to be seen with a dashing admiral of the fleet.'

I thought she was laying on the charm exceedingly thick, but Lord Snetton had consumed some considerable quantity of spirits and was not at his most perceptive. Instead of dismissing her statement, he accepted it, nodding sagely. 'Well, my dear, t'was not long before we were married, and her joyous company made me a new man.' He smiled at the memories, but then a shadow crossed his face. 'It was not to last. She began to hear things, to see malevolence and jealousy in the shadows. She was convinced it–it was the presence of my former wife, and nothing I could say would convince her otherwise.'

I held my breath, for I was certain Roberta would explain the reason for our attendance at the house the day before. But instead, she merely stroked the admiral's hand.

'In all my years serving in the Royal Navy, I never ran from a fight,' said Lord Snetton quietly. 'The French, the Spanish, the Russians...I've faced 'em all, dammit, and I never turned tail. But this–this madness of Hattie's was something foreign to me. I took to staying at my club, drinking too much and sleeping away from home.' He swallowed. 'I ran away and hid like a craven coward.'

Roberta moved closer, putting her arm around the old gentleman's shoulders, and this small gesture of comfort triggered a wave of emotion. Lord Snetton leaned forwards, burying his face in his hands, his body racked by sobs. 'There there,' murmured Roberta. 'You did nothing wrong by your wife, sir, for I swear there was nothing you could have done to help her.'

Profoundly moved by this heart-wrenching tableau, I could only pray the professor did not take this most inopportune moment to present his Lordship with an invoice for ten pounds. But instead, the professor took my arm and led me from the room. 'This is a terrible tragedy,' he whispered, once we were standing in the hallway, 'but there is nothing unnatural here, and I believe our business is done.'

I winced at his close proximity, for the smell of fish was as strong as ever. 'You don't think this was the work of a vengeful spirit?'

'It is more likely the old goat killed this woman himself.' The professor saw my shocked expression. 'Don't be fooled by his tears, my boy. Murderers cry too, you know.'

'But–'

'If he did kill her, that's for the police to determine.' The professor eyed me with a most calculating look. 'D'you think you can get the ten pounds out of him?'

'Me!' I said, aghast. 'I could no more ask that broken gentleman for money, than...than...' My voice tailed off as I reached for a suitable comparison, and then it came to me. 'Than I could load and fire a broadside single-handed!' I finished.

'And so I bid *adieu* to my ten pounds, unless Roberta thinks to charm it out of him.' The professor harrumphed. 'Well, I am not waiting for his Lordship's tears to dry. I shall take the omnibus this instant, and you will see Roberta home once she is quite finished with her charitable works.'

Before I could say anything, the professor turned and left, striding along the corridor towards the kitchens. Fragments of broken vase and wood panelling, the result of Lord Snetton's wild gunfire, crunched under his feet, and once the scullery door closed I was quite alone. I glanced into the sitting room, where Roberta sat with Lord Snetton, and I decided to allow the grief-stricken gentleman a little privacy.

While they were occupied, I would take myself upstairs to inspect the bedroom where poor Lady Snetton had breathed her last. After all, the professor had dismissed an unnatural hand in Lady Snetton's death without so much as a cursory investigation. This, then, was a chance to determine the truth on my own.

Before going upstairs I paid a visit to the kitchen, my intention being to borrow one or two items from the haversacks. The spectacles with the mismatched lenses, for one, and also the professor's weapon, so that I might defend myself if the need arose. I decided to take the trap, and the lantern-like enclosure it was suspended within, but I left the repaired netting and the patterned discs, for I had no instruction in their use. Then I spotted the metronome device with its three needles, and on a whim I took that also. By now my hands were full, and so I transferred items between the haversacks until mine contained the few devices I required, while Roberta's bulged with the equipment I intended to leave behind.

I glanced around the deserted kitchen before leaving, and it struck me as strange that the cook, at least, was not present. Had the grieving Lord Snetton dismissed the servants for the day, or had every one of them given notice after the lady of the house had been found dead? A thought occurred to me, and I crossed to the hob and cautiously placed my hand on the enamelled surface. It was quite cold, which meant the oven had not been lit that day. The staff, then, had been dismissed before dawn...or perhaps the night before.

I frowned as I spotted a milk churn near the pantry door, lying on its side. The contents had spilled, and I wondered what the short-tempered cook I'd met the day before would have to say when she saw it. Quite a lot, I guessed. Then I looked at the pantry door again, and a cold chill ran up my spine. What if the pantry contained something larger than game birds and cured meats? What if it contained the lifeless bodies of the cook and the scullery maid?

I approached the pantry slowly, hesitantly, and my fingers shook as I reached for the doorknob. My heart was in my mouth as I turned it, and I eased the door open inch by inch, fearing what I might see.

Yeowl!

I leapt back as a fast-moving shape launched itself from the pantry, almost knocking me over in its bid for freedom. It was a tabby cat, ears laid flat against its skull as it raced for the door, paws scrabbling on the hard floor. At that moment I don't know which of us was more frightened...myself, or the unfortunate cat.

I took a deep shuddering breath and turned to the pantry, opening the door fully. The insides were in disarray, thanks no doubt to the cat, but to my relief there were no human victims within. I managed a rueful smile, for I recognised that my recent experiences with ghostly apparitions were leading me to imagine the worst kind of horrors behind every harmless door.

There was nothing else of interest in the kitchen, and so I slung the haversack across one shoulder and took the hallway to the front door. On the way I looked into the sitting room, where I saw Roberta engaged in conversation with Lord Snetton. His mood appeared to have brightened considerably, and he was speaking animatedly of his late wife. Roberta, for her part, shot me a meaningful look as I passed the open doorway. A look which all but demanded I rescue her. A look which I ignored, for I needed her to hold Lord Snetton's attention whilst I inspected the upstairs bedroom.

22

Once upstairs I located the master suite, which looked almost exactly as it had the day before. However, despite the late afternoon sunshine leaking through gaps in the shutters, the room was filled with an air of sorrow and despair. The bedclothes were drawn back, and I imagined I could see an indentation in the bed where the unfortunate Lady Snetton had breathed her last.

Shivering, I turned away from the four-poster and approached a nearby desk. Here, I extracted various items from my haversack, placing them carefully so as not to mark the polished wooden surface. After I had placed the trap and the metronome, I gripped the sword in my left hand and donned the dichromatic spectacles. I was not sure what to expect as I surveyed the room through the red and black lenses, and I held the weapon at the ready and prepared to defend my very life from any vengeful spirit that might present itself. A small voice inside my head told me I was being exceedingly foolish, and that I should have left the investigation to one more capable than I. However, the professor had already departed, and Roberta was all but chained to Lord Snetton, who showed little inclination towards giving up her company. Another voice, this one tinged with jealousy, suggested that the wealthy admiral might already be picturing Roberta in the role of his third wife, but I quickly pushed the uncharitable thought aside. She was a sturdy young woman, and I had no doubt that Lord Snetton would receive a swift punch to the nose if he made an untoward suggestion of that nature.

Once I'd cleared my mind of misgivings, I stood on the spot and scanned the room with my glasses, inspecting every nook and cranny. In the professor's study, the spirit had been cloaked inside a deep black cloud, and so I paid particular attention to deep shadows. I assumed phantasms came in all sizes, and I did not want to miss even the smallest if it was hiding in that room.

I reached the end of my arc, having scanned every inch of the room without success. To make doubly sure, I moved to a new location and repeated the process, but there was nothing to be seen. Relieved, I relaxed my deathlike grip on the weapon. Although I was no expert, I was convinced there were no phantasms lurking in that quiet, sad room.

Removing the spectacles, I placed them next to the trap and turned to the metronome device. Roberta had described it as a sort of detector, and I could see now that each of the three hands was secured with a miniature clasp. I freed them in order, just as she had done the day before, and was surprised when they failed to move as much as a whisker. The key turned easily as I wound the device, until I felt the spring tighten to capacity, and still the hands did not move. I gave the largest a gentle push with my fingertip, but after giving an inch it shuddered to a halt.

By now I was convinced the room was as free of spirits as it was of prancing horses and marching bands. It seemed Lady Snetton's death could be explained by natural causes, brought on perhaps by the strain of sharing her residence with the vengeful presence of

Lord Snetton's first wife.

I crossed to the window and peered through the shutters at the street below, wondering how long it might be before Roberta and I could leave this place and make our way to the underground station.

Tick!

I turned quickly at the sudden noise.

Tock!

It was the metronome! I could see the large hand moving from side to side, slowly at first, but getting faster all the time. Then the middle hand joined in, adding its own noise to the first. And finally, as I crossed the room for a closer look, the smallest needle began to swing to and fro, moving even faster than its companions.

I reached out and turned the device, as Roberta had done the day before. Moving it one way slowed the needles, while moving it the other made them swing like fury, until I worried they would fly off completely. Then, after I'd aligned it once more, the hands began to move so quickly they were but a blur. A haze began to rise from the device, and I felt rising alarm as I detected a smell of burning. I picked the device up, intending to slow the frantic motion with my fingers before locking the hands once more, but the metronome was so hot it burnt my fingers.

Shocked, I let go, and the device clattered on the hard wooden floor. The hands flew off, skating across the polished floorboards, and the metronome spun like a top before finally coming to rest on its side. In a panic at the damage I'd caused, I crouched to pick it up, using my coat for insulation. But when I gathered the thing, it was now as cold as a block of ice!

I set it down on the nearby desk, and could see frost glittering on the face. Then I remembered the missing needles, and I crawled upon hands and knees, seeking beneath various pieces of furniture until I had located all three. The largest had a bend at the very tip, but I straightened it without trouble, and then I returned to the desk and attempted to refit the hands. Each had a square hole bored through its thickest portion, a hole which fitted over the stepped peg protruding from the lowest point of the metronome's face. Once all three were positioned I latched them securely, and replaced the metronome in the bag.

Unfortunately, I did not know whether the metronome had signalled the presence of an ancient, malevolent danger, or whether I had merely set it up incorrectly. And, if I was foolish enough to describe the device's reaction to either the professor or Roberta, they would soon discover that I had been careless enough to damage it.

Caught in a bind of my own making, I decided to remain silent for the time being. And so, after gathering the materials and tools I had brought with me, I took to the stairs and returned to the ground floor.

Roberta was in the corridor, and she was surprised to see me descending the stairs. More surprised still, when she saw the haversack over my shoulder. 'Whatever are you doing?' she demanded.

'I was inspecting the bedroom,' I whispered, lest our host overhear me.

'There's no need to lower your voice. Lord Snetton just left the house in order to make funeral arrangements.'

'Was his mood improved by your ministrations?'

Roberta gave me a look. 'He spoke to me of his wife, if that is what you're asking.' Then she glanced up the stairs. 'I promised his lordship we'd leave immediately, but do you think we ought to...?'

'There is no need, for I found neither evil spirit nor phantasm.'

'I am pleased you have already learned the difference between the two,' said Roberta.

I kept my silence, for I suspected there was none, and she was merely chiding me after I'd suggested that Lord Snetton had received more attention than perhaps was proper.

'Incidentally, my father will be pleased with the outcome of this visit,' said Roberta.

I thought of the damaged metronome. 'Are you certain?'

'Most definitely. Lord Snetton agreed to pay us ten pounds the moment he receives an invoice.'

'Why, that is wonderful news!'

'Indeed,' remarked Roberta. 'It was worth a little attentiveness on my part, wouldn't you agree?'

'I'm sorry. I spoke out of turn. I was just...' I hesitated. 'I was concerned for you, that is all. There have been two Lady Snettons already, both of whom met untimely ends. I did not want you to...er...'

'Me? *Marry?*' Roberta laughed. 'Mr Jones, you may rest assured I have no intention of chaining myself to any man!'

I did not know how to respond to this, so I indicated the corridor. 'Shall we? Your father left already, and I see no reason to remain here a moment longer.'

'You feel it also?' Roberta looked up at me searchingly. 'A cold, unfriendly chill, like the inside of a tomb?'

'Indeed I do.'

'Then let us collect our things and depart this sorrowful house. Hopefully, never to return!'

We arrived home an hour later, and it was a relief to step into the now-familiar surroundings of the professor's house. There was no hint of the bone-chilling cold I had experienced at Lord Snetton's, nor the air of sadness and loss.

Roberta sought out her father, intending to give him the good news about the ten pounds she'd been promised, while I took our haversacks upstairs and left them at her bedroom door. I feared a heated discussion once the metronome was unpacked, but I hoped Roberta would think any damage had been caused within the haversack. I knew it was cowardly to avoid confrontation, but I was new to the household, and I feared they would dispense with my services if I did not live up to expectations. In time to come, once I'd succeeded in proving my worth, these little mistakes and mishaps would not be cause for such alarm.

After leaving the haversacks I took the stairs once more, this time to my bedroom. I removed my travel-stained coat and brushed it vigorously, before hanging it carefully in the wardrobe. Then I washed my face with cold water, and smoothed my hair with the flats of my hands, all the while studying my less-than-impressive reflection in the small mirror. I recalled Roberta's uncontrolled laughter at the notion of marriage, and I wondered whether she'd been giving me a none-too-subtle hint. I could almost hear her speaking the words: *Do not expend any effort in that direction, Mr Jones, for you and I are quite unsuited to one another.*

Still, I had employment, and regular meals, and a roof over my head, which is more than could be said for a vast proportion of the city's inhabitants. I also had a number of troubles requiring my attention, and my time was better spent on those than agitating myself over matters of the heart.

I recalled the mysterious box concealed in my desk drawer, and decided to inspect it that instant. Barely had I taken two steps towards the door, however, when there was a knock. 'Yes?' I called out. 'Come in!'

The door opened, admitting the maid, Elsie. She carried a silver tray, and upon it, a sealed envelope. 'Begging your pardon, but there's a letter for you. Hand-delivered, it was.'

I took the envelope and thanked her, and she was just turning to leave when I saw my name scrawled across the front. I recognised the style immediately, and a cry escaped my lips. It was from the scar-faced man!

'Is everything all right, sir?' asked Elsie, her thin face exhibiting concern.

'Yes, yes. Run along now.'

She hesitated a moment, then turned and left, closing the door behind herself. As soon as I was alone, I tore into the envelope with shaking fingers, pulling out the folded sheet of parchment within. It was barely a quarter of a page, but that was all that was required for the brief instruction written in the same bold hand:

Crown and Feather

Nine p.m. sharp.

My heart hammered in my chest. I had yet to secure any kind of drawings for the scar-faced man, and now I must obtain something of value before nine! The professor and Roberta were both home, and Mrs Fairacre and the maid would be moving around the house as they prepared and served dinner. With a sinking feeling, I realised my chances of obtaining a prize for the scar-faced man were something approximating zero.

Then I recalled the locked box once more. That was the ticket! Open it, and there were sure to be items inside I could trade for my parents' safety.

Quickly, I stuffed both envelope and note into my pocket, and then I donned my spare coat and left the bedroom for the floor below. Barely had I stepped off the staircase when I heard the dinner bell, and I cursed under my breath at the timing. I could not forgo the meal without drawing attention to myself, and in any case I had not eaten a bite since lunch. No, I would have to take dinner with the professor and Roberta, and immediately after I would beg their leave and tackle the mysterious box.

23

It was a shame I was in such a hurry at dinner, for Mrs Fairacre had outdone herself. A large platter of roast beef sat on the sideboard, with thick-cut slices exhibiting just the right amount of pink in the centre. To round out the feast there was a dish of roast potatoes, a tureen brimming with fresh garden peas, and a jug full of steaming hot gravy.

The professor was in attendance, and for once he was not hidden behind his newspaper. He'd donned a smoking jacket of antique vintage for the occasion, the fabric consisting of a diamond pattern picked out in orange thread. With dark purple lapels and cuffs fashioned from plush velvet, the extraordinary piece lent him a certain air of gentility. It also lent him a vibrancy that was most troublesome to the eye, and I avoided looking at him as much as possible.

Roberta was absent, and when the professor helped himself to a platter and began to eat, I felt I should enquire as to her whereabouts before I, too, began my repast.

'Roberta is getting ready,' replied the professor proudly. 'This evening my daughter attends the theatre with a friend.'

I was surprised, for Roberta did not strike me as the theatre-going type. Also, the professor had placed special emphasis on the word 'friend', and I pondered the significance. Was it some beau she was stepping out with, of whom I had been hitherto unaware? I was still thinking on the matter as I began my meal, and the excellent food barely registered.

The dining room fell silent for some time, with nothing but the clink of cutlery to disturb us. Despite the lack of conversation, the professor behaved as though in high spirits, occasionally humming to himself, while at other times he gave a brief utterance of joy and slapped his thigh. I had little doubt this remarkable transformation in his demeanour was due to Lord Snetton's willingness to pay the oft-lamented ten pounds, for the professor's love of money was only exceeded by his enthusiasm for a restorative pint or so of neat brandy. As for myself, I'd been hoping for Roberta's company at the dinner table, for it would be my last chance to converse with her before I had to face the scar-faced man.

Then I brightened, for if Roberta was attending the theatre, it would give me the perfect opportunity to sneak a diagram or two from her bedroom! I would copy them as quickly as possible, adding my own embellishments, and there would be time aplenty to return them before I left to meet my tormentor at the Crown and Feather.

Some of my enthusiasm must have transmitted itself to my face, for I noticed the professor studying me. 'You look uncommonly pleased with yourself,' he remarked.

'The beef is excellent, sir.'

'The very best,' agreed the professor. 'Did I not tell you Lord Snetton would pay his bills? See? This is the result.'

I distinctly recalled him stating the direct opposite, and at great length, but I decided not to mention it. However, I hastened to set him straight on one matter. 'Sir, are you aware I have not yet drawn up the invoice?'

'No matter,' he said, waved his hand. 'With these wealthy clients it's money in the bank, Mr Jones. Money in the bank!'

I wished I shared his confidence, since I knew first-hand that few of the professor's clients troubled to pay their bills, and what meagre funds they did remit rarely made it to the bank. However, I did not wish to dampen his good mood, and once again I held my tongue.

We ate in silence until our plates were almost clean, and I was about to finish my meal when there was a rustle behind me. I turned, and my eyes almost started from my head as I saw a beautiful woman in the doorway. 'Good heavens!' I exclaimed, as I recognized Roberta. Her working clothes and heavy boots had been whisked away, replaced by a fashionable skirt and gleaming shoes. Her hair was done up with ribbons and a bonnet, with ringlets framing her face, and her cheeks were graced with the merest hint of rouge. I was quite entranced at the heavenly creature standing before me, and barely noticed as a morsel of potato and gravy slipped off my fork and landed in my lap.

Roberta looked nervous in her finery, and she greeted me with a shy smile. 'How is dinner, Mr Jones? It smells divine.'

'It is!' exclaimed the professor, before I could answer. 'Roberta, my dear, are you sure you won't join us?'

'I dare not, for I would incur Mrs Fairacre's displeasure should I manage to spill gravy on my skirts.'

'Yes, of course. In any case, I suppose Charles is due any moment.'

Charles? My stomach lurched at the name, my euphoria dissipating to leave a sour sensation in my stomach. Was this Charles a family member like cousin Edgar, or something else entirely? I did not believe for an instant that Roberta harboured feelings for me, but I'd hoped that our friendship might blossom into something more as we faced dangers and perils together. Now, those hopes had been dashed, and I was disappointed that she had not thought to mention this rival, even in passing. It was none of my business if Charles were courting her, of course, but I felt it would have been merciful if Roberta had set me straight a little sooner.

I decided I did not want to meet this Charles, and I finished my dinner promptly. 'I'll bid you both a good evening,' I said, my manner a little stiff. 'Professor, I will attend to the accounts tonight as promised.'

'Do not trouble yourself, Mr Jones, for the bookwork can wait until morning,' said the professor expansively.

'That is kind of you, sir, but I am eager to continue my work.' I hesitated. 'I may pass by the Crown and Feather this evening, just for a half hour or so.'

'My dear boy, you need not advise me of every outing. After all, you are not a prisoner here.' The professor looked thoughtful. 'You know, it is some time since I visited an alehouse. I have half a mind to accompany you.'

My heart sank, for this would truly be a disaster. The scar-faced man would be waiting for me, and should I appear in company with the professor, he might decide to murder us both! But what could I say to prevent the meeting? Then I caught Roberta's eye, and she must have noted my alarmed expression for she interjected on my behalf.

'Father, I will not have you trawling alehouses after the knock you took this morning. I insist you stay home and rest.'

The professor opened his mouth to argue, but Roberta hadn't

finished.

'When Charles and I return later this evening, you will be here to greet us. Is that clear?'

'But–'

'I insist!' Roberta indicated her fancy skirts. 'This was your doing, was it not? Would you like me to develop a headache and refuse to go out at all?'

The professor knew when he was beaten, and he backed down immediately. 'Of course, dear. I shall remain here like your dutiful and obedient father.'

'I am glad to hear it.'

I was relieved too, for disaster had been averted. However, I was puzzling over something Roberta had alluded to. It seemed the professor had organised her night at the theatre, and I wondered whether this Charles fellow was a business associate of his. Or perhaps the man had ties to a wealthy family, and the professor was hoping to gain introductions through Roberta. My spirits rose at the thought, for that was an entirely different situation. She wasn't courting, she was the unwilling player in her father's plans!

Roberta had been eying the sideboard while these thoughts had been tumbling around inside my head, and now she uttered a mild oath and took up a plate.

'Dear, your skirt!' protested her father.

'Hang the finery,' growled Roberta. 'I'm hungry.'

I felt an inner glow at her rebellious words, for *this* was the Roberta I knew. I wanted to remain there, to spend as long as possible in her company before she had to leave, but time was passing and I had much to do. 'I wish you both good evening once more. Roberta, I hope you enjoy the theatre.'

'Endure,' she said, looking up from her meal.

'I'm sorry?'

'I shall endure the theatre, and enjoy returning afterwards.'

The professor sighed at this, and I took my leave before they started another argument. As I climbed the staircase to my study, I found myself wishing that I was the one escorting Roberta to the theatre. Touring actors had visited my home town on occasion, but I had never experienced a performance in a London theatre. But to be frank, it was not the theatre that interested me, but Roberta's company.

I reached my office and sat in my chair, and within moments I'd extracted the locked box from the lower drawer. I decided to carry it to my bedroom for closer inspection, for my window looked out on the road and I would be able to witness Roberta's departure. At that point I would enter her bedroom to secure the drawings I needed.

I placed two ledgers on top of the box and tucked the whole under the flap of my coat, disguising it as best I could. Then, praying I was not seen, I left my office and mounted the stairs as quickly as I dared.

I reached my room without incident, and I carried the box to my bed, concealing it under the counterpane. Next I moved a side-table to the window, placing it so that I would have a view of the road. Finally, I adjusted the gaslight, turning it up so that I might see better.

Preparations complete, I moved the metal case to the side-table at the window, where I sat down to give the lock a thorough inspection. There were two dozen buttons, each of which could be centered, or positioned up or down. Each could be pressed in, or left flush with the surface. And the button to the far right acted as a reset, moving the rest to their default position.

If zero represented the default state, then there were five other states the button could be made to represent: Centered and pressed-in, up and flush, up and pressed-in, and two more with the button in the lower position.

Six states per button, and twenty-four buttons? Why, the number of combinations was immense! My heart sank, for I knew it could not be guessed. Then I brightened, for I suspected it could not easily be memorised either. Surely the owner would have left themselves an *aide-memoire*? A diagram or drawing, perhaps disguised or concealed? Not on the case itself, for that would be obvious, but it might be elsewhere in my study.

I got up, intending to seek out the answer that instant, and then I happened to glance out of the window. What if Roberta left while I was away from my post? If so, I would not know whether she was still in the house when I attempted to obtain the diagrams from her room.

I decided to take my chances. If I left my study door open as I searched, I ought to hear the disturbance from the hallway below once this Charles fellow arrived. Forewarned, I could then return to my own room to observe their departure.

As I descended the stairs I formed a mental picture of Charles. I saw him as a pasty-faced individual with a receding chin and protruding teeth. He would have wispy sideburns and a loud, unpleasant voice, and were it not for his money Roberta would have nothing to do with him.

It took me but a moment to reach my office, where I quickly took stock of the furnishings. Aside from my desk there was the bookcase containing ledgers and paperwork, some of which did not appear to have been disturbed for years. There was also a corner stand with a number of well-thumbed books, and two paintings on the wall. One depicted two ships of the line at the Battle of Trafalgar, their guns recoiling as mighty broadsides belched fire and smoke. Most of the portholes were closed, no doubt a result of the pitched battle, and through those which remained open I could just see the fierce expressions of the sailors 'tween decks. The other painting could not have been more different, for it captured a peaceful country scene with a girl in flowing skirts watching a number of dairy cows in a field. I looked closely at both pieces of artwork, especially the frames, but there were no markings. I even lifted the paintings from the wall, turning them to inspect the rear, but they were completely unremarkable.

I picked up each book on the shelves, bending them gently against my thumb in order to flick rapidly through the pages, but observed nothing of significance. I moved several ledgers, but only succeeded in raising a cloud of dust. Slowly, I was coming to believe that the search was hopeless, and that the locked boxed was destined to remain so. If I wasn't so afraid of harming the contents, I swear I would have pitched it out of my fourth-floor window to burst it open on the ground far below.

I spent a few minutes inspecting the desk, particularly where the sides met the top, but there were no clues scratched into the woodwork. Finally, I went through the drawers, even lifting them out to check the sides, the back and the underneath.

Nothing.

Defeated, I decided my hopes of finding the code had been wildly optimistic. Perhaps the owner of the box had memorised it after all, for the combination would be no easy thing to conceal. Any representation would require three rows with two dozen markings in each, which was a substantial thing to hide from prying eyes.

At that moment I heard a commotion from the corridor below, including laughter and greetings and a hearty male voice. I was tempted to take the stairs to the landing, so that I might obtain a glimpse of this Charles character...until I imagined the embarrassment should someone spot me hiding there.

Instead, I left my study and took the stairs to the top of the house. I hurried to the window in my bedroom and peered out, and to my dismay I saw a magnificent coach-and-four in the road below, attended by a driver and a liveried footman. The horses had matching black plumes upon their heads, and the lacquered carriage shone like a mirror under the nearby streetlamp. Several passersby stared at the overt display of wealth as they hurried by, for such a coach was not a common sight outside the wealthiest parts of the city. Little wonder the professor had encouraged the outing, for the patronage of such a wealthy family might swell his coffers considerably.

I saw a young boy clothed in rags approaching the carriage, presumably to beg a copper or two, but before he could say anything the driver casually flicked his long whip in the lad's direction. The loud crack was audible even from my lofty perch, and the startled boy, who could not have been more than ten years of age, ducked his head and scurried away like a frightened rat. The footman called something after the unfortunate lad, and the driver laughed.

What a pleasant pair, I thought sourly, even though the encounter was a common occurrence all over the city. Then I saw the footman stand to attention, the driver sitting ramrod-straight, and seconds later I spied Roberta and Charles strolling along the path to the iron gates at the road. From my angle I was looking almost directly down on them, but even so, I decided Charles was a most unsuitable sort. From his foppish hair to his broad-shouldered blue coat, there was much to dislike about him. Had I been able to make out any other details, I am certain I would have disliked those also.

Roberta, on the other hand, was a picture of loveliness in her flowing skirts. I pressed my nose to the cold pane of window glass as I tried to take in every detail, and once again I wished *I* was the one escorting her to the theatre. She walked arm-in-arm with her companion, who suddenly threw his head back and laughed long and hard at some quip. As for myself, I had never felt less like laughing in my entire life.

They reached the carriage, where Charles waved the footman away so that he might assist Roberta up the step himself. She gave him a grateful smile, and that was my last glimpse of her before she disappeared within the spacious carriage. Charles followed, and the footman closed the door and folded the step away before taking his seat beside the driver.

Then, with a crack of the whip and a whinny from the horses, the carriage pulled away from the house and disappeared into the night.

Dispirited, discouraged and dismayed, I turned from the window. My nine o'clock meeting with the scar-faced man was a mere ninety minutes away, further adding to my gloom. I remembered his gleaming knife, and the body of Jules Hartlow found floating in the river, and I shivered. There was no time for self-pity, for I knew I would be renewing my acquaintance with the late Mr Hartlow if I did not stir myself.

24

I took the stairs down to Roberta's floor, where I crossed the corridor and opened her door. I slipped inside and closed the door behind me, short of breath and with my heart thudding in my chest. I had dreamt up an excuse in case anyone should find me there, a fabrication involving a missing invoice, but I hoped I would not have to put it to use. For one thing, Roberta would contradict my story once she returned home.

I stood for a moment, regaining my poise, and then I approached the workbench. It was strewn with odds and ends of materials, and mysterious tools, and tangled wire, and I wondered why she did not maintain a working space in the basement. But then my gaze fell on the prize, which was a pile of crumpled diagrams in double foolscap. I leafed through them quickly, selecting two of the simpler ones as being the most suitable for copying. I folded them small and crammed them into my coat pocket, before hurrying to the door.

I peered out through the tiniest crack, ensuring the corridor was clear, and then hurried to the stairs and ascended to the next floor. Here, I collected writing materials and a blank sheet of parchment from my study, before heading further up the stairs to my own room with my loot secreted about my person.

I did not relax until I'd closed the bedroom door behind me. Then I placed the items I'd gathered on the small table near the window, drew up a chair and set to work on crafting a new set of diagrams from those I'd borrowed.

Both of the purloined drawings were of the same device, which appeared to have several moving parts arranged in a circular pattern. There was no explanation as to its purpose, but that did not trouble me. One drawing was more elaborate than the other, as though it were a refinement of the original idea. Regardless, I took elements of both drawings as I crafted my own version on the blank piece of paper. It was a good twenty minutes before I had something that approximated Roberta's original design, without copying it precisely. Next, I turned my attention to the measurements. On Roberta's plan they were expressed in fractions of an inch, and the entire machine would have sat on the palm of one hand. I wanted to show something far more impressive to the scar-faced man, so I changed all the measurements to feet and yards. This made my version of the machine around a hundred times the size of Roberta's, and in total it would be twice the height of an adult. Let Mr Scarface chew on *that*, I thought to myself. Why, if he were foolish enough to build the enormous contraption, it would cost him a small fortune for the materials alone!

Roberta's device was meant to be fashioned from bronze, but I changed mine to good strong oak. Had I not done so, the machine in my diagram would have weighed as much as the great bell of the Clock Tower, and required even more metal.

I spent some time adding meaningless tables of figures to the margins of the drawing, along with notes and comments on the construction. So distracted was I that I barely noticed the passage of time, and I was shocked to discover it was almost thirty past eight. I set the plans aside to dry, for it was too soon to fold them away, and decided to spend a few minutes on the combination to the locked box. I took another sheet of parchment and drew a pair of parallel lines across the page, then crossed them with twenty-three short vertical lines. This formed a rough representation of the lock mechanism, and all I needed – *all* I needed! – was the correct pattern. A dot or a cross in one of the three vertical spaces would indicate whether a button were pushed in, as well as its vertical position - up, down or centered. To experiment, I drew several circles with my quill, and as I inked them in, it created a pattern eerily similar to notes on sheet music. Could that be the answer? But then, none of the books in my office had anything to do with music.

As I studied the drawing, with its intermittent dots and blank squares, I felt the first stirrings of recognition. Not music, but a similar pattern which I had seen only recently. I tried to grasp the memory but it slipped away, and the harder I tried, the more it hid away in the shadows. Black dots inside squares, displayed in three rows! Where oh where had I seen such a thing? And why was I picturing tiny figures with fierce faces?

All of a sudden it came to me, and I leapt to my feet with a cry of triumph. I crossed the bedroom at a run, hauled the door open and ran downstairs at top speed. On the next floor I burst into my study, where I almost ran into the desk in my haste. Off-balance, I skirted the desk and fetched up at the rear wall, where the paintings were hanging. I had no interest in the country scene, and instead turned to the one depicting the Battle of Trafalgar. I leaned closer to study the ships, paying particular attention to the three rows of guns. My excitement grew as I saw the round black muzzles protruding from the square gunports like...dots! And many of the gunports were closed, which would never happen in a true sea battle.

Certain I had it now, I lifted the painting off the wall, tucked it under my arm and ran for my bedroom.

I laid the painting on my bed and fetched the locked box, sitting down and placing the heavy metal case in my lap. My fingers shook as I copied the pattern of open gun ports, sliding this button up, that button down, and pressing them in to match the arrangement in the painting. Once finished, I held my breath and waited for the lock to activate. Nothing happened, so I turned the case on its side and tried to pry the lid open, without success.

I glanced at my watch and swallowed. It was a quarter to nine, and I had to leave immediately if I was to make my appointment with the scar-faced man. On the other hand, I suspected the drawing in my pocket might not be enough to satisfy him. If I could only persuade the obstinate case to yield its secrets!

I felt a rising panic as I realised the painting might be a red herring, for I had wasted what little time remained trying to open the case. But I was reluctant to let it go, for I was convinced I'd hit upon the solution. Had I made an error copying the pattern? No, I double-checked the buttons, and their positions were a perfect match for the open gun ports in the painting.

I placed the locked case on the bed, set the painting beside it and stood up. For now, I would cover both with the counterpane, and would return them to my study after my meeting with the scar-faced man. Assuming I survived the meeting, that was. To improve my chances I decided I would steal one of the smaller cubes from the sitting room as I left the house. Someone might see me taking it, and even if they did not the cube would likely be missed, but I had no other option.

I moved to the foot of the bed and bent to take hold of the counterpane, and as I straightened I glanced at the painting and the case lying beside it. From my position the painting was now upside-down, and the pattern on the case was a mirror image in the horizontal plane. Quickly, I glanced over my shoulder, towards the small shaving mirror affixed to the wall. Could that be the answer? Requiring that the pattern be reversed...now that would put almost anyone off the scent!

By this time I knew I would have to run all the way to the Crown and Feather, but I simply had to try that case again. So, I detached the mirror from the wall and carried it to the bed, where I held it in such a way it reflected the hulls of the two ships. Then I copied the new pattern to the buttons on the case.

My finger was trembling as I pressed in the final button, but to my relief my efforts were rewarded with a solid *chack!* The lid popped open half an inch, and I set the mirror aside and eagerly opened the case the rest of the way, scarcely able to believe I had cracked the code. Inside was a polished wooden box, taking up almost all the available space, and I groaned at the sight. If this too was sealed with a mysterious lock, I swore I would hurl it at the wall until I succeeded in smashing it open!

But no, there was a simple latch which opened easily, and when I lifted the lid I discovered a shape wrapped in velvet, about two hand-spans in size. Beside it was a leather tobacco pouch, which rattled when I picked it up. It was heavy, and at first I believed it to contain coins, but when I opened it I discovered it was full of ammunition. Two dozen brass cartridges at least, with dull lead bullets peeping out of the ends.

Now I noticed the smell of machine oil, and I was not entirely surprised when I unwrapped the large shape to discover a revolver. It was a wicked-looking thing with a short barrel, the wooden grip worn smooth with use. I took it from the velvet cloth, holding it gingerly at first, for I was not in the least accustomed to firearms. But my confidence grew as I felt the weight of the weapon in my hand, and I had no trouble picturing the scar-faced man cringing before me as I threatened to shoot him.

Unfortunately, that was little more than a fantasy. I could threaten the man as much as I liked, but it was all to nothing unless I was prepared to carry out my threat. I could not shoot a man in cold blood, and even if I convinced myself it was for my own defence, the other members of the scar-faced man's organisation would immediately know who the culprit was. I would be powerless to stop any reprisals against my parents and myself.

I was about to replace the gun and close the lid when I decided instead to take the weapon with me. If the meeting turned sour I would point it at the scar-faced man to scare him away. Then I would travel home, to my family, using the first available method of transport. If rogues arrived to harm my parents, well, in that case I was certain I would be able to use the gun.

Satisfied, I tucked the heavy revolver into my pocket, and then I added the tobacco pouch with the cartridges, for there would be no time to return for them if I were forced to flee.

It was now five minutes to nine, and I closed the case and hurriedly threw the coverlet over it. Then I doused the gaslight and left my room, the heavy pistol swaying and bumping against my hip with every step.

25

The night was clear with no trace of fog, which was to my advantage given the haste with which I had to navigate the poorly-lit streets. I had encountered the professor on my way out of the house, which had not only delayed me a minute or two, but had also made it impossible for me to snatch one of the metal cubes from the sitting room. Before that, I had also returned Roberta's drawings to her room, replacing them more-or-less as I had found them. Which is to say, crumpled and tangled amongst the many items on her workbench.

Now, not only would I be late, but I also had nothing to offer the scar-faced man aside from my hastily-drawn fake of a diagram. I realised it had been the height of foolishness to think my plan might work, and I now feared the ruthless villain would take one look at my amateur scribblings before knifing me on the spot.

The closer I drew to the Crown and Feather, the greater my desire to turn and run in the opposite direction. The revolver was a deadweight in my pocket, thumping painfully against my hip, and my intention to threaten a hardened criminal with the weapon now seemed like complete madness. Why, he could probably tell it was not loaded at a glance!

As I turned into the high street I heard a hubbub of noise from the alehouse, which was even busier than it had been during my last visit. Crowds spilled onto the street, and I could see two men engaging in a bare-knuckle fight, much to the delight of the drunken revellers. The punch-drunk adversaries were goaded by the crowd in turn, and I had no doubt wagers had been placed. Then I stopped, for two constables in distinctive blue uniforms were watching the fight from the opposite side of the street. They did nothing to intervene, and indeed, from the way they were driving at the air with their fists, mimicking the boxers' moves, I guessed they were as invested in the outcome as most of the crowd appeared to be.

I realised I may have acted suspiciously by stopping dead in the street, and I resumed progress towards the alehouse. Skirting the shouting, heaving crowd, I made the entrance and recoiled at the stench of sweat and stale beer that met me. There was a large crowd inside, filling the tables and lining the walls two deep, and my heart hammered as I stood there surveying the scene. Had the scar-faced man already seen me? Was he approaching me from behind at that very moment? I turned on the spot, but none of the people milling around had the man's terribly disfigured face. I felt out of place, and there was nowhere I could sit nor stand that would make me any less so.

Then, without warning, I felt a hand gripping my elbow. 'Do not look round,' hissed a low voice. 'Pass me what you have, and quickly now.'

My blood ran cold at the menace contained in that voice, and I reached into my coat and withdrew the folded plans I'd drawn earlier. Taking them out, I held them over my shoulder, where I felt the parchment snatched from my fingers.

'What do you call this?' hissed the voice.

'I–it's all I could secure in the time available to me!' I stammered. Even there, amongst the heaving crowds, I feared the savage thrust of a knife in my back. 'I swear, I could not lay hands on any more!'

'Gimme your pocketbook, or...'

I waited for the rest of the threat, but instead I felt the grip on my elbow relax. Someone leaned against me, hard, and it was all I could do to maintain my feet. Then the deadweight shifted, and I turned cautiously to see what was happening. Directly behind me was the scar-faced man, one arm around the waist of a man I'd never seen before, supporting him. This second man, with dirty, straw-coloured hair and a rather coarse appearance, was slumped as though asleep, and had it not been for the scar-faced man I was certain he would have fallen to the ground in a dead faint.

The scar-faced man half-carried, half-dragged his companion to a nearby wooden pillar, where he set him down, none too gently. The unconscious man's head slumped, and he almost toppled sideways before coming to rest in a most uncomfortable-looking position. As the scar-faced man bent to arrange the drunk properly, I saw his coat hang open, revealing his clenched right hand. It was gripping a long, bloodied dagger, and with a sick feeling I turned to look at the 'drunk'. He wasn't unconscious...the scar-faced man had just murdered him in the middle of a busy alehouse!

The scar-faced man casually drew his coat together, then twitched my folded parchment from the victim's fingers. He straightened, fixed me with a meaningful look and nodded towards the door.

I stared at him, aghast, and the scar-faced man frowned at me before opening his coat a fraction of an inch to display the handle of his knife. Then he nodded at the exit once more, and this time I obeyed with unseemly haste. If my adversary was capable of killing a man right here, in the midst of a crowded alehouse, there was nowhere I would be safe.

Once outside, I turned to my left and made for the alley. I was physically shaking, for while I had witnessed death before, it had been the peaceful conclusion to a life, either from ill health or old age. Never had I witnessed cold-blooded murder, and the sight of the freshly-killed victim slumped against the pillar would haunt my dreams for the rest of my life.

I felt sick, too, for I suspected I was about to meet a similar fate. At that moment I would gladly have stolen a dozen of the professor's metal cubes, along with every bronze cylinder from his study and the spectacles from his very nose.

Until that moment I'd harboured a faint suspicion that the scar-faced man might be a plant of the professor's. The man could have been part of some elaborate ploy to test my loyalty, to see whether I would give up the secrets I'd promised to keep. Indeed, this suspicion had been on my mind when I copied Roberta's drawings, rather than simply stealing the originals. But now, with murder committed, I realised this was no ploy.

I was still alone in the alley, the scar-faced man not yet having appeared, and as I stood there quivering with fear my fingers closed on the revolver in my pocket. The cartridges and pouch were in the opposite pocket, and in my desperation I was willing to attempt loading the weapon right there in the darkness. But it was too late, for a shadow fell across the alleyway, and I swallowed nervously as the scar-faced man advanced on me.

'Lucky for you I was present,' said the man conversationally. 'But a moment more, and that thief would have had your wallet.'

'D—did you have to k—kill him?'

In return, there was a shrug. 'Quieter and more efficient than a brawl. And, unlike Mr Jules Hartlow, there was no need to tip his body into the Thames.'

'So you claim that murder also? What sort of devil *are* you?'

'Not the devil, although some have me a close relative.' The scar-faced man bent at the waist, giving me an ironic bow. 'William Sykes is the name.'

'And no doubt Nancy is tending to your supper at this very moment,' I said sarcastically, since Bill Sikes was a famed villain from one of Mr Dickens' novels. Then I remembered to whom I was speaking. 'Oh! I–I did not mean–'

Sykes gestured. 'A *nom-de-plume*, obviously, but it will suffice.'

'And who am I in your sorry tale?'

'You, Mr Jones? Why, you are my obedient terrier. Now, I have much to do this evening, and I would appreciate a conclusion to our business. What marvels do you bring me from the professor's workshop?'

'You already have them,' I said, in a steady voice. 'That parchment contains plans for a tremendous device, the likes of which has never been seen before.' This was no lie, for I had only just drawn the machine with my own hands.

Sykes unfolded the parchment and tried to discern the contents, but to no avail. In the near-total darkness he might as well have been looking for a black pearl in a coal cellar. 'You bring no mechanical devices? No other information?' he demanded, folding the plans once more.

'I am watched all hours of the day, particularly by the housekeeper.'

'Is that so?' mused Sykes. 'Perhaps I should dispose of the formidable Mrs Fairacre.'

I was surprised he knew the housekeeper's name, and thus more details of the professor's life than I realised, but I was shocked far more by his threat of harm. 'I will get more!' I said quickly. 'I promise you, I'll bring something extraordinary next time.'

Sykes eyed me thoughtfully, then nodded. 'Gather what you can, for my patience runs thin. If you disappoint me again, it will not go well for you.'

'Yes, of course. I will do as you ask.'

'Go, then. And I warn you, not a word to a soul!' He drew the knife, the fresh blood like pools of ink. 'I cut Hartlow's throat to show you I meant business. The professor will read of another death in tomorrow's newspaper, and that will be your final warning. The one after that will be your own.'

He stepped aside to let me past, and I hurried from the alley to rejoin the crowds in the street. Another fight was in progress, and not one person paid me the slightest attention. The policemen were still present, but I gave them a wide berth. If I went to them with a tale of a scar-faced man named Sykes, and spoke of the murder I'd witnessed in the nearby alehouse, I suspected they would question my sanity whilst treating me as their chief suspect.

As I left the death and madness behind I felt a growing weakness in my legs, and by the time I reached the professor's road I was shivering uncontrollably. The strain of serving both the professor and Sykes was taking its toll, and I knew that I must soon find a path out of the deadly maze. If not, I feared it would not take Sykes' dagger to finish me, for I would simply expire of my own accord.

As I hurried along the road, lost in my myriad problems, I was scarcely aware of the coach standing outside the professor's house. I was still fifty yards away, on the opposite side of the street, but as I got closer the impressive vehicle loomed in my consciousness until I could ignore it no longer. Eventually I came to a halt almost directly opposite. I remained there, hidden in the darkness between streetlamps, for I had no wish to encounter Roberta at that moment. I especially did not want to meet Charles, for introductions would follow and I would surely be found wanting if any comparison were made. After all, he was the son of a wealthy family, while I was a penniless bookkeeper who was spying on my employer at the behest of a cold-blooded murderer.

Then I saw movement within the coach, and I stared in shock at the scene which met my eyes.

The coach lanterns were lit, and I could see the interior clearly. Roberta and Charles were sitting in the carriage, with Roberta occupying the side closest to me. They appeared to be talking, and then, as Roberta made to get up, Charles leaned across to embrace her. She turned away quickly, and he only managed to kiss her cheek. When he tried again, she opened the door and clambered out of the carriage, skirts and all.

The footman leapt down from his perch and hurried to help, but Roberta brushed away his hand and strode right past him. Behind her, Charles leaned out of the open door and raised his voice. 'Your father needs my family's patronage, Roberta. Consider that before you choose to spurn me!'

Roberta stopped beside the horses. 'Do you know what you can do with your desires?' She growled. Then she made an uncouth suggestion of a most intimate and anatomical nature.

This was too much for Charles. Whatever his designs on the fair Roberta, it was now certain they would not come to fruition. Angrily, he withdrew into the carriage, slamming the door and rapping the head of his cane on the roof. The driver cracked his whip, and Roberta was almost bowled over as the horses leapt forward. The footman was forced to leap onto the running-board so as not to be left behind, but my gaze was on Roberta, who had recovered her balance and was now standing in the middle of the road. I was relieved she was not harmed, and furious at the man who had placed her in such danger.

As the carriage drove off I saw Charles inside, sitting very upright in his seat. He looked angry and frustrated, and I could not help noticing that he had the face of a man used to getting his own way. I suspected Roberta had made an enemy of the arrogant young man, even though she was entirely blameless.

Roberta was facing away from me, still in the middle of the street, and as she took a step towards the far side of the road I could stand it no longer. 'Roberta!' I called. 'Are you hurt?'

'Why, it's Mr Jones,' she said brightly...a little too brightly. 'Did you witness my little drama?'

'I was returning home when I saw you almost run down,' I said, which was almost all of the truth. 'I did not wish to intrude, but–'

'Come, I cannot stand in the street all night. Join me, and we will enter the house together.'

I needed no second bidding, and when I reached her I offered my arm, which she gratefully accepted. Walking in close proximity, we passed through the iron gate and took the path to the front door, where we were met by the professor. 'I thought I heard a commotion out here,' he said, squinting at us in the darkness. 'Roberta? Charles? Is that you?'

'It is Mr Jones and I,' said Roberta. 'We returned at the exact same moment, and I asked him to see me to the door.'

She said nothing of Charles, and I said nothing at all. I had noted the look of surprise on the professor's face, quickly followed by a look of disappointment at my presence, and I guessed he saw me as a poor substitute for the wealthy suitor. Then he saw the way Roberta and I had linked arms, and his expression turned to one of alarm. 'Come inside quickly, or you'll catch your deaths in the night air. And Mr Jones, you must run along upstairs now to complete that work you promised.'

He ushered me away, almost shooing me down the hall, and I had no opportunity to say goodnight to Roberta. I did look back as I climbed the staircase, but Roberta had already entered the sitting room.

With the recent excitement I had all but forgotten Sykes and his cold-blooded murdering ways, but it came back with a vengeance as I climbed the stairs in the darkness. I felt like a condemned man being led to the scaffold, and I could almost feel the noose of rough hemp tightening around my neck.

Once I gained my room I prepared myself for bed, for the day had been a long and busy one and I was in desperate need of rest. I lay in bed for some time, thinking on the day's events, until eventually a fitful sleep overtook me.

26

It was the dead of night, and I was the sole passenger in a rowboat, the grizzled oarsman grunting with effort as he hauled on the blades. With each stroke, water ran like blood from the oars, trickling back into the river with an unpleasant gurgling sound. As for the river itself, it was as flat as a millpond.

I did not know why I was seated in that old wooden boat, nor where the oarsman was taking me.

Then, as if by magic, there was someone seated beside me. It was a woman wrapped in a heavy boat cloak, her face hidden by folds of oiled canvas. I fancied it might be Roberta, and my heart leapt at the thought, but when she turned her face to me, it was the sorrowful visage of Lady Snetton. She looked pale and wan, and there was an unnatural tightness to her expression. Then, without warning, she parted the boat cloak to grip my forearm with a claw-like hand.

'You must choose between them, for one must die.'

She spoke with a voice as cold as the grey dawn, and the words made my skin crawl even though I did not know to whom she referred. Then the grip on my arm relaxed, the lady dissipated into the mist, and I was alone on my seat once more.

'Comin' up to your stop,' called the oarsman. 'Better get yoursel' ready.'

I looked at him, and to my astonishment I saw the boatman was Charles. But now the man's face was disfigured with a terrible scar, and I almost retched as I saw it pulsating with live maggots. I turned away from the horror, and that's when I spotted figures in the river nearby, floating face-down. I could tell at a glance that they were the professor and Roberta, and at the sight of their lifeless corpses I got to my feet in alarm, making the boat rock and sway in a most dangerous fashion.

'You can only save one,' Charles told me, although he now spoke with Lady Snetton's voice.

The professor and Roberta were alive? Yes indeed, for I could see each of them moving, albeit so weakly it seemed they were all but lost. The boat drew closer, speeding up, and all of a sudden I was clenching a boathook in both hands. 'Slow down!' I cried to the oarsman, but instead our speed increased further. I turned to shout at Charles, to order him to stop, but discovered I was completely alone in the boat. Even the oars had vanished.

By now the boat moved faster than ever, with bow-waves curling away from the scarred wooden prow. The little craft raced towards the bodies in the water, aiming to pass directly between them. I braced myself with the boathook, swinging it from left to right and back again and I tried to decide which drowning victim deserved my help.

And then I woke.

I woke with a start, my heart thumping wildly, my room in total darkness. I did not know what hour it was, but there was an eerie howling outside as though the hounds of hell had been set loose. A sudden bang, sharp and loud, had me clutching at the covers.

Then I heard rain lashing my window, and it was apparent a

storm had rolled in over the city. There was another bang and I realised the shutters were slamming repeatedly against the window as they blew back and forth in the howling wind. I got up and padded across the wooden floor in my bare feet, and as I threw open the window I was stung by the driving rain. I stretched for the shutters, leaning above the long, unbroken drop to the garden below, and that's when I saw him.

Outside, in the street, a tall man in a top hat was standing in the middle of the road, looking up at me. He was a misty, half-seen figure in the storm, and even though I tried to make out his face, it was hidden in deep shadow. Squalls tore at his cape, which fluttered in the wind, but neither wind nor driving rain appeared to trouble him. Indeed, he stood there observing me as though it were a sunny day without a cloud in the sky.

The scrutiny unnerved me, and I felt the world tipping. With a shock, I realised I had let go of the shutters, and was leaning further and further over the drop. The ground far below seemed to beckon, urging me to take the plunge, to end my problems once and for all.

A flash of lightning speared through the heavy skies, briefly illuminating the slick rooftops and rain-swept roads with intense, stark white. In that instant, the figure in the street simply vanished.

I realised what was happening, and I renewed my grip on the shutters and closed them firmly, latching them in place. Then I closed the windows and stood with my back to them, breathing hard, drenched by rain and shivering with cold. I had almost fallen, I knew that for certain, but what unearthly power had taken over my mind? Who was the mysterious figure in the street? It was not Sykes, nor Charles, of that I was certain.

But I fancied I recognised the man, and I suspected it might have been...Lord Snetton?

Still shivering, I dried myself as best I could before returning to my bed. I cocooned myself in the blankets and huddled up for warmth, but there was a deep chill in my bones that I could not dispel. And, above all, I could still hear Lady Snetton's final words to me.

You can only save one.

'Good Lord, we are in the midst of an epidemic!'

The professor, Roberta and I were at breakfast, and the morning sun shone through the bay windows in the dining room. There was no sign of the previous night's storm, although the three of us all exhibited symptoms of a certain lack of sleep. Upon entering, Roberta had given me a warning look, which I took to mean that I should not discuss her *contretemps* with that scoundrel Charles the evening before. Or, perhaps, I was not to discuss the manner in which I had accompanied her to the front door, lest I manage to upset the professor. Or maybe I was not meant to speak of any subject whatsoever, just to be safe?

In the midst of my attempts at not speaking, the professor's voice spoke very loudly indeed.

'Do you mean a plague, father?'

'No, it's an epidemic of murders!' The professor jabbed at the newspaper. 'Lord Snetton has vanished, nowhere to be seen, and two of his servants lie dead. They were discovered in the cellars of his house with their throats cut. Why, the poor innocent souls must have lain there even as we spoke with the murderous villain!'

The blood froze in my veins. 'Wh-what of the other servants? Are they accounted for?'

'It was the cook and the scullery maid they found. The housemaid was found wandering the streets, but they say she's a gibbering wretch who has quite lost her mind.'

'And they suspect Lord Snetton?' I could not believe the upright gentleman we'd met the day before had murdered his own servants. He had been distraught and sad, not enraged. 'How do they know he is not also a victim?'

'The bodies had been there a day or two, most likely coinciding with the death of his wife. They now claim Lady Snetton might have been strangled, so perhaps the old devil was discovered in the act by his own servants, and was thus forced to silence them too.'

I said nothing, even though the scenario seemed unlikely in the extreme. If Lord Snetton were responsible he would have fled two days ago, for who else would the police suspect in this tragic case but the master of the house? By remaining, he had all but fastened a noose around his own neck. I glanced at Roberta, but she was staring at her plate with a distant look in her eyes. Her breakfast was untouched, and she sat as still as a statue. Whether this was caused by the horrible news of the deaths or Charles' beastly behaviour towards her the night before, I could not hope to guess.

Then I recalled the parting words from Sykes, the scar-faced man. He told me the professor would read of another death, and here there were *two* more. Had he ended more innocent lives just to make certain I got the message? But why would Sykes attack members of Lord Snetton's household?

The professor was still reading, and now he exclaimed once more. 'They found another body in the river last night! Another unfortunate young man cut down in his prime. Oh, whatever is the world coming to?'

This was Sykes' work, I was sure of it. At first I thought it might be the body of the murdered thief from the tavern, but I realised it could not be so. The thief would have been found where I'd last seen him, for Sykes could not have spirited him out of that busy place unseen. 'Do they give his name?' I asked the professor.

The professor looked at me. 'Why do you ask? Do your acquaintances regularly appear in the Thames with their throats cut?'

'Yesterday it was Mr Hartlow,' I said evenly. 'I am hoping this latest victim was not another of your applicants, for if so my own life might be in danger also.'

'Yesterday was pure coincidence,' said the professor, with an impatient gesture. 'This will turn out to be some vagabond, or the result of a deadly dispute.' The professor resumed his perusal of the newspaper, only to snort under his breath. 'An entire wagon of timber was stolen overnight. Planks, joists and everything! Is nothing safe from...' His voice tailed off, and then he exploded. 'Listen to this. Just listen!' Holding the paper to the light, hands shaking with anger, he began to read. 'Wayward spirits? Ghostly visitors? Write now for professional assistance. Modern methods. Discretion assured.' Having finished, he glared at us, demanding our reaction. 'Well?'

'It was inevitable,' said Roberta calmly. 'We could not hope to keep the field to ourselves for long.'

'It's an outrage! I will sue for infringement of my patents.'

'You have not obtained any patents. You feared the government clerks would sell your ideas.'

'I will send these crooks out of business! Ruin them!'

'Let them be, father. They do not have access to your vast store of knowledge, nor your working methods.'

I had yet to contribute to the discussion, because an unpleasant idea had been worming its way into my brain. Who did I know that had been trying to access the professor's store of knowledge? Who did I know that was prepared to kill to learn the professor's working methods? William Sykes, of course, and I was placing that knowledge directly into his hands! At least, he believed I was, which amounted to much the same thing. I comforted myself with the thought that the drawings I'd given him had been faked by my own hand. Sykes could advertise for business all he liked, for he would not be catching spirits with the rickety contraption I had sketched out.

The professor opened his mouth to resume his rant, only to close it again as Roberta spoke first. 'I think I will rest upstairs,' she said, her voice tired and drawn. 'I am out of sorts this morning.'

'But, my dear!' exclaimed the professor. 'You have not touched your breakfast.'

'How can you think of eating, when there is misery and horror and murder all around us?'

The professor shrugged. 'One must struggle on.'

'For now, you must face those heroic struggles without me.' Roberta got up, and I pushed my chair back and stood.

'Perhaps you should organise another evening with Charles,' said the professor.

The look on Roberta's face spoke volumes, but she quickly suppressed it. 'I would prefer to maintain my own social diary, if that's quite all right with you,' she said coldly.

'Er…of course, of course.'

Roberta left, and I retook my seat. After her footsteps had faded, the professor cleared his throat. 'Mr Jones, I must caution you about any intentions you may have towards my daughter.'

I had just taken a bite of toast, and at his unexpected words I choked and spluttered, spraying crumbs across half the table.

'I have high hopes for Roberta's future,' continued the professor. 'She is an intelligent girl, perhaps a little headstrong, and with a suitable match I have no doubt she will rise through the ranks of society.'

I was still struggling to breathe, but even so I was taken aback by the professor's total misreading of Roberta's nature. A suitable match? Why, only yesterday she'd declared she would be chained to no man! No, Roberta was most at peace when forging metals, and designing machinery, and using her intellect to catch spirits. Hers would not be a life of society events, and tearooms and theatres! 'But sir,' I managed at last. 'What of your business? You need Roberta to carry out your work!'

'What indeed?' said the professor sadly, and then he sighed. 'Mr Jones, you have perused my accounts. You are well aware that my finances have shaky foundations, to say the least.'

He was right in this, for expenses outstripped income by a wide margin. In fact, I had been wondering how he was going to pay my wages, meagre though they were.

'Do not try to convince me otherwise,' said the professor, raising one hand to forestall any argument. 'I was banking on Lord Snetton's payment, and with this latest news it seems I shall never see those oft-promised funds. Even if the man succeeds in avoiding the police, and thus his execution, he will be in hiding for the rest of his life. But should Roberta find a suitable match...' The professor left the words hanging before continuing in a low voice. 'You think ill of me, but I do not suggest a marriage of convenience. I want her to find happiness, and joy, and love, yes, but it should be with someone of means.'

I was silent, even though this barb was for my benefit.

'As for my own situation, I care not a fig!' said the professor, his voice rising. 'I will cope with the vagaries of life, but I will *not* see my daughter in the poorhouse, nor reduced to begging. You see, Mr Jones, If she marries well she will not have to struggle each day, as I was forced to during my earlier years.'

'Roberta will never agree to it,' I said firmly. 'Why, she would rather be poor than be married to a scoundrel like Charles!' Even as I spoke, I realised I had said too much. The professor, upset though he was, pounced on my words.

'Scoundrel? What do you mean scoundrel?'

'He, er...' I gestured helplessly, for I could not bring myself to describe the scene in the carriage. 'Charles made...certain advances upon Roberta,' I said unwillingly. 'When she refused, he lost his temper. I–I was returning from the alehouse, and he departed at such speed his carriage almost ran Roberta down.'

'And yet she said nothing of this?' The professor looked at me with a kindly expression. 'Septimus, tell me man to man. Do you exaggerate the situation for your own ends? If you confess now, I will not hold it against you.'

'Sir, I promised Roberta I would not speak of the matter, and but for my slip of the tongue I would have said nothing. I regret that you learned of this from me, but I swear it's the truth.'

As I spoke the blood had drained from the professor's face, vanished but for twin patches of red upon his cheeks. Then, without a word, he turned his attention to his breakfast. I saw him butter his bread as though slashing weeds, driving his knife back and forth with such vigour that he tore one slice in two. I don't believe I had ever seen a man so angry, and I worried lest the professor's heart gave way right in front of me.

So, it was not the most opportune moment for Mrs Fairacre to appear, as silently as ever, with the news that two policemen were on the doorstep.

27

The professor and I remained seated as Sergeant Parkes and Inspector Cox entered the dining room. The latter drew up a chair and sat down, facing us both across the table, while the former cast a hopeful look at the sideboard. Unfortunately for him, and fortunately for the professor, there were no sausages going spare, for today's breakfast had consisted of nothing but toast.

'I am delighted to see you both again,' said the professor, sounding anything but. 'It's gratifying that you find time to visit me when you must be swamped by all these unsolved murders and daylight robberies.'

Cox's jaw tightened at the slight, but his voice was calm when he spoke. 'Tell me, sir, why did you visit the Snetton residence yesterday? If you were trying to gain my attention, it worked admirably.'

'I had business with his lordship,' said the professor loftily. 'At its conclusion, my staff and I immediately left the premises.' Here, he tapped the newspaper. 'Had I known your men neglected to find a pair of victims lying quite dead in the cellar, I would have chosen to meet Lord Snetton at his club instead.'

I felt the professor was taking things a little far, for he was goading the policeman mercilessly. On the other hand, his were not the words of a guilty party, and I was certain the professor knew that. But would Cox think the professor already knew that, and therefore conclude that the professor might be guilty just because he appeared not to be? And would the professor, knowing this…But by now I'd tied my mind in knots with negative and double-negative, knowing and not knowing, and I decided there was no simple answer to the question. I only hoped that the professor was not going to give the police reason to look into his affairs, for I certainly did not want them looking into mine.

It was at that moment that I remembered the revolver. The night before, I had been so distracted by Roberta's plight at the hands of that rotter, Charles, that I had quite forgotten to return the pistol and cartridges to their proper place. What if the police insisted on searching my room, and found the gun sitting in my coat pocket? My stomach sank at the thought. It was not illegal to own such a weapon, but I, as a bookkeeper, was not the sort of person who would do so. The weapon might lead to suspicion and awkward questions, and perhaps a journey to the police station for an unpleasant interview at the hands of the sergeant.

I noticed Parkes regarding me from his position across the room. I looked away quickly, but out of the corner of my eye I saw him writing something into his notebook.

Meanwhile, Inspector Cox was addressing the professor. 'Sir, those bodies were not present when my men searched the house,' he said quietly, and without emotion. Nothing seemed to trouble the inspector, who invariably spoke softly and patiently.

'You cannot think I carried the poor wretches there myself?' protested the professor, who lacked patience at the best of times, and needed only the hint of an excuse to raise his voice. 'Why, I took the omnibus! D'you think I had a body under each arm? Eh? Is that it?'

'Of course not, sir. But a carriage was observed at your door last night.'

'You *spy* on me?' demanded the professor, half-raising from his chair.

'We have men in the area.'

'I'll have you know that carriage belonged to my daughter's young man! Not that it's any of your business, but Charles is the son of a wealthy family, and he was taking her to the theatre.' Not content with that, he proceeded to name the family, and I saw a flicker of surprise in Cox's expression. 'Yes, *that* family,' crowed the professor. 'D'you think they used a coach and four to distribute murder victims around the city?' He stabbed his finger on the newspaper. 'Why, perhaps they used it to make off with these stolen building materials! I'm certain they could attach a half-dozen oaken beams to the roof of their fancy carriage, given enough rope.'

Cox sat unmoved throughout the professor's onslaught, and when the older man ran out of wild claims he resumed his questioning as though nothing had been said. 'A local washerwoman has been interviewed, and she revealed that a young man seemed uncommonly interested in the Snetton household. From the description, that young man appeared to be your Mr Jones.' Here, Inspector Cox turned his attention on me for the first time, fastening me with a level gaze that I found distinctly unnerving. 'Do you have any comment, sir?'

'I wanted to know if Lord Snetton was home,' I replied.

'And this meagre fact was worth a handful of coins?'

'The woman had several children with her. Two of them had no shoes, and I felt sympathy towards their plight.'

'Oho!' said the professor. 'Do not admit to caring for others, Mr Jones, for the policemen here will find reason to arrest you for such aberrant behaviour! If, that is, they're not out botching murder investigations.'

I wished heartily that the professor would cease his interjections, for I felt they would not end well for either of us.

Meanwhile, Cox switched tack without warning. 'Are you familiar with the Crown and Feather, sir?'

The professor glanced at me, but I avoided meeting his eye. 'I have taken ale there on occasion.'

'Last night being one of them?'

'I may have happened by.' I made a show of dredging my memory. 'Yes, I did visit last night. There was a large crowd spilling into the street.'

'Around what time was this, sir?'

'Some time between eight and ten,' I said, deliberately widening the hour to avoid pinpointing the precise time of my visit.

'Did you observe a fight in the street?'

'You could ask your policemen about that, for I saw two of them stationed across the road.'

Cox and the sergeant exchanged a glance, and I wondered whether the police in question had revealed their presence to their superiors. Or perhaps the Inspector already knew the precise time his policemen had been there, in which case I had been too clever by half.

'What's this all about?' demanded the professor suddenly. 'Is there a law against drinking in alehouses now?'

'Last night, at the Crown and Feather, a patron was stabbed and left to die before several dozen witnesses.'

'My goodness,' said the professor, in mock surprise. 'A murder in London? How is such a thing possible when the police are here to protect us?'

'Mr Jones,' said Cox, ignoring the professor. 'Did you witness anything unusual?'

'Inspector, there were a hundred people or more crammed into that alehouse last night,' I protested. 'One could barely move in the crush, and I would not have noticed if Queen Victoria herself put in an appearance!'

Cox frowned. 'I'll ask you not to use Her Majesty's name in that fashion. Now please answer the question.'

Chastened, I nodded. The professor had a gift of needling the policemen without offending, but my own effort had been clumsy in comparison. 'I did not see anything untoward,' I said quickly.

The inspector regarded me coolly, and I looked steadily back at him. I had a trick I employed when I wanted to mask my expression, and it involved summing an imaginary column of pounds, shillings and pence in my head. I made it through two entire columns, double-checking the results, before Cox nodded and turned his attention to the professor. 'Sir, do you have any knowledge of one Arthur Staines?'

'None whatsoever.'

'Are you certain? I believe you interviewed him for the position of bookkeeper earlier this week.'

'I did?' The professor thought for a moment. 'It's possible, of course, but I don't recall the name. Can you describe him?'

'Indeed I can. He was a young man of twenty-three, five foot six in height, and he was in the habit of wearing eyeglasses.'

'I have encountered many such men,' said the professor with a shrug. 'Unless you can be more explicit...'

'He did have one distinguishing feature.' Cox drew a thumb

across his neck. 'He had a large incision across his throat. You couldn't miss it, as it was deep enough to strike bone.'

The professor paled. 'The murder victim from today's newspaper? That was Mr Staines?'

'Indeed. And from your expression, I'm guessing you now recall the young man in question.'

'Why yes. He was an applicant, but I did not find him suitable. Mr Jones here won the position, as I'm sure you're aware.'

'Professor, in the course of my enquiries I discovered that you also considered Jules Hartlow for the same job. Yet you failed to mention this significant fact during our previous interview.'

'You cannot expect me to remember the name of every man or woman I encounter!' cried the professor. 'In any case, all the applicants were in perfect health after leaving my house. Aside from pure coincidence, how can you think to link me with their unfortunate deaths?'

'I do set much store in coincidence,' said Cox quietly. 'And professor, I would like the names of the other unsuccessful applicants, if you please.'

'Mrs Fairacre will write them down for you, although I can think of no reason why they might be singled out by a vicious murderer.'

I sat in silence, torn by conflicting emotions. I knew the reason the applicants been singled out, and it was all due to the scar-faced man, William Sykes. At that moment I would have revealed all to the police, had I but known the man's true name. As it was I had nothing more than a *nom-de-plume* and a description, and while the police blundered around making enquiries of the mysterious Sykes, I suspected he or his cronies would quickly put an end to my beloved parents. Despite this, I still would have spoken out but for one fact. I knew there was no danger to the surviving applicants, for Sykes had promised to end *my* life next.

'Inspector, are you quite done?' asked the professor. 'The hour marches on, and I really must return to my work.'

'And what work is that exactly?' Cox asked him.

'I am a specialist in fine metalwork, and the fabrication of intricate mechanical devices.'

'To what end?'

'None. They serve a decorative purpose.'

'Would you show me?' asked Cox.

The professor was taken aback. 'You wish to poke around in my study? My workshop?'

'If you would be so kind.'

'Well!' said the professor, most put out. 'Why don't you search the entire house while you're at it?'

'Thank you sir. I was hoping you'd agree.' With that, Cox signalled to his sergeant, who tucked away his notebook and left the dining room. 'It won't take long,' said the inspector, oblivious to the professor's shocked expression. 'The sergeant and I brought along half a dozen constables for the job.'

'You planned to search my house all along?' demanded the professor.

'I did indeed,' said Inspector Cox. 'And sir, in case your servants are in cahoots, know that I have constables stationed at the exits to ensure any evidence remains on the premises.'

'But this is monstrous!' cried the professor. 'It's an absurdity! A complete waste of time!'

'It's our time to be wasted,' said Cox mildly.

'But whatever are you hoping to find? A bloodied dagger, perhaps, or a confession written in the blood of my victims?'

'I'll know when I see it.' Cox got up and turned for the hall, but the professor hadn't finished.

'Wait just one moment, Inspector! My daughter is resting upstairs, and I demand that you let me speak with her, so that she might dress appropriately. I will not have your constables gawking upon her night-things.'

'Very well. You may fetch her downstairs, but I want all three of you in here for the search. Understood?'

'Yes, of course.'

'And you will be careful with our belongings?'

'Yes, sir. You have my word.' Cox hesitated. 'I know this is an imposition, professor, but my methods involve eliminating suspects so that I might narrow my investigation.'

'It seems to me you should be preventing your suspects from eliminating any more victims,' said the professor tartly. 'Oh, go on with you. Turn my house upside-down. We have nothing to hide!'

All this time I was thinking of the revolver in my room, and I wondered whether I might volunteer to fetch Roberta in the professor's stead. Perhaps a remark about the steep stairs, and his aging legs? If I flew upstairs I might have enough time to warn Roberta *and* reach my own room so as to conceal the pistol before the police came looking. Why, maybe I could throw the thing out of my window, and the pouch full of cartridges along with it!

But no, it was impossible. It would have been strange indeed if I had volunteered to enter a woman's bedroom while she was

240

sleeping, and in addition I was certain the professor would have had something to say about it!

So, I was forced to sit and fret while the inspector went to organise the sergeant and the professor went upstairs to warn Roberta. Within moments I heard a rumble of heavy boots, and then policeman after policeman tramped along the professor's hallway on their way to the rest of the house. One was sent into the dining room, and after directing a curious look in my direction, he busied himself inspecting every nook and cranny in the room. Halfway through this process the sergeant looked in, checking on the constable's progress before departing to oversee the search in other parts of the house. Then, worried though I was about the revolver, I realised the professor had bigger concerns than I. How would he explain the rows of metal cylinders in his study, and the mysterious cubes in the sitting room? What about the spirit traps, and the glasses with the mismatched lenses? The police inspector was not a fool, and would recognise them as tools and containers, not the decorative trinkets the professor claimed them to be.

But even were he armed with this knowledge, what could the inspector deduce from it? Why, he would think the professor some kind of madcap inventor with a machine shop in the cellar and bats in the belfry! The British Isles were packed with such people, each striving to invent newer and ever-more-elaborate marvels, from cheaper methods of picture photography to sturdier bicycles, from electric telegraphs to steam-powered vehicles which could travel on the roads themselves. To whit, a man or woman with a thirst for knowledge and the skills to make their mad inventions a reality!

I did not think the inspector would hit upon the truth, not in a million million years.

The constable finished his search of the room, and for a moment

I thought he was going to search me. However, it did not occur to him, and he left to make a report to his superiors.

At that moment the professor arrived in the dining room with a somewhat dishevelled Roberta in tow. She gave me a brief smile, then sank into a seat, folded her arms on the table and rested her head. 'Poor dear,' murmured the professor. 'I was forced to wake her from deep slumber.'

'How goes the search?' I asked him.

The professor snorted. 'These men should be out catching real criminals, not disturbing the lives of law-abiding citizens.'

'Are they being particularly thorough, do you think?'

At that, he gave me a curious look. 'Why? Do you have something you don't wish them to find? Salacious sketches, perhaps, or exuberant letters from a young woman?'

The truth was far worse, and so I refrained from answering.

'I should like to ask Mrs Fairacre for a pot of tea,' mused the professor. 'Do you think the police will permit it, or would they beat me back with their truncheons?'

'Father, do stop needling the police,' said Roberta, her voice muffled. 'In fact, please stop speaking altogether, for you are making my headache worse.'

'Yes dear.'

At that moment the sergeant looked in. 'Who uses the study on the third floor?'

The professor turned to me, and even Roberta raised her head from her arms to give me a curious look. 'Er, that's mine,' I said. I was puzzled, for there was nothing unusual in that office. After all, I had searched it myself just the night before!

'Would you come with me, sir?' asked the sergeant.

'Now wait just a minute,' said the professor. 'What's this all about?'

'I'm askin' the young gentleman, sir.' The sergeant turned to me. 'Quickly, son. I got men waiting.'

From his expression, it was not a request to be denied, so I got up and followed him from the room. Outside, he got me to lead the way, and as I climbed the stairs I heard his heavy tread behind me. Oddly, I was not feeling the slightest bit nervous for my only concern was the pistol, and that was in my bedroom.

When I reached the study I found two constables inside, one of them crouched behind the desk. He was jiggling the lower drawer, which rattled to his touch but refused to open. 'Would you mind, sir?' said the sergeant, motioning me forward.

I complied, and the constable moved aside to give me room. It took but a moment to operate the trick handle, and then I opened the drawer to reveal the metal box within. 'Do you want me to lift it out?' I asked the men.

The sergeant shook his head. 'Step back, sir, if you don't mind.'

I obeyed, and watched as they took the box from the drawer and placed it on the desk amidst the ledgers and paperwork. I had not troubled to lock it the night before, and so the sergeant had no trouble opening the lid. I hid a smile, for I imagined his disappointment at the empty interior. I would have bet a pound to a penny that he expected to find some clue that would link me to the murders.

So, imagine my surprise when the sergeant reached into the box and carefully took out a long, bloodstained dagger.

28

I stared at the bloodied dagger in horror, for I recognised it immediately. It was the knife Sykes had used to stab the poor unfortunate in the tavern. But for it to appear right here in my desk...why, that meant Sykes or one of his cronies had been skulking around the professor's house in the dead of night!

At that moment I had other concerns than Sykes though, for two constables promptly took hold of me, twisting my arms painfully behind my back so that I could not move so much as a muscle. Then Sergeant Parkes addressed another of his men. 'Find the inspector and get him here quick.'

'Yessir!'

The constable departed, his boots rattling the floorboards. Meanwhile I was still eyeing the murder weapon clutched in the sergeant's meaty hand. How the devil had it arrived in my office? And more importantly...*why?*

'Simpkins,' said Parkes, addressing a fourth constable. 'Go and close the dining room door. The inspector won't want the professor or his daughter giving us lip when we take this one away.'

The constable nodded, and he too ran off on his errand. Then I caught the import of the sergeant's words. 'I'm sorry...did you say you were taking me away?'

The sergeant graced me with an unpleasant smile. 'Ho yes, my lad. The Inspector will be glad to get you off the streets. Very glad indeed.'

'But I haven't done anything!' I protested.

The sergeant snorted. 'Hear that, lads? He ain't done nothing!'

The constables gripping my arms laughed, and I felt my world tumbling around me. 'But–'

'You'll hang for these murders,' said the sergeant conversationally. 'Pretty daft, killin' all those applicants so's you'd get the job. Who'd 'ave thought?'

'But they were killed *after* I was employed!'

'Tell that to the judge, my son. Now button yer lip, or I'll shut your mouth for you.'

I would have protested further, but there was a commotion as Inspector Cox arrived with the two other constables. I felt a glimmer of hope, for surely things would now be straightened out? I started to protest my innocence immediately, but Cox motioned me to silence, and the two men holding me increased the pressure on my arms. The inspector walked straight past me to take the dagger from the sergeant, inspecting it closely.

'It's the murder weapon, sir,' said the sergeant.

'I can see that, Parkes.' Cox handed it back and indicated the metal box. 'In there, was it?'

'Yessir.'

Unhurriedly, Cox lifted the lid and peered inside. He ran his hand over the lining and inspected his fingertips, then picked the box up and took it to the nearby gaslight to see into the interior more clearly. Then, with a glance at the sergeant, he reached inside and withdrew a folded slip of paper. He shook it one-handed to open it up, the box being under his other arm, and then glanced at both sides. 'You read this, I take it?'

'Er–'

Wordlessly, the inspector held the note out to Parkes. 'Do so now.'

The sergeant took the note and held it at arms length, squinting slightly as he made out the words. 'You're next,' he intoned. He turned the paper over, then looked at Cox. 'You're next? What does it mean, sir?'

'It means you can release Mr Jones, sergeant.'

'But we only just caught 'im!'

'You certainly did. Unfortunately for you, this man is not the killer.'

Reluctantly, Parkes nodded to his men. 'All right, you heard the Inspector. Let go of 'im. And don't stand there gawking, search the rest of the 'ouse!'

The constables released me and left, and after Cox set the box down on my desk, he finally turned his attention to me. 'Mr Jones, I believe you have a story to tell. Would you prefer to reveal everything here in your study, or back at the station?'

I realised I had no choice, and my shoulders slumped in defeat. 'Very well,' I said quietly. 'Let us speak.'

'Excellent.' The inspector gestured at Parkes. 'Send someone to fetch me a chair, and afterwards you can take the constables back to the station.'

'What about the search, sir?'

'I have what I need.'

'And the professor?'

'Ensure you have a man at the dining room door. I want the rest of the family safely where they are for the time being.'

'Yes sir.'

Moments later a constable returned with a chair, and then the inspector and I were left alone. Cox moved my own chair out from behind the desk, and then indicated I should sit. He faced me, taking out a notebook and a short lead pencil, and after a brief pause gave me an encouraging look. 'Mr Jones, I'd like you to tell me everything. Take your time, and please don't leave anything out.'

After a moment's hesitation, I began to recount my story.

'He gave his name as William Sykes,' I began, 'although he admitted to me that it was a *nom-de-plume*. He bears a terrible scar down one side of his face.'

'From a blade?' asked the inspector, who was busy taking notes. 'Or was it an injury from machinery, perhaps?'

'How would one tell the difference?'

'A blade leaves a clean cut with defined edges. Wounds from machines can be jagged, as the skin is frequently torn from the face.'

I winced as I recalled the spinning lathe Roberta had used in the cellar, for I had just pictured her comely features disfigured in the same manner as Sykes' scar. 'A machine, I should say.'

'Still, it doesn't entirely rule out a military man,' murmured Cox, as he wrote down the details. He glanced at me, then explained further. 'Explosions can also cause jagged scars. Mortar fire and the like.'

Cox was being so genial towards me that I felt completely at ease sharing information with him. A part of me knew his friendly manner was a ploy to make me talk, but after holding so many secrets it was a relief to unburden myself. Because of this, I had already decided to reveal everything. Everything, that was, except for the precise nature of the professor's business. Let the professor explain that, if he cared to, for I would not break my promise.

'How do you know this Sykes is the murderer?' Cox asked me.

I hesitated. If I told the inspector I had witnessed the death, would I get myself into trouble for not reporting it?

'If you were not involved, you have nothing to fear,' said Cox, guessing at the reason for my silence.

Quickly, I told him of the events inside the Crown and Feather. When I revealed the manner in which Sykes had left the dead man sitting propped against a wooden column, the inspector betrayed his surprise by whistling quietly. 'A ruthless killer, and a bold one,' he remarked. 'But tell me this. How did you first come to know of Sykes, and why were you meeting?'

I explained about the note I'd received, and when I explained that Sykes wanted me to steal drawings and devices from the professor, Cox looked at me like I was the madman. 'Are you trying to tell me this fellow is killing and threatening and planting bloodied daggers because he wants the secrets to the professor's decorative trinkets? Carved metal boxes and little brass cylinders?'

'The professor is an inventor, and very secretive about his work.' With good reason, I thought, but I did not elaborate. Instead, there was a more pressing matter I needed to discuss. 'Inspector, Sykes threatened to harm my parents if I did not comply with his wishes. If you cannot catch him quickly, and round up all his men into the bargain, I must ask that you let me return home so that I might protect my family.'

'Men?'

'Why yes. He led me to believe there was an organisation behind him.'

Cox smiled at me, shaking his head. 'He would say something like that, wouldn't he? Keep you on your toes, when like as not it's just him.'

'But what if it's the truth? Inspector, if there's anything you can do to protect my parents–'

'I will send word to the local police. Don't concern yourself in that regard.' Cox glanced at his notebook. 'Now, what else do you have?'

'Sykes told me that he killed Jules Hartlow,' I said quietly.

The inspector looked surprised. 'Did he now?'

'A–and I think he might have killed Arthur Staines as well. Last night...he warned me there would be another death in the newspaper.' I looked down at the floor, lowering my voice. 'I thought it was just a threat,' I said quietly. 'Had I known he really meant to kill again–'

'Don't trouble yourself, Mr Jones. Had you come into the station with this story, it would have been dismissed as lunacy. You would not believe the number of crackpots who spin tales of such-and-such threatening a neighbour and the like.' Cox leaned forwards. 'Shall I tell you how I see things?'

'Please.'

'I surmise that William Sykes learned of the earlier murders before they appeared in the newspaper, and claimed the credit in order to scare you. He did kill a man in the Crown and Feather last night, but that man was known to us. The dead man was a nasty piece of work, Mr Jones, and the world is better off without him.'

'But the dagger...it was left in my study! He knew exactly where I work each day!'

'It's likely he's visited this house before. Business dealings with the professor, perhaps.'

'So the professor might know him?'

'Indeed. In your place I would have gone to the professor immediately. But, of course, you were motivated by concern for your parents, and one must make allowances.' Next, the inspector returned to my description of Sykes, ensuring I had shared every detail. When we'd finished, he closed his notebook with a snap, tucking it away. 'We will put a description about and see whether we can't snare this fellow. But if he should get in touch to organise another meet, you must report it to the police immediately. Is that clear?'

I nodded.

'We will surround the place, and the moment you identify Sykes to us, we'll take him.' Cox stood, and he gripped my shoulder. 'With any luck, this will be over soon. Now, I must speak with the professor to see whether he has any knowledge of Sykes.'

'D–do you have to do that?'

He frowned at me. 'Don't you want to find this killer?'

'Yes, but if you reveal my involvement...well, the professor has a temper, and if he's shouting at me, he won't be assisting you.'

Cox's lips twisted in amusement. 'Yes, well, I'm sure I can ask him about Sykes without mentioning you. After all, we don't want you getting fired just yet, do we? You'd be no use to Sykes then, and no use to me either.'

The inspector directed me towards the door, and we took the stairs to the lower hallway. He nodded to the constable at the dining room door, who stood aside to let us through.

'I must protest at this treatment!' cried the professor, immediately he saw us. 'Held prisoner in my own home? Why, it's unconscionable!'

'If you'll just sit down a moment...' began Cox.

'Sit down? *Sit down?* I've been doing nothing but sit down for the best part of an hour, and I'm telling you I'm sick of it!'

'I have one more question for you, and then my men and I will leave you in peace.'

This quietened the professor. Well, a little at least. 'Go on then. Ask this precious question.'

'Do you know of a man with a scar all the way down one side of his face?' Cox indicated which side he meant by drawing a finger down his cheek.

'No. Should I?'

Cox shook his head. 'It's not important. It came up during my investigation.'

'There,' said the professor. 'And now you can leave. I'm sure you don't need me to show you the door, as you've used it all too frequently these past few days.'

The inspector gave him a quick nod, offered Roberta a far more gentlemanly bow, and then gave me a significant look. 'No doubt I shall hear from you soon,' he said, and then he collected the constable at the door and departed.

'Well,' said the professor.

'Father, don't start,' said Roberta. 'The police are only doing their job.'

'Yes, and which job is that?' He turned to me. 'And you, sir. Why did they need your presence upstairs?'

'The inspector had a few questions about the ledgers, that's all. I did not divulge any information about your business, you can be sure of that.'

'Glad to hear it,' remarked the professor. 'Well, the day is already half gone and I'm behind with everything. Everything, I tell you! Roberta, would you be so good as to–'

'Father, please,' groaned Roberta. 'Just let me have one hour of peaceful sleep.'

'Hmm, yes, of course.' The professor looked at me. 'Mr Jones, you will help me in her stead.'

'Help with what, sir?'

'Oh, don't worry, my boy. It's nothing too taxing, else I wouldn't ask. Come, let us retire to my study.'

The last time I'd met the professor in his study he'd released a spirit and stunned himself into near-unconsciousness, so I followed him out of the dining room with some trepidation.

'Good luck,' called Roberta.

I took little comfort from her parting words, and as we made our way to the study I asked the professor about the nature of our forthcoming work.

'I have assembled a machine of Roberta's design,' he told me. 'The parts were ordered from half a dozen suppliers, so that none had any inkling of the whole.'

'I believe I saw the invoices upstairs,' I said. 'The casting and machining of various metal components, if I recall.'

'Of course you did. Well, Roberta and I fabricated much of the machine here, from connecting pins to bearings to copper wire. But alas, this new device must be powered by an electrical charge.'

'How will you do such a thing?'

'Aha! I read several fascinating reports from America on the subject of electrical energy, and I was lucky enough to secure one or two basic sketches. From these, Roberta and I developed a second machine to power the first. We built an electrostatic generator, Mr Jones, and I believe it is the first of its kind in all of England!'

His words were like a foreign language to me, but when we reached his office and showed me the rough sketches, it all became clear. 'The rotating portion generates electricity!' I said, as I studied the faint pencilled lines. 'It's sent along these wires, and from there it can be used externally.'

'That's very good!' he said, looking at me in surprise. 'Very few are that intuitive, young man!'

I thought he might be patronising me, but I realised he meant it. Then I saw something on the diagram which seemed off, somehow. Inefficient, that was it. 'Sir, this section here, near the handle. Why is there no reducing gear? It would double the speed of the, er, spinning part.'

Now he looked at me in complete astonishment. 'Mr Jones, that is the same modification Roberta suggested! Are you sure you have no training in engineering?'

'I am just a bookkeeper, sir. But I confess, I do see patterns in numbers, and these diagrams are merely numbers expressed in lines, arcs and circles.'

The professor was silent at this observation, and he remained so as he took up a wooden crate and removed the lid. I thought I might have offended him, but then I realised he was deep in thought.

'Come and look at the generator,' he said at last. 'Tell me what you see.'

I approached his workbench, where he'd set down a wondrous gadget about the length and height of a loaf of bread. It was quite clearly the machine from the sketches, and with its gleaming bronze parts, coiled copper wires, and polished wooden crank it was a beautiful device indeed. The professor ushered me closer, and encouraged me to turn the device on the workbench so as to inspect it from every angle. 'It's the most amazing instrument I have ever seen,' I murmured.

The professor looked pleased. 'We are lucky the police did not break it apart with their clumsy searching. Now tell me, do you see anything that could increase the output?'

I guessed he meant the electricity generation. 'Is it not sufficient?'

'Sadly, no. Let me see, where did I put...aha!' He pounced on another crate, this one pushed under his workbench. Hauling it out, he took out another device and placed it next to the first.

This new machine was a quarter of the size of the first, and looked like a segmented orange balanced on a child's spinning top, with both enclosed within a metal frame. There was a clear piece of crystal in the centre of the orange, attached to it with fine wires, and as I stared at the contraption I realised there was something strangely familiar about it. Had I seen it in the professor's study before now? No, I did not think so.

Then it hit me. This was the exact same machine displayed in Roberta's drawings from the night before. The drawings I had taken and modified to create a fake diagram for Sykes.

'So, what do you think of this one?' the professor asked me.

'The workmanship is remarkable,' I said. 'But sir, what does it do?'

'I'm glad you asked, Mr Jones. When you captured a spirit earlier, what was the most difficult part of the operation?'

I thought back to my fight in this very room. 'The phantasm was only visible at close range,' I said. 'Outside that range, I could only see a pitch black fog.'

'Precisely!'

'Is this some kind of illumination device?' I asked, turning to the machine. If so, the outsized version I gave Sykes would light up the night sky for miles. Of course, to activate it, he would need an enormous amount of power.

The professor snorted. 'You think I'd waste my time and money on a glorified street lamp? No, my boy, this is not a light. Come now, use that brain of yours and consider the design.'

I examined the item from every angle. 'I should imagine this central part would spin, given sufficient power, and that would cause a disturbance of an electrical nature.'

'Very good.'

After that I was stumped, so I hazarded a guess. 'Does it repel spirits, like the tip of the weapon you used yesterday?'

'No, it's the opposite,' said the professor triumphantly. 'It attracts them, like a venus flytrap with its prey.' He pointed. 'You see? Spirits are drawn to this point, and from there it's a trivial matter to scoop them up.' Then his face fell. 'Unfortunately, it consumes more power than I have available, and I've not been able to run the machine for more than a second or two at a time.'

'And the crystal? Is it some valuable specimen which is hard to obtain?'

'No, it's an ordinary piece of glass,' said the professor. 'Fired, then allowed to cool.'

At that, my worry only increased. I'd given scaled-up plans for this device to Sykes, and I'd been hoping the gem in the middle would be impossible for him to obtain, especially as he'd need one around six inches across. Now, it seemed, he could obtain such a crystal with little trouble. 'So tell me, professor. What would happen if you built a machine of a similar design, but made it even larger?'

He shook his head. 'Double the size, and the power requirements would be squared.'

'Let's say you could power it. Hypothetically.'

The professor thought for a moment. 'The attraction field would increase substantially, of course. You'd draw in spirits from an area measuring dozens of yards, instead of a few square feet.'

'And if the machine were, say, six feet across and ten high?'

At this, he laughed aloud. 'Why, you'd need the power of a thousand steam locomotives for a device of that size. And electrical power at that!'

Relieved, I turned back to the generator.

'Of course,' continued the professor, 'if one *did* manage to power such a monstrous contraption, every spirit, evil shade and phantasm would be drawn to it from across the length and breadth of England. Could you imagine the chaos if such a thing were unleashed upon the heart of London?'

29

With the professor's doom-laden words still ringing in my ears, I approached his hand-cranked generator to see whether I could find a way to increase its output. Now, I was not versed in engineering or the mechanical arts, but recent events had shown me that I possessed a certain instinct. As I viewed the machine I tried to think of it in terms of numbers and equations, with variables for every part.

I was still considering these when the professor cleared his throat. 'Mr Jones, I just want to say that I'm very pleased with your dedication thus far.'

This gave me pause, for my first thought was of Sykes and the drawings I'd copied for him.

'There was a young man before you, you know,' said the professor. 'A cousin of Roberta's on her mother's side.'

'Do you mean Edgar?' I asked him. I was still busy inspecting the machine, but if the professor was willing to volunteer information, I was not going to stop him.

'Yes, that's the lad. I suppose Roberta told you about him.'

'She only told me that he died.'

'Hmph.' There was a pause. 'Well, I might as well tell you, for it will serve as a cautionary tale. I was against hiring him from the start, for Edgar was a cunning sort. And, sure enough, I began to notice items disappearing.'

I started guiltily, which was unfortunate because at that moment I'd been holding two slender wires apart. One pulled clear of its connector, and I fumbled to rejoin it before the professor noticed.

'I thought he was selling the items to line his pockets, but his plans were grander than that. Would you believe he hoped to set up in competition to me? Me, with a lifetime of experience! But Roberta and I knew nothing of this until it was too late.'

'What happened?'

'Much as you'd expect. He stole plans from Roberta and vital pieces of equipment from me, and then he tried to construct a simple machine of his own. Of course, the foolish boy got it all wrong, and he unleashed a phantasm which promptly took his life. Then his unstable contraption of a machine exploded, and they do say the flash lit up half of London.'

'I'm sorry to hear of your loss.'

'My only loss was the equipment,' said the professor curtly, which to my mind was somewhat callous. 'Edgar was a thorough disappointment, and he deserved everything that came to him.'

I wondered whether he was warning me, in an oblique fashion. But instead, he praised me.

'Now you, Mr Jones, you are clearly a cut above. An upright sort.' The professor clapped me on the shoulder. 'I am so pleased we met, and I believe you will become a tremendous help to my little enterprise.'

It was lucky I was inspecting the machine, for had I been looking into the professor's eyes I'm sure my guilty expression would have betrayed me. The professor and Roberta had taken me in and treated me well, and I was repaying them by becoming another Edgar. I felt like a heel of the worst kind, and I wished heartily that Sykes had never been born. Without his evil shadow clouding my very existence, I could have been truly happy in the professor's household.

'Now, what have you noticed so far?' asked the professor, turning once more to the task at hand.

'There are only three ways to increase the output of this generator,' I said. 'The first is to make the machine larger.'

The professor shook his head. 'I do not have the funds, the materials, nor the time.'

'The second is to rework this central part, so that it runs more efficiently.' Carefully, I withdrew the core of the machine, which was a cylindrical rotor studded with dull grey squares. The wooden handle was attached, as was the gearing mechanism, and I held the piece of machinery in both hands lest I drop it. 'If these squares were larger–'

'Impossible,' said the professor. 'Those form part of the armature, and each took days to fashion.'

I gestured at the wooden handle. 'The only remaining option is to spin the central portion at higher speed.'

'I have already geared it so high that it takes two strong arms just to turn the generator over. Any more, and it will be completely immobilised.' He looked at me hopefully. 'Are you sure there is no other way?'

'I'm sorry, but those are the only options I have identified.'

'Then it seems I have reached the limits with this design,' said the professor despondently. 'I shall have to start from scratch once I have the means to do so.'

As he spoke I was inspecting the wooden handle, and I frowned as I noticed the method by which it was fastened to the central shaft. Remove the handle, and the shaft could be turned mechanically. Turned, perhaps, by the same power Roberta had used to drive the lathe in the cellar. It would not be portable, but it would most certainly serve to power the attracting machine which the professor was so keen to test. 'Sir, I have an idea.'

'Good man! I knew you'd hit upon the answer. Do tell, or I shall drag the information out of you.'

Quickly, I told him about my idea, and his eyes lit up instantly. 'That is genius!' he declared. 'Come, let us not waste a single moment. To the cellar!'

We left the study with our equipment, the professor cradling the generator in his arms while I bore the delicate attractor machine. As we entered the hall we encountered Mrs Fairacre carrying away the remains of the breakfast things. She took one look at the outlandish machines and gave a sniff of disapproval, before marching away with her head held high.

'That good lady is not overly impressed with my chosen occupation,' whispered the professor. 'She fears it will end me one day.'

I guessed that the housekeeper's concerns arose out of her feeling for him, but I was not crass enough to say so.

We took the corridor to the cellar door, which I held open so the professor could take the stairs with his larger, more cumbersome load. I followed, and noted that heat rose up the narrow stairs despite the fact the equipment was not in use. 'Do you keep the boiler running at all times?' I asked the professor. 'Only I notice you purchase a lot of coal.'

'Mrs Fairacre sends a girl down to light the furnace in the mornings. It's an expense, certainly, but if Roberta or I need to carry out our work we cannot afford to wait several hours for steam to build.'

We reached the foot of the stairs, where we placed the equipment on a nearby workbench. The professor set to work on the generator's wooden handle, removing it before fitting a collar to the exposed shaft. He seemed to be in good spirits, and he kept up a chirpy commentary as he worked. He was convinced the spirit attractor would lead to a change in his fortunes, and he spoke of building several of the devices once he had sufficient funds. After that, he envisaged hiring additional workers that could be despatched to all points of the city, thus servicing a large number of clients at once.

I did not ask him how he intended to power all of these devices, and contented myself with listening to his grandiose plans.

I did not have anything to do at first, but soon the professor had me forming narrow strips of metal. There were several of these, and I guessed they would be used to hold the generator down. Meanwhile, the professor worked on the lathe, preparing the axle so it could be attached to the generator shaft.

It took perhaps an hour, but this part of our work was finally completed. After that, the professor used an auger to drill four holes in the surface of a sturdy work table. 'Do not tell Roberta,' he panted, as he applied himself to the labour. 'This is a favourite of hers, but it's just the size we need.'

'What exactly is a favourite of mine?'

We both started guiltily, and then turned to see Roberta descending the stairs. I was glad to see she looked rested, but I'm certain the professor wished she had slept for another few minutes. He was trying to stand in front of the bench, the augur concealed behind his back, but it was a waste of time because Roberta merely had to crane her neck to look past him. 'I see the woodworm have been particularly active this time of year,' she remarked.

'I'm sorry my dear, but this old bench had to be sacrificed in the name of scientific advances. Needs must, as they say.'

'Indeed they should, for I will need a new bench and you must pay for it.'

I interrupted quickly, before their dispute scaled into a full-scale argument. 'Roberta, your father and I are attempting to increase the output of the electrical generator by attaching it to the spinning end of the lathe.'

Roberta's eyebrows rose at this news, and she looked from the generator to the lathe and back again. Then she inspected the metal strips I'd fashioned on the professor's instructions. 'These will not hold,' she said flatly.

'They will suffice,' said the professor.

'I assure you they will not.'

'And I say they will!'

'They won't, not even if you drilled holes in that block of wood you call a head and attached these pieces with half a pound of screws.'

The professor was taken aback at her vehemence. 'As you appear so convinced of yourself, I would ask you to explain.'

'This metal has been infused, father dear. It is so brittle as to be useless, and your precious generator would have come loose, flown through the air and likely taken your heads off.'

Chastened, the professor took the strips from her hand and discarded them. 'Perhaps, now you are here...' he began.

'I will attend to it.' Roberta looked at me. 'Was this your idea?'

'The metal?'

'No, attaching father's generator to the lathe.'

I nodded, and in return she gave me a smile. 'I shall have to be careful, or you will put me out of work.'

'Never!' I protested. 'Why, your drawings and diagrams are the most amazing work I have ever seen.'

'Really?' asked Roberta, raising one eyebrow. 'And when did you have occasion to study them?'

I felt a chill as I realised I had trapped myself. 'I saw a few pages when we visited your room together. It was just a quick glance, if I'm completely honest, but–'

'–but you thought to compliment me, regardless.' She gave me a look. 'You will not win my favour with honeyed words, Mr Jones, particularly false ones.'

'I apologise.'

'Do not fret, Mr Jones,' said Roberta, giving me a smile. 'My father and I adopt a brusque manner when working, and you will get used to it soon enough. A sharp tongue and a kindly heart, that is our way!' Roberta left me to rummage in a set of shelves nearby, before returning with four metal pieces, each two inches across and twelve long. 'Now take these and bend them to match father's originals. You may find them harder to work, but they will be stronger for it. Afterwards, we shall drill them out and attach them to my poor workbench.'

I nodded, and soon I was busy at the arbor press. The metal was indeed harder to bend, but eventually I had all four pieces prepared. Afterwards, Roberta took an auger and a small can of mineral oil, and we took it in turns to work small fastening-holes through the metal.

The professor had finished lining up the generator with the lathe, and he was slowly turning the shaft by hand to inspect the joint for straightness. I understood why, since the lathe would be spinning at high speed and the slightest distortion might tear the delicate generator apart.

Roberta took him the metal supports, and they were still fastening the generator when Elsie, the young housemaid, came down the steps with a platter of thick sandwiches, a jug of beer and three glasses. 'Mrs Fairacre's compliments,' she said, 'and she thought lunch might be welcome.'

'Welcome indeed!' cried the professor. 'Come, let us eat and we'll finish the task afterwards.'

Elsie was looking around for a clear spot to place the tray, but in vain.

'Why, if only we had that workbench of mine,' said Roberta, fixing her father with a glare.

In reply, he swept a shelf clear with his arm, sending pieces of metal and stray items clattering to the floor. Elsie winced at the noise, then advanced carefully with the tray, trying not to step on the scattered odds and ends. She set it down, then bobbed her head at the professor. 'Begging pardon, but Mrs Fairacre says there's a storm brewing. She asks if you want the shutters drawn.'

'Most definitely,' said the professor. 'Please ask her to attend to it immediately, and when you speak with her, be certain to thank her for the sandwiches.'

'Yessir.' Elsie departed, but only after a backward glance at the mess she would probably have to tidy later. In that moment I resolved to pick the items up myself, for it hardly seemed fair to burden the girl with the result of the professor's ill temper.

The professor was eager to fire up the generator and test his spirit attractor, and he wolfed his sandwiches down before I had finished my first. He was still dashing crumbs from his coat as he crossed to the steam distributor, where he tapped a glass-fronted gauge before adjusting the wheel on a pressure valve.

'He'll choke on his meals one of these days,' muttered Roberta. 'Just look at him. He's like a child of five.'

She spoke with affection, despite the words, and I noticed that she too was eating with unseemly haste. The sandwiches were delicious, consisting of thin-sliced salted ham between hunks of crusty bread, the whole flavoured with hot mustard. I washed mine down with a glass of ale, and had barely done so when I discovered I was sitting alone. Roberta had gone to the lathe, where she was inspecting her father's work. She turned her back to him to make an adjustment or two, so that he would not observe her.

The professor spun a large valve wheel attached to the wall, and steam hissed and whistled as it filled the pipes leading around the cellar. These rattled and banged, and I saw jets emanating from several joints where the lead solder must have developed minute cracks from the stress.

Meanwhile, high above the professor's head, a large axle parallel to the ceiling began to turn. This axle was affixed to a large worm gear in the corner, which turned a second axle leading to the lathe. The speed of both axles increased with the steam pressure, until they were spinning so fast I could feel the rumbling of their bearings transmitted directly through the soles of my shoes. Plaster and soot rained down from the ceiling, and I eyed the brackets restraining these heavy, fast-moving axles with some trepidation. If they were to come free...

'Ready!' called the professor, and Roberta sprang into action. She took hold of the big lever beside the lathe and pulled down hard, engaging the broad driving belt. The lathe hesitated, then began to spin faster and faster, and as it did so I saw a glow emanating from the generator attached to the far end. The speed increased further, and I saw the device straining against the metal brackets I'd fashioned earlier. The workbench shook and shuddered, and I feared it might not hold.

The professor left his post and hurried over to the machine, stopping to collect a small burlap sack on the way. This looked heavy, despite its modest size, and the professor winced as he braced himself. He staggered towards the workbench containing the generator and swung the sack forward in one quick motion, laying it across the braces near the foot of the workbench's legs. The weight of the sack dampened the shuddering immediately, and, having averted catastrophe, the professor now turned his attention to the generator.

Roberta watched him from her position at the lever, where she waited in case the lathe had to be stopped in a hurry.

There were two electrical leads attached to one side of the generator, each terminating in an insulated clamp. The professor took a clamp in each hand and struck them together briefly, causing a fat blue spark. Then he turned a fierce grin on Roberta, and a grateful one on me. 'My boy, you are indeed a genius!' he shouted, raising his voice over the hiss of steam and the rumble of machinery. 'There should be sufficient power here, of that I am certain!'

'Sufficient?' cried Roberta. 'That seems far too much power to me!'

The professor ignored her, and he crossed to the shelf where he'd deposited the attracting machine earlier. He took it up carefully, using both hands, and carried it to the generator with all the solemnity of a midwife handling a newborn. He laid it down on the workbench, and proceeded to attach the first of the two electrical cables.

'Father!' shouted Roberta. 'Let me slow the lathe a little.'

During my brief period of employment with the Twickhams I had come to view the professor as an impatient sort, little given to lengthy deliberations even when his life was in mortal danger. Such proved the case in this instance, for he ignored his daughter's advice and connected the second cable to the attractor machine without a moment's hesitation.

Instantly, the clear gem at the heart of the device glared like the midday sun, bathing that dank, grimy cellar with an unnaturally bright light. I shielded my eyes, as did Roberta, while the professor, who was standing so much closer, squinted through his fingers. At that moment all of us saw the exact same thing. The segmented orange shape began to spin, faster and faster, and as it did so the light gleaming from the gem began to turn to the deepest, darkest night.

This darkness quickly spread throughout the cellar, much like a bottle of ink tipped into a pool of water. Now, instead of shielding our eyes, we were forced to peer into the gloom just to make each other out. As my eyes grew accustomed I realised the darkness was not complete, for it was shot through with shimmering waves of violet and dark red.

Roberta waited no longer. She pushed upwards with all her might on the handle controlling the lathe. The thick band driving the machine slowed and stopped, but to my astonishment the lathe did not. Indeed, the machine now seemed to be powered by the spin of the generator rather than the other way around. The generator was no longer turning motion from the lathe into electricity, it was receiving energy from Lord knows where and using it to spin the lathe!

Roberta pulled on the handle and then raised it once more, but to no effect. Then, in the near-darkness, I saw that the cables leading from the generator to the attractor machine were glowing red. The latter was still spinning, emitting that strange black light, and I wondered whether it was drawing power from some hitherto unimagined spirit world and sending that power to the generator. In effect, the attractor device had turned the generator into an electric motor of sorts!

The workbench had been shaking wildly under the immense rotational forces, and all of a sudden the brackets I'd fashioned gave up the struggle. One of them snapped, and a split second later the generator spun free, tearing away from the connecting cables to smash against the wall. There was a shower of hot metal fragments, and I ducked as the spinning shaft flew past my ear with a loud humming noise. There was a crash behind me as it hit the wall, and further patterings of metal as bits and pieces of the ruined generator came to rest.

Meanwhile, the two cables attached to the attractor where whipping around in mid-air like angry snakes, sparking and crackling every time the ends approached each other. The professor was almost caught once or twice, and he stepped back hurriedly to avoid injury.

The attractor was still spinning wildly, with no signs of slowing, and the gem was now turning to a dark purplish colour. Now and again there was a flash of blood red lightning, and one of these narrowly missed the professor before striking a cupboard pushed against the wall. There was a bang, and a hole the size of my fist appeared in the wooden door.

'Shut it down!' screamed Roberta. 'Shut it down before it does for us!'

The professor turned a ghastly look on her. 'I agree with you wholeheartedly, my dear. But...*how?*'

30

Bolts of red lightning speared out of the attractor machine, striking walls and furniture alike, and for the first time in my life I understood what it might be like to face enemy fire. The professor was much closer to the machine than I, and far more likely to be hit, but he appeared incapable of movement. It was as though the strange lights and bursts of energy emanating from his machine were too shocking for him to comprehend, and so he could only stand there staring foolishly at the thing.

Roberta had no such trouble. She leapt from her position at the other end of the lathe, dodging forks of deadly red lightning as she made for her father. Upon reaching him she spared no time for niceties, instead dragging him bodily away from the madly spinning device.

Even as they withdrew, a ghostly, insubstantial shape began to emerge from the attractor. At first it was a twisted hand, with long fingers and ragged nails, and to my horror I realised this hand was twice the size of any I had seen before. The hand appeared to be clawing at the air, like a drowning man striving to reach the surface, and soon a second hand joined the first. Then a face appeared, its features horribly stretched. The head turned this way and that as though struggling to breathe, the distorted, gaping mouth exhibiting teeth like tombstones. A thick tongue protruded from the mouth, flailing around like a freshly beheaded snake, and as I gazed in horror upon this apparition I suddenly realised it had *seen* me.

The spirit fastened me with a hungry look, and it redoubled its efforts to free itself, desperately trying to enter our world so that it might rend the very soul from my living body. I was frozen to the spot, completely unable to move, but out of the corner of my eye I saw Roberta leave the professor and run for the far end of the room. Here, near the coal chute, there stood a half-barrel containing various tools and implements. Selecting a sledgehammer, Roberta held it up to inspect the big, heavy head. Then she gave a nod, and turned a grim look on the machine from which the malevolent phantasm struggled to emerge.

'No!' I whispered, for I dreaded what might happen. Even if she avoided the slavering phantasm, the sparking electrical cables and stray bolts of red lightning would end her life for certain. But the spirit held me in its gaze, and I found I could not move a muscle.

Roberta let out a great cry as she raised the sledgehammer above her head, and I guessed then that she was about to charge. The spirit turned its deadly gaze upon her, and I knew with stone cold certainty that she would be dead in seconds. Even as she faced the thing, it stretched out its hands to her, willing her into its embrace.

However, in turning to her, the spirit had released me. Freed of the mental bonds, I was on the point of charging it myself, but I knew that would end in my own death as well as Roberta's. Instead, desperate now, I cast about me. My gaze fell on the original strips of infused metal which Roberta had discarded. I retrieved them with a cry of triumph, drawing my arm back and hurling the first piece directly at the spinning attractor machine.

I missed.

In despair, I watched the bent piece of metal strike the wall and spin away, landing harmlessly on the floor. Meanwhile, Roberta had begun her charge, and was already halfway across the cellar with the raised sledgehammer at the ready.

I threw the second piece of metal, willing it towards the target. This time it grazed the machine before slamming into the wall, and I heard the ringing noise above the hiss of steam and the rumble of machinery. By now Roberta was almost upon the phantom, and I knew I had but one chance remaining.

I drew my arm back, sighted, and hurled that piece of metal harder than I had ever thrown anything in my entire life. My arm near popped from its socket, and the momentum bent me double until I was looking down at the floor. I heard a clang, and then an unholy scream rent the air. I looked up, praying it was not Roberta, and to my delight I saw she was unharmed. The spirit though...now that was another matter. My throw had lodged the piece of metal into the very middle of the attractor machine, shattering the glowing crystal and jamming the orange-segment shape so that it spun no more. The red lightning ceased, and the dark, purplish light was being drawn back into the device as though acted upon by a powerful force. As for the spirit itself, it was no longer menacing us, but instead desperately clawing at the air as it strove to maintain its place in our world. It was failing, and the more it was drawn back into the broken machine, the more it screamed and wailed in anger and frustration. The noise set my hair on end, and I tossed aside the last remaining piece of metal and clamped my hands over my ears.

Then, after a brief flash of light, the terrifying spectre was gone.

The sparking cables were now lifeless, and lay flat on the workbench. The machine smouldered gently, with no signs of the purple light nor deadly bolts of lightning.

That final explosion had thrown Roberta to the floor, and I hurried over with my heart in my mouth. Fortunately, she was only winded, and I helped her to sit up, supporting her weight in my arms. She sat there but a moment, before brushing me aside and struggling to her feet. Before I could stop her, Roberta took up the sledgehammer and, ignoring her father's cry of anguish, brought it down on the attractor. She hit it again and again, demolishing it completely, and then, for good measure, she smashed the workbench into kindling also. When she was done she scattered the pieces before setting the sledgehammer aside. She was breathing heavily, and her face was a mask of anger as she turned to confront her father. 'You old fool!' she cried. 'Did I not tell you there was too much power?'

I expected the professor to counter vociferously, as was his fashion, but he looked shaken and said nothing.

'You mess with things you do not understand!' continued Roberta. 'Why can you not be content with catching the spirits already present in our world? Must you now bring new and ever-more-dangerous horrors into being?'

'I–I'm sorry,' muttered the professor.

Roberta gestured at the shattered machinery. 'Just because something can be designed and built, it does not mean you should do so!'

'Yes dear.'

The professor was contrite, undoubtedly. But I could tell his scientific brain was excited by the implications of this new discovery. There was a certain gleam in his eye, and I guessed he was already working on plans to capture the half-seen phantasm which had almost crossed the barrier into our world. It was plain to see he was excited by the untold horrors lurking around us, and I could not imagine him giving up the hunt so easily.

At that moment he stooped to gather a fragment or two of his destroyed machine, inspecting the pieces closely, and Roberta promptly ordered him out of the cellar. He left unwillingly, protesting all the while, but she had up a fearsome temper, and in addition was taller and stronger than her aged father. She'd also taken up the sledgehammer once more, holding it in both hands, and that seemed to settle the matter.

'The old fool,' she growled, once he'd departed up the stairs.

I said nothing, for it was not my place to do so.

Roberta turned to me, and her manner softened a touch. 'That was a good throw, Mr Jones. I believe you saved the day.'

Happy with her praise, I smiled.

'Oh, do not look so pleased with yourself,' she said, her expression once more forbidding. 'If you had not aided my father in the first place, none of this would have happened. In future, I ask that you consult with me before suggesting changes to the professor's machinery.'

'Yes, of course.'

'I know you meant well, but witness the result.'

I did not point out that she'd helped to connect the generator to the lathe, and had not objected to the idea at that time. I also wondered whether her anger was partially due to the fact that I had solved the professor's energy problem where she had not.

But Roberta had finished chiding me, and we turned our attention to the chaos and disorder which had befallen the cellar. It took us an hour or more to sweep up the debris, straighten the shelves, reassemble parts of the lathe and return every tool and item to its rightful place.

Once we'd finished, Roberta indicated the stairs. 'You should attend to your bookkeeping duties while I have words with my father. And if I were you, I'd ensure the door to your study was firmly closed, else you may hear an argument so heated it would put a thunderstorm to shame.'

I did not even reach my office, for I had no sooner left the cellar than I met Elsie, the maid, on her way back from the front door. Roberta strode by, leaving the two of us alone, and then Elsie offered me a folded slip of paper. 'He said to give this to you immediately,' she told me.

My head thudded as I took the note. Was it from Sykes? Or was Inspector Cox summoning me to the police station for more questioning? 'W—who was it? Who left it?' I asked, staring at the note in my hand. I had not yet opened it, and I was debating whether to throw the thing onto the nearest fire. Perhaps then I could pretend I had never received it.

'Just a boy, sir. He was paid a penny to deliver it, real urgent like.'

'Thank you, Elsie.'

The maid left for the kitchen, and I stood there alone in the darkened hallway. Then, knowing I was only delaying the inevitable, I unfolded the note and read the contents.

Meet at the Crown and Feather, 3.30 p.m. I have questions.

Below was a symbol with two triangles entwined. Sykes! And what sort of questions did he mean? Did he know I'd spoken with the police?

I guessed it was already mid-afternoon, and when I pulled out my pocket watch I received a nasty surprise. It was a quarter past three, and I knew for certain I could not reach the police station before the allotted time, let alone speak with Cox and inform him of the meeting with Sykes. Not only that, but the meeting would take place in broad daylight, which meant that even if the police could organise themselves in a matter of seconds, which was clearly impossible, there would be no darkness to hide their presence.

By setting the meeting so soon, Sykes had inadvertently avoided Cox's trap. I only hoped he did not know of Cox's plans, or else I would meet a swift and brutal end. Likewise, I would be killed if Sykes knew I'd spoken with the police. Presumably the outcome would be equally fatal if I did not answer Sykes' questions to his satisfaction.

In fact, I was beginning to suspect there was no scenario in which I might survive the meeting.

So, why not go to the police station instead, and trust Cox to send police to search the area around the Crown? Because Sykes would see them coming, that's why, and would almost certainly elude them. And the next time he crept around the professor's house in the dead of night it would be to murder me in my own bed. If he happened to wake Roberta or the servants, he might just kill them also.

I glanced towards the nearby stairs. Should I take the revolver? In all the excitement I had not yet returned to my room, and the weapon would still be concealed in my spare coat. I could attempt to load the thing, and then shoot Sykes if he came at me. I decided to do so, for without a weapon in my pocket I was not sure I'd be able to summon enough courage to attend the meeting in the first place.

I dashed upstairs to my room, crossed to the wardrobe and reached into my coat. My fingers closed on thin air, and I frantically searched the other pockets lest I'd chosen the wrong one. Then, in desperation, I grabbed the coat from the wardrobe and shook it upside-down, even though I was not certain what this would achieve. After all, the heavy revolver and the pouch full of cartridges could hardly have been caught in the lining.

'Have you lost something, Mr Jones?'

I leapt into the air and spun around, the very picture of a guilty man. Standing in the doorway was Mrs Fairacre, her face as expressionless as usual. 'Why yes indeed,' I declared. 'It was just some change from my pockets, but I am certain it will turn up.'

Mrs Fairacre stood with her hands behind her back, but now she withdrew them. The pistol lay on one palm, the bulging leather pouch of shells on the other. 'I had Elsie remove these from your room when the police arrived.'

Questions fired at me from all directions. How had Elsie known about the weapon? Why was Mrs Fairacre returning it? And why hadn't anyone gone to the professor...or the police? Then I saw a hint of a smile playing on Mrs Fairacre's lips. 'Come now, Mr Jones. I have work to do, and I cannot tarry all day while you collect your thoughts.'

'But–'

Impatiently, she strode into my room, almost slapping the pistol and pouch into my open hands. 'I've seen far worse in this house,' she said conversationally.

'But–'

'Do you intend to shoot the professor or Miss Twickham?'

'N–no, of course not!'

'The servants, perhaps? Or me?'

I shook my head emphatically.

'Then it's none of my business, is it?' Mrs Fairacre was about to leave, but something in the way I was staring at the revolver stopped her. 'Do you know how to use it?' she demanded.

'Er–'

Impatiently, she took the pistol from my hand, then expertly flipped out the chamber. Next, she bid me open the pouch, and, taking a small handful of cartridges, she slotted them home one by one. Finally, she spun the chamber and snapped it home with a flick of her wrist, before holding the pistol towards me, butt-first.

Open-mouthed, I could only stare.

Mrs Fairacre smiled. 'I was a nurse in the Crimea, Mr Jones. I learned a thing or two at the British Hotel, let me tell you.' Then her smile faded, and she shook her head slowly. 'So many young men lost,' she murmured. 'So many.'

There was a sad tale there, I was sure of it, but I was far too polite to enquire.

Mrs Fairacre shook herself, dispelling her memories of the war. 'Perhaps next time you will seek a better hiding place,' she remarked, and so saying, she spun on one heel and marched from my room.

I was left staring after her with a slightly dazed expression. Then I realised I had only minutes to reach the Crown and Feather. I took the loaded revolver gingerly, depositing it in my pocket, and then placed the pouch full of shells into my spare coat and tossed it across the bed. The better hiding place could wait until later...if I survived this latest meeting with Sykes.

There was no sign of Mrs Fairacre as I descended the staircase, but I did hear a terrific shouting match from the professor's study as I approached the front door. The words were indistinct, but Roberta and her father appeared to be sorting out their differences in typical fiery fashion. I was only glad I held the pistol, because I dreaded the outcome if either of them were in possession of a deadly weapon at that moment.

Once outside, I bent my head against the rain and hurried towards the road, seeking a suitable gap in the busy traffic so that I might cross. Heavy goods wagons rumbled by, along with the occasional omnibus, nimble hansom cabs, drenched-looking barrow boys and the usual flood of labourers, merchants and tradesmen heading to and from their places of work.

As I stood there, I felt a hand grip my elbow. At the same moment, something pricked me in the side. 'Turn left and start walking. Make a fuss and you'll die where you stand.'

The voice was low and menacing, but I recognised it for all of that. It was Sykes, and he had a knife pressed to my ribs.

We walked together for some time, the point of the knife pricking my skin with every step. The revolver was heavy in my pocket, but I knew that if I tried to draw it, and then turn and shoot, I would be dead before the manoeuvre was half completed.

We continued through the rain, until eventually we turned north, taking a narrow lane towards Kensington Gardens and Hyde Park. I saw the trees and shrubbery ahead, and wondered whether Sykes was leading me to a quiet spot where he could finish me unobserved. But his note mentioned questions! If we stopped to converse, then maybe I could back away a pace or two in order to use my gun. The shots would be loud, attracting instant attention, but I was confident I could lose myself in the crowds.

Then I thought of the bullets striking Mr Sykes, tearing into his flesh one after the next, driving him backwards until he fell to the ground, lifeless. I felt sick at the very idea, and I knew that I could not fire the weapon unless I was absolutely certain I was about to die.

We reached a park bench under a tree, where Sykes bid me sit. Rain pattered on the ground, and larger drops fell from the leaves, falling all around. Sykes took the seat alongside me, the knife aimed at my ribs, and I glanced at him and tried to determine his intent. His hair was slicked down around his face like that of a bedraggled rat, and my heart sank as I met his eyes, for his gaze was hard, flint-like and unwavering. If I did not answer his questions promptly and accurately, I had no doubt he would drive the knife into my chest.

'Are you going to behave?' he asked me.

I nodded.

He withdrew the knife and tucked it inside his coat, putting it away but keeping it within easy reach. He then took out a folded sheet of parchment. It was crumpled and much-used, and as he opened it up I recognised it as my own work. But now the diagrams I had drawn were extended, with countless notes scribbled in the margins, and new measurements, and additions that I could not quite make out. I realised that he had taken my drawing most seriously, and I wondered how far he'd progressed with building the thing. And also, what might happen when he discovered it could never work. 'Here,' he said, pointing to the centre of the diagram. 'What is this, and of what material is it made?'

I knew what he wanted, having seen the professor's much smaller version of the actual machine working before my very own eyes. Sykes was pointing at the crystal in the centre, which the professor had assured me was merely a piece of glass. I debated lying, telling the man it was some hard-to-obtain gemstone, but quickly decided against it. If he thought it was difficult to lay hands on, he would probably charge me with obtaining the part from the professor myself! 'It is a piece of ordinary glass,' I said quietly. 'I believe it serves to refract the light, and nothing more. Of course, I am no expert—'

'Clearly.' Sykes eyed me thoughtfully. 'Does it really need to be this large?'

'I–I don't know.'

'No matter. I will test on smaller sizes at first, and one piece at a time will see the wall built. But I must hurry, for the storm approaches! Yes yes, the storm. Hurry my boy, hurry!'

By now Sykes appeared to be speaking with himself, and I wondered whether his mind was as damaged as his face. Then he looked at me, focussed once more. 'After this, we shall never meet again. You have played your part, Mr Jones, and I thank you.'

Surprised beyond measure, I stared at him.

'Go!' he commanded me. 'Go back to your precious Roberta and her impatient, arrogant father.'

I stood quickly, scarcely believing it was over. Meanwhile, Sykes brandished the parchment at me. 'You may reveal your part in this if you dare, but I would advise against it. You see, late this evening, when those fools discover what I have achieved, they will curse your name until the end of time.'

I backed away slowly, moving my hand to my pocket. My fingers closed on the revolver's grip, and I stood there, hesitating. Draw the gun, fire a shot or two, and even I could not miss at this range. Sykes would be finished, and I would be free. On the other hand he had just released me, unharmed. Further, he had promised to leave me alone in future, although I did not trust him in the slightest. When his machine failed to work, I suspected he would seek retribution, or additional materials. Then, we would begin all over. So why not end it now?

Because I was a law-abiding man, that's why.

Turning, I walked away quickly, turning my collar up against the rain. I glanced back once, to make sure Sykes was not following, but the bench was empty and there was no sign of him anywhere. Relieved, I lengthened my stride, determined to reach the professor's house before I drowned.

On the way I considered reporting to the police station, to inform Cox of this latest development. In the end I decided against it. First, because I had the loaded revolver in my pocket. Second, because there was little to tell the inspector, aside from the fact Sykes was building some gimcrack machine based on my forged copy of an unfinished diagram. A machine which would probably crumble before he finished it, and which in any case could never be powered up. And finally, because I wanted to put the whole mess behind me once and for all.

31

Dinner was a sombre affair, with the professor and Roberta refusing to speak with each other. I was the only one in good spirits, and it was a relief when we finished our repast and departed the dining room. There was a huge flash of lightning and a rumble of thunder as I took the stairs to my study, and I resolved to double-check the shutters in my bedroom so that I would not be woken if the wind got up in the night.

After two or three hours of peaceful bookwork I doused the gaslight, tidied my desk and went upstairs to my bedroom. The maid had dried my coat, laying it out neatly on the bed, and I carried it to the wardrobe and hung it with the rest of my clothes. I had unloaded the gun earlier, but had not returned it to the locked metal box in my study. I still feared Sykes might gain entry to the house, perhaps for revenge, and knew I would have no compunction shooting him if he appeared in my bedroom. So, I'd concealed the pistol underneath my bed, with the pouch of cartridges close at hand.

A lightning flash lit my room, and seconds later a peal of thunder rumbled across the city. I went to my window and gazed out on the rain-soaked streets, with gaslights casting their dim glow and the occasional lighted window a yellowed rectangle of domesticity in the gloom. Then I opened my windows and leaned out to pull the shutters to, fastening them securely. Another flash lit them from without, and I felt the old painted timbers shiver as thunder followed.

Then, satisfied I'd done all I could, I prepared myself for bed and turned in.

I awoke with a start, and to my horror I realised someone was kneeling over me, shaking my shoulder. Instinct took over, and I pushed the shadowy figure away with all my might. As they vanished over one side of the bed, crying out in alarm, I rolled off the other side, reaching around desperately for the hidden gun. Even as I did so I heard my adversary dive across the bed, intent on reaching me once more.

With my brain foggy from sleep I'd forgotten the gun wasn't loaded, and when I jumped up and pulled the trigger, again and again, there was only a succession of mechanical clicks. At that same instant I heard a woman's voice directly in front of me.

'*Septimus!*'

Then came a flash of lighting, which glared through the shutters to render my room with bands of stark white. In the brief glow I saw Roberta's startled face mere inches from the end of my gun. Her hair and face were wet, as though she'd been lashed by the rain, but it was the wide-eyed stare that stilled my heart. Sickened, I realised I could have shot her dead right there in my room, and I threw the gun onto the bed as though it were suddenly red hot.

'Where did you get that thing?' demanded Roberta, seemingly more worried about my possession of a gun than the fact I'd tried to shoot her.

'I–I–'

'No matter,' she said brusquely. 'You must come downstairs quickly. We need you.'

'What time is it?'

'Late. Come, get dressed and follow me.'

I looked down at my nightclothes, then at Roberta.

'Hurry, Septimus. Lives may be in the balance!'

She showed no sign of leaving my room, and her urgency left me no choice. Still half-asleep, still mortified by my precipitous actions with that thrice-cursed revolver, I crossed to the wardrobe and removed my nightshirt, grateful the darkness hid my naked form. Then, as I was reaching for my clothes, another flash of lightning lit the room, revealing me to Roberta in all my modest glory. I was standing with my back to her, and as she did not make a comment I hoped she had not noticed. Fortunately there were no more ill-timed lightning flashes, and soon we were descending the stairs together, myself with cheeks glowing from the heat of embarrassment. No more was said about the gun, but I resolved to lock it away at the earliest opportunity. As for my temporary nakedness, nothing was said of that either, and thoroughly relieved I was too.

The professor was in the hallway, bleary-eyed and wearing a faded dressing-gown. With him stood Mrs Fairacre, whose clothes exhibited signs of having been outside in the storm. She was speaking in an animated fashion, her famous reserve nowhere to be seen. 'And I'm going to keep saying this until you believe me, you obstinate man!' she cried, thoroughly worked up. 'I swear I saw one of your ghosties in the street!'

'But my dear woman, that's quite impossible!' replied the professor. 'Why, without the right glasses...'

'Don't dear woman me,' said Mrs Fairacre. 'And I don't need your fancy glasses to see evil. The Lord strike me down if it isn't so!'

I felt this a rather unfortunate turn of phrase, given the lightning storm raging across the city, but the housekeeper was not to be pacified.

'You take those funny machines of yours into the street,' she demanded, all but prodding the professor in the chest. 'You take those gadgets and you catch this wild spirit before it does harm to some innocent!'

Roberta hurried past me and put an arm around Mrs Fairacre's shoulders. 'Come, why don't you and the professor retire to the sitting room? Perhaps you could both take a little brandy while Septimus and I handle this matter.'

The housekeeper looked from Roberta to me and back again. 'Septimus, is it?' she said. 'Very well. It's a harsh night for old bones, anyways, and I won't say no to a restorative.'

The professor brightened at the mention of brandy, and the pair of them retired to the sitting room, from whence I soon heard the clink of glasses. 'That's put them out of the way,' muttered Roberta. 'Now, Mr Jones, you and I should attend to this wayward spirit.'

'I don't mind if you call me Septimus,' I ventured.

She smiled. 'I might just do that, given I've seen you as naked as the day you were born.'

I stood there, mouth open, until she took my arm and half-dragged me to the professor's study. Here, she gathered several items, placing them into a haversack which I held open for her. 'Is it usual for spirits to be seen abroad like this?' I asked her, eager to change the subject.

'Nothing is usual when it comes to spirits,' she declared. 'My father and I are pioneers in the subject, yet you could publish a twenty-volume encyclopaedia containing all the knowledge we have yet to gain. More, probably.' Roberta looked around. 'That will do for now. Hopefully we will take this spirit quickly, and then return here and use the detector to seek any others.'

I was silent, for all of a sudden I remembered that I had attempted to use that same detector at the Snetton house, and that I may have broken it. I had not yet found the courage to tell Roberta, and I decided this was not the moment. No, I would confess all when she tried to use it, and only if it did not work.

We left the study and made our way to the front door, passing the sitting room on the way. The professor and Mrs Fairacre were seated together on the chaise, brandy glasses in hand, and the housekeeper appeared to be sharing a particularly humorous story. The professor slapped his knee, bent double with laughter, and Mrs Fairacre patted him on the back in a most tender fashion. I looked away quickly, embarrassed at witnessing their interaction.

'She cares for him a great deal,' murmured Roberta. 'They're a foolish pair, if I'm honest. He cares for her, but is blind to her devotion, while she is far too correct to declare her feelings for him. I suppose one day I shall have to sit them down and straighten things out, but in the meantime they circle each other like nervous debutantes.'

She opened the front door and we were met immediately by

driving rain, which lashed the ground and hid the street from view. 'I glanced out earlier,' said Roberta, raising her voice over the noise. 'You won't be surprised when I tell you I saw no sign of Mrs Fairacre's 'ghostie'.'

Braving the rain, we hurried to the iron gate and thence into the road. I stepped forward, intending to cross, and in that instant my world exploded in a shower of sparks and stars. I was hurled backwards, stunned, and I landed full-length in the muddy, puddle-strewn road, rolling over and over.

Through my pain I was dimly aware of a horse and carriage speeding past, hooves thundering and wheels rumbling on the road. There was a scream also, from behind me, and then I was lying on my back with the rain hammering my face.

Roberta crouched over me, her face white with shock. She was shouting at me for being such a fool, and then, in a panic, she turned and screamed for help. I had never seen her so upset, and a small part of me was pleased at her reaction. Unfortunately, the greater part of me hurt like the dickens.

Dimly, I became aware of the unpleasant cold seeping through my clothes, and I wished someone would pick me up, strip me down and lay me before a nice warm fire.

I think I passed out then, for my next recollection was Mrs Fairacre kneeling in the road beside me, with no concern for the mud and the streams of water running down the road. Her firm, expert hands felt every inch of me, and then she turned to Roberta and the professor, who were standing nearby. 'Nothing broken, thank goodness.'

'Will he live?' demanded Roberta.

'He's bruised and battered, but yes indeed. Come, let's get him to his feet.'

I cried out in pain as they helped me up, for my entire body was aflame. Slowly, with Roberta supporting one side and Mrs Fairacre the other, we limped towards the house, every step a shooting agony.

'Brandy,' said the professor. 'He must have brandy.'

'Did you leave any?' Roberta asked him.

'My dear, I am never without.' The professor hurried ahead, and by the time I reached the sitting room he had a large glass brimming with spirits. He held it to my mouth and I took a deep draught, and after that my body really was aflame, only this time it was from the inside out. I coughed and spluttered, and the professor tried to help by thumping me on the back.

This caused me even more pain, and Mrs Fairacre knocked his hand aside. 'Are you trying to kill the boy, you old fool?'

The professor retreated, and Mrs Fairacre looked me up and down. 'Those clothes will have to come off, and you'll need warming.' She nodded towards the glowing embers in the fireplace. 'Professor, will you wake Elsie and get her to build up a fire?'

'Oh, don't trouble her!' said Roberta. 'I will tend to it myself.'

'Good lass,' said the housekeeper. 'Now, let's see about these things.'

Then, to my discomfort, she removed my coat and shirt, while behind us Roberta stoked the fire until it was blazing. Next went my trousers, and as I stood there in my underthings, I felt Mrs Fairacre's hands exploring my ribs. 'You're going to be a riot of bruises,' she remarked. 'Roberta, will you fetch this young man some clothes?'

Roberta nodded, and left the room.

'What sort of fool crosses the road without looking first?' Mrs Fairacre asked me. 'You'll be no sort of husband to that girl if you're dead, will you?'

Sore and bruised as I was, I still managed to turn my head to stare.

'Oh come now,' said the housekeeper briskly. 'I wasn't born yesterday. You and she will make a perfect match one day, and don't you worry about the professor. He may think his daughter'll do well with some hoity toity lordship or other, but Roberta wasn't born to that nonsense.'

Stunned into silence, I could only stand there, swaying slightly in the heady warmth of that room. At that moment Roberta came back with my clothes, and she averted her eyes as I dressed. By now the brandy was taking effect, and despite the heavy knock I was beginning to feel like my old self once more. Briefly, I wondered whether the professor's brandy contained something extra, because he kept saying it was a restorative and that most certainly appeared to be the case. But that was a question for later, because at this moment we had more important matters to deal with.

Once dressed, I turned to Roberta. 'Come, let us find that spirit and capture it.'

'You cannot possibly venture out after that terrible accident!' she said. 'Why, I saw you thrown ten feet through the air!'

I flexed my arms and raised my feet one by one, trying not to wince at the pain. 'As you can see, I am perfectly fine,' I lied. 'Please, we must catch that spirit, for I would never forgive myself if it escaped thanks to my own foolish error.'

'If you're quite sure...' began Roberta. 'I mean, it's very brave of you.'

I saw the look of admiration in her eye, and at that moment I dare say I would have ventured from that room with four broken limbs. The warmth of the brandy, the heat from the fire and, above all, Roberta's approval, had all combined to make me feel invincible.

So, leaving Mrs Fairacre with a knowing grin on her face, Roberta and I headed out into the rain once more.

She'd collected the haversack at the doorway, and now she took my arm and walked close beside me, but whether to provide support or to prevent any more foolish accidents, I could not say. 'Mrs Fairacre said the spirit was heading...' Roberta's voice tailed off, for there was no need to say any more. The two of us stood together at the gate, and we were oblivious to the rain as we gazed upon the scene which met our eyes.

The street was deserted...of living beings, at least. Instead, at least a dozen ghostly phantasms were gliding along the rain-swept road, arms outstretched and ragged scraps of clothing billowing behind them. They were stretched out in a line, and even as we watched, another half-dozen followed them by. Their figures were indistinct, fuzzy around the edges, but I could make out the worn faces of the elderly, and the small, tragic figures of long-departed children.

Roberta looked down at the haversack, then back at the two dozen spirits majestically drifting past, and I could tell what she was thinking. Herding just one of them would be difficult, but to step out amongst this many was tantamount to suicide.

There was a flash of lightning in the distance, and the spirits seemed to be drawn towards it. They altered direction to pass directly through the row of houses opposite, and then Roberta and I were alone.

'Something calls them,' muttered Roberta. 'But what could it be?'

Even as she spoke, I knew. With growing dread I realised it had to be Sykes and his newly-built machine. The machine for which I had drawn up plans. The machine which I had designed to be a hundred times larger than the specimen the professor had built.

'Wait here,' said Roberta urgently. 'Father must see this, for he alone will know what to do.'

She left me there, and I found myself looking left and right into the darkness. What if I slipped away now, before I was forced to explain my part in all of this? I could find somewhere to spend the night – a hedgerow if necessary – and then make for my parents' house in the morning.

Then I cursed my cowardly thoughts. I was the cause of this latest madness, and I would face my obligations however onerous they might be.

Roberta returned soon after with the professor in tow. By the time they reached me, another pair of spirits had appeared, and the professor watched in silence as they passed through a house on the opposite side of the road. Moments later there was a bright flash of lightning, followed by a rumble of thunder.

'You see? It's almost as though your attractor is still operating,' said Roberta at last.

The professor gave her an aggrieved look. 'How can it be, when it lies in pieces?'

'Regardless, it was not powerful enough for this. Why, you'd need a machine ten times larger.'

'Or one hundred,' said the professor slowly, and he turned to look at me. 'Mr Jones, I recall you asking many questions about just such a machine. Something scaled up to six feet in height, you said.'

'But sir, the power requirements would make such a thing impossible. You told me so yourself!'

'Indeed. It would require the power of a thousand locomotives. Why, you could never hope to concentrate such an enormous amount of energy into one single location.'

There was another flash of lightning.

'Is it my imagination,' said Roberta, 'or is each lightning bolt striking in the exact same place?'

Flash!

This time there was absolutely no doubt, for the unimaginably powerful fork of pure energy was sustained for several seconds, twisting and crackling violently before it finally disappeared.

'Oh, Mr Jones,' groaned the professor, after the deafening peal of thunder finished beating upon our ears. 'Whatever have you done?'

32

We were seated around the dining table, with Roberta and the professor opposite me like judges at a court-martial. I only hoped they did not have black caps to wear after the process was complete, although I was not optimistic.

'This is your one chance, young man,' said the professor, his face like stone. 'You must speak the truth so that we might undo your deceitful actions.'

'Father,' began Roberta. 'Perhaps we should tackle the–'

'Silence!' The professor banged his fist on the table. 'I will have the truth, Mr Jones!'

I could see no way out, and so I recounted everything, from my first meeting with Sykes to my very last. I spoke tersely, summarising heavily, for frequent lightning flashes glared through the closed shutters and I knew time was pressing. The professor sat silently throughout, not making a single comment, but it was Roberta's reaction that tore the heart from my chest. Rather than suppressed anger, or dismay, she merely regarded me with pity.

By the time I had finished the sorry tale, barely ten minutes had passed.

'Right,' said the professor, his voice abnormally calm. 'I will deal with you later, but first Roberta and I must find out what hellish device you have unleashed on the world. And then we will put a stop to this Mr Sykes, and his machine along with him.'

'Sir, I beg you...let me help!' I pleaded. 'I know I've let you down, but–'

'Let me down?' demanded the professor. 'Let me *down?*' he cried, his voice rising. 'You have not just let me down, you have stolen my secrets and revealed them to my competitors, and you *still* had enough bare-faced cheek left over to attempt to ingratiate yourself with my daughter!'

Embarrassed and mortified, I sat shrouded in misery. No matter what I did, I knew the professor would sack me and Roberta would never speak to me again.

'Father, you are being unfair,' began Roberta. 'Mr Jones did try to fool this Sykes fellow, after all.'

'No! Do not stand up for him.'

'And as for ingratiating himself, nothing could be further from the truth. Mr Jones has been the model of respectability, and you can have no complaints in that direction.'

Briefly, I recalled the moment when I'd disrobed in front of Roberta, the lightning illuminating every curve and sinew of my body. If she brought *that* incident up, I suspected the professor would take up a poker and run me through on the spot.

'I will not have you defending him,' said the professor sharply. 'My mind is quite made up.'

'Of course,' said Roberta soothingly. 'But Mr Jones knows the design of this monstrous machine, and he could at least serve as an observer.'

'Well...'

'And he alone is able to recognise this William Sykes.'

Given Sykes had a vicious scar, easily visible, I felt this argument carried little weight. But the professor merely nodded, and I realised he was genuinely considering enlisting my help. I was about to plead my case once more, but Roberta saw me preparing to speak and gave me a tiny shake of the head. Then, master of controlling her father that she was, she continued.

'We shall need quite a lot of equipment, and Mr Jones can carry it for us.'

'If he doesn't make off with it, so as to sell it to the highest bidder,' muttered the professor, but his protests were symbolic now, and it was clear he'd already given in.

'Come, Septimus.' Roberta stood. 'Let us collect our things, and then the three of us will face this new challenge together.'

The professor did not object, and so I followed her from the room. Once outside, I turned to offer my apology, only to stop dead when I saw her look of contempt.

'Do not speak to me,' she hissed savagely. 'You have betrayed my father and you have betrayed my friendship. If you know what is good for you, you will aid us this evening and then depart this house forever. After that, you can be absolutely certain I do not wish to see you ever again, not for as long as I might live!'

I was still reeling from Roberta's menacing words as we gathered up the equipment. She barely spoke to me throughout, and whenever she was forced to communicate she maintained a cold, detached tone. In the dining room I'd been convinced that Roberta was firmly on my side, and that she would talk her father around just like she always did. Of course, there would have been a few days of strained relations with the professor afterwards, but I was certain I would prove my worth to him eventually.

But now it seemed Roberta had fooled me too, for she was even more incensed with my betrayal than her father had been. She'd soft-spoken him only to obtain my help with Sykes and his infernal machine, but afterwards I would be dismissed and shunned by both her and the professor.

Once we'd collected the equipment I ran upstairs for the pistol and ammunition, for I had no desire to meet Sykes without some kind of weapon at my disposal. Then, upon my return, Roberta and I met the professor at the front door. He took one look at me and snorted, and then our little procession left the house and made for the road. On the way, whilst still in the garden, the professor reached into his coat and took out a stoppered glass bottle. 'While you were busy I brewed this rather potent elixir.'

'Really, father,' said Roberta. 'Would you have me bring a magic wand as well?'

'No, no, you don't understand. This will keep minor spirits at bay, for they will not approach anyone wearing it.'

'Wearing?' demanded Roberta. 'Are we to pour it upon ourselves?'

'A dab here and there will be more appropriate, since there is so little to go around.' The professor removed the stopper, and Roberta and I instantly recoiled at the foul smell.

'Father, did it *have* to smell like raw fish?' she complained.

'You'll thank me when it saves your very soul,' said the professor. He covered the neck of the tiny bottle with his finger and tipped, then dabbed the fingertip onto his neck and clothes, repeating the dose several times. Then he offered the bottle to Roberta. After some hesitation she applied the foul-smelling brew, and then she looked at me. I expected her to pass the bottle, but instead she reached out and shook the contents onto my hair and clothing, getting several drops on my face for good measure. As she handled the bottle back to her father, I was certain I saw a smile lurking on her lips.

Then we left the garden, the three of us smelling like a steaming great heap of fish guts. The rain was lighter, thank goodness, but I was so dispirited by the Twickhams' dislike of me that even a thorough drenching couldn't have made me feel any worse.

'Mind the traffic,' said Roberta curtly, as we approached the road.

I thought she'd found a speck of concern for me, but her next words dispelled that notion.

'If you step in front of another horse, it'll waste even more time.'

'Some people are just careless,' muttered the professor, and he signalled to an approaching cab.

I recalled one or two occasions where he'd blithely stepped into the road without looking, getting roundly cursed in the process, but he seemed completely unaware of the hypocrisy.

The cab swept past, muddy water flying up from its wheels, and I saw a couple huddled within. They were using a cloak to keep the worst of the rain and dirt at bay, and then they were past and I saw no more. The professor muttered under his breath, and Roberta turned on him. 'Did you really expect to find a cab this late at night? Why, most of the drivers will be home sleeping!'

'As we should be,' growled the professor, and he gave me a dark look.

Another cab approached, eventually, and this time it came to a halt before us. The driver looked on as we loaded the equipment, and then the three of us crowded into a narrow seat designed for two. 'Where to guv?' demanded the driver, once we were settled. The look on his face told me he'd caught a whiff of our fishy scent, but a fare was a fare and he did not comment.

The professor pointed. 'Follow that lightning!'

After a surprised glance at the three of us, the driver shrugged and clicked his tongue at the horse. The cab lurched off, and soon we were moving quickly through the wet, empty streets. The lanterns on either side of the carriage picked out falling raindrops, but their illumination barely reached the horse's swaying rump.

We travelled without speaking, our journey accompanied by the rhythmic sound of hooves, the rumble of wooden wheels, and the patter of rain on the roof. Occasionally a bolt of lightning rent the horizon, followed shortly after by a loud thunderclap. Of spirits and phantasms, there was no sign.

Roberta sat in the middle, pressed against me, and I could feel her warmth through my clothes. Unfortunately, that was the side of my body which had been struck by the passing carriage earlier, and every movement of the cab caused me to draw in my breath with pain. I'd also suffered numerous small puncture wounds from Sykes' dagger, when he'd accosted me and led me to the park, but these were literally pinpricks in comparison.

We'd been moving for around half an hour now, and were appreciably closer to the lightning. Each flash was followed almost instantaneously by an ear-splitting bang, and even the weary horse was beginning to start and shy with every fresh assault on the senses. Eventually, the driver was forced to stop. 'I can't get any closer,' he shouted. 'Horse'll bolt otherwise.'

The professor paid him, and we clambered down with our bags.

There were two knapsacks, and Roberta took one and silently handed me the other. The professor led the way down a narrow alley, carrying his weapon with the forked tip. Halfway along, a spirit appeared without warning from within the grimy brick wall, and he thrust at it with the weapon. Sparks flew, and the spirit fled instantly. 'Did you see that?' cried the professor exaltedly. 'These mindless phantasms are no match for my scientific prowess.'

We continued down the alley until we reached a large warehouse. The hair on my head felt like it was standing on end, and I jumped as a tremendous bolt of lightning flashed down. The noise was indescribable, like a ship's broadside at close range, and I clamped my hands to my ears.

'What's that up there?' shouted the professor, pointing at the roof.

We all saw it: a metal pole extending skywards, with a thick cable leading down from the lowest end before vanishing through the brick wall. This cable glowed with heat, and no wonder as it was carrying repeated bursts of energy from the lightning. The bricks around the mounting were seared and blackened, and I wondered how long it might be before the structure was destroyed by the unfathomable power.

'We must get inside quickly,' said Roberta. 'It's far too dangerous out here.'

Knowing what might await us inside, I felt it might be equally dangerous within, but I said nothing. In the meantime Roberta had found a door, and she opened it without hesitation, leading us into the large building.

I'm not sure what I expected to see, but the sight that met my eyes was like nothing I'd experienced before. The interior of the warehouse was a large, empty space, apart from the huge machine sitting in the dead centre. This machine was a copy of the professor's attractor, only built to a far larger scale. It stood over six feet tall, with an outer cage of thick oak beams and an inner fashioned from a framework of iron. In the middle, supported by this heavy cage, an orange-segment rotor was spinning so fast the very air hummed. I could just make out a large piece of glass twice the size of my fist at the very core of the machine, and even now the first vestiges of darkness were beginning to reach out from the heart of the machine. This spreading darkness was shot through with flashes of red and purple, which bathed the interior of the warehouse with unholy light.

'It's a copy of my attractor!' cried the professor. 'But heavens, what a size!'

Then a figure stepped from the shadows, and my heart near stopped as I recognised the scar-faced man. Sykes seemed amused at our presence, laughing to himself as he saw our haversacks and the professor's sword weapon. 'You poor fools!' he cried. 'Do you think to stop me with such trinkets? Why, my machine will tear the very soul from your bones!'

I expected a robust reply from the professor and Roberta, but instead they seemed completely dumbfounded. Rooted to the spot, they stared at Sykes as though in a daze. The man's scar was vivid in the unearthly light from the machine, but that was hardly terrifying enough to affect them so. For an instant I wondered whether some property of the machine had frozen them, but then the professor suddenly came alive.

'No, it cannot be,' he declared, stirring himself at last. 'It's impossible!'

Roberta seemed even more surprised, and she barely managed a strangled cry. 'Cousin *Edgar*?'

33

Of the four people present I think I was the most surprised of all. The scar-faced man, William Sykes...*he* was Roberta's cousin Edgar? The man who used to work for the professor, and who attempted to steal his secrets? The man who went mad and scrawled *KILL THEM ALL* right across the ledgers? The man who sneaked into the house at night and left a bloodied dagger inside the very desk he once used? No wonder he'd known where my study was, for it was once his very own!

Then I frowned, for something had occurred to me. The professor and Roberta had both told me Edgar was dead. Clearly this wasn't the case, so why had they lied to me? And why had Sykes himself–Edgar, rather–told me he'd been confined to an asylum?

I was still puzzling over this when I heard an unexpected sound. It was the professor, and he was laughing.

'Edgar, you're a complete fool. Why, you could barely tie your own shoclaces without making a complete hash of things, and you will never convince me you built this...this contraption by yourself. Who are you working with, eh? Who's really behind this?'

'Oh, you'd like to believe that, wouldn't you?' said Edgar coldly. 'Once, you belittled me at every opportunity. You treated me like a wayward child, and would not entrust to me a single one of your secrets. And then, when I sought to branch out and learn on my own, you accused me of theft and set the police upon me! Well, look upon my creation now! See what I have constructed with my own two hands!'

The professor did look, and he did not seem particularly impressed. 'Shoddy workmanship. Inaccurate joints. Rough-hewn timbers, more suited to roof beams than the purpose to which you've put them. Yes, maybe you did build this thing after all.'

I groaned, for the professor was engaging in his favourite sport: needling his enemies. But surely this was the worst possible time?

'Mock me all you want!' cried Edgar, a light of madness in his eyes. 'You enjoy catching spirits, do you not? Why not try your hand at the horrors soon to emerge? Do you think that feeble weapon of yours will hold back the powerful phantoms about to descend on us? Why, you will scream and scream with impunity as these denizens of the darkness tear your daughter's life from her very body!'

The professor turned to Roberta. 'The poor boy was never particularly adept at composition, was he? His prose was always a touch overblown for my taste.'

This aside seemed to tip Edgar over the edge, and he advanced, screaming at us. 'An ancient power grows stronger by the minute, and you can do nothing to stop it,' he spat. 'Soon, it will consume every soul in the city, and after that, the entire world!'

'If you say so,' murmured the professor.

All the time they were arguing, the machine's hum had been growing louder, and now the sound of it was beating at our ears.

Darkness was spreading from the spinning crystal heart of the huge device, and I felt an unnatural chill in the air.

'They're coming!' shouted Edgar. 'And before they feast on the rest of the planet, they will take your souls. I will seal you into this building and watch your doom, for that is my revenge!'

I'd slipped my hand into my pocket during this outburst, and now I withdrew the gun. Edgar saw it, and froze. Roberta frowned at it, and then at me. And the professor merely stared. 'Good heavens!' he said.

'Oh, so that's where it got to,' said Edgar, quite unconcerned. 'I sought to retrieve it the other night, but you seem to have beaten me to it.'

I pointed the gun at him. 'Turn off that machine.'

'No.'

Frowning, I raised the gun, aiming directly at his head. 'I said to switch if off.'

'And I said no no no,' replied Edgar, in a chirpy, sing-song voice.

'Septimus, you can't shoot him,' muttered Roberta.

'But we must stop that thing!' I cried, nodding towards the machine. Already I could see the shadowy, indistinct forms that were struggling to emerge, and I knew that before too long we would be overrun. I was tempted to empty the revolver at it, but I was not sure I could hit anything at that distance, and I certainly wasn't going to approach any closer. In any case, the machine had already stored a vast amount of power, and who knew what kind of explosion I might unleash?

'Look out!' cried Roberta suddenly.

I spun around and saw a spirit coming straight for me, its blank eyes fixed on my face, and its hands outstretched as though it were going to strangle me. Then I heard the professor's warning cry, and when I turned again I saw half a dozen spirits coming towards the three of us. The professor raised his weapon, ready to fight, but then the phantasms slowed their progress towards us, until they were circling us without drawing closer. Now and then, one would make a move towards us, only to recoil.

'It's that foul fish-guts potion of yours!' cried Roberta. 'It's working!'

I heard an angry howl, and turned to see Edgar practically gnashing his teeth. He looked like a spoiled little boy refused a treat, stamping one foot and shaking his fist at us. The transformation from the cool, collected Sykes was all but complete, and I wondered how the man had held himself together in my presence. I guessed that meeting the professor and Roberta had shaken his mind loose, and he was now little more than a raving lunatic.

Then the spirits ceased circling us, and instead headed directly for Edgar. He took one look at their long-dead faces and clawed hands and fled. Moments later, we heard a solid thump as the outer door closed, followed by the troubling sound of a bolt shooting home. Edgar had departed, but he'd also trapped us with the active machine and the hungry spirits.

'Never have I been so fond of rotten fish,' muttered Roberta.

'Such a fool of a boy,' muttered the professor. 'Now, let us stop this machine and leave this place.'

'Yes, but how?' demanded Roberta. 'I would need a mallet the size of a coal shed to smash this machine.'

'I could try shooting the crystal,' I suggested.

'Do not even think of it,' warned the professor. 'There will be no destroying or shooting or smashing of any kind until I've made a proper inspection.' Warily, he approached the machine, and when he judged himself close enough he gave it a thorough looking over.

Then he turned to face us. 'This is quite the worst workmanship I have encountered in my entire life. It might bring a few stray spirits from nearby hauntings, but I'd stake my life on the fact that it would never, and I mean never, bring spirits into this world from the next.' Here, he paused to gaze upon our faces. We, in turn, were staring in rapt fascination. Heartened by our avid attention, the professor continued. 'All we must do is knock out one of these poorly-made pins, and I assure you this entire contraption will fall apart before our very eyes. Now, I suggest that we–'

What he was about to suggest we would never know, because the professor now realised that Roberta and I weren't so much gazing at *him* in rapt fascination, but rather the machine *behind* him. Indeed, it was not the machine itself which we found so interesting, but the pair of clawed red demons that were even now emerging from within it. Fully twelve feet tall, with broad faces and arms as thick as tree trunks, these were no mere phantasms but seemingly living flesh and blood...if such an evil-looking creature even had blood.

These arrivals were directly behind the professor, and Roberta and I were so overcome by the horror we were quite unable to speak. They rose higher and higher, towering over him, and then some shadow or change in the light alerted the professor to his danger. Our wild gestures and pointing fingers may also have given him a clue. Thus the professor turned, sword at the ready, to come face to face with the two huge demons. Then, very slowly, he lowered the sword and backed away.

One of the demons sniffed the air, and I hoped with all my might that these creatures were as averse to the professor's potion as the earlier spirits had been. My hopes were dashed when the creature slowly and deliberately ran a forked tongue around its gleaming red lips.

'This would be an excellent time to stop the machine,' called the professor nervously, as he backed away from the demons.

I knew he was right, but at that moment the machine was just behind the giant creatures, and to reach it we would have to first defeat them. Meanwhile the menacing creatures continued to advance on the professor in a most unhurried fashion. There was no reason for haste, since they had us trapped in an enclosed space with very little in the way of defences. First, we possessed an electric sword that would barely register against their scaly hides. And second, a revolver wielded by a bookkeeper who had never fired a gun in his life. We weren't so much trapped, as enclosed in an oversized feeding trough.

I feared the professor would be torn asunder before my very eyes, his innards splashed across the floor. Then, these creatures would come for me, ripping into my battered and bruised body with those piercing claws. And finally, the pair of them would corner Roberta, and who knew what terrors these slavering otherworldly beasts might subject her to before she too was torn limb from limb?

I was tempted to fire my gun, but the professor was bravely taunting the beasts with his sword, waving it at them whilst calling them every name under the sun, and I was worried I might accidentally shoot him. He'd retreated from the machine, leading the creatures away, and that's when I realised his intent. With the way clear, Roberta could approach the thing and bring it to a stop! I looked to her, but she had come to the same conclusion as I, and was already in motion.

Then one of the beasts spotted her. It turned away from the professor, who redoubled his efforts to attract its attention, but to no avail. The beast took one step towards Roberta, and I realised it would end her quickly if I did not intervene. So, I raised my pistol, sighted along the barrel, and squeezed the trigger.

The shot was tremendously loud, and the gun bucked in my hand, almost leaping free. As the smoke cleared I saw the beast was now looking directly at me...and it had murder in its yellowed eyes. Where the bullet went I had no idea, but at least the creature had abandoned Roberta. I encouraged it further by waving the gun and shouting at the top of my voice.

The beast lowered its head and began to stalk me, padding along on its clawed feet. It was as tall as a horse standing on its hind legs, and with its barrel chest and thick legs it looked twice as sturdy. I had no hopes of surviving the thing, should it get close enough, and I decided to save my ammunition until I was looking right into its eyes.

I heard a muffled thud, and I looked around the creature to see Roberta hammering at a joint with a block of wood. I saw her intent, for if one part of the machine were to collapse, the rest would fly apart from the stresses of the spinning core. What those same forces would do to Roberta when they were unleashed, I did not wish to consider. She clearly wasn't thinking about the outcome either, for she was raining sickening blows on the machine without pause, as though determined to smash the entire structure to pieces with her bare hands.

I was still looking at Roberta when I heard the professor cry out. Turning, I saw him pinned on the ground, the beast crouched over him like a hound from the depths of hell. I raised my gun and sighted, but my hand shook and half the time I was looking at the beast over my sights, while the other half I seemed to be aiming at the professor. Then, out of the corner of my eye, I saw the beast closest to me spring into action.

Turning towards it, I had to raise my gun near-vertically to bring it to bear, for the beast was in the midst of a tremendous leap. Then, as it descended towards me, I closed my eyes, turned my head and pulled the trigger as fast as I could.

The first five pulls on the trigger yielded deafening explosions. The last three, mocking clicks. Then I was cannoned into by the huge creature, and the gun flew from my hand as I was thrown to the floor. I rolled as I hit, more to protect my already-damaged side than from some form of acrobatic training, and even as I rolled away, over and over, I felt the ground shake as the beast thudded down.

I risked a look, and saw the huge red creature lying face down, limbs twitching. I thought it might rise again, come after me, and I looked around for the revolver so that I might quickly load it from the pouch in my coat pocket. Then I saw my gun, and my heart sank. It was wedged between the monster's knee and the floor.

'Help!'

The faint cry came from my left, and I turned to see the professor still trapped by his beast. But instead of ripping his chest open to devour the contents, as I expected it to do, it was holding one clawed hand above the professor's face, palm down. I thought I saw a shimmering light between them, and I wondered whether it was trying to drain the professor's very life force.

I glanced again at the beast I'd felled, but it lay still aside from the occasional twitch of a limb. I hurried closer, and then took my life into my hands as I crouched next to that hideously muscled leg and tried to retrieve the gun. Pull as I might it would not come free, and so I was forced to take the scaly leg between both hands and lift it with all my might. The second it shifted I swept the gun from underneath with my foot, and then I released that horrid limb and took up the weapon once more. With fumbling fingers I loaded cartridges, spilling several in my haste. After three I gave up, snapping the weapon closed before charging the professor's beast. This creature was intent on its victim, and did not even look round as I skidded to a halt, aimed the muzzle of my revolver at the side of its head and pulled the trigger.

Three shots rang out, and the creature toppled off the professor to lie hunched on the floor, quivering and jerking in its death throes. The professor moved weakly, and I was about to crouch beside him to offer my help when I realised more of these creatures might yet emerge from Edgar's contraption. I loaded the gun, fully this time, and then set it beside myself as I checked the professor. He looked dazed, but I was pleased to see a flicker of recognition in his eyes. I was no medical expert, but when I checked his body for wounds there were none that I could see.

'Look out, it's coming apart!'

Roberta's cry was barely in time. I turned to see one support from the machine's outer frame flapping wildly, the six-inch oak beam moving like a twig in a hurricane. Roberta was scrabbling backwards on all fours, trying to get clear, but had barely gone six feet when the entire ramshackle machine was torn apart. Solid oak beams flew outwards like oversized javelins, scattering smaller pieces all over the floor. One of these struck Roberta on the side of the head, luckily just a glancing blow, but it was enough to knock her unconscious. Others slammed into the walls, some piercing the brickwork with ear-shattering blows. Just as I thought the worst was over, the spinning array of orange-segments at the heart of the machine lurched free.

The core spun like a top, moving first this way and then the other. I thought it was going to run into Roberta's unconscious form, and feared the fast-spinning segments would chew her body apart. Fortunately, it ran into fallen debris, and changed direction. Still spinning at hellish speed, the core moved towards the nearest wall, where it struck with a chattering sound before disintegrating against the brickwork. Fragments flew the length and breadth of the warehouse, and it was a miracle none of us were struck.

I began to breathe again, until I realised the only illumination in the room had come from the machine's core, and now that it was destroyed the warehouse was in near darkness. Worse, I could see a dozen phantasms advancing on us, splitting up so as to reach the three of us at once. The large demons were dead, but it seemed the spirits had not finished with us yet. These were visible to the naked eye, and I guessed they were more powerful than any phantasm I had encountered before.

I looked around for the professor's sword, but it was hopeless. Why, I could barely see a hand waved in front of my face! And as for the pistol, it was worse than useless against ghosts. I began to back away from the encroaching spirits, but to either side of me I knew the professor and Roberta were both lying helpless. I had a vague idea of the professor's location, and as he'd been carrying the sword I decided to try and reach him. Movement was next to impossible, and I stumbled over fragments of the machine, tripped on pieces of wooden beam, and almost rolled my ankle on a stray metal bolt, which skidded from underfoot as I trod on it.

Then my foot encountered something soft, and I crouched to feel the professor's unconscious form. Working outwards, I sought the weapon he must have dropped nearby. All the while I glanced over my shoulder at the spirits, which were steadily moving closer. They made no sound, and to me that was all the more frightening.

I got further and further from the professor, while the three groups of spirits advanced on each of us. Even as I felt around, my desperation growing, I saw the first group reach Roberta. I prayed the awful fish-scented elixir would deter them, but either it had worn off, or these phantasms were stronger-willed. They didn't even hesitate, their ghostly fingers reaching for her, clutching at her unconscious body, and I saw one phantasm reaching right into her chest. I wanted to run across, screaming at them, but I knew that sword was our only hope. Without it, we were all doomed.

To my horror I saw that ghostly hand withdrawing, and a gleaming strand of light came with it. Roberta's back arched, her chest thrusting upwards, and I saw her moving uncontrollably as the very soul was torn from her body. Then I heard the professor groaning nearby, and I turned to see a spirit perched above his chest also, tugging and pulling at a similar strand of light.

I knew instinctively that once the bond between that strand of light and the host body was broken, there would be no coming back. At that point, Roberta and the professor would be dead.

I cast around frantically, with no thought for my own safety, and I cried out with relief as my fingers encountered something cold and narrow. I felt along the thing in both directions, and when I felt the leather-wrapped grip I realised to my delight that I had finally located the professor's sword. Standing up, I activated it and brandished it at the closest spirits, all of which drew back in fear.

That's when the true horror of the situation dawned on me. Already, the strand from Roberta's chest was weakening, and I knew she had but seconds to live. But she was sixty feet to my right, while to my left, forty feet in the opposite direction, lay the professor. His strand too was weakening, and he was just as close to death.

I knew then that I could only reach one of them in time. I knew then that one of them was going to die.

Just as the woman in my dream had warned me: *You can only save one.*

34

With no time for a rational decision I let instincts take over, and suddenly I was running towards Roberta, shouting and brandishing my sword. As I sprinted across the warehouse floor, the tails of my coat flapping behind me, I tried to justify my decision. Roberta was younger and fitter than the professor, and if I managed to revive her, the two of us might still save him. She had more life ahead of her. The demon might have quite taken the professor's wits away, leaving him as near death as made no difference.

All of these excuses sounded weak, even to me, but I refused to admit to myself that maybe, just maybe, I was choosing to save Roberta because of some ill-fated romantic notions on my part.

I took the last three steps towards the spirits menacing Roberta, my sword raised to strike. In that split second the terrifying tableau was imprinted on my mind. A vibrant cloud of pure energy was coalescing in mid-air between the three spirits, and it was connected to Roberta by a thin, twisting spiral of the same material. On the ground, Roberta was turning her head this way and that, mumbling incoherently as her back arched to an impossible angle. While the first spirit continued to draw this life force from her very body, the other two spirits appeared to be suckling on the cloud of energy, as though trying to consume Roberta's essence.

Well, I would soon put a stop to that!

The forked tip of the sword plunged into the first spirit, and there was a vivid flash as it pierced the filmy, veil of a body. The spirit flew back like a curtain blowing in the wind, distorted and flapping wildly in its desperate attempt to escape. The other two were still feasting, and I turned the sword on them, jabbing and thrusting like an enraged musketeer. Sparks flew from the tip of my weapon, and the ghostly spirits retreated instantly, disgorging long streamers of Roberta's life force. Even as I stood over her body, defending her from the phantasms, she relaxed her spine. Then, to my eternal relief, the coalescing energy cloud began to return to her, seeking its rightful home.

I glanced across at the professor, and to my despair I saw three spirits heading away from him. Even at this distance, I could see they carried his life force with them, the vibrant cloud entirely in their possession with no trace of connection to the professor's inert body. Slowly, they descended into the floor itself, until they disappeared. The professor was gone, then. Lost to us. Only his body remained, lifeless and somehow smaller and more vulnerable than I expected.

I was struck forcibly by his death, but there was no time to grieve. We had been facing nine spirits in total, and the three I had not yet faced were approaching me from behind. Also, the three I'd driven away from Roberta were growing bold, returning inch by inch. I stepped over her and waved the sword at the spirits as they got closer and closer, but even though the forked tip made contact, it no longer had any effect. My heart sinking, I realised Roberta and I would soon join the professor if I did not think up a new defence.

Flash!

Lightning struck the building, infusing the remains of Edgar's machine with power. The thick wooden beams were long gone, but the metal cage, bent and twisted, sparked and crackled with electrical energy. It was maybe twenty feet behind me, and it gave me an idea.

I crouched, taking Roberta's hand firmly in mine, and slowly I dragged her backwards across the wooden floor. The spirits drifted after us as we made for the ruined attractor, all six now having joined forces. Now and then one of them darted forward, and I jabbed wildly with the sword to keep them at bay.

I could now hear the crackling of the ruined machine right behind me, the metal frame still drawing power from some unknown source. Touch it, and I knew Roberta and I would be killed instantly. But that was not my intention.

Judging I was close enough, I turned to examine the charred and twisted remains of the machine. Metal bars protruded from the wreckage, fat electrical sparks arcing between several of them to fill the air with noise. Then I turned to look at the advancing spirits, and to my horror I saw that they had hemmed us in, pinning us against the device. Even now, two of them were preparing to drive their ghostly hands into Roberta's chest, and another was reaching for me. They were so close they overlapped, forming a glowing wall of ghostly bodies.

I looked down at the sword, then over my shoulder, and I knew this was our only chance. Taking the sword carefully by the leather-wrapped grip, I touched the metal pommel against the nearest piece of metalwork. There was a crackle as they made contact, and I almost dropped the thing as I felt a surge of immense power through the grip. The sword glowed as tracers of electricity ran up

316

the blade, and all of a sudden the forked tip of the weapon shone like the midday sun, bathing the gloomy interior of the warehouse with wholesome golden light. This grew brighter and brighter, forcing me to narrow my eyes to mere slits, and then six bolts of lightning shot out from the end. Each took up a phantasm and drove it backwards in a heartbeat, shredding the ghostly bodies like dandelion heads, and leaving only the merest trace of the foul beings twisting and tumbling in the glare.

The golden glow faded, with only the crackling, sparking machine behind me to light the scene. I discovered the sword had grown red hot, the heat even now radiating uncomfortably through the leather wrapping, and I dropped the thing hurriedly. Then I crouched next to Roberta, feeling her wrist for a pulse.

'Septimus?' she murmured.

Relieved, I broke into a smile. 'They're gone,' I said.

'And father?'

My heart stilled, for in the events of the past few minutes I had entirely forgotten the professor. 'I–I'm sorry. He–'

Roberta threw off my hand and struggled up. 'He what?'

'The spirits.' I hung my head. 'They...took him.'

'No!' she breathed. Before I could stop her, she scrambled to her feet and ran towards the professor's crumpled form. She threw herself upon him, her head to his chest, and my blood ran cold as she let out an unearthly, wailing cry.

I felt my heart go out to Roberta as she sobbed uncontrollably, her face buried in her father's chest. I wanted to approach, to offer what little comfort I could, but I knew there might still be danger lurking in that accursed warehouse. The stronger spirits had been vanquished, but lesser phantasms might be surrounding us at that very moment. The first we would know of it would be their cold, ghostly touch.

As Roberta's cries of grief rang out, I made my way to the haversacks containing our equipment. I searched them quickly and located the spectacles with the twin lenses, which I pressed to my nose. Then, with my nerves a-jangle, I scanned the gloomy interior of the warehouse for enemies. I saw Roberta immediately, her body enveloped in a vibrant aura. Then I frowned and looked again, for there was a second aura beside her, lying on the ground. I removed the spectacles, looked with my naked eye, then replaced them. There could be no doubt, it was the professor's body giving off the aura, faint though it was. I was on the point of crying out to Roberta, but then my hopes were dashed as I realised it was no more than a latent image. My face grim, I turned away to inspect the rest of the warehouse, verifying that we were indeed alone.

Or were we?

I looked towards a nearby section of floor, an area through which I knew the phantasms had carried the professor's life force. The merest hint of a glowing line protruded through the floor, a strand as thin as sewing cotton. I approached cautiously, and observed that the line led away towards Roberta and the professor. I peered over the top of my glasses at it, lest it were merely some trick of the light, but it promptly vanished. Then, using the eyeglasses once more, I began to follow the thin, winding trail. As I approached Roberta she turned her tear-stained face towards me, and that's when I noticed the terminating point of this fine strand of light. It was attached to the professor!

I dropped to my knees, hardly daring to hope. Easing Roberta aside, I pressed the side of my head to the professor's chest, listening intently.

Nothing...nothing...nothing...*Thud!*

I waited several seconds for a second beat, just to confirm my suspicions, and the moment I heard it I turned to Roberta, taking her hands in mine. She stared at me in confusion, and I could barely form the words as I burst out with the truth. 'Your father's life force is still attached, albeit by the thinnest thread imaginable. Roberta...he lives!'

Roberta stared at me, then bent to listen for herself. 'Oh, you surely are a tough old goat,' she murmured lovingly, and then she stood, suddenly businesslike. 'Come, we must hurry if we are to save him.'

'Yes, but to where?' I asked. 'They carried his life force directly through a solid floor!'

'And what do you think lies beneath that floor?' demanded Roberta.

I hazarded a guess. 'A cellar?'

'If so, there will be a trapdoor.'

I picked up the sword and handed it to her, and then I took the revolver from my pocket. It was useless against spirits, but I knew Edgar might still be lurking. If he tried to prevent me from saving the professor I would shoot him dead without hesitation.

Together we made our way around the perimeter of the warehouse, stepping over fallen oak beams and scattered bricks. Finally we found what we were looking for: a square trapdoor with a recessed iron handle. We lifted it, only to turn our heads as a dank smell rose from the darkness below. 'A cellar, or a sewer?' I remarked.

There were wide steps below, rough stone ones, and Roberta and I descended them arm in arm. I still wore the glasses, but the glow from the sword's forked tip gave just enough light to see by. When we reached the bottom we turned left, away from the wall, and Roberta gripped my arm. 'Do you see it?' she demanded.

I did indeed, for the faint trail came through the ceiling above and led away into the darkness. After pointing the way, we followed the trail for a dozen steps or more, passing several broken, rotting barrels alive with the rustle and scurry of rats. The trail seemed to grow lighter as we continued, and then it stopped completely. I removed the glasses to see a brick wall across our path, stretching from one side of the cellar to the other.

'Well?' demanded Roberta.

I turned to her, my buoyant mood suddenly brought low. 'It goes right through,' I said quietly. 'I'm sorry, Roberta. I think...I think we really have lost him.'

She snorted. 'Really, Septimus? You give up so easily?'

'I do not wish to!' I said heatedly. 'But you and I cannot pass through solid rock!'

'You would think so, but I have lived in this city longer than you. Come, there is still time.'

Taking my hand in hers, she led me up the steps and out of the cellar. In the warehouse we paused only to collect our things, and then I looked towards the professor's unnaturally still form. 'Should we...I mean, do you think it will be all right to leave him?'

'It pains me, but we cannot take him with us,' said Roberta evenly. 'In any case, first we must escape this prison ourselves, for if I am not mistaken dearest cousin Edgar locked the door as he departed.'

She was correct, because the metal entry door was sealed tight. After giving it a hefty kick or two, Roberta uttered an oath. Then she turned to look along the brick wall, which had been pierced in several places by oak beams from the destroyed machine. 'Help me lift one of those,' she said. 'Perhaps we can finish the job it started.'

We laid down our weapons and picked up the nearest beam, staggering under the weight. We carried it away from the wall, and then ran towards it with the beam held under our arms in the manner of a battering ram. We were aiming at a section which had already been holed, and the end of the beam struck the damaged brickwork with a sickening blow, knocking a dozen bricks flying. Repeating our efforts, we soon made a hole large enough to climb through. Roberta scrambled through first, and once she was on the other side she took the haversacks from me. Then I followed, clutching the weapons.

The rain and thunder had ceased, but the air was chill and a dense mist rose from the cobbles, making it hard to see. Each streetlamp was like a beacon in the darkness, and we hurried from one to the next, completely alone in that deathly quiet part of the city. I glanced around, still fearful that the scar-faced man might seek his revenge on us.

'Edgar does not have the brains for this,' said Roberta suddenly.

'What do you mean?'

'He was not a great thinker,' she said. 'In addition, he was a follower, not a leader. Septimus, there is someone else behind all of this, you may take my word on it.'

'Someone worse?' I asked her. 'That idea is troubling indeed.'

'Whoever it is, they will not take my father from me,' declared Roberta, her face grim and determined. 'Ah, here is our destination.'

— 35 —

I stopped, for directly ahead of us was the red brick building of a station. The name above the entrance read Westminster, and there were metal gates below, closed and padlocked. Beyond these was Stygian darkness of the most oppressive kind. 'The underground!' I said in astonishment, for suddenly all was clear. 'But...it's closed for the night!'

'You think I mean to buy tickets?' asked Roberta, with a weak smile. She led me towards the locked gates, and after looking up and down the road to make sure we were not observed, she set to work with a slender piece of metal taken from the knapsack. It took her a minute or two, but eventually there was a metallic click and the padlock came free. The chain rattled as she withdrew it, and then we passed through, quickly closing the gate behind us.

'Replace the padlock, but do not close the hasp,' Roberta told me. 'We may have to leave this place in a hurry.'

I did as I was told, and then we took the steps down to the platforms, our footsteps reverberating around the big tiled area. At the bottom Roberta climbed down onto the tracks without hesitation, then held her hands out so that I might pass down the equipment. I joined her, and she pointed down the tracks towards the gaping mouth of the tunnel. 'We go that way.'

'I hope they're not running any trains,' I muttered, as we strode along parallel to the rails.

'Do not concern yourself about those. Rather you should be seeking my father's trail.'

'Yes, of course.'

We walked on, with only the noise of our footsteps on the clinker to break the silence. Roberta guided me, walking close, for my vision was badly affected by the lenses in my spectacles, and in addition I was peering to my left and right as I tried to pick up the trail. Deep within, I feared the spirits may have carried the professor's life force to some deep dark hole far below the Earth, in which case he was already as good as dead. But I said nothing, for there was still a slender hope and I did not wish to trouble Roberta unduly.

'Do you see anything?' she asked me in a whisper.

I shook my head.

'Tell me if you detect the slightest hint of a trail. I do not care if you are mistaken.'

'Are you sure you don't want to wear these?' I asked her, indicating the glasses.

'No, I trust you.'

My heart warmed at her words, and I redoubled my efforts, staring into every shadow with my eyes open wide. I scarcely dared blink, even though they watered from the effort. And then, as I was beginning to lose hope, I saw it. 'There!' I muttered, pointing at the faint strand of light which emerged from the curved brick wall. 'It leads away from us, down the tunnel.'

'Faster,' said Roberta, and she all but dragged me along with her.

I was following the trail, and after two hundred yards or so I took Roberta's arm. 'Left here,' I whispered, pointing.

There was a big opening in the tunnel wall, surrounded by unfinished brickwork and piles of broken earth. All of a sudden I recognised the place, for we'd passed these diggings on the way to the Snetton house just a day or two earlier. It was the new underground tunnel, the one where a collapse had killed several workers.

'In there?' Roberta asked me.

'I'm afraid so.' Then I noticed something even more troubling. 'The line we're following...it's getting thinner.' It was true, for now I could barely see the fine thread in places, as though it were stretching to breaking point.

'We must hurry!' said Roberta desperately.

We had no choice, and so we strode into the diggings with no regard for our own safety. There were tools stacked against the walls, and fortunately there were flickering oil lanterns to illuminate the way, the glass in the frames dirty and stained. I wondered why there were not gas lights instead, but then I imagined the danger if one should go out. The tunnels would fill with explosive fumes, which would be ignited by the first train to pass by.

Then we rounded a bend, and I saw a patch of ghostly light ahead. Three phantasms were drifting along the tunnel, heading away from us, and they bore the professor's life spirit between them. Beyond, further around the corner, a dull red glow lit the tunnel. 'Do you see them?' I asked Roberta.

'I do indeed,' she muttered grimly, and she tightened her grip on the sword.

We caught up, moving as quickly and as silently as possible, and more details were revealed to us. There was something wrong with the life force they carried, for instead of a gleaming, coalescing ball of vital energy, it was weak and dull. It seemed a life force could not survive long outside of the host body, and vice versa.

'They're killing him,' growled Roberta. 'I must put an end to this.'

'That weapon alone will not stop them,' I said. 'In the warehouse, I had to add power from your cousin's machine to defeat the phantasms attacking us.'

She stopped dead and looked at me. 'Could you not have mentioned this a little earlier? At times, Septimus, I really do wonder about you.'

'I'm sorry, I–'

'No matter. Help me with the things.'

We placed the knapsacks on the ground, and Roberta used the light of a nearby lantern to dig out the items she needed. A handful of metal discs, the trap with its suspended cylinder, and the small glass vial with its stopper...she placed them in a line, then retrieved a tool with a bulbous handle and wide jaws at both ends. Finally, she took out the net made from copper wire.

'Do you think those will work?' I asked.

'I believe you will have your answer a few minutes from now.' Roberta gathered the items and stood. 'Leave the rest here,' she told me.

I took the net and the discs, and we set off after the spirits. They were drifting slowly along the tunnel, following a gentle curve to the right. Ahead of them was that baleful red glow, and as we got closer I turned to Roberta. 'Where do you think they're taking your father?'

'They are not taking him anywhere,' she said firmly. 'Even if I must stand my own body in the way.'

'Yes, but–' I gestured towards the glow. 'What lies around the corner? Do you think it is the men at the tunnel face?' Even as I asked the question, I knew it could not be so. The red light was like the gleam of an open furnace, not the flickering yellow of candles and lanterns.

'It's possible that light shines from a rift,' said Roberta slowly. 'A gateway between worlds, like those which the attractor devices created. You recall the glimpse of a hellish domain, with countless spirits striving to pass through?'

I shuddered, for the memory of the red demons was still fresh. Then I saw the error in her argument. 'But Edgar's machine was on the surface, and here we are below ground. Are you suggesting there is another of those devices in the underground tunnels?'

'No.' Roberta indicated the ceiling, ten or fifteen feet above. 'I'm suggesting we are somewhere beneath the warehouse, and that the red glow ahead of us may be positioned *directly* beneath.'

'So even now, more of those foul demons might be gathering around the corner?'

'At this moment they are not our concern, for I plan to save my father first,' said Roberta firmly. 'If there is a greater evil beneath the streets of London, we will need his help to defeat it, for you and I cannot hope to prevail on our own. For that we shall need powerful weapons, stronger equipment, and every ounce of knowledge my father possesses.'

By now the spirits were just ahead, and they'd just detected our approach. Two of them turned to meet us, while the third continued onwards with its prize. 'We will capture them quickly,' said Roberta. 'Unfurl the netting, and do not let those spirits touch you!'

I did as I was told, while Roberta set the trap on the ground and inserted a fresh, empty cylinder. Then she took the discs, and with a series of overarm throws she placed them neatly ahead of the spirit carrying her father's life force. When it reached the discs it came to a stop, turning uncertainly from side to side. Roberta took one end of the net, and we took several paces away from each other, stretching it out. Then we advanced towards the pair of spirits nearest to us, the net held between us at the height of our waists.

They reversed direction, gliding backwards towards their companion, their features stretching into distorted caricatures of human faces. One moment they appeared to be elderly ladies, and the next one of them was a crying child while the other was a middle-aged man with whiskers. But no matter which face they presented, their eyes were black, bottomless pits.

We were still driving the spirits backwards towards the line of discs, which lay in the dirt at various angles. Some of these discs reflected the weak light from the oil lamps nearby, while the finely traced lines on the rest gleamed at me from the shadows. They had powers though, that was undeniable, for the retreating spirits came to a halt as though they'd encountered an invisible barrier. Roberta and I continued to approach, and now she unstoppered the small glass bottle with her teeth and threw the contents ahead of us. Thick purple smoke boiled across the ground, quickly filling the tunnel, and the spirits began to shrink within themselves, getting smaller and smaller. The one cradling the professor's life force bent its head and began to feed on the dull, glowing cloud in its arms, and as it did so it began to grow once more. The other two saw this, and moved towards it so that they too might feast on the professor.

Roberta was having none of this. Gripping the strange tool with its open jaws, she released the net and sprang forwards, leaving whirling eddies in the thick purple smoke at her feet. Then, as she reached the spirits, she thrust at them one-two-three with the device, eliciting a sharp crackling noise from each. There was an unholy wailing noise as the spirits were stretched out, the lower portion of their bodies drawn towards the trap like water to a hole in the ground. The metal cylinder at the heart of the trap began to gleam as it consumed its prey, and the more it gleamed, the faster it drew the spirits in. Soon there was only a head and shoulders for each of them, the rest being stretched out thin over a span of twenty feet or more. Then these too were drawn into the trap, and the cylinder's gleam went out.

The spirits having vanished, the professor's weak life force now swirled in mid-air, suddenly freed. For a moment it seemed to hover, moving this way and that, and then it stretched past us at tremendous speed, heading back up the tunnel. The swirling cloud thinned until none remained, and I turned to watch the tail end vanishing up the tunnel like a thrashing, transparent snake.

'Were we in time?' I demanded of Roberta. 'Did we save him?'

'Oh, I hope so.' She dropped the tool into my hands. 'I must go and tend to him. Please...will you gather my things and follow?'

'Of course!' I cried. 'Go!'

She needed no second bidding, turning and running back along the tunnel until she disappeared around the curve. I prayed she would find the professor made whole once more, and with a wry grin I wondered whether she'd thought to bring any brandy, for he was certain to ask for it.

Then I turned to my task, folding the net and picking up the now-featureless discs from the earthen floor. My final task was to collect the trap, and as I did so I studied the cylinder suspended within. Three powerful spirits trapped in one metal core! Would it hold, or would they explode outwards to consume me? Even as I watched, it shook savagely, and I almost dropped the trap in surprise. I recalled the shattered cylinder I'd seen several days earlier, when the professor and Roberta had returned from their cleansing at Lady Fotherington-Eames' residence. That one had failed with but a single spirit inside.

In the end I wrapped the trap tightly inside the copper net, reasoning it might afford me a few seconds of warning should the spirits escape their bronze prison. I shouldered both knapsacks, and was about to follow after Roberta when I happened to spy the red gleam further along the tunnel. She'd indicated that the three of us would be returning this way, assuming her father was fit enough to do so. We would return with weapons, and stronger traps, and we would be going further around that corner to face the unknown horrors which had crawled into our world through Edgar's rift.

So would it not make sense for me to take a very quick, very cautious look?

There was a risk I would have to flee back down the tunnel with a score of slavering demons at my heels, but it would be worth it if I returned with valuable information. The number of enemies, for example, and perhaps a description of their appearance. I knew it was the right thing to do, and so I set the haversacks against the wall and began my stealthy approach to the curve in the tunnel and the baleful red gleam beyond.

The closer I got to the bend in the tunnel, the louder my footsteps seemed to become, and the more certain I was that I would be heard. I stopped once or twice, knowing it was madness to continue, but I had an overwhelming need to see what terrors might await the three of us when we returned.

I had the revolver in one hand, still fully loaded in case I encountered Edgar. As for spirits, if I ran into a less than human opponent I resolved to turn and run until my legs would carry me no further.

As I reached the gentle curve I pressed myself to the smooth green tiles lining the wall, continuing around the corner in a crabwise fashion. In the newspapers, I'd seen claims that these underground tunnels would serve the city for a hundred years or more, and I wondered what marvels might exist in the year nineteen hundred and seventy-one. I would never know, of course, but I only hoped these people of the future did not have to face a world ravaged by foul spirits and demons. For if they did, the blame would lie entirely with me. Why, I should have taken a knife to Edgar the first time I met him, and then none of this would have happened!

I pushed these self-recriminations aside, and continued creeping along the wall. As I did so, the scene ahead came into view, and what I saw froze me in place.

The tunnel broadened into a large cavern with a high ceiling, which I guessed was to be a new station for the underground. But at this moment, instead of passengers, the entire cavern was filled with ghostly apparitions. There were spirits of all sizes, and they whirled clockwise around the circular area as though blown by a powerful wind. Only they moved in complete silence, and there was not even the hint of a breeze on my cheeks.

This gathering of spirits was revolving around something hidden in the centre of the cavern, something that glowed with the baleful red light that had attracted me here. I squinted to determine the source, and through the whirling clouds of gauze-like spirits I made out a narrow oval shape floating in mid-air, around eight feet tall with indistinct edges. The red light came from within, and the effect was like peering through an open door into a boiler's fire box. I had seen something similar in the professor's cellar, only on a much smaller scale. It had come into being when he'd started his attractor machine, opening what looked like a gate into a hellish, otherworldly place.

This, then, must be a portal, and it could only have been opened by Edgar's scaled-up version of the professor's machine. It was a rent in the very fabric of our world, and the power it exuded was drawing spirits and phantoms from all over the city. But had anything come through from the other side?

There was a temporary gap in the whirling spirits, and at that moment I saw more details. The first was a wooden bench, low to the ground, and upon it lay a motionless figure, bound hand and foot. Light from the portal gleamed on naked flesh, but at this distance I could not see whether the person was male or female. Standing beyond this unfortunate was my nemesis, Edgar, and reddish light glinted on the cruel, long-bladed knife in his hand.

But the scar-faced man was not alone. Standing on the near side of the bench, looking down at the victim, was a tall man, elegantly dressed in coat and tails. He carried a cane and wore a top hat, and looked for all the world like a dandy out on the town. I had a sudden crazed notion that this was Charles, Roberta's suitor, but I dismissed it. This man was taller, and I could see grey hair beneath the brim of his hat. Even as I watched, he signalled to Edgar, then gestured at the unfortunate tied to the bench.

To my horror, Edgar crouched and drew his knife swiftly across the naked victim's throat. Blood welled up, deeper and redder than that hellish light bathing the scene, but the poor victim of his blade did not move. Were they bound so tightly as to make movement impossible, or had they mercifully been reduced to unconsciousness before they were brutally slain?

I recoiled in horror at the ghastly sight, and as rivulets of blood ran down the victim's neck to splash on the ground beneath the wooden bench, a cry escaped my lips. It was not only the horror of the murder that shocked me, but also the sudden widening of the portal, for it had grown larger at the moment of the killing.

Unfortunately, I had larger concerns than the growing portal. The moment I cried out, the tall, well-dressed man turned in my direction, looking directly into my eyes. His face was twisted by blood-lust and fury, but I knew him all the same.

The man with the top hat, the man directing Edgar, was none other than Lord Snetton.

36

I stood rooted to the spot, shocked beyond measure. Lord Snetton! *He* was behind the killings? Was Edgar nothing more than a hapless pawn in his master's devilish plans?

Snetton's features relaxed as he spied me, and suddenly he smiled. It was not an evil sneer, but the self-confident look of a man completely in command. And, to prove it, he raised his cane and pointed the tip at me. Instantly, the whirling phantasms formed into a stream, and after a half-circuit of the cavern they came straight towards my location. Edgar, meanwhile, sprang right over the unfortunate victim and started to run towards me. There was an intent look in his eye, and he gripped that knife as though he were most desperately keen to use it.

I did not hesitate. I turned and fled, my feet slipping and skidding on the loose soil underfoot. As I did so, Lord Snetton laughed long and hard, the sound magnified by that huge chamber. The echoes chased me along the tunnel, but I dared not look back because I knew what I would see...an army of spirits, each and every one of them ordered to chase me until I dropped, exhausted beyond measure. And then, when I could move no more, they would strip my life force and carry it back to their master so that he might feast on it. And afterwards, would Edgar take my near-dead body and tie it to that bench, in order to finish me utterly and completely?

But for now I was ahead of the spirits, and the scar-faced man with his bloodied knife, and I ran for all I was worth. The revolver was in my hand, and as I ran I pointed it behind myself, firing off two shots in the hope they would dissuade my human pursuer at least. The reports were deafening, and as the echoes faded I heard fragments of tiles smashed from the walls, and the whine of spent bullets ricocheting down the tunnel.

I ran on until I saw the haversacks propped against the wall where I'd left them. Was there anything inside I could use? There was no time for nets, and the small discs had been drained of their power, but Roberta's curious tool might hold the spirits at bay while I held Edgar off with my pistol.

I was approaching the bags fast, and had to make a decision. Unfortunately, I still had no idea how close my pursuers were. I risked a glance, and then came to a halt, breathing heavily and surprised beyond measure. In the distance, the spirits had turned about and were streaming back to the chamber. And of Edgar there was no sign. I squinted into the ill-lit tunnel, wondering whether a lucky shot had killed the man, but there was no crumpled body lying on the earthen floor.

I guessed that Snetton had called his forces back, perhaps because he was far more eager to open the portal than to waste time pursuing a mere onlooker. After all, should he succeed in opening that portal, thus permitting countless demons and horrors to pass into our world, I had no doubt there would *be* no more onlookers.

I was deeply troubled by what I had seen, but also relieved I was not to be hunted down and killed just yet. Taking up the bags, I slung them over my shoulder and hurried along the tunnel towards the exit as fast as my legs would carry me.

I reached the empty station and hurried up the steps, the knapsacks like lead weights across my shoulders. I did not think I had ever run so far nor so fast, and despite the chill night air I was panting like a dog on a hot summer day.

Once in the street I turned for the warehouse, my intention being to meet Roberta and – hopefully! – the professor. I would reveal the horrors I had witnessed below, and then the professor would build a contraption to seal the rift while Roberta and I dealt with Edgar and Lord Snetton.

I knew this was a gross oversimplification, and despite the severity of the situation a wry smile came to my lips. Why, one might as well reattach a severed leg with a tot of brandy and a handful of good wishes! Then I recalled the poor unfortunate victim of Edgar's knife, and my smile slipped. Suddenly I saw an alternative ending, one in which the professor was already dead, and I would be forced to watch as Roberta was tied to the wooden bench, before her throat was slit from ear to ear right before my very eyes.

By the time I reached the warehouse, my mood was dark indeed. It grew even more so as I stumbled around the darkened interior, calling Roberta's name as loudly as I dared. No matter how much I called, there was no reply. I found the spot where the professor had lain, and to my relief he was not there. This gave me great hope, for I could not imagine Roberta carrying him into the streets. Therefore, he must have been revived!

I turned for the exit and made my way into the road. The lightning and thunder had long since ceased, but a light rain was falling and the glow from the streetlamps barely lit the wet pavement. There was not a soul to be seen, which was not surprising as the storm had been a powerful one. In addition, many were no doubt cowering in their homes after witnessing spirits drifting through the very streets of the city. Some might have seen their loved ones having the life force torn from their bodies, as I had witnessed with Roberta and the professor.

Fortunately, there was no sign of any further spirits, and I surmised they were all circling Lord Snetton's half-opened portal beneath the streets of London. So, I turned up my collar, hunched my shoulders beneath the weight of the haversacks, and started walking in the direction of the professor's house.

I kept up a fast pace, for I had important news to share and I knew that portal would open wider and wider the more victims Edgar sacrificed. Would it take two lives to open that hellish gateway? Three? Half a dozen? I did not know, but the scar-faced man was a monster, killing without hesitation, and I had no doubt he would slaughter innocents until the required outcome was achieved.

It took me a good twenty minutes, but finally I turned into the professor's road. Even as I did so, I saw Roberta and her father passing through the iron gate in front of the house. Roberta was supporting the professor, who seemed barely conscious, and I redoubled my pace to meet them.

'Where have you been?' demanded Roberta, giving me an angry look. 'You were supposed to collect the things and catch me up!'

'I'm sorry, but the horrors I witnessed–'

'Never mind that now. We must get him inside.'

The professor murmured something, and I bent closer. 'What is it, sir?'

'Bran...dy,' muttered the professor.

'He's been saying the same thing these past ten minutes,' said Roberta. 'I swear his blood must be swimming in it.'

At the mention of blood I recalled Edgar's ruthless killing, and I knew there was a matter I had to raise with some urgency. 'Lord Snetton is behind this,' I said. 'I witnessed it with my own eyes.'

Roberta was silent, her face drawn.

'He had Edgar with him,' I continued. 'They're opening a portal in the tunnels, and they sacrificed a victim before my very eyes. As the poor soul's life was extinguished, the portal opened wider. I–I think, if they kill enough...'

By now we had reached the front door, which opened before us. Mrs Fairacre saw the state of the professor and immediately took charge. 'What have you done to the poor fellow *now?*' she cried, as she helped him to the sitting room. 'And what is that awful smell of fish?'

Roberta and I followed but she promptly ushered us out again, flapping her hands at us. 'Leave him be! Go on, out with you!'

And then she closed the door in our startled faces, shutting us out.

'Will your father be all right?' I asked Roberta.

'He is stronger than he looks,' she said stoutly.

Her words were encouraging, but I noticed she had not answered my question. Then she led me to the dining room, where I leaned the haversacks against the wall and sank gratefully onto a chair.

Roberta took a seat beside me, looking into my eyes. 'Tell me what you saw. Leave nothing out.'

I did as she asked, quickly recounting the hellish scenes I had witnessed. She winced when I recounted Edgar's murder of the victim, and shook her head slowly as I told her of the portal and the massed spirits doing Lord Snetton's bidding. 'No doubt the souls of Snetton's wife and servants were among them,' she said quietly. 'Those unfortunates, as well as the spirits of Jules Hartlow and Arthur Staines and many others slaughtered by that evil duo.'

'And the victims of the underground collapse,' I added. 'It's possible Edgar tampered with the tunneling equipment. Weaken a support here or there, and it would not have been particularly difficult to cause the roof to cave in.'

'Then we must put a stop to it. Do you still have the revolver?'

'Indeed I do.'

'When we encounter Lord Snetton and Edgar again, I would ask you not to shoot.'

'But–'

'Septimus, it is plain to me that an evil spirit has taken each of them over. They are not acting of their own free will, and if you kill their host bodies you will be murdering innocent men.'

'I witnessed Edgar murdering a helpless victim. Are you saying it was not his fault?'

'Somewhere inside his body, his own spirit may be screaming to get out. Deep down, he may be as sickened as you are at the killings, but completely helpless against the evil that has taken up residence.'

Or maybe Edgar and Lord Snetton are just evil, I thought, for I did not believe a man could be forced to commit such horrors against his will. Why, if such were the case, every murderer brought to the Old Bailey would be crying that it was not his fault, and that evil spirits made him do it! There would be no justice for any crime, and the very fabric of society would be torn asunder.

'I see you doubt me,' said Roberta. 'I do not seek to excuse my cousin, and nor would I spare him if these horrors are truly his own fault. But I beg you to consider the possibility before you shoot him dead. Will you promise me?'

'Very well, you have my word.' I said reluctantly. 'But if any of us are in mortal danger, I will fire bullet after bullet until the gun is empty. You have my word on that also.'

Roberta looked like she might argue, but such was my resolve that she let it lie.

'What can we do to meet this horror?' I asked her. 'Is there equipment we can build? Potions that might help us? A more powerful weapon, perhaps?'

Slowly, she shook her head. 'This situation is entirely new to me. To be honest, I am reaching in the dark.'

These were not the words I wished to hear, for I'd been hoping Roberta might have an effective solution to the problem.

'Father does have a number of old books in his study,' she said suddenly. 'We should see whether we can identify the portal you saw.'

'You're not suggesting there is more than one kind?' I asked her in alarm.

'Oh yes. The barrier between our world and the next is thin and easily broken. Blood sacrifices are commonly used to create these gateways, but there are many different rituals. If we can identify the ritual in use, it will make it easier to close the rift. If not, we might be forced to employ more direct measures. Measures almost as unholy as those employed to open the rift in the first place.'

I did not ask what those direct measures were, although I guessed she meant sacrifices. To think I, a simple bookkeeper, would be exposed to such an outlandish situation. Why, the knowledge of a hellish dimension parallel to our own would drive most souls to madness!

We hurried to the professor's study, and on the way I glanced towards the sitting-room door. It was firmly closed, and I hoped Mrs Fairacre was being successful in her attempts to revive the professor, for I knew we were lost without him. Cantankerous he might be, and somewhat over-confident and hypocritical too, but while Roberta was most capable in the matter of spirits I suspected we would need the professor's superior knowledge.

Roberta took down an armful of dusty books and laid them on the professor's workbench, and then we took a pile each and began our search. I could not believe the horrors displayed upon those pages, for there were sketches of tortured souls with their limbs being torn from their bodies, pages of aberrant and deviant behaviour the likes of which I had never before seen, let alone imagined, and far, far worse. Foul creatures lurked on every page, and the sickening images got more terrifying and depraved the further I got. I glanced at Roberta, concerned that she might be as sickened as I, but her face was calm and expressionless. 'What of this one?' she asked me. 'Is this similar to the gateway you observed?'

It was not. For one thing, the portal in the drawing had flames spreading out from the perimeter. For another, it was set into a solid wall, and appeared to be no more than half the height of a man. I told her so, and she turned the page without comment.

We finished the first two books together, and set them aside to start on the next. By now I was beginning to despair, for time was passing and for all I knew Lord Snetton and Edgar were murdering more and more victims. I felt we should be gathering weapons, and demanding to speak with the professor, and even, dare I say it, calling on Inspector Cox and Sergeant Parkes and the rest of the

Kensington police force.

But deep down I knew Roberta was right, for my impatience would only lead to more deaths. Hers, mine, the professor's…and any policemen who tried to apprehend Lord Snetton and his scar-faced accomplice. To put it plainly, we could not fight back until we knew what we faced.

'Is this similar?' Roberta asked me.

I looked over her shoulder to see a drawing of some poor unfortunate being put to death in some arcane ritual, with robed figures surrounding him. Behind them was a portal shaped like a narrow oval. 'That's close to what I observed.' I glanced down at the text, but the language was unfamiliar to me. 'What does it say?'

Roberta shook her head. 'It is beyond my knowledge. We need my father.'

'Then let us hope Mrs Fairacre has worked some magic,' I said quietly.

At that moment we heard footsteps, and then the professor himself marched in as bold as you like. He looked to be in perfect health, aside from a somewhat pale face, and when he got closer I understood why. My nose wrinkled, for there was a cloud of brandy fumes following him about.

'Father!' cried Roberta, and she hugged him tight. 'We were so worried about you!'

'There, there. Don't make a fuss, my dear, or you'll have me off my feet.' The professor seemed pleased at the attention, despite his words, but then he saw me. His expression altered instantly, from fatherly affection to cold anger. 'I see the traitor is back. What a shame the spirits did not take him instead of me.'

'Septimus helped to save your life,' said Roberta.

'It is his fault I needed saving in the first place.'

'Yes, yes, but please save your recriminations for later. Mr Jones spied out the enemy, despite the danger, and he brought back news!' Quickly. she recounted what I'd told her, although she added several embellishments which made me out to be far braver than I had actually been. But she knew her father well, and the more she revealed about my adventures, the more his expression altered. At the end, he was on the point of clapping me on the shoulder, but I was not yet forgiven and he satisfied himself by giving me a curt nod.

Then Roberta showed him the drawing in the old book, and he whistled quietly. 'Are you sure?' he asked me. 'This is not another mistake on your part?'

'The rift was near identical.'

'And Lord Snetton!' murmured the professor. 'I knew all along Edgar could not have worked alone. The boy has the brains of a cabbage.'

'He's hardly a boy,' protested Roberta. 'He must be thirty-five if he's a day.'

'He will always be an insignificant pipsqueak of twelve to me,' growled the professor. 'Getting mixed up in this nonsense. What would your poor auntie have said?'

'Never mind auntie.' Roberta pointed to the book. 'How do we stop them? Or rather, *can* we stop them?'

'Lord Snetton may have more than just Edgar at his beck and call. There may be a legion of helpers spread across the city, all of them possessed.'

Roberta stared at him.

'On the other hand,' said the professor, 'it's possible we have run headlong into Lord Snetton at the very beginning of his crazed plans. Either way, we shall need every resource, every scrap of knowledge, and every willing helper we can lay hands on.' He looked at me. 'I have not forgotten your betrayal, Mr Jones, but I need you for the moment. We shall suspend hostilities, you and I, but once this evil is defeated you will leave this house and never return.'

'I understand, sir.'

'Good.' The professor donned a pair of reading lenses, studying the text before him. 'Hmph,' he muttered. 'Interesting. Very interesting indeed.'

As he turned the pages, murmuring under his breath, Roberta took my hand and squeezed. 'I will talk to him later,' she whispered, so quietly I almost didn't hear. 'Do not worry.'

'What?' demanded the professor. 'What was that?'

'Nothing, father. Please, keep reading.'

'Then stop interrupting my thoughts,' snapped the professor. 'Instead of fussing around me, why don't you take Mr Jones and fashion a brand new trap?'

'I have spares already.'

The professor shook his head. 'This one must be larger and stronger to contain the evil I have in mind. I suggest a vessel twice the size, with walls three times as thick. I shall also require two dozen infused discs, and you can add every spirit in the house to the pour.'

Roberta glanced at the racks of metal cylinders on the nearby shelf. '*All* of them?'

'Did I not say so? Now go, go before I lose my place once more!'

We beat a hasty retreat after Roberta collected the racks of cylinders. As we strode down the corridor the shiny bronze vessels rattled in the wooden racks, as though the captured spirits were trying to escape. 'How many do you usually include when you make the discs?' I asked her.

'Two have always sufficed for anything we've encountered before.'

We eyed the cylinders, of which there were three dozen or so. The professor had told Roberta to use all of them, and I suddenly appreciated the scale and power of the enemy we were facing. 'Do you...do you believe we will prevail?' I asked her.

She gave me a confident smile. 'Of course! To admit doubt is to court defeat. Now hurry, we must get to work before father comes to find us.'

37

It was two hours later, and the cellar was as hot as a furnace. Roberta had worked non-stop melting, pouring and shaping metals, while I stamped out discs, cleared bronze shavings from the machinery and helped her in any way I could. There was a sense of urgency to our work, because we knew Lord Snetton would be striving to finish his ritual before we returned to try and stop him. As the hour grew late I raised the subject of calling in the police, but Roberta was adamant that we should not.

'We'd be sending them to their deaths,' was her only comment, and she turned away to continue her work.

We had not heard from the professor, and I hoped he was as busy as we were.

Once she'd fashioned the large bronze cylinder the professor had requested, Roberta constructed a makeshift cage to support it. We scavenged materials from all over the cellar to build the cage, and then Roberta strung it with fine copper wire to suspend the cylinder. She was just fastening the ends when we heard footsteps, and I turned to see the professor coming downstairs to join us. He carried a bundle of cloth under one arm, wrapped around something slender and long, and there was an excited expression on his face. 'Come and see what I have brought to aid us in the coming battle!' he declared, and he proceeded to lay the bundle on a workbench. Unwrapping the fabric, he revealed...three poorly-made swords constructed from wood. I could not see the reason for his excitement, for these did not look remotely dangerous, and indeed they appeared to have been fashioned from scraps of glued-together kindling. There was writing along each blade, but this was in the same script as the book Roberta had shown me earlier, and I could not read it.

I wanted to ask the professor if these wooden swords were the sum total of his two hours of labour, but I was already in his bad books and said nothing. In any case, he seemed inordinately proud of the things and I did not want to bring him low. Roberta, on the other hand, had no such qualms.

'What have you there, father?' she asked him. 'Do not tell me those sticks are fuel for the boiler, for I do not require any more at this moment.'

'Sticks?' demanded the professor, looking most annoyed. He brandished one of the wooden swords, and light glinted off the engraved lettering. I say engraved, but to be honest it was more a series of wayward scratchings. 'These are no sticks! They are weapons carefully constructed to match the specifications in ancient tomes, and they feature additions developed by my own hand.'

Roberta eyed the so-called weapon critically. 'Let us hope the enemy does not possess a box of matches.'

'Would you cease harping on the wooden construction for just one moment?' growled the professor. 'It is not the blades, but the runes that appear therein which give these weapons their power. They will keep at bay the most powerful spirits!'

I looked anew at the weapons, seeing them in a different light. It appeared they were not for cutting or thrusting, but for brandishing in the face of a ghostly enemy, and with that in mind I deduced they would indeed prove useful. Assuming they were not brandished too vigorously, of course.

'Is that the new vessel I see?' demanded the professor. He laid the sword with the others, carefully, and crossed to the workbench to inspect Roberta's handiwork. 'I would have strengthened the cage a little more, were I in charge of the construction. And these joints in the corners...they seem rough and unfinished.'

I felt this criticism was unwarranted, as *his* handiwork could have benefited from a great deal of strengthening and finishing. But again, I left the rebuttal to Roberta.

'It will suffice,' she said.

'Then we are ready.' The professor took a deep breath and looked towards the stairs. 'Out there, we face the greatest challenge of our lives,' he said, in the manner of an orator giving a performance. 'We must face this evil and defeat it, for if we fail the entire world may fall. We may suffer grievous wounds in the process, and the inhabitants of this fair city may never know the sacrifices we made, but in the end we shall hold our heads high and know that we did our duty for queen and country!'

'Bravo!' I cried, moved by the professor's stirring speech.

Roberta, meanwhile, turned to me with one eyebrow raised. Then she collected the large trap and strode towards the stairs. Deflated, the professor gathered up the wooden swords while I placed the metal discs I had fashioned into a leather bag, pulling the drawstring tight. As I did so, the heavy bag slipped from my fingers, bursting on the floor and scattering discs to all corners of the room.

The professor watched me scurrying around collecting the discs, and as I passed close by he shook his head slowly. 'May my end be quick and painless,' he murmured.

It was now the early hours of the morning, and there was little chance of our securing a cab. Each of us held one of the professor's long wooden swords, the strange lettering gleaming in the darkness, and so it was probably just as well. In addition, the professor carried his forked weapon from a leather belt, the tip sparking from time to time. As for myself, I bore the heavier of the two knapsacks, the strap chafing my shoulder despite the thickness of my coat.

To increase our misery a light drizzle began to fall, the moisture quickly soaking into our clothes. We must have made for a miserable sight as we strode the city streets and byways, and our mood was not improved by the thought of the danger we faced.

Finally, after an interminable walk, we turned into the road with the underground station. Here we stopped, for two shadowy figures were at the metal gates, one of them bent to inspect the lock. My heart thudded, for at first I believed them to be our enemies, Lord Snetton and Edgar, but then I saw the uniforms. 'It's the police!' I whispered. 'They have seen the open padlock!'

'Wait here,' murmured the professor. Before we could object, he handed Roberta his wooden sword and approached the policemen. I thought he intended to disarm them with a few well-chosen words, or perhaps draw them away from the gate so that Roberta and I might enter.

Instead, as they turned to look at him, the professor drew the pronged weapon and pressed it to each policeman's chest in turn. They shook and quivered briefly, with sparks running up and down their bodies, and then they fell to the ground to lie inert.

Roberta and I stared at each other, then ran towards the gate. The professor was crouched over the unconscious policemen, and as we approached I heard him muttering to the nearest. 'Eat all my sausages, would you?'

'Father!' hissed Roberta, scandalised. 'You cannot attack policemen!'

'Your statement is demonstrably inaccurate,' said the professor haughtily. 'Now help move them inside, lest more of these interfering peelers come to foil our plans.'

We did as we were told, dragging both policemen through the gate before laying them out on the floor. Roberta moved them onto their sides, confirmed they were breathing, then rounded on her father. 'You will be jailed for this if they catch you!' she hissed.

'This pair will not be catching anyone,' said the professor. 'Now do come on, or Snetton will open his rift and we shall be facing hordes of slavering demons instead of two dozen relatively harmless spirits.'

Harmless? I was glad he thought so, especially as those same spirits had succeeded in stripping his life force earlier, leaving him for dead. But there was no time to dwell on this, because the professor had already lowered himself to the tracks, and was now striding towards the underground tunnel.

Roberta and I followed, catching up with the professor, and the three of us moved to the narrow path beside the railway tracks. Here, the ground was packed dirt, and we walked in relative silence. Ahead, in the distance, I could already make out the baleful red glow which I knew emanated from Lord Snetton's portal. Was it my imagination, or did it seem brighter than before?

'What was that?' muttered Roberta suddenly.

We stopped to listen, and then we all heard it. Someone had just coughed, and the faint sound came from the tunnel ahead of us.

'A guard?' murmured the professor. 'A wise precaution, I suppose, and yet another impediment to our success.'

I crouched and moved closer to the tunnel wall, and as I did so I saw the man framed against the distant red glow. He was perhaps fifty yards away, leaning casually against the tunnel wall, and he appeared to have a long wooden club in his hand. This was leaning casually across one shoulder, and it looked a heavy and substantial weapon. In addition, the man was tall and well-built, and more than a match for any of us. I beckoned to the others, and they crouched beside me to look for themselves.

'My sword is useless against that bruiser,' said the professor. 'He has the reach on me, and would smash it with that club of his before I could get close.'

'I have the revolver still,' I murmured in reply.

The professor shook his head. 'Fire a single shot in these tunnels, and you will attract more enemies to our position.'

'What if I walked up to him and threatened–'

'I have an idea,' said Roberta. 'Come, we must get closer.'

She said no more, and the three of us moved along the tunnel in a crouch, placing our feet carefully. Once we were twenty yards from the man, she stopped, sinking to the ground. I heard a faint noise, and saw her turning over pieces of clinker in the nearby rail bed. She found what she was looking for, and handed me a substantial piece of stone roughly the size of my fist. Then she took the pronged weapon from her father, taking a firm hold of the grip.

'On three!' she whispered. 'One, Two, Three!'

I stood there with the piece of stone in my hand, unsure what I was meant to do. Roberta, meanwhile, looked displeased.

'Mr Jones,' she hissed. 'I know you did not attend university, but when my father and I hired you as a bookkeeper we assumed you could at least count to three.'

I mumbled an apology.

'Perhaps, instead of berating the poor boy, you should tell him what you require of him,' whispered the professor.

'Is it not obvious?' Roberta gestured at the stone and explained patiently. 'On three, I want you to throw that past the guard. When it lands it will make a noise, and he will turn to investigate. I will hurry up behind and subdue him.'

I wanted to tell her I was not the man for the job, and that my throwing accuracy was questionable at the best of times. I wasn't even certain I could reach the man, let alone throw the heavy stone beyond him. But there was no time to explain, since Roberta had started counting once more.

'One. Two. *Three!*'

I threw the stone as hard as I could, quickly losing sight of it in the darkness. We all held our breath, and then we heard a solid thud. The guard's head jerked sideways, and he promptly fell in a heap.

Roberta lowered her weapon. 'That will do just as well, I suppose.'

I worried I might have killed the man, but when we reached him he was already recovering and clutching at his head. Roberta, unmoved by his pain, pressed the forked tip of the sword to his chest, and the man jerked violently before lying still.

'That's the spirit,' growled the professor, showing not the

slightest concern for our latest victim. 'And now, let us confront the chief architects of this evil plan!'

38

We reached the turn in the tunnel, and the three of us gazed in horrified awe upon the scene beyond. The portal was now several times larger than when I had last laid eyes on it, and the edges had begun to revolve slowly, leaving swirling eddies of blood-red light in mid-air. The centre opened on a fiery landscape, where a jet-black sky was shot through with lightning bolts exhibiting the hue and gleam of polished rubies. There was movement in that landscape, and my mouth turned dry as I saw the horde of unholy creatures impatient to emerge from that hellish portal. Some latecomers fought their way to the head of the heaving mass, and I saw several of these evil denizens torn apart by tooth and claw before my very eyes.

Meanwhile, three dozen spirits whirled around the chamber on our side of the rift, as though guarding Lord Snetton from intruders.

Slowly, silently, we withdrew around the corner to confer.

'There is but one way to win this battle,' murmured the professor, sounding quite shaken after the horrifying sight. 'We must eject the invading spirit from Lord Snetton's body and capture it in the trap.'

I looked around the corner once more. Lord Snetton stood near a mound of ten or twelve naked cadavers, and even now Edgar raised a bloodstained knife to slaughter the latest victim. Edgar's scar gleamed in the light from the portal, and fresh blood soaked his shirt from wrist to shoulder. Once more, I drew my head back around the corner. 'Oh for a rifle, and one trained in its use,' I muttered.

The professor shook his head. 'Lord Snetton is possessed, and shooting him would only kill the unwilling human host. The demon inside him would break free, seeking another to inhabit.'

His meaning was clear. Kill Snetton, and one of us would likely be possessed by the spirit now occupying him. 'What if we knocked him unconscious?' I asked.

Roberta snorted. 'Your last throw was a miracle. Do not expect a repeat.'

I looked down at the wooden sword in my hand. 'Professor, are you certain this will keep those spirits away?'

'I built that weapon myself,' said the professor, in a stuffy tone. 'Of course it will work!'

'Then I'd ask you both to wish me good fortune,' I muttered, and before they could stop me I shrugged off the haversack and charged around the corner into the chamber.

'No!'
  'Stop!'

I heard the professor and Roberta cry out, but I was beyond caring. If I could subdue Lord Snetton somehow, the other two could use their traps and devices to draw the evil out of him. If Edgar came at me with his dagger, I promised myself I would shoot him dead. As for the spirits whirling around the chamber, I could only hope that the professor's faith in the wooden swords was not misplaced, and that I would be able to keep them at bay.

As I ran, I suspected that none of the above would come to pass. Deep down, I guessed that I was sacrificing myself, but as the cause of so much trouble I felt that my loss would be worth it...as long as it tipped the scales.

I had barely entered the chamber when I was beset by spirits, and I held up that fragile wooden sword to meet them. To my surprise, the runes scratched into the blade glowed with fierce light, and the spirits were quite unable to pierce the invisible shield surrounding me. By now I was running fast, and the angry phantasms circled me like huge moths around a lantern,

Ahead, Lord Snetton and his depraved, murderous assistant had become aware of the disturbance, and they both turned to face me. Snetton seemed entirely unconcerned as I closed the distance between us, and my confidence faltered at his look of disdain. As for Edgar, his expression was intensely ravenous, as though his very soul cried out for fresh blood.

At this moment I realised my plan could have done with a little more thought and a little less action. I carried the revolver in my left hand, but if I shot either of the men I would quickly be overcome by the evil spirit inhabiting them. And as for the sword, I might as well attack them with a sheet of parchment.

Snetton's smile widened at my approach, as though he'd read my mind. Edgar, meanwhile, had abandoned his victim and was coming for me with his knife. He was five or six paces behind Lord Snetton, and I was running headlong towards both of them.

With only a split second left before reaching them, I decided to use the only weapon remaining to me. Lowering one shoulder, I charged the slender figure of Lord Snetton, and as we collided I hurled him backwards. His top hat went one way, his cane the other, and then we were both tumbling over and over in the dirt.

I ended up face-down, and a fast-moving shadow alerted me to the danger. Rolling over, I was just in time to avoid Edgar and his bloodied dagger. The force of his thrust drove the blade into the dirt, and I lashed out with my shoe, kicking his hand as hard as I could. There was a satisfying snap as the blade broke off, and I regained my feet and backed away, revolver at the ready as Edgar tossed aside the haft of his knife.

I had lost my wooden sword in the melee, and all of a sudden I was surrounded by glowing phantasms, their hollow eyes and wide open mouths screaming of their past lives. Their hands grasped for me, and I found myself frozen to the spot, unable to move an inch as glowing fingers passed through my clothes and into my chest. There was a wrench deep inside, and then I could only watch in horror as a fine, bright strand was pulled twisting and turning from my chest. My vision began to fade, and I was on the point of collapse when I heard a roar of anger.

'Back, you foul demons. Back, I say!'

The spirits scattered as though blown by a gale, and my vision returned as the twisting strand of glowing light snapped back into my chest. The chill that had been upon me was dispelled, and I turned to see Roberta and the professor either side of me, their glowing wooden swords held high.

By this time Lord Snetton had recovered, and he took up his

black cane and pointed it at Roberta. 'Come closer.'

I laughed, for he might as well have ordered her to fly.

Edgar was on his feet, and he crouched as though he were about to spring. Lord Snetton stilled him with a gesture, then smiled at Roberta. 'Come, my dear. Join us.'

To my surprise Roberta took a step forward, and quickly I reached out a hand to stop her. She shook me off and took another step towards Snetton, somehow under his power. She was fighting with everything she had, and from the expression on her face it was clear she was moving against her will. The professor and I took a step towards her, intending to pull her back, but Snetton gestured at us with his cane and I felt a fiery agony in my veins. The pain was excruciating, and I had no choice but to retreat. The professor tried again, but was forced to his knees as a second wave of agony rippled through his body.

I raised my pistol, intending to shoot Snetton no matter the consequences, but the revolver's grip glowed with searing heat and I was forced to drop the weapon. Despite the terrible pain I was fully aware it was a trick, an illusion, but it was so real I could almost smell my own flesh burning.

By now Roberta was close to Lord Snetton, and he had her turn to face us. Then, very deliberately, he raised a gloved hand to her throat, pressing his thumb and fingers to the arteries in her neck. 'I shall starve the blood from her brain,' he told us conversationally. 'Once she has fainted, my associate will bind her to the bench you see behind me. Then, with great pleasure, I shall observe while he cuts her throat.'

I took a step forward but Lord Snetton's cane jerked instantly, and a wave of sheer force hurled me backwards to land in the dirt. As I lay there, ears ringing, I heard his final words as though from afar.

'Her sacrifice will be sufficient to open the portal you see behind me, and then this pathetic world of yours is finished.'

I raised my head, and to my dismay I saw Roberta's eyelids fluttering as she began to lose consciousness. But it was the pleading look in those eyes that struck me the hardest, and I knew that I must help her no matter the cost. Then I frowned, for she slowly closed one eye before opening it again. What madness was this?

Her head dropped forwards, her body instantly going limp. Lord Snetton was supporting her, and he staggered as her weight came to bear. That's when I recalled the pleading look, and I realised she had not been pleading for me to save her, but instead had been warning me she was about to fool Snetton!

I cast around me, and saw a gleam of metal nearby. It was the pistol, and it was lying half-covered in the dirt nearby. I stretched out a hand and took it up, then looked to the professor. He was two paces away, his face haggard as he watched his daughter's supposedly-unconscious form, since he was completely unable to help her. 'Professor!' I croaked.

He glanced at me, then at the gun in my hand. 'You cannot harm an evil spirit with that,' he hissed.

'A distraction. Please.'

He turned to look at Lord Snetton, and I could read his thoughts. We were done for, even if he saved Roberta. But then his jaw tightened, and he nodded.

I expected him to run at Snetton, but instead the professor reached into his coat and took out a hip flask. He took a decent draught, smacked his lips, and then drew his arm back and hurled the silver flask directly at Lord Snetton. It flashed past his head, causing the man to start, and in that instant Roberta elbowed him firmly in the stomach and broke free. He made a desperate grab for her, and I rolled onto my haunches, brought the gun up and fired three shots.

The first bullet missed completely, but the next two caught Lord Snetton in the chest, and red blossoms appeared on his crisp white shirtfront as though by magic. The cane fell from his grasp and he dropped to his knees, a trickle of blood already forming at the corner of his mouth. Then, slowly, he fell face-forward into the dirt.

There was a howl of dismay, and I turned the gun to cover Edgar, whose face was a twisted mask of hatred. Then I became aware of two things. First, the portal had just widened appreciably, and twisted limbs and clawed hands were already reaching through as the denizens on the other side strove to enter our world. And second, a glowing red cloud was pouring from Lord Snetton's mouth and nose. It whirled this way and that as it rose into the air, before it selected its victim and darted straight towards me.

I was still on my haunches, gun in hand, and saw I had no chance of escaping the advancing red cloud. Roberta, however, had not given up. Reaching into her pocket, she took out a handful of infused discs, and with a series of rapid throws she managed to land several between me and the approaching phantasm.

It continued to advance, and for a second I thought the specially-crafted discs would have no effect. But then, at the last second, the evil phantasm drew back. Then it abandoned me and darted towards the professor. Roberta threw more discs, quick as a flash, and they fell in the dirt in a rough circular pattern, until the spirit was completely surrounded.

I heard a thin howl of frustration that set my hair on end, but there was no time to think. Edgar had picked up a second knife, and was advancing on Roberta from behind. There was murder in his eyes, and I had no doubt that one more death would open that terrible portal. I stood, raising my gun, but I knew it was no use. Shooting him dead would be just as effective, and the portal would open all the same.

In all of this, I'd forgotten the professor. That worthy now ran past me, pronged weapon in hand, and Edgar turned from Roberta to face this new threat. I could see the madness in his eyes, could see his desire to slaughter this new enemy, but there was something else too. With Lord Snetton dead, and the spirit master trapped, Edgar now faced three opponents alone.

To my relief, he uttered an oath at the professor, then turned and fled down the tunnel.

'Roberta, quick!' shouted the professor. 'We must trap Lord Snetton this instant, before he escapes once more.'

They dragged open the knapsacks and tipped out the contents, grabbing the now-familiar pieces of equipment. I was given the netting, and as I unfurled it I admired the way Roberta and the professor went about their task so calmly and efficiently. All this time, the portal stood open nearby, and to my eye it appeared to be getting larger even without the sacrifice of fresh victims. What if the thing could grow to completion under its own steam, and the sacrifices merely speeded the process? I glanced up to see the two dozen or so spirits hovering overhead, which were still keeping their distance from the professor's wooden swords. Perhaps their presence alone was enough to power the opening of the portal?

By now Roberta and the professor were ready, and the former was approaching the angry red cloud with the curious open-jawed tool held ahead of her.

'Be careful,' called the professor. 'This is no ordinary spirit. It is stronger than anything you've encountered before.'

'Thank you, father,' muttered Roberta, eying the spirit which had been freed by Lord Snetton's death. 'I am well aware of that.'

The spirit railed at its prison, darting from one side to the other and occasionally even managing to extend a shadowy extension of itself between the discs. It withdrew again quickly, although it seemed to reach a little further and remain outside the circle a little longer. Much more of this, I thought, and the spirit would escape completely.

But I was forgetting Roberta. She approached the circle, almost taunting the spirit with her nearness, and as it reached a tendril toward her she gripped it with the tool, drawing it towards her. Some property of the tool caused the spirit to contract, and it grew brighter and more intense as it coalesced on the tip of the curious tool.

Once it was gathered up in its entirety, Roberta strolled casually to the large trap and pressed the tool against the metal cylinder. There was a keening wail, and the spirit vanished within.

'Well done, my dear,' said the professor. 'Very well done indeed.'

There was a disturbance overhead, and the spirits whirling near the ceiling of the large chamber separated all of a sudden, flying off in all directions. They went right through the roof, vanishing completely, and my heart sank at the sight. Two dozen spirits let loose in the city? That would be a cleansing job and a half!

The professor, though, was as pleased as Punch. 'Fly away, my beauties,' he murmured. 'Fly away, and you'll fill my purse as I catch each and every one of you.'

'Father,' muttered Roberta in mock disgust. 'Have you no shame?'

'I only hope they settle with rich families,' said the professor. Then he looked at the portal. 'It's a crying shame we won't be paid for closing that monstrosity,' he grumbled.

'How will you do it?' I asked him.

In reply, he approached Roberta and gestured for the trap. She held it up so he could reach inside, and after a struggle he removed the thick cylinder from its mountings. 'Let he who opened it close it again,' he intoned, and he drew his arm back for a throw. Then he paused to look at me. 'I think perhaps you have the better arm.'

'I assure you I do not,' I declared.

He smiled, then threw the cylinder, hard. It flew into the centre of the portal, end over end, glinting in the hellish red light. Then, with a final flash, it was gone. Instantly, the portal closed like a giant eye, and we were left in comparative darkness. It was as quiet as a tomb, and our faces were barely visible in the dim glow of the construction lanterns.

Then, all of a sudden, I heard voices and heavy boots...many of them. 'It came from this way sir,' echoed a voice from the nearby tunnel. 'You men, spread out there!'

'The police are here!' hissed the professor. 'Let us gather our things and make ourselves scarce, for I have no wish to spend the next week explaining all of this to Inspector Cox and that dullard Parkes.'

39

As we walked home I noticed a blush to the sky, with dawn not far off. We were all exhausted from our efforts, but even so we had spent the journey reliving the recent battle in excited voices. Roberta and the professor showed no ill-effects from the trials we had faced, and I felt the warmth of their companionship as we strolled through the deserted streets. I wished it could continue forever, but it was with a heavy heart that I remembered I was to be cast from their employ. At that moment I would have given anything to remain, but I had betrayed these good people to the scar-faced man, and would have to pay the price. 'What of Edgar?' I asked suddenly. 'Surely we cannot let him escape?'

'Do not trouble yourself over that fool,' said the professor. 'Roberta and I will hunt him down eventually, and then we shall trap the spirit living within.'

I was silent, because already the professor was omitting me from his plans. Then I recalled an earlier conversation. 'Why did you tell me Edgar was dead when you first employed me?'

'We believed it to be true,' said the professor. 'The police found several charred bodies at the site of his first experiment, and since he was never seen again it was assumed he perished. Instead, it seems he adopted a new name and went into hiding.'

'Should we tell the police he's alive? He's a dangerous man, and he might kill again.'

'And what would you tell them? That Edgar conspired with Lord Snetton to summon ghosts and phantasms? That he served as right-hand-man to a foul being from beyond? Why, they would commit the three of us to the Bethlem Hospital, assuming they did not jail us for Lord Snetton's death.'

'Especially if those police you attacked with your weapon happened to recognise you,' murmured Roberta.

The professor ignored her and turned to me. 'I know we have had our differences, my boy, but you acted bravely today and I thank you for saving Roberta's life.'

'It was my pleasure to help, sir. I would do it again in an instant.'

'Sadly, you will not have the chance,' he said, a little stiffly. 'I have not forgotten that it was your actions which brought this mess upon us in the first place.'

The mood soured after this proclamation, and we walked the rest of the way in silence. There were people about now, with early-morning deliveries already under way, and I knew the streets would soon be bustling. For myself, I just wanted to curl up in bed.

We finally arrived home, where the professor let us in.

'Mrs Fairacre and the maid will be sleeping,' whispered Roberta. 'Do try not to disturb them.'

The professor turned to me. 'You may spend the night, but I want you to pack your things when you awaken. Tomorrow, you must leave.'

I turned to Roberta for support, but she said nothing. So, I turned from the two of them and stumbled towards the staircase, feeling low and unwanted. I had hoped Roberta might put in a word for me as she had promised, but it seemed she was as determined to see the back of me as her father was. This was hardly surprising, for he had almost died as a result of my betrayal.

Slowly, I climbed the steps to my room, and on the way I wondered what the next day might bring. There was no guarantee the professor would pay me for my three or four days service, but if he did I resolved to take the first train home to my parents. Once there I would comply with their wishes, and take the first steps towards settling down with the wealthy merchant's rather dull daughter. It was not the life I wanted, but it seemed I no longer had a choice.

After readying myself for bed, I crossed to the window and gazed out upon the city. It looked peaceful in the the first grey light of dawn, and I wondered what the sleeping inhabitants would think if they knew of the horrors that had threatened to overwhelm them. The events of the past few days had been terrifying to me, but they had also opened my eyes to a new world of excitement and danger. And to think I once found maintaining accounting ledgers and summing dry columns of figures satisfying work!

No, I would welcome more of the same danger, especially if it involved working closely with Roberta.

Then I sighed, for Roberta was as lost to me as the professor and my short-lived employment.

Before retiring I took the pistol from my coat, ensured it was fully loaded, and tucked it under my pillow. The professor and Roberta did not seem to think Edgar would return, but I was not taking any chances. As for shooting Roberta by mistake, I was not the slightest bit concerned about that, for I knew she would not be visiting my room again.

I woke late the next day, refreshed and alert. I must have slept eight hours straight, and it was after midday by the time I stirred from my bed. Below, I could hear noises from the rest of the household, and I wondered whether the professor might soon hammer on my door to request my immediate departure.

The last vestiges of sleep fled, and I was up in an instant. My mood had been optimistic upon waking, but it soured quickly as I fetched my valise, laid it on the bed and began packing my things. After checking on top of the wardrobe and beneath the bed, I remembered the pistol under my pillow. I did not want to return it to the locked box, for Edgar knew the combination and might return to take the thing. Instead, I tucked it into my case with the leather pouch of cartridges.

I left my room the instant my packing was complete, for I saw no reason to delay my departure. Taking the stairs, I reached the ground floor and made for the dining room. I was hungry, and I hoped the professor might grant me a final breakfast before I departed. Also, I greatly desired to see Roberta one more time. I would not make a fool of myself by pleading my case, but I did want to say a final goodbye.

I passed the professor's study on my way to the dining room, and I glanced in to see him at his desk. He was reading a newspaper, and such was his concentration that I dared not disturb him. Instead, I continued to the dining room, where I was met by the mouth-watering smell of breakfast.

Roberta was at the table, a substantial plate of food before her, and she smiled warmly as I entered. 'Mr Jones! I feared you'd slipped away from us in the night. Did you sleep well?'

I was saddened by the formal manner in which she addressed me, for until recently she had taken to using my given name. However, I did not let my expression betray my feelings. 'Indeed I did, and thank you,' I said brightly. 'And yourself?'

'Like a babe in arms.' She gestured at the sideboard. 'Please help yourself. Father is deep in his works, and the food will probably go to waste.'

I needed no second bidding, and I set my valise against the wall and took up a plate. Moments later I returned to sit at the table with a substantial breakfast before me.

'Goodness,' said Roberta. 'Is that to last you all week?'

I reddened. 'If you wish me to put some back...' I began.

'Of course not! It's good to see your appetite has returned.'

I couldn't help noticing that the food on her own plate was untouched, and she seemed to be in no mood to eat. Then again, given the perils of the day before, perhaps it was to be expected.

The dining room fell silent as I turned to my food, and so it was that I heard the lightest of footsteps approaching. I looked up to see Mrs Fairacre in the doorway, and my heart sank. Surely it was not the police again? But no, it was worse. Far, far worse.

'Roberta, I've laid out the blue skirt for your luncheon, but do you have a preference as to the bonnet?'

'None,' said Roberta quietly. 'Any will do.'

'Very well. But do get changed soon, or you'll be keeping your young man waiting.'

Mrs Fairacre departed, and I held my silence for as long as I could.

But eventually, I simply had to know. 'You have a luncheon?' I asked her lightly. 'Is that why you do not eat?'

'Yes, and before you ask, it's with Charles.' She smiled weakly. 'At least it will be daylight this time.'

I knew it wasn't my place, but I could not believe the professor was forcing her to meet the man once more. 'Charles is a thorough cad,' I muttered. 'I'm sorry, but you should tell the professor you refuse to–'

'My father doesn't know,' said Roberta quietly. 'What's more, I would trouble you not to tell him.'

I was taken aback, and it must have showed.

'Charles has promised introductions, and they would mean the world to my father.'

'But his behaviour towards you is despicable!'

Roberta smiled at me. 'Did you not see me elbow Lord Snetton in the midriff? Do you truly believe a dandy like Charles would get the better of me?'

She had a point, and all of a sudden I felt better. She would play Charles the way she played her father, and would extract from him the utmost without giving up a single thing in return. Then I heard a knock at the door, and my confidence evaporated.

Soon after, Mrs Fairacre returned with Charles. Accompanying them was a liveried footman, with white gloves and a nervous, set-upon manner. I wondered at his presence, for there was no luggage to be carried.

'Roberta, such a delight,' said Charles, with an elaborate bow. He was a handsome devil with a lean, tanned face and he carried himself with an air of supreme confidence. Naturally, I detested him on sight. Then, after a sidelong glance at me, he gave Roberta a superior smile. 'My dear girl, are you brought so low you must dine with the servants?'

'Mr Jones is in my father's employ,' said Roberta.

'Smythe here is in *my* employ, but you don't see me taking breakfast with the wretched fellow.'

At the mention of his name the footman all but cringed. In that moment, I guessed at the horrors of employment with a bully like Charles. But Charles had spotted my valise, and didn't notice his servant's reaction. 'My dear Roberta, how perceptive of you!' he cried. 'I was going to ask you to pack some things for the weekend, and it seems you anticipated my wishes!'

'Weekend?' said Roberta. 'What do you mean, weekend?'

'Why, our suite at the Grande, of course. If we're going to do this thing, we might as well do it in style, what?'

Roberta stared at him, and as I realised what Charles was hinting at I felt a red rage come upon me. Muttering an oath, I pushed my chair back and stood up, ready to wipe the knowing smirk from the man's arrogant face.

'Oh, do tell him to sit down,' drawled Charles. 'If a servant of mine acted so impudently, I'd thrash him half to death.'

My fists were clenched, and I was about to launch myself at him when the professor entered. 'What's all this noise?' he demanded. 'Can't a man read his morning paper without...' Then, as he noticed Charles, his voice tailed off. 'What are you doing here?' he asked coldly.

'I bring introductions, my good man! Friends of mine, good families all, and every one of them requiring your particular...services.'

The professor brightened, and he didn't seem to notice the

thunderous expression on my face, nor the thoughtful, angry look on Roberta's.

'Now, Roberta and I will be away for the weekend, but I promise that upon our return I shall–'

'You'll be what?' asked the professor, his eyes narrowing. 'Did you just suggest that my daughter accompany you like a...a cheap floozy?'

'Come now, we're men of the world,' said Charles, with a knowing smile. 'She has little else to commend her, but who can resist a little fun now and then?'

I cried out in rage and leapt forward, only for the professor to restrain me. I struggled to break free but he was stronger than I expected.

Charles laughed in my face. 'Have patience, my dear fellow! Perhaps the fair Roberta will allow you to dip your wick once I've broken her in.'

Unseen by him, Roberta had risen from her chair. Now, very politely, she tapped him on the shoulder. He turned, and as he did so she punched him right in the nose, putting her shoulder behind the blow.

I had witnessed the occasional boxing match in my time, and a heavyweight champ would have been proud to lay such a punch. The unpleasant dandy was thrown clear off his feet, and he fetched up against the nearby wall with a terrible crash. But his woes had not yet ended, for a painting, loosened from its hanger, dropped like a stone, the frame landing across the top of his head with a loud thud.

Dazed, Charles dashed the back of his hand across his face, and it came away bloodied. No wonder, because his nose was bent sideways and was running like a leaky tap.

'Keep your damned money, and tell your stuck-up family they can go to hell!' shouted Roberta, angrier than I'd ever seen her. 'My father and I will manage without you, even if it means begging in the streets!'

There was a shocked silence, and then the footman sprang forward to help his master up. Once upon his feet, Charles shoved him away and turned on Roberta, drawing his hand back to strike her. I was nearest, and I spun the man round and pushed him backwards, again and again, until we fetched up against the far wall. Then I took up a poker and held the blackened tip under Charles' misshapen nose. 'Leave this house this instant, or it will end badly for you,' I growled. 'One word of this to anyone, and I will hunt you down and flay the skin from your bones. Understand me when I say I have nothing to lose. Nothing!'

I put everything I had into the threat, and Charles crumpled like a piece of wet parchment. Eyes wide and fearful, he nodded quickly before turning and stumbling for the hall, blood dripping from his damaged nose. The footman was all but grinning with delight, but he straightened his face quickly before following Charles from the room.

Mrs Fairacre looked in at that moment, attracted by the uproar. She saw Roberta wincing and massaging her hand, and hurried across to help her. Meanwhile, the professor clapped me on the shoulder. 'I see you do have some backbone after all, Mr Jones. Of course, if I were a younger man I'd have given him what-for myself.'

'Of course, sir.'

Then the professor spotted my valise. 'All packed and ready, eh?'

'Yes sir.' Deep inside, hope welled. Surely now he would allow me to stay?

'Mrs Fairacre will send a runner for a cab,' said the professor, crushing my hopes. 'You can finish your breakfast in the meantime.'

I turned to Roberta, and I noticed her looking at me in confusion. 'Mr Jones, would you say that behaviour was out of character?'

'No,' I said firmly. 'Charles is a thorough cad.'

She smiled. 'I meant your behaviour, Septimus. The way you lost your temper and threatened him.'

'I'm sorry, but I feel it was justified.'

'All the same, I'd like to check something before you leave.'

I sat down and ate a few mouthfuls of breakfast, but in truth my appetite was gone. Fortunately, Roberta came back quickly, and to my surprise I saw she held the spectacles with mismatched eyeglasses. She put them on and studied me through the lenses, and then she gave a cry of alarm. 'Father, you will not believe this! Mr Jones is *possessed!*'

'What is it you say?' demanded the professor. 'Possessed?'

'It's the truth!' declared Roberta. 'Poor Septimus carries a minor spirit within him. It must have guided his actions all along!'

'Let me see!'

The professor reached for the glasses, but Roberta swatted his hand away. 'Will you take my word, just this once?' she demanded.

Chastened, her father nodded. 'It all makes sense now,' he said slowly. 'The cowardice, the craven behaviour...what other evidence did I need? I should have known the boy wasn't a traitor!'

'Come, Septimus. Come quickly, and I will rid you of this demon immediately!' Without waiting for an answer, Roberta took my hand and practically dragged me from the room.

'I'll help you!' called the professor.

'No! I can manage on my own.'

'But–'

'Father, do you truly believe I need your help?' By now Roberta and I were climbing the stairs, and the professor's protestations faded. When we reached her floor she opened the door and led me to the bed, where she forced me to sit. By now I was in a blind panic, for I could almost feel the tendrils of an evil spirit invading every part of my body. How long had it been there? How long had it been driving my every thought?

Meanwhile, Roberta had closed the door, and now she wedged a chair beneath the handle. I grew truly frightened, because I guessed she'd trapped me in that room so that my controlling spirit would have no escape. The extraction was going to be bad, truly bad, and I felt my heart pounding as I imagined the horrors to come.

Now Roberta was at her workbench, rummaging amongst the equipment. She picked up several tools, some with curved blades and others with pincer-like ends, and not one of them gave me any comfort. Then she took up an object and came back to the bed. It was a bronze cylinder, of the sort used to capture spirits, and as she sat next to me I could not take my eyes off the rounded, gleaming vessel. Soon, the monster inhabiting me would be drawn out, kicking and fighting, and then it would be trapped in that vessel for all time.

And what of me? Would I feel any different? 'W–will it hurt?' I whispered, my eyes wide.

Roberta looked at me. 'Will what hurt?'

'Removing my spirit. Freeing me from this evil possession.'

'Oh Septimus, you complete fool. There is no spirit!'

I stared at her, stunned.

'It's a ruse,' she whispered. 'And do please keep your voice down, lest father hear your idiot questions and guess at the truth.'

'A ruse?' I breathed. 'But...' Then, all of a sudden, I realised just how adroitly she'd played her father this time around. If he believed I'd betrayed him while under the influence of a spirit, he could no more blame me than he could Mrs Fairacre! I stared at Roberta in admiration, and not for the first time I realised she truly did have the mind of a criminal genius. 'So what do we do now?' I whispered.

'Now we sit for a while. A few minutes should suffice, and then I shall inform my father that the extraction was successful. He will apologise to you, and after that he will ask you to stay on with us.'

I lowered my head, quite overcome. 'Thank you,' I murmured.

'You are most welcome.'

'But you do leave me a little confused, for yesterday you told me you never wished to see me again.'

'I was angry then, and rightly so. I was growing to like you, just a little, and when I learned of your betrayal it was a horrible shock. But you really had no choice, and you did your best to satisfy Edgar while protecting my father, and I decided you were not so terrible after all.'

'Just a little?' I asked.

'I'm sorry?'

'You said you only liked me a little.'

'If you press me, Mr Jones, I dare say I won't like you at all.'

We were sitting close together on the edge of the bed, and in that moment I turned to look at her. Without hesitation, she leaned in and kissed me full on the lips. My eyes widened in surprise, and then, as the kiss lingered I closed them tight and let myself be carried away. A heat spread throughout my body, and my heart beat so fast it threatened to leap out of my chest.

Then, all of a sudden, there was a sharp knock on the door. 'Roberta?' demanded the professor. 'How are things proceeding?'

I had drawn back in shock, but Roberta put her hand behind my neck and drew me closer until our foreheads touched. 'Things are proceeding well, father,' she called out. 'They are proceeding very well indeed.'

'Tell Mr Jones...tell Septimus I am truly sorry. Tell him I should not have doubted him. Tell him he can stay, with my blessing. And...do make it up to him, won't you?'

'Oh, have no fear, for I intend to do precisely that,' called Roberta, and then she drew me gently towards her so that we might resume our kiss.

About the Author

Simon Haynes was born in England and grew up in Spain. His family moved to Australia when he was 16.

In addition to novels, Simon writes computer software. In fact, he writes computer software to help him write novels faster, which leaves him more time to improve his writing software. And write novels faster. (spacejock.com/yWriter.html)

Simon's goal is to write fifteen novels before someone takes his keyboard away.

Update 2019: goal achieved and I still have my keyboard!

New goal: write thirty novels.

Update 2020: Enigma in Silver is #29...

Stay in touch!

Simon's website is spacejock.com.au

Author's newsletter: spacejock.com.au/ML.html

Facebook: facebook.com/halspacejock

Twitter: @spacejock

Acknowledgements

To Andrew, Angelika, Ann, Annette, Barbara, Bill, Cindy, Corey, David, Deanne, Debby, Gary, Helen, Ian (in advance), Jack, Jan, Jenny, Joan, John, Jon, Keith, Ken, Larrie, Luke, Lynne, Mike, Nathan, Nancy, Neville, Pat, Patrick, Paulette, Peter, Phil, Phillip, Robert, Roger, Selene, Steve, Sue, Susan, Terry, Tony, Tricia (Hi Mum!), Val and Vince, thanks for the awesome help and support!

THE HAL SPACEJOCK SERIES

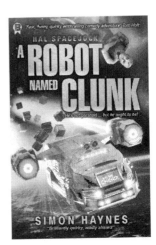

"Brilliantly quirky, wildly absurd"

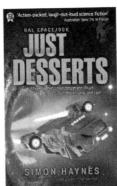

"The perfect blend of adventure, conflict and laughable moments"

but wait...
there's more!

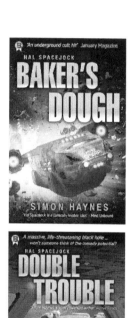

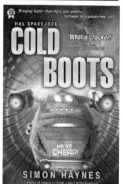

Available in Ebook and Trade Paperback

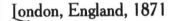

THE
MYSTERIES
IN METAL
SERIES

London, England, 1871

When I applied for the position of book-keeper with Professor Twickham and his daughter, I lied about my qualifications.

As it turns out, they lied about the job for which I was applying.

Had we not been so untruthful with each other, there might have been fewer night terrors stalking the inhabitants of the City.

Fewer unexplained disappearances. Fewer deaths.

Now, nobody is safe from the creeping horrors we've unleashed.

With no time to spare, we face an impossible task: we must discover the mysteries in metal in order to right this wrong.

But is it already too late?

Ebook and Trade Paperback

THE
SECRET WAR
SERIES

What happens when you're worth more dead... than alive?

When a decorated fighter pilot goes missing, his death is quickly turned into propaganda, inspiring fresh recruits to feed the war's voracious appetite.

Sam Willet is one such recruit, but she's different.

Different because the missing hero is her brother, and Sam has questions.

Questions nobody wants asked.

Questions that will probably get her killed.

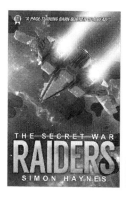

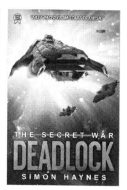

Ebook and Trade Paperback

THE
HARRIET WALSH
SERIES

It's Harriet Walsh's first day as a Peace Force trainee, and she's given a simulated case to solve. Simulated, because Dismolle is a peaceful planet and there's absolutely no crime.

Well, almost no crime.

You see, Harriet's found a genuine case to investigate, and she's hot on the trail of a real live suspect.

Which is a shame, because her crime-fighting computer is so basic it doesn't even have solitaire.

Coming 2020

Ebook and Trade Paperback

THE HAL JUNIOR SERIES

Hal Junior lives aboard a futuristic space station. His mum is chief scientist, his dad cleans air filters and his best mate is Stephen 'Stinky' Binn.

As for Hal ... he's a bit of a trouble magnet. He means well, but his wild schemes and crazy plans never turn out as expected!

Hal Junior: The Secret Signal features mayhem and laughs, daring and intrigue ... plus a home-made space cannon!

THE
DRAGON & CHIPS
TRILOGY

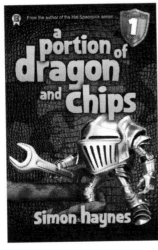

Ebook and Trade Paperback

A mild-mannered old robot has just been transported to a medieval kingdom, and things are quickly going from bad to worse:

A homicidal knight is after his blood - or the robot equivalent.

A greedy queen wants to bend him to her will.

A conniving Master of Spies is hatching his own devious plan for the mechanical marvel.

And worst of all, there's nowhere to get a recharge!

"Laugh after laugh, dark in places but the humour punches through. Amazing!"

Printed in Great Britain
by Amazon